THE SULLEN HILLS

THE SACRED TEARS TRILOGY

Book 2

~

THE SULLEN HILLS

RODERIC GRIGSON

rodericgrigson.com

ISBN: 978-0-6481183-1-2

Published by Roderic Grigson

Cover design & illustration, interior formatting & maps
Mark Thomas / Coverness.com

DEDICATION

'The Sullen Hills' has been almost 5-years in the making. It was stillborn as a part of my first book 'Sacred Tears', which had to be trimmed by a third to meet some arbitrary publishing guideline.

Then it was ignored for the better part of two years while I wrote my second book 'After the Flames', which consumed all my energy at the time.

It was finally given a life this year thanks to the help of my friends from the writing group 'The Scribe Tribe', and the efforts of my dear wife Menaka, who reads and comments on all my drafts.

And thank you to all my readers who have waited patiently to know what happened to Samir, the young man I met all those many years ago in Beirut, who has been the inspiration for all my stories.

It is my joy to present the next portion of his life.

- Roderic Grigson, October 2018

i

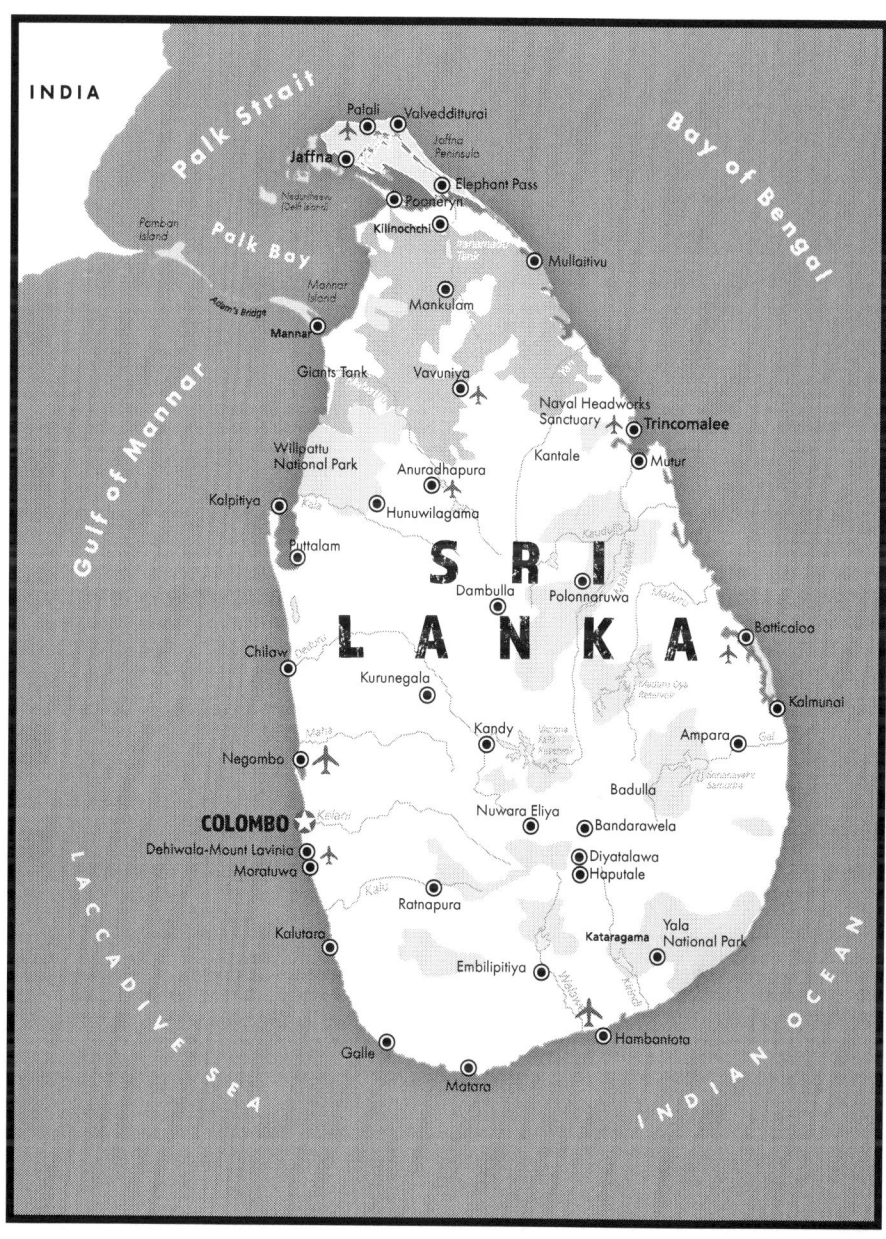

INDIA

Palk Strait

Bay of Bengal

Palali
Valvedditturai
Jaffna
Jaffna Peninsula
Elephant Pass
Nedunheevu (Delft Island)
Poonaryn
Kilinochchi

Palk Bay

Pamban Island

Adam's Bridge

Mannar Island

Mullaitivu

Mankulam

Mannar

Giants Tank

Vavuniya

Naval Headworks
Sanctuary
Trincomalee

Gulf of Mannar

Willpattu
National Park

Anuradhapura
Kantale
Mutur

Kalpitiya

Hunuwilagama

S R I

Puttalam

Dambulla
Polonnaruwa

L A N K A

Batticaloa

Chilaw

Kurunegala

Kalmunai

Kandy

Ampara

Negombo

COLOMBO

Badulla

Nuwara Eliya

Bandarawela

Dehiwala-Mount Lavinia

Diyatalawa
Haputale

Moratuwa

Ratnapura

Kataragama

Yala
National Park

Kalutara

Embilipitiya

Galle

Hambantota

Matara

LACCADIVE SEA

INDIAN OCEAN

S R I   L A N K A

| National Parks | | Main Cities & Towns |
| Vanni Area | | Airports |

0   20   40 km
0   20   40 mi

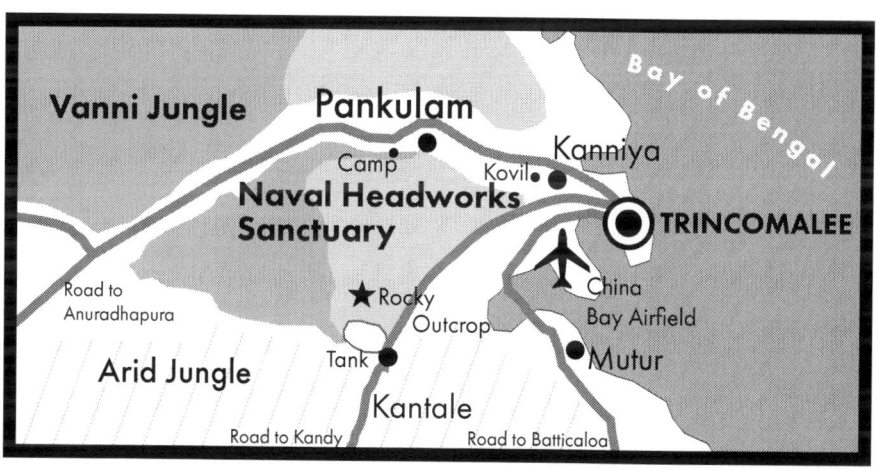

MAP OF NAVAL HEADWORKS SANCTUARY

 Towns & Villages    Main City   Airport

CHAPTER ONE

JAFFNA, NORTHERN PROVINCE

Two young women walked past the beggar in the searing heat, bright saris skimming the dirt. One carried a black umbrella to shield them both from the ferocious midday sun. The beggar watched as they chattered, walking, almost floating, up the hot, dusty road, seemingly oblivious to the old-fashioned bicycles and noisy three-wheelers weaving and clattering around them.

The beggar rubbed his arms restlessly. He was risking his life in the Tamil heartland while the militants stepped up their attacks on the military and grew in confidence. Bombs had been going off across the country and he was ordered by his army handler to find out what the Tamil Tigers were up to.

The shade from that morning had long disappeared, and dark, wet patches of sweat stained his grimy shirt. For two hours he had sat on the street corner next to the *thea kade* -tea-house, watching the market entrance across the street, his wooden bowl on the dirt footpath in front of him, collecting alms and intelligence.

The beggar's body ached. His current mission started two days earlier and he'd hardly slept during that time. Local rivalries, trigger-happy security forces and increasingly aggressive militant gunmen made moving around dangerous and unpredictable. Forced to take a slow, roundabout route to escape the notice of the men who controlled the streets around the military-occupied sixteenth century Dutch Fort, he had only reached the tea-house that morning.

It was fortunate that his disguise as a beggar allowed him to blend in with the locals. It was becoming more and more difficult to leave the army camp without being seen. Only the military dared to venture out into the city in force when they needed resupply, and to escort fresh troops from their main base in the north.

He had overheard gossip in the town that the young men who made up the bulk of the militant organisation were preparing for an offensive by the army. He had seen bricks knocked out of walls, places from which to observe the alleys and roads around the camp. The holes dug into gardens and at the side of roads indicated that they were preparing to lay mines and booby traps. From what he was seeing, the well-armed militants would not give up the town easily. He had also observed men removing railway sleepers and train tracks into overloaded lorries which headed north. He knew they were being used to fortify strong points around the main military base with its small airfield and access to the sea.

The colours of the morning gave way to the white heat of the mid-afternoon as the beggar struggled to stay focused.

'Mukesh, here!' The beggar snapped out of his stupor when a voice called out to him imperiously in Tamil. The tearoom proprietor beckoned from his darkened sanctuary behind a rough wooden counter. Dressed in a checkered blue sarong and a white shirt, he stood out brightly in front of the cave-like interior of his shop. The man's thin black moustache almost blended with his upper lip giving his hollow-cheeked, elongated face a touch of menace.

The beggar was used to the man's ways. The proprietor offered him a drink whenever he felt like it, sometimes when he showed up, sometimes later. The beggar made it a habit of changing his begging routine every few days. Being in the same place at the same time every day made it easier for his enemies to find him. Sometimes he'd be at the tearoom in the morning, sometimes after midday. That way he could watch out for the watchers.

The beggar grunted as he pushed himself up off the ground, using the stick he carried to keep himself balanced. The fragrance of the tea wafted across his face as he accepted the small glass of dark steaming brew. He bowed his head in thanks before leaning on the stick and limping back to his mat. He groaned as he sank into the warm sand and stretched his injured leg in front of him. He sipped the sweetened tea appreciatively; he had not drunk anything since morning.

Born to a Sinhalese bus driver and a Tamil tea plucker from the hill town of Haputale, he had spent most of his adult life locked in a high security prison near the southern port city of Galle. Badly injured during the Marxist uprising more than ten years ago, the beggar had rehabilitated himself, working as a servant for the Sinhalese soldiers who guarded the prison. Fluent in both Tamil and Sinhalese and with a basic understanding of English, he had been recruited by the military to gather vital intelligence. After a few weeks of intensive training in surveillance and counter-surveillance tactics, he was sent to the north to collect information on the militant groups who were moving about the town quite openly.

Mukesh's body ached. Moving his good leg more comfortably under him, he rotated his shoulders, his eyes darting around the street as he did. It was long past lunchtime, still many hours away from a tasty rice and curry meal at the camp he had left two days ago. Another three hours outside the market before he would move, first to a busy temple a few streets to the west to lose himself in the crowd, and then to carefully make his way back to the heavily fortified army camp as darkness fell, always watching to be sure that no one was following.

His eyes narrowed, his heart skipping a beat, as two men came out of the market and paused by the side of the road. Mukesh hunched forward, beads of sweat suddenly forming on his forehead.

The dark, round-faced man with the thin moustache Mukesh had seen many times before. His name was Shankar and he had been under observation by the military after his name was linked to the temple massacre in Anuradhapura. The man always moved around on a motorcycle making it impossible for anyone to follow, but he occasionally came to the market where Mukesh had seen him.

It was the other man who made Mukesh instantly afraid. A heavy, thickset man with a bald head, the operative knew of him only as Balan. The man stared in his direction and Mukesh forced himself to avert his eyes, his body stiffening with tension.

The last time Mukesh had seen the man was when he witnessed a body being dumped in a pile of garbage near the university. Around midnight, an old Austin A40 had pulled up opposite the beggar as he slept under a jasmine creeper. Mukesh watched in the shadow of the bush as two young men dragged a body from the back seat, throwing it on top of the mound of steaming refuse. Mukesh had glimpsed the cruel face of the man who had been driving and he had never forgotten his eyes. He had reported the incident to the Captain the next day and was ordered to find out who he was. Mukesh had learnt that the man was an enforcer in the militant Tiger organisation, a nasty piece of work, responsible for many murders. It was rumoured that the man spent most of his time in India. No one wanted to talk about him. The Captain would want to know that the man was back in Jaffna.

Mukesh's heart thumped uncontrollably as he sensed the two men coming in his direction. He forced himself to avoid looking at them, doing his best not to fidget, trying to relax his body and keeping his face angled downward. Sweat trickled off his face onto the few coins in his bowl. He only looked up, hand outstretched, as the two men passed him.

'Something for a crippled brother,' he grimaced wanly. 'Just a coin to buy some food.'

The two men ignored the beggar's plea and walked into the tearoom, calling out for two orders of milk tea. They sat at a plastic-covered table near the entrance, just a few metres from the beggar. Mukesh inhaled deeply. He didn't realise that he had been holding his breath. Behind him, he could not hear their talk for the loud clatter of a metal spoon against an enamelled jug as the proprietor prepared the frothy brew.

Mukesh adjusted himself carefully, turning his body slightly so he could see into the tearoom. The two men sat, their heads close together as they sipped their milk tea. Seeing Balan with Shankar confirmed Mukesh's fears that the Tigers were up to something soon. The Tigers were the largest of the militant groups still opposing the government and were also the most ruthless. Mukesh had noticed many more young men than usual hanging around, some even carrying weapons openly, and it seemed that the Tigers were gathering their forces to oppose the military. It was a major change in their behaviour as they had never taken on the army directly in the past, content to use hit and run tactics to keep the soldiers off balance.

Mukesh hated the Sri Lankan Tamils with their airs and graces. Just because they had come to the island thousands of years ago didn't mean that they were a superior race. They were all Tamils, weren't they?

The Tamils working on the tea estates where Mukesh was born were brought from India by the British to work on the plantations as indentured labourers. They lived a life of squalor and poverty, the local Tamils treating them worse than the British did. He remembered how hard his mother had to work plucking tea from the steep, tea covered hills around Haputale. And then she was refused citizenship while he was in prison and was forced to go back to India where she died. When Mukesh was approached by the army Captain it wasn't difficult to say yes. They had wanted him to become an informer, and for that he would be released from prison.

Mukesh tensed as the two men got up and walked outside the tearoom. They stopped opposite him, forcing him to look up. Balan's eyes were hard-edged as he studied Mukesh closely.

'What's wrong with you,' he scowled down at him. The man had a high-pitched, irritating voice which was out of character compared to his size.

Mukesh's heart pounded. He tried not to think about what would happen if they found out what he was doing.

'I was shot by the army during the southern uprising,' Mukesh spat, hoping that the man would not see through his disguise. 'I have lost the use of my right leg.' He had learnt that telling the truth was the best cover story you could have. It had served him well up to now, earning him pity and alms from traders and householders who knew his story.

'How were you involved?' Balan asked, staring at the beggar across the width of pavement. 'The Sinhala uprising had nothing to do with us.'

Fingers of ice raced up and down his spine. Mukesh needed to be careful not to arouse any suspicions. In the early seventies a student uprising driven by Marxist ideologies had ripped the southern portion of the country apart. The government, taken by surprise, had reacted savagely, deploying the security forces and putting down the rebellion by killing many of the mostly Sinhalese rebels. Although the uprising was not supported by the Tamils, parts of the central highlands were affected, dragging some Tamil youth into the conflict.

Mukesh adjusted his injured leg. He could feel large beads of sweat running down between his shoulder blades. 'I was going to Balangoda with my mother,' he responded bitterly. 'The army found weapons in the bus we were in and arrested everyone who was young. I was shot when I resisted.'

Balan wrinkled his brow, tightening his lips and glancing at Shankar. Mukesh tensed. He could see that the man was not convinced.

'Where are you from?' Shankar asked suspiciously. 'You're not from around here.'

Mukesh had trouble breathing. His chest tightened, his heart racing uncontrollably. He worked hard to try and disguise the Indian accent he had picked up from his mother, but it came out during times of stress or nervousness.

'My mother is from Haputale,' he shrugged nervously. 'She worked on a tea estate as a tea plucker.'

Nothing Mukesh had said so far was untrue.

'What are you doing here?' Shankar asked disbelievingly. 'It's a long way from your home.' The Enforcer's eyes narrowed at Shankar's question. He stared at Mukesh suspiciously.

'I went to India when we were promised money and citizenship,' Mukesh said bitterly, sweat streaming down his face. He had used this story many times before and came out quite convincingly. 'But we were cheated and treated like dirt, so I came back by boat.'

Mukesh had heard stories about the estate workers bound for India, standing in groups at the railway station, surrounded by bulky parcels and trunks. The men speaking in subdued voices, the women crouching with their arms on each other's shoulders crying helplessly.

'I am trying to collect money to go back to my family.' It was all part of his cover story to account for the time he spent in prison.

Shankar nodded silently. It was well known that the governments of India and Sri Lanka had colluded to send thousands of Indian Tamils working in the tea estates back to India. For many who went back, the rehabilitation schemes were simply inadequate. They were run by corrupt officials who took their money and did not provide the economic and social security benefits they had been promised.

Shankar reached into his pocket, then extended his hand. A few coins clattered into the beggar's bowl. 'The Indians are no better than the Sinhalese,' he said looking away into the distance. 'They want us to do their bidding. I don't trust them and neither does *Anna*.'

Shankar motioned to the Enforcer and the two men moved away from the beggar, stepping onto the street. Shankar raised his arm to stop the flow of bicycles and three-wheelers and crossed, heedless of the honking and cursing of the drivers. Balan glanced back in Mukesh's direction saying something to Shankar before the two of them disappeared around the corner.

Mukesh slumped back, both relieved and worried. He breathed out silently, not daring to look up, concentrating on the coins in the bowl. *That was close,* he thought to himself. *Am I being paranoid?*

No! I need to be very careful ... the game has changed. Shankar's reference to *Anna* was significant. He had to be referring to the leader of the militant organisation whom the militants referred to as 'Big Brother'. Shankar obviously knew him.

Mukesh knew his time was up. The two men would not forget him and would question why he was still around. *With Balan in town I must ask the Captain for another assignment.* But first he needed to get out.

Jaffna town had become a place where everybody watched everyone else. The town was thick with informants and if Shankar or Balan decided Mukesh needed to be watched, it would be almost impossible to get back to the army camp in the Fort without tipping someone off. *It will not be easy!*

Mukesh looked around casually. The market across the street was emptying, the crowd almost imperceptibly starting to thin out. The vegetable and fruit vendors, sensing the rush was over, called out bargains in loud voices, encouraging late arrivals to consider their goods. No one seemed to stand out of the crowd, but Mukesh knew better than to ignore his instincts.

Mukesh shifted uneasily trying hard to steady his fast-fraying nerves, unable to stop thinking about the risks he would have to face trying to get back while being watched. It was still far too early to leave without raising suspicions ... the last thing he wanted to do was to make their job easier by leaving in a panic.

He took a deep breath, letting it go in a hiss ragged with tension and fear. *I can't put this off any longer*, he told himself. The chances of being caught doubled the more he waited. *I have to go soon.*

CHAPTER TWO

COLOMBO, WESTERN PROVINCE

Shafts of bright sunlight spilled across the busy thoroughfare, framing dusty walls smothered with Jasmine creepers, their white flowers tinged with brown from the delayed monsoon rains.

A white-gloved waiter placed a glass of fresh pineapple juice and a bowl of peanuts on the table in front of Priyani and Preethi. The large air-conditioned room was a relief from the sweltering heat where they had taken refuge after spending the afternoon shopping.

Priyani cupped the cool, ice-filled glass in her hands, sipping the fruit drink appreciatively. The old-world Victorian-era hotel anchored one end of the Galle Face Green, an open expanse of land which stretched for a kilometre opposite the Hotel along the coast. A favourite watering hole for the rich and famous, the Galle Face Hotel stood right next to the Indian Ocean and salt spray thrown high by the constantly breaking waves frequently stained its white wooden shutters. They sat in the Wine Lounge which led off from the main hotel lobby. It's teak wood floors and panelling, coupled with the rich scent wafting through the lobby, gave the lounge a mood of casual elegance and luxury. Priyani's favourite spot in the hotel, it allowed her to watch the endless parade of hotel guests and visitors through its arched doorways.

Preethi pulled the bowl of peanuts towards her taking a handful before reaching into her bag and pulling out a fashion magazine which she placed on the table between them. She frowned. 'I want it to look exactly like this but it's not available in Colombo.' Preethi was getting married in a few months' time and was searching for a saree to wear during her homecoming. 'I'll have to ask *aiya* to get it in India.'

Priyani smiled fondly at her friend. Preethi was a very determined person and she would leave no stone unturned to get what she wanted.

'When is Nihal going to India,' Priyani asked. Preethi's older brother was always traveling somewhere on business. 'Will there be time to get it before the wedding?'

'Yes,' Preethi mumbled, her mouth full of peanuts. 'He's going to Madras next month. But I heard that there is a shop in Pettah that might have what I want. You feel like going there now?' she asked hopefully.

A wave of laughter and happy chatter made the two girls raise their heads. On the other side of the lobby, a bride and groom were posing for their wedding photographs. The bride dressed in a white *Osariya* saree bedecked in gold and pearl necklaces, wore the traditional gold *Nalalpata* on her forehead studded with ruby red precious stones. The groom wore the traditional *Mul Anduma* with its ornate four-cornered head piece. Hotel guests paused to watch the happy young couple on the elegant spiralling staircase.

Priyani felt a twinge of envy which she quickly suppressed. David had not formally proposed to her although it was understood that they would be married one day. It had been almost three weeks since she had seen him and

Priyani missed him desperately. She only saw David on the occasional weekend when he came back to Colombo. Priyani instinctively picked up her cell-phone hoping there would be a message from him, but she would have heard the beep.

Priyani saw Preethi looking at her curiously as she placed the phone back in her bag. 'What?' she asked, rolling her eyes. They had been friends for many years and Preethi knew her very well.

'Just give him some time,' Preethi said. 'It cannot be easy for him up north.' Preethi had the habit of seeing through her sometimes.

Priyani nodded, her eyes moistening as she looked through the tall open windows towards the sea. She knew that David wanted to spend more time with her in Colombo. But peace talks between the government and the Tamil militants had failed, forcing him to spend most of his time in the field.

Priyani's life changed dramatically after they had met, and she learned to conceal her anxiety whenever he went to the north. Knowing that David had a dangerous job did not make it any easier. She remembered the time that he had rescued her from the Black Tigers, following the men who had kidnapped her for three days in one of the most inhospitable regions of the country.

Her parents no longer objected to her relationship with David. She had moved out of the family home into a flat in Cinnamon Gardens where her brother Rohan and his wife Janaki lived. The relief agency she worked for demanded more of her time and she rarely visited the refugee camps anymore. Being tied to a desk in the city did not sit well with her, but as the head of the agency in the country, her job was to raise and allocate funds and take care of the paperwork that crossed her desk. Having a brother who worked for the President helped her to deal with the government officials who always had their hand out for bribes, but it was tedious work. She had everything she wanted, well, almost everything!

Priyani felt claustrophobic and wanted some fresh air. 'Ok, I am game,' she said trying to be cheerful. 'Let's go to Pettah before we go home. We can catch a taxi outside.'

Preethi grinned at her, waving at the waiter to bring the bill. 'Let's go near the red mosque. The shops around there will be open till six, so there's enough time.'

Priyani knew the area well. The Bombay Sweet shops she used to visit as a child with her uncle, especially the one near the red mosque, had the best tasting *samosas* she had ever eaten. Once in your mouth, the meal of vegetables wrapped in a thin sheet of flour-based pastry and deep fried till crisp, exploded into a kaleidoscope of different spicy flavours when they were eaten hot, and preferably, with a thick homemade chilli and tomato sauce. She remembered washing it down with a mixture of rose water and milk, ice cream and jelly called a *faluda* which had her hooked for life.

A smudge of black cloud on the horizon brought the promise of rain as they stepped out of the hotel lobby. Kites whirled their way drunkenly across the sky while a few hardy office workers strolled casually on the esplanade from buildings in the Fort. The shade from young coconut trees planted along the edge of the open park provided some relief to a group of students dressed in white playing a game of cricket on the hard-baked earth.

The ancient doorman who had been working at the hotel for over forty years blew his whistle summoning a taxi to the large entrance portico.

'Take these two young ladies to Pettah,' he told the taxi driver, 'and wait for them. You'll get another fare from me if you do.' The taxi driver nodded his head and watched while Preethi and Priyani climbed into the cramped vehicle.

'Where in Pettah do you want to go?' he asked, looking into the rear-view mirror at the two girls.

'It's near the central bus station,' Preethi said. 'On Muhandiram's Road, between the bus station and the mosque.'

The taxi driver nodded his head as he nosed his vehicle into the streaming traffic on Galle Road.

As they drove past the open green towards the old Parliament building, a large passenger liner was leaving the harbour. Tugboats fussed around the gleaming white ship with the P&O insignia on its funnel. Passengers crowded the decks watching the shoreline as the ship, blowing its siren imperiously, moved majestically into deeper water.

~

The taxi slowed down to a crawl opposite the railway station as people, anxious to get home, streamed across the wide junction from office buildings in the Fort.

'I forgot it was almost rush hour,' Priyani said looking out of the window as the taxi inched forward. Women dressed in simple cotton saris and others in skirts and blouses, mixed with men in white shirts and dark trousers darted across the road into the railway station, anxious to catch the 5:20 train heading to the southern suburbs.

'It'll be fine once we get past the station,' Preethi said, grimacing at the crowd. 'The bus terminal is just ahead.'

They passed the railway station and the worst of the crowd when a bright orange-red flash followed immediately by a loud clap of thunder filled the inside of the vehicle. The taxi shook violently and through the front windscreen Priyani watched a dark mushroom cloud of smoke and debris rise into the air.

It's a bomb, the thought flashed through Priyani's mind. She had overheard her brother on the phone that morning discussing a bombing incident outside Colombo a few days ago. It seemed that a new bombing campaign had been started by the Tigers again.

Pandemonium reigned as stunned pedestrians ran away from the area of the blast, some looking over their shoulders in panic, crashing into each other and vehicles on the road. Car horns blared loudly, and three-wheelers tooted their horns, but the traffic had come to an abrupt stop and was not moving. The taxi driver cursed loudly in Sinhalese, beating his hand incessantly on the horn.

'Stop doing that,' Priyani snapped, glaring at him angrily. She looked

13

around at Preethi who sat with her mouth open clutching her bag. 'It looks like a bomb has gone off.'

Priyani looked around. They were stuck in the middle of the road, surrounded by other vehicles. 'We'll have to get out and walk,' she said. 'Otherwise we will never move.'

Priyani opened the taxi door and stepped out onto the road looking in the direction of the bomb blast. Her view was obscured by other vehicles, so she stepped up onto the taxi doorframe hoping to get a clearer view of what was happening. The central bus station was clearly visible with several shops on the ground floor on fire. Buses and other vehicles near the centre of the explosion burned fiercely. The Bank of Ceylon building next to the bus station, with its shattered windows looking dark and deserted, had several fires burning out of control.

There had been a spate of bombings around Colombo a few months before, but the authorities had assured everyone that they had caught the men responsible and it was safe once again to move around the city. Priyani looked back. Cars, buses and other vehicles jammed the road behind them.

The wailing sound of sirens in the distance snapped Priyani out of her trance. 'C'mon,' she said, reaching into the taxi and grabbing her purse. 'We've got to get out of here.' Preethi nodded her head and scrambled across the back seat towards Priyani.

The taxi driver looked back at them angrily. 'Where are you going?' he shouted. 'You owe me money.' Priyani opened her purse and grabbed a couple of bank notes. 'This should be enough,' she said, handing the crumpled notes to the man. The taxi driver glanced at the notes and nodded.

The two girls locked arms and moved towards the curb closest to them. Their path was blocked by other vehicles, the gaps between them too small to squeeze through. Priyani looked around. The only way they could get out of the traffic jam was to cross the concrete centre divider onto the other side of the street which was free of oncoming vehicles.

Priyani pulled Preethi back towards the centre divider. 'Let's get to the other side,' she said. 'We'll walk to the railway station and try and catch a taxi there.'

Negotiating the low centre divider was easy. They crossed the almost empty road towards the pavement filled with shopkeepers and pedestrians standing and staring towards where the bomb had exploded.

The walk to the Fort Railway station was quick. They flagged a three-wheeler that had just dropped a fare outside the station. The driver thankfully agreed to take the two girls to Cinnamon Gardens.

CHAPTER THREE

JAFFNA LAGOON

The sun had struggled all day behind heavy rain clouds, finally succumbing to the quick onset of darkness common in the tropics. The monsoon-night darkness was broken by a twinkling of lights, low in the water, coming from fishing hamlets lining the shore of the lagoon.

The town of Jaffna they were heading towards was an inky pool of darkness. Except for a few military bases, the land across the lagoon was under the Tiger's control. The crossing was a risk they were taking as the militants also used the open water of the lagoon to cross to the mainland in small boats.

The star-shaped fortification at the northern edge of the lagoon adjoining the town was held by a reinforced detachment of the Sri Lankan army. The militants who surrounded the old Dutch Fort attacked anyone who ventured outside, forcing the army to resupply the garrison by helicopter or by boat. High

Command had stopped using helicopters after the militants moved a heavy machine gun into the town making it extremely dangerous for helicopters to land. That didn't leave many options to resupply the garrison as bringing supplies across the lagoon was always risky. The heavy naval boats often got stuck in the mud and came under fire from the Tigers who patrolled the shallow reef bound coast line.

David felt his heart beat against his chest. The light flow of air off the lagoon did little to prevent the sweat that ran down his back. He flexed his cramped legs and arched his back, reaching behind him to adjust the position of the backup automatic pistol that was tucked in a holster at the small of his back. He'd never got used to the feeling of a weapon there, especially when he was sitting. It ground against his spine with every movement.

David didn't mind the feeling of discomfort. It reassured him and reminded him that the mission could turn quite ugly. The navy had recently discovered on old naval charts, a long narrow channel in the lagoon built by the Dutch over two-hundred years ago. This allowed the Fort to be resupplied from the mainland without the boats getting stuck in the mud. The military used the channel sparingly. They did not want the militants to find out that it was being used to resupply the garrison. It had taken a call from the General in Colombo for the Sector Commander to relent and allow the two of them access.

The lagoon was still, with hardly a ripple. The moon was thankfully behind the clouds, making their boat impossible to see in the blackness. The rise and fall of music coming from somewhere across the lagoon drifted faintly across the oily black water. The officer suddenly sat up straighter when a faint throbbing sound seemingly coming from the right, rose and fell with the light breeze. The young Petty Officer faintly outlined against the lighter darkness of the night sky, raised his hand with his head cocked to one side. The two naval ratings dressed in dark blue uniforms stopped paddling and everyone froze in place.

The officer searched the darkness, his head tilted to catch any sound coming across the water. He signalled to the helmsman to swing to the left. He then pushed his paddle into the water and leant forward, stroking the water powerfully. The two seamen in the boat followed suit and the little craft sliced through the water with surprising ease heading west, away from the peninsula coast line.

Everyone in the boat had instinctively bent forward lowering their profile as they moved away from the channel. After five minutes of steady rowing the officer signalled with a closed fist for his men to stop paddling.

David strained to hear any sound. Only the lapping of small waves against the sides of the boat disturbed the stillness of the night. For a moment he thought he heard something, but it was just the murmur of the light wind in his ears.

The officer waited a while longer and signalled to the right and the naval rating controlling the small tiller swung the boat back in its original direction. The naval officer turned his head catching David's eyes. 'We're not going to land by the Fort,' he whispered, his sweaty face gleaming in the dark. 'I'll drop you off at the causeway.'

It wasn't a question and David nodded without saying anything. The Sector Commander had been adamant that, despite being ordered to get David and Sarath across to the Fort, he was not going to risk being discovered using the channel. Because of this uncertainty, the naval officer commanding the small boat had been ordered to use the alternative landing site.

The four-kilometre-long causeway connecting the island of Kayts to the Jaffna Peninsula had been abandoned after army patrols came under intense fire from the militants making it too dangerous to use.

This will complicate things, David thought. The Jaffna entrance to the causeway was only a few hundred metres from the Fort and it was possible for a small group of men on foot to reach their destination in the dark without being seen. If they were going to use the causeway, they needed a couple of hours of darkness to negotiate the narrow road to the spit of land that connected it to the peninsula and reach the Fort. Sunrise was around six, but they needed to get into there before the false dawn.

David struggled to concentrate as he watched the naval officer signal his men to propel the flat bottom boat forward. He had been in the field for over three months and badly needed a break. Although trained by professionals both technically and tactically for war, nothing had adequately prepared him for combat. He dealt with death daily and it sucked the life out of him.

For about the hundredth time in the last half hour the foremost thing on his mind was not getting caught. David knew that anything could happen now that they were within rifle range of land. He was desperate to talk to his operative and find out what the Tigers were up to. The man had sent a cryptic radio message saying that he had seen someone important and urgently needed to report, but he wanted to do it face-to-face. The man who had been operating undercover for the last three months was one of the best field operatives they had. David was prepared to put up with his demands, but he'd make sure it wouldn't happen again.

The army were preparing plans to take back control of the peninsula and very soon newly-trained and equipped troops would be deploying into the area. David should have been at the Fort two days ago, but the Sector Commander had refused permission to let him cross. 'It's getting more and more difficult to get supplies across without being seen,' he said shaking his head. 'They don't know about the channel and I want to keep it that way.'

It was a few hours before sunrise when, with a final pull of the paddles, the boat coasted to the edge of the low causeway. Small blocks of coral and granite lined the road allowing David and Sarath to access the causeway directly from the boat.

The two men knelt on the rocks as an unpleasant odour of bird droppings and dampness permeated the area. David wrinkled his nose in disgust as he scanned the causeway, sensing the boat pulling away quietly behind him. It would be back in twenty-four hours to pick them up.

David pulled a short-range radio from his vest and keyed the pre-arranged frequency.

'Base-Actual. Charlie-Niner. Over.'

A hiss of static answered the call. David repeated the message. He breathed a sigh of relief when the radio crackled to life.

'Charlie-Niner. Base-Actual. Report status. Over.'

'Base-Actual, using alternate. Confirm. Over.'

'Charlie-Niner, confirm alternate. Base-Actual. Over.'

The two of them were dressed in black fatigues and carried suppressed automatic rifles. A small knapsack on their backs held a medical kit, three days of food, and water supply. A holstered pistol, a sheathed fighting knife and spare ammunition magazines, fitted in pouches on their tactical vests, completed their gear. David scanned the road in both directions before stepping out carefully on the rocks that lined the sides of the road. Sarath followed David a few metres behind. There was a good chance that the militants had mined the road and David felt much safer walking on the slick rocks, even though the chances of slipping and injuring themselves were high.

David knew they couldn't stay out in the open for long. Shivers ran down David's neck, heightening his senses as he felt the tension of how close he was to the enemy. David was glad that Sarath was with him. Second in command of the Special Operations Team David commanded, they had been together for a few years and had become friends out of necessity. Visiting the old Fort was not as dangerous as some of the missions they had been on, but it was reassuring to have someone of Sarath's calibre to watch his back.

It was dawn when the two of them reached the open ground where the road from Jaffna entered the causeway. Sunrise wouldn't be far away. The noise of crickets and cicadas increased in volume as they reached an area of overgrown grass and low bushes lining the sides of the empty road. His feet scuffed the earth as they eased their way off the road. Their senses heightened! This is where they would be spotted by anyone watching if they weren't careful. Small wildlife rustled around them as they crawled on their bellies along the edge of the lagoon below the height of the road. The Fort was less than a couple of hundred metres away when they turned east.

They needed to be careful as they were between the militants and the soldiers in the Fort and could easily be mistaken by either. The soldiers would be expecting them, but David did not want to risk being shot at by mistake.

David pulled out the radio and pressed the submit key.

'Base-Actual, light the way. Charlie-Niner. Over.

There was no response on the radio. David stared at the Fort whose outline was becoming visible with the lightening of the eastern sky behind it. He knew that Sarath would be watching his back.

There! A light flickered briefly low down by the water's edge next to the rampart wall. David tapped Sarath on his shoulder. Moving small branches and fronds aside, the two men, almost bent in two, moved cautiously towards the spot. David kept a firm grip on his automatic rifle. Making contact in the dark was always fraught with danger. All it took was one trigger–happy soldier.

David continually scanned for threats, pausing at the edge of the open ground leading to the moat surrounding the rampart. The soldiers must have been watching as a shape detached itself from the darkness of the wall and waved them forward.

The officer whom David had met before recognised them. 'You took your time,' he said, lowering his weapon. 'Did you run into any trouble?'

David could sense other soldiers around him but could not see them. He shook his head. 'No, just the navy being bloody minded.'

He couldn't help but think that the Sector Commander had ordered the naval officer to drop them off at the causeway. What mattered was that they had reached the Fort and he would be able to talk to his operative.

CHAPTER FOUR

COLOMBO

David walked back to the Galle Face Hotel after his meeting with the Colonel. He had taken a room at the hotel when he had arrived the previous evening from his mission to the north. David was so tired he had gone straight to bed and slept like a baby. He woke up late that morning, just in time for his meeting at the army headquarters on Slave Island, a ten-minute walk away. He had called Priyani at work before he left and was disappointed that he could not talk to her. He was hoping that she had got his message.

A white gloved waiter placed a bowl of peanuts on the table in front of him, looking at him enquiringly. 'I am expecting someone to join me,' David said, looking up at the waiter. 'Can you bring us two glasses of fresh pineapple juice with ice.'

David sat in the Wine Lounge which led off from the main hotel lobby. Its teak wood floors and panelling gave the lounge an old-world sophistication and class. The hotel staff were all well trained, some had been working there for many years. The waiter nodded and left him.

David pulled the bowl of peanuts towards him and took a handful. He sat back on the comfortable chair crunching on a peanut, his mind going over what the Colonel had said to him at their meeting.

'We're in the final stages of preparing to take back the peninsula,' the Colonel said, studying David over his wire framed glasses. 'Troops are being moved by sea to Palali and will kick off the first phase of the operation in two weeks' time.'

David was not surprised at the news. He had heard that the President had ordered the armed forces to step up their campaign, and planning had been underway for a while to wrest control of the Jaffna Peninsula from the Tigers.

'This will be a combined assault using elements of the army, navy and air force,' the Colonel continued. 'The reports you brought back from Jaffna indicate that the militants have established numerous fixed defensive positions to fight from. They think it will stop us but in fact it will make it easier.' The Colonel frowned when David raised his eyebrows questioningly. 'We are arming our ground troops with rocket propelled grenades and rocket launchers which should make it easier to take these positions out. We will also use helicopters and planes to target the strong points outside the built-up areas.'

'That's not going to be easy,' David said, his eyes narrowing in concentration. 'According to Mukesh, they have constructed many of these strongpoints at road junctions where there is already a civilian presence. Others are built in places close to schools and temples.'

The Colonel stood up and paced across the room. 'Yes, there will be civilian casualties, no doubt, but we will warn them to evacuate the areas where these strongpoints are located until the campaign is over.'

David loved the army and particularly liked serving with his men, but he was not totally happy with the way his life was panning out. Adding to his frustration was the fact that decisions were being made at high levels without proper consultation with the troops on the ground.

The Colonel raised his hand when David opened his mouth to speak. 'Before you say anything more the decision has been made and we'll handle whatever happens.'

David didn't say anything, realising that the Colonel was not in a mood to argue. The Colonel stared at him for a moment and he nodded when he saw that David wasn't going to speak.

'Now,' he said. 'I want to discuss what your team's role will be. We want to take out as many of their leaders as we can before the assault begins. We have had reports of significant militant activity around Trincomalee and we believe they will launch an attack on the town to divert our attention away from Jaffna.'

David concentrated on what the Colonel was saying. The tactics made sense and he trusted the Colonel. He had taken command of the northern sector when David was a Lieutenant and promoted him to Captain when David proved himself in the field. The Colonel didn't seem to care that David was Burgher, a descendant of the Europeans who ruled the island for over four centuries. The army was now predominantly Sinhalese and only the very capable from outside the largest ethnic group were ever promoted. The Colonel wanted results, highly valuing David's ability to analyse and assess the militants' capabilities and vulnerabilities from his own unique perspective.

The Colonel stood up and walked in front of a large floor to ceiling map of the island taped onto the wall. 'We don't have the manpower to fight them on two fronts,' he said, waving his hand at the map. 'So, we're targeting their leaders to prevent them from causing us trouble in the east.'

The Colonel turned to David. 'I want you to take your team to Trinco. We have learnt that the militant area leaders will be meeting in the jungle just north of the naval sanctuary. We want you and your men to take out everyone at that meeting.'

David steepled his hands thinking. *It wouldn't be easy!* He often led his team on intelligence gathering missions into territory controlled by the enemy and while the Colonel regarded these missions as extremely dangerous, David knew the Colonel was confident in his ability to complete a mission.

'How sure are you that this information is correct?' David questioned. 'What's the source?' David had learnt the hard way to never completely trust the information unless he knew where it came from.

'The information has been reliable in the past,' the Colonel assured him. 'We have a mid-level operative in one of the smaller militant groups and all indications are that they are preparing for some sort of attack.'

David nodded. He knew not to ask more questions. The less he knew about the intelligence source the better.

'You have two days to prepare,' the Colonel said, observing David's reaction. 'This is an opportunity we don't want to miss.'

David sipped his drink, glad he had some time off in Colombo before having to leave. He didn't have to worry about his team as they were always on a semi-permanent state of readiness. They were often called, sometimes without any warning, to carry out important assignments and he had sent them a message before leaving headquarters, to prepare for an urgent mission in the north.

David looked towards the hotel entrance. He had not seen Priyani for over four weeks and hoped that she was not out of town. He had known Priyani from the time he went to school. She was the sister of his best friend who had lived just a few houses away in the suburb of Ratmalana. David had lost touch with Priyani when he joined the army and had been smitten when he saw her after many years, dancing with her father at a charity ball organised by his mother.

Ah, there she is! David grinned when he saw Priyani get out of a taxi that had just pulled up at the entrance. She was dressed in green slacks and a batik blouse with dark motifs of the same colour. Her black hair was loosely puffed into a long pony tail which swayed gracefully behind her as she entered the hotel lobby.

Priyani smiled delightedly when she saw David in the lounge, waving to him before moving around a family that were posing for photographs on the elegant spiralling staircase. She moved like a trained athlete, her clean, lightly tanned skin glowing with health. David stepped out to meet her, taking her in her arms, pressing her slim, hard body to him.

Priyani looked up at him, touching his cheek with her long fingers. 'Oh, David. What's happened to you?' she asked with quick concern flaring in her huge eyes. David didn't understand what she meant before realising she had not seen him for a while. Most of that time he had been in the field, not eating very well, the stress of constant vigilance. He had lost weight and it must have shown on his face.

'It's been quite a busy period,' David said enjoying the feel of Priyani's body against him. 'There's lots going on. I am sorry it's been so long.'

Priyani hugged him fiercely. 'I missed you so much,' she whispered, low enough for no one else in the room to hear and reached up with her mouth for his. Her kiss was soft and warm; her body melting and trusting against his. She smelt clean and fresh, and faintly of crushed jasmine. He felt himself physically aroused by her and wanted to reach out and touch her face, to feel the warmth and glossiness of her skin.

Priyani broke gently from his embrace feeling his desire, keeping those slim, strong hips pressed against him for a second. 'Come,' she said, turning away and leading him to where he had been sitting.

They were more than friends. They had become lovers after David had rescued Priyani from the terrorists who had taken Eileen, the European head of the refugee agency, and Priyani into the northern jungle as hostages.

Their lives had changed dramatically since that incident. David found himself spending more time in the field. The capability he had demonstrated by tracking and killing the terrorists had come to the attention of the President. Ever since that incident, his team was always the first to be picked for any dangerous mission.

Priyani sat beside David on the deep leather couch. 'Tell me please, David,' she said, holding onto his arm, 'what has it been like?'

David gave Priyani a summary of what he'd been doing the past few weeks without going into any details. It was a rule of his not to hide anything from her. He'd seen the strength in Priyani when she was taken prisoner by the Black Tigers and knew that keeping anything from her would only make her more determined to find the truth.

Priyani took in a deep breath when David finished talking, hugging his arm in understanding. She knew he had a dangerous job and had come to accept it.

A burst of laughter and happy chatter made them look up. The family had finished with their photographs and were moving past the lounge.

'When do you have to go back?' she asked. Being the daughter of a retired army Colonel, she was familiar with the demands her father's duties had placed on the family and how her mother had coped.

'I have to be in Trinco the day after tomorrow,' David answered. 'I am sorry we don't have much time together.'

She looked at him frankly and openly. 'So, we have two days and we should not waste them,' Priyani said, motioning to the waiter hovering in the background. Her eyes were the colour of wild-honey, dark brown and flecked with gold. David felt a shiver run through his spine. He paid the waiter conscious of Priyani watching him.

David took her by the hand and walked down the long narrow corridor towards the Regency Wing. Priyani walked in silence beside David, moving with a flowing, long-legged grace. Beneath her blouse her arms were delicately sculpted from toned muscle, her waist narrow, her breasts small and unfettered, their lovely shape pressing clearly through the fine material. David respected her silence, pleased to be able to spend the time with her.

The room was on the first floor overlooking the Indian Ocean. A black and white ship was just pulling out of the harbour. Passengers lined the rails as the big liner shook off its attendant tug boats, pulling away into the deep ocean.

Priyani locked the door behind them and walked over to David slowly.

27

Her eyes were dark and unfathomable. A pulse slowly throbbed on her long graceful neck.

David took her into his arms and kissed her gently. Her chin lifted slightly as her lips parted slowly, softly, to his. She pushed him away and loosened her hair, turning her back to him as she undid the buttons of her blouse, beginning at her throat and working down. She slipped the light material from her shoulders and reached down to undo the clasp on her slacks which dropped with a rustling sound around her ankles.

Her smooth, lightly tanned flesh gleamed through the fall of her dark hair as she kicked off her sandals and turned back to face David.

She wore green panties and a gold chain with a heart shaped locket around her long neck. Her small perky breasts, with prominent nipples already fully erect were the colour of dark strawberries. Her satiny skin tanned to a light mahogany showing off her flat stomach. Her lips were parted slightly, and her eyes were soft and glowing. David felt aroused by the look on her face.

'You look beautiful ...'

His words were stopped by the warm pressure of her lips on his. There was nothing tentative about her kiss. She took it for granted that he wanted this as much as she did.

David smelt her, a light summery perfume that seemed to come from her hair. He resisted the temptation to press his face into it. He could feel the warmth and suppleness of her flesh through his clothing.

His lips parted, and her tongue found his, teasing him with light strokes. She leaned into him, pressing herself against him. Her breasts crushed against his chest and David could feel her nipples hard and tight through the layers of clothing that separated them.

He lifted one hand and cupped her breast, the pad of his thumb rubbing across the hard peak. She gasped against his mouth and shifted her position to give him better access.

'I have wanted to do this ever since I saw you this morning. You looked so good in your uniform …' she whispered.

David gathered Priyani in his arms and walked over to the huge mahogany bed in the centre of the room. He lay her down gently and began to remove his clothes, almost falling over in his haste to remove his boots.

Priyani lay on the bed propped up on one elbow, her lower body under the cotton sheet watching David as he crawled in beside her.

They made love as the sun set outside, creating long darkening shadows across the room. 'I love you,' she cried at the very end, her voice hoarse from exertion.

CHAPTER FIVE

CENTRAL HIGHLANDS

Mukesh left Jaffna before the army offensive began. The Captain had refused to tell him anything, but he didn't have to be too smart to figure that something was going to happen. Even the Tigers knew that an attack was imminent. It had become too dangerous to leave the Fort as the army garrison were under constant watch.

The prospect of being trapped in the Fort did trouble him a little. Mukesh had seen the Tigers lay anti-personnel mines and other explosive devices in the lanes and alleyways opposite the stronghold and he knew it wouldn't be long before one side or the other would initiate some action.

In many ways, the fighting was probably inevitable. The respective ideologies of the political parties wrestling for control were not even so fundamentally different that they couldn't be reconciled. But a fierce dislike and deep suspicion seemed to exist between the local Tamil community and the Sinhalese controlled military which represented the government.

Mukesh had been evacuated out of the Fort in the boat that brought troop replacements and supplies every alternate night. The Captain had organised it and had asked Mukesh to take a long break and report back for duty when he was ready.

It had taken him almost a week to get to the hill country. The monsoon rains had begun to sweep across the southern escarpment bringing normal life on the tea estates to a complete stop. Rivers overflowed, and trees fell, making some roads impassable. He had waited in Kandy until the rains finally stopped and the roads were cleared. He had caught the first bus out of the city going up into the hill country. The bus was full of people, even the aisle was packed. Mukesh pushed himself to the back of the bus, joining the men hanging onto straps suspended from the ceiling.

Forested hills rose vertically from valley floors filled with rows of pale green tea bushes as the bus wound its way up the hilly road. It was early in the morning and hundreds of women added bright specks of colour to the landscape as they began the daily harvesting of the leaves by hand. Mukesh had a sister who lived on a tea estate near Haputale with her husband and young daughter. He had not seen them for a while, so he decided to visit them.

Rani was a tea plucker and she had always welcomed Mukesh to her home, but he had stayed away because he didn't like her husband. Kanan drank heavily, always quarrelling with his wife when he was drunk and Mukesh suspected that he beat her.

Mukesh had almost forgotten how they lived. He had taken a well-worn path through the trees by the side of the road to where the workers lived. In two lines, a pair of long, low buildings built by the British more than a hundred years ago faced each other across a narrow strip of cobbled ground. The corrugated iron sheets on the roof were weighed down by large rocks. Patches of stone and plaster, fallen away from the stained walls were crudely plugged with mud and grass. Each building had twenty doorways, each leading to a separate dwelling. Not a single doorway had a door to it. Bright saris of red, green and purple hung on washing lines. Litter fluttered around the area between the long, narrow, dilapidated structures. Scrawny looking chickens wandered the compound, scratching around the garbage that lay heaped in piles at both ends. Pots clanked, and a smoky haze floated across the lines. The smell of something cooking drifted after it.

Most of the tea pluckers and labourers were Tamils of Indian origin - people whose forefathers were brought from India by the British to work the estates.

The room they lived in was small and dark. It was where the family cooked, ate and slept. There was no electricity or running water, the two toilets outside were shared by all the families. Three steps led up to the front entrance. On either side of the steps were raised cement platforms, the front corners of which held wooden beams that supported a leaning thatched roof. These platforms were used to entertain any visitors who would drop in during the evening for a cup of tea or to sit and talk.

Mukesh looked at the early morning sunlight streaming through the trees. Six days of doing nothing. For once he was glad that he had decided to spend some time with Rani and her family. It had been so long since he'd seen them. He had not had a chance to unwind since he'd been shot and put in prison.

His sister had been happy to see Mukesh, fussing over him constantly since he arrived. Kanan, his brother in law, had looked morosely at him after coming back from working in the fields that day. Mukesh never understood why his parents had chosen Kanan to marry his sister. The man was always drinking and complaining about something. He had brightened up when Mukesh gave Rani a handful of notes to buy kerosene, cooking oil and flour from the estate store.

What made Mukesh enjoy his time here most was his niece, Savitri, Rani's daughter. Savitri was six years old, her hair falling over her shoulders in two thick black plaits fastened with bits of thread. She was a happy child, so full of life. Savitri never walked, she skipped, she danced and sang for him. The dogs loved her, wagging their tails and yapping when she came outside, leaping up at her, rolling on the ground so she could rub their bellies. She wasn't supposed to touch dogs, for they were unclean; but she did so because she loved them, and they knew it.

Smiling in pleasure he folded his arms beneath his head and closed his eyes. These days he was content to relax, spend time with his niece and relish the food his sister made. Sitting on the stoop, watching the activity around him and drinking tea – he couldn't think of a better start to his day. Finishing his tea, he climbed to his feet and entered the doorway.

Rani was in the area used as a kitchen - no surprise there – stirring something vigorously over the wood fire. Her hair was completely black, her skin stretched tightly across raised cheekbones. The huge diamond stud embedded in her nose gave his sister a rather cute look, although she would scold him if he'd say anything. She wore a plain green and red cotton sari she favoured, the loose end tucked in at the waist. Her multi-hued glass bangles interspersed with gold ones, jangled in rhythm to her stirring.

Mukesh's stomach growled in response to the delicious smells. Walking behind Rani, he put out his hand to grab a freshly fried vadai.

Rani slapped his hand away. 'How many times do I have to tell you I have to offer it to the Gods before you can put it in your mouth?'

Mukesh grinned as she continued to mutter under her breath about badly raised boys turning into grown men.

He breathed in the aroma. 'What is that curry? Cabbage?'

Rani swung her head around, a look of disbelief across her face. 'See what happens when you stay away for so long? Forgotten all your vegetables. You have lived with the locals for too long.'

Mukesh laughed out loud. Nothing had changed. He remembered how his mother talked about the Sinhalese – the local people on the island, even though she had been married to one. Rani was becoming just like her.

'You are up!' Kanan scowled from where he was sitting at the back of the room. Mukesh hadn't seen him there and tried not to sigh out loud. The man irritated him. Mukesh thought Kanan had gone to work but realised it must be the weekend and he'd have to put up with him all day.

CHAPTER SIX

KALPITIYA REFUGEE CAMP

Sami walked back to the refugee camp as it was getting dark. He carried a small plastic bag with a handful of fresh squid. The fishermen had allowed him to pick a few of the smaller catch from the net, waving him away when he offered them money. He had gone to the beach to talk to some of the refugees who worked as casual labourers for the fishermen, helping them to haul in the catch and repair their nets.

The camp was occupied by people the government unfeelingly called "internally displaced persons". They were Muslim families who had been evicted forcibly from their homes in Mannar by the Tamil Tigers, who had ordered them to leave the area or face certain death. Sami was the Coordinator of an overseas-based relief agency that ran a local medical clinic and provided schooling to the children living in the refugee community. The refugees who had left their homes with only what they could carry struggled to make ends meet. They supplemented the meagre allowance given by the government by working with the local fishing communities. They cleaned and mended the fishing nets and boats, while others helped gather the onion harvest in the nearby fields or collected salt from the salt pans along the coast.

Even though Sami was kept busy by his work with the refugees, he had started to feel that his life was like a piece of driftwood floating aimlessly across a vast ocean. He couldn't stop himself from thinking that he had failed, failed the people who believed in him, especially his sister, who was struggling to deal with the loneliness and uncertainty about their mother.

Sami remembered clearly the day that he had decided to break away from the Tamil militant group. Born to a Malay father and a Muslim mother, he had been brought up following the teachings of the Prophet Allah. He had agreed to take on the relief coordinators job to look after the Muslim refugees and had done the best he could. Now he'd have to protect his own family.

Gravel crunched underfoot as he approached the two-room hut he shared with his sister Suria. The small, rectangular houses the refugee's used were built of concrete cinder blocks and corrugated-iron roofing, consisting of only two rooms and an outhouse.

The outline of two men coming out of a building a couple of doors away made Sami pause in the shadow of a coconut palm. Sami had heard complaints from a few of the refugee families that a local gang was taking advantage of them, demanding money and other favours in return for the protection they offered. He watched as the two men walked onto the road, their voices raised in laughter. The men did not notice that they were being observed and passed within a few metres of him, not conscious of his presence.

Sami stepped out of the shadows and moved silently towards the hut he occupied with his sister. He paused at the door, looking towards where the men had gone before slipping inside the small building.

Suria kneeled on the floor as if in prayer, face to the ground, her hands cupped over her ears, sobbing. Sami ran to her and cradled her in his arms. 'Why are you crying?' he asked, looking around. He saw that the table they used for eating was on its side. 'What happened?'

'Where have you been?' she cried. 'Two men came here wanting money. They threatened to hurt me if they didn't get what they wanted.'

Sami felt the blood rush to his head. 'Did they touch you?' he asked breathlessly. He was ashamed of himself. A deep, deathly shame he'd never felt before. He should have been here protecting her.

Suria shook her head. 'No, no. They didn't hurt me,' she said breathlessly. 'They knocked over the table and I gave them what money I had, so they went away.'

Sami cradled his sister to his chest, his thoughts full of relief and red-hot anger. He wanted to go after the two men he saw on the street and teach them a lesson, but it wouldn't be the smart thing to do. They belonged to a gang run by a man named Mahen. They would come back with more men and he couldn't risk Suria getting hurt.

'Don't cry,' he said calming himself with difficulty. 'I promise it won't happen again. I'll take care of it.' Sami knew he couldn't fix this by himself. He would follow the rules laid out by the relief agency and report it to the police, again, but this time he'd make sure that they listened.

Suria continued sobbing. It broke his heart to listen to her cry. She had always been his little sister and he somehow felt that he was letting her down. Sami knew that she was very unhappy, missing their mother, who had decided to remain with her parents in Jaffna.

'Suria, listen,' he said, stroking her hair, holding her close to him. 'I know you are unhappy because you are missing *amma* -mother. You know the last letter we got from her said that she is doing well. Priyani is visiting the camp next week and I'll speak to her about trying to get them out of Jaffna.'

Eventually Suria calmed down and Sami let her go. He upended the table and placed the bag on it. 'I brought some *dallo* -squid, for us to eat,' he said, looking at Suria. 'Can you prepare it for dinner?'

Suria sniffled, her face swollen with tears. She took the bag from Sami and walked to the next room. The room at the back where they slept, had a small kerosene single burner cooker that they used to boil water and cook any food. Sami thought about the home they had left empty in Colombo, frowning when he realised one of the table legs was loose. He yearned to be back in his familiar surroundings, but he knew not to push his luck. He'd been lucky not to get sent to jail for joining the Tigers and fighting the army. He really didn't want to draw any attention to himself.

So much had happened since the skirmishes with the military on the Western Highway. He had gone back into the jungle to extricate his men from the situation he'd left them in. He had been almost paralysed by exhaustion after their escape to Kilinochchi. It had taken almost a day and a half of hard travel through the scrub jungle to get back to the highway from Mannar.

Leaving his sister Suria behind with David and Priyani that day had been difficult. Not that he did not trust them to keep his sister safe. The Captain was very capable as Sami had discovered. But it was separatist territory and he was not certain that a Tiger patrol would not pass by.

Sami had watched when the three of them were picked up by the army patrol. Sami was hidden a hundred metres away, concealed by the leafy branches of a Mara tree. He felt a choke of emotion as he watched Priyani, her arm around Suria, help her climb into the truck. Priyani worked as the coordinator for the relief agency whom he now worked for and was one of the hostages Sami and the army Captain had freed from the Black Tigers.

Sami's thoughts turned to Danika as they often did. He wondered what she was doing, was she even alive? His relationship with the leader of the small team of women sent to support them was strange. She had been hard and uncompromising when they had first met in Jaffna, even to the point of being rude to him, treating him like she would a servant. But he had sensed a softening in her attitude and even friendliness, although she ferociously guarded her independence and the other women in her team.

All that was irrelevant right now, Sami sighed. He had an immediate problem he needed to solve. He would use cunning and guile before resorting to brute force and violence. He wondered for a moment whether he should contact his uncle Saheed who was an officer in the Sri Lankan Artillery Regiment but discarded the idea immediately. Sami had never shied away from danger and this was just another challenge for him to overcome. But he needed to be careful. The men whom he had to deal with would not show any mercy.

CHAPTER SEVEN

TRINCOMALEE

Dark clouds filled the horizon when David looked down at the green paddy fields passing slowly beneath. Ragged lines of women harvested the long stalks of rice in the afternoon sun, wrapping them into bundles and leaving them to be collected by the men. The area was irrigated from the ancient reservoir at Kantale that collected water from the Mahaweli river which flowed out to sea not far away.

To the left, the vast expanse of dense, arid jungle known as the Vanni covered most of the north-east of the island. The thick vegetation spread far to the north, unbroken except for patches of open grassland and glinting bodies of water. The army had found it increasingly difficult to enter the area without running into the Tamil Tigers who controlled all the main roads and tracks in this mainly undeveloped territory.

David was struck by a guilty pang at the thought of Priyani back in Colombo. He had delighted in her company and although the time they spent together was short, he was able to wind down completely and forget the war. Priyani had been quiet and unusually pensive when they said their goodbyes that morning. David had promised himself while driving away that he would grab the first opportunity to get out from under the tremendous burden his current role placed him in.

David shook his head to clear his thoughts. *Snap out of it!* He couldn't go into a war zone in this frame of mind. It was a good way to get himself killed. He needed to get his head in the game and concentrate on what he was sent to do.

David forced himself to think of the mission. As accustomed as he'd become to the thought of the separatists gaining control of parts of the country, David still struggled to accept the idea of a rival power establishing itself on the island. Putting aside his own access to top secret information, there was simply no avoiding the conclusion that the militant Tigers were preparing for a major confrontation with the government forces in the north. They either wanted to break the rule of law on the peninsula or hurt the authorities so badly that the government wouldn't be able to recover for years.

But David had little thought for the wider issues of the war right now. His attention was focused on the jungle he was heading into with his team. He had read reports of a significant build-up of Tigers in the eastern district close to the port city of Trincomalee. Control of this area would give the Tigers a clear view of the harbour and put them within easy reach of the Sri Lankan navy ships. It would also place them directly under the flight path of aircraft landing at the China Bay air force base. The city's population was a mix of Tamil, Muslim and Sinhalese, and tensions were high. At a recent strategic briefing he had attended in Colombo, it was assessed that the situation in Trincomalee, with its strategically sensitive harbour and potentially volatile ethnic mix, was a particular area of concern.

David reflected on his orders. They were to destroy the militant camp and its inhabitants, and to make every attempt to capture one for interrogation. The orders were contradictory, but David felt cold and functional, ready to do the job he had been trained for. They would have to infiltrate the camp first and grab a militant before destroying it. David knew that once the firing started there couldn't be any hesitation whether to shoot to kill.

Next to him in the military helicopter sat Sarath. They were joining the rest of the men who were already deployed outside Trincomalee. The area they were targeting was a remote range of low hills north of the Naval Headworks Sanctuary where there had been sighting of militant movements. The sanctuary was filled with wild elephants, leopards, sloth bears and other nocturnal animals making it difficult to move around stealthily.

The clouds had lowered and darkened when the helicopter flared for a landing at the China Bay Airfield. It started to rain when David and Sarath were driven in an army jeep to the staging area where they met the rest of the team. David had picked eight men to go into the jungle with. The rest would remain at base as a backup and provide security when they returned.

The afternoon rain eased shortly before the team was dropped off on a track that joined the Kandy Road, south of the little hamlet of Palampodduru. These forest tracks were made with tree trunks placed lengthwise. To stop the trunks from being washed away by rain, wooden logs were placed across them and the spaces in between were filled with soil which was then rammed in. Roads built like this were redone each year after the rainy season was over. This may sound easy, but the work involved was back-breaking.

They moved quickly off the track in the dark and stopped under the wide branches of a tall Mara tree. The late afternoon showers had left the trees dripping with water and the half-moon that appeared occasionally from behind the dark clouds had just enough light filtering through them to see a few metres.

David paused to wipe his face across the sleeve of his faded jungle green shirt, feeling the prickle of his thick stubble through the fabric. The temperature under the canopy was in the high eighties by his estimation, the humidity of the monsoon jungle leaving the smell of wet leaves and dirt hanging in the air. The call of a startled peahen on the tree above them froze them in their tracks. Even this far south of their objective it was not smart startling any wildlife into activity.

Indika, who was their designated point man, ghosted forward after the bird settled, slipping into the shadows without a sound. A tall man, Indika moved like a cat, ducking smoothly under branches, stepping fluidly over logs and avoiding any jungle debris that would make a sound if stepped on. David followed, staying close, sensing his men moving in behind him.

The hoarse rasping call of a leopard not far away froze them in place. A fierce nocturnal hunter, it would do them no good to run into one that night. Indika paused like a deer, listening and scenting the air around him. David sank to his haunches, his palms sweaty on the rifle he carried. After what seemed like an eternity, Indika moved forward again, away from where the sound came.

The jungle was not quiet. Rustling sounds from the dense undergrowth around them and the branches above kept the whole team on edge. The loud trumpeting of an elephant warning a predator away made David almost jump out of his skin.

The humidity of the forest had made them uncomfortable and wet beneath their tactical vests and David was thankful when he followed Indika up an incline and onto the long grass of a clearing. He'd worked up a sweat walking uphill and the back of his legs ached. The sky was lightening above, showing that dawn was near.

The outline of a rocky outcrop on a small hill rose suddenly from the surrounding jungle in front of them. It had taken most of the night for them to make their way to the bottom of the low range of craggy hills, not more than two hundred metres tall, the hills marching gently towards the north-east.

'We'll rest up here,' David said, looking over his shoulder at Sarath.

'Indika, you scout around to make sure we are alone.' Indika nodded at David, slipping back into the jungle at the edge of the clearing. 'Sarath you take first watch and wake me in two hours' time.'

∾

David's eyes burned, and his head fell leaden. The sun had struggled all day behind heavy monsoon clouds, finally succumbing to the quick onset of darkness common in the tropics. Annoyed by the constant hubbub of monkeys and birds, David had finally fallen asleep after his stint on guard duty and woke up with a blinding headache. He gulped down two aspirin from a bottle he always carried in his pack as he listened to a report from Sarath.

Indika had spotted what looked like the camp under the jungle canopy about a kilometre away during one of his perimeter patrols. It was exactly where the informer had said it would be. Indika had watched it from the crest of a nearby hill and had noticed that the camp was quite active with many comings and goings. He had spotted two sentries, one to the south at the base of the hill he was on and another to the east.

David looked at his compass and peered through the trees. 'Indika, I want you to take out the sentry near the hill as that will be our point of approach.' David didn't think that capturing a low-level sentry would give them the intelligence they needed. He wanted someone who was part of the meeting and would know what was happening.

'Once you do that, take Jaya and stop anyone escaping to the north. Make sure you stay back from the camp so that you won't be hit by our fire.'

'The rest of you come with me.' David waited a few moments. 'I will infiltrate the camp and grab one of them. Only after I do that is anyone to open fire.'

The stars that night looked brilliant and familiar, the three-quarter moon occasionally covered by high, scudding clouds. David looked around at his men, their faces dark with camouflage cream, only the white of their eyes looking intently at him. They had been together for almost three years and he trusted them with his life. 'Any questions?'

Not hearing any, he nodded at Indika who slipped silently into the jungle. They would give Indika enough time to take out the sentry before following.

It was almost an hour before David heard the double click on the radio. 'Ok, that's it,' he said, looking around. 'Remember what I said about waiting until I give the signal.'

Easing through the undergrowth, they moved much slower knowing that that any unusual sound would alert the camp. Indika joined them after twenty minutes of picking their way through the jungle. He led them until the low glow of a fire behind a clump of trees, and the sound of quiet voices made them spread out. David settled behind a collapsed tree trunk and peered over its top, closing one of his eyes so he wouldn't lose his night vision completely.

David could see the fire and the shape of someone sitting next to it but could not make out how many others there were. He looked around and saw that Sarath was not far from him. David crawled over to him, putting his head as close as he could to the Sergeant's face. 'Disperse the men and tell them to be ready. I am moving closer to the fire,' he whispered. 'Watch my back.'

David slithered over the tree trunk hoping that there weren't any snakes around. They usually hid under fallen trees during the day and came out to hunt at night. He crawled forward slowly using his elbows and knees to move forward a few centimetres at a time. He was able to make out the sound of at least half-a-dozen voices as he got closer to the fire.

An empty lean-to made by weaving low branches together appeared out of the darkness in front of him. It was about twenty metres from the fire. A bulging gunny sack hung from one of the branches and a piece of cloth, neatly laid out on a bed of leaves, was ready for its owner to lie on.

David was contemplating what to do when a shape detached from the darkness around the fire and moved towards the structure. A voice called out from the fire and the response was inaudible.

It's a woman, David realised, hearing her voice. *This is going to make it interesting.*

David knew that women cadre served with the militant forces in various capacities. Recently he had heard from an informer that they had formed into a fighting force and were training somewhere in the Vanni jungles.

The woman dressed in a dark uniform knelt outside the lean-to, adjusting the cloth on the ground before crawling onto it. She curled into a sleeping position, her back to David.

Time passed slowly as David waited for the camp to fall asleep. The woman lying in the shadow of the lean-to had not moved at all. The glow from the fire had dimmed down to coals before he decided to move. Slinging his rifle quietly over his shoulder he crept forward centimetre by centimetre until he was right next to the structure. David could feel the blood pounding in his ears, amplifying with every movement he made. Quietly untying the knot from the scarf around his neck, he gathered himself for a moment and launched himself on top of the woman, crushing her with his weight.

The woman exhaled audibly as the air was forced out of her. David clamped his hand down on her face with his scarf, smothering her.

The woman gasped loudly for breath, her eyes wide open in shock by the sudden assault. A voice called out from the fire and the woman tried to respond through the scarf covering her face. David clubbed her on the side of the head with his forearm quietening her. He crouched on top of the woman, his knees pinning her arms to her sides. He reached around, unslinging his automatic rifle and switching the selector to the semi-automatic firing position.

A voice called out again and David made out the shape of two men as they left the circle of firelight, walking towards the lean-to. David saw that one of the men carried an AK-47 automatic rifle, distinct by its curved magazine, hanging by a sling on his shoulder.

David cantered his aim at the body mass of the man carrying the rifle and pulled the trigger twice, swinging the rifle from right to left. Both men dropped immediately. Gunfire erupted around him, the rifle flashes silhouetting the trees around the camp.

The surprise was total. No return fire came their way. David heard his men moving forward in a line clearing the camp site as they did. The air smelt of cordite when the firing eventually died down. They would need to head out quickly in case there were other militant units around, but the men would check the bodies for identification and documents first. They knew the procedure to follow and how much time they had.

David stayed where he was. The light from the fire reflected off the woman's face when he looked down at her. She had stopped struggling when the gunfire started, and he could feel her body tremble in shock beneath his when he reached down and ripped open the top buttons of her shirt. A glass vial, not larger than the size of the top joint of his little finger, hung between her small almost pubescent breasts. David grabbed the cord, ripping it off her neck and stuffing it into one of his pockets. He had neglected to properly search a young militant he had captured once before, and the boy had bitten into the vial which contained a cyanide capsule, killing himself within seconds.

David patted the woman down, finding a knife on a belt around her waist which he tossed into the undergrowth. Other than the knife, she was unarmed. David turned her around roughly and tied her arms beneath her back.

'If you remain still you won't be hurt,' he whispered in her ear. 'Do you understand?'

The woman nodded, her eyes wide in terror. Grabbing her body, he lifted her onto his shoulder and moved quietly away from the camp.

He felt his men fall in protectively around him as they moved quickly back over the low hill, across the open grassland and into the safety of the jungle.

CHAPTER EIGHT

KALPITIYA REFUGEE CAMP

Priyani made sure she was in the relief agency office before Sami and Suria got there. She had left Colombo long before dawn to get to the small fishing village on the central west coast. Negotiating the many roadblocks and security checkpoints in and out of the city took time, especially after the bus station bombing.

'Ah, Suria,' she said, coming around the desk and hugging her. 'I have been looking forward to seeing you. How have you been doing?' Suria clung to Priyani like a long-lost friend.

Sensing that something was not right Priyani grasped Suria by both her shoulders and looked into her face. 'What's wrong,' she asked. Seeing that Suria's eyes were full of tears she looked questioningly at Sami. 'What happened?'

Priyani's eyes narrowed as Sami described the incident with the local gang.

'So, have you lodged a complaint,' she asked.

Sami nodded. 'I went to the police station and lodged an official complaint,' he said, 'but it's a waste of time. Mahen has paid the local constabulary to ignore complaints from the refugees.'

This wasn't the first time Priyani had experienced this kind of situation. It made her blood boil. 'That's not right,' she said angrily. 'Can't we go to the Station Commander?'

'I did,' said Sami. 'I spoke with the Sub-Inspector and I heard that Mahen was taken in for questioning. But I am not sure for how long he'll be locked up,' Sami shrugged. 'You know how these things work.'

Priyani nodded. 'I can get Rohan to talk to the District Superintendent.' Her brother worked for the President and would have the authority to speak to someone at that level.

'Yes,' Sami nodded. 'I think it'll be worth the effort. I did what I could do from here, but he could be released any day.'

Priyani leaned back in her chair. *I must do something for them.* Their father and brother had been killed at their place of business during the riots and the house they had lived in had been partially ransacked. It was time she pulled some strings!

'I don't think this whole situation is working too well for you is it?' she asked studying Sami.

Priyani nodded after seeing the look on Sami's face. 'Yes, I thought so. I will talk to Rohan again and try and get you moved back to your home in Colombo. But it may take a bit of time.'

'Have you heard from your mother?' she asked. 'We have lost touch with our contacts in Jaffna after the Indian army came. I don't think any of the refugee services in Jaffna are working right now.'

Sami had taken his mother and sister to Jaffna to be safe from the troubles in Colombo. But the situation in Jaffna had become worse and he'd decided to get his family out when he found out that the Tamil leadership had decided to evict all the Moors living in Jaffna. The news had shocked Sami. There were thousands of Moors living in Jaffna, some families had been there for centuries. His grandparents were very old and had lived in Jaffna all their lives. He did not think they were capable of living anywhere new at their age. It was the turning point for him. It had shaken his belief that he was doing the right thing by fighting someone else's war. He didn't trust the Tigers anymore and had decided to leave the organisation.

His mother had refused to leave her parents when Sami had arranged for his family to escape from Jaffna by boat. She had sent word that she'd try to get out with them. She had saved some money and her plan was to pay a truck driver to extricate them.

'No, we have not heard anything for a while,' Sami shrugged. 'I was hoping you would have some news.'

'We haven't either,' Priyani said. 'But there is a new group of refugees from Jaffna who have arrived in Kilinochchi and also in Trincomalee. The refugees are being processed and I'll keep a lookout for their names on the list.'

CHAPTER NINE

COLOMBO

'*Kohomada Mahathaya* –Hello Sir?' Asilin greeted David as he walked through the front door into the cool hall. David had just returned from the north after attending an intelligence briefing. He had come to his parents' home in the southern suburb of Ratmalana after the meeting concluded early.

Asilin was a small woman. The top of her head was well below the level of David's chin. Until about ten years of age David hadn't understood the class system in the country. He had always thought of Asilin as a part of the family until he learnt the role of a servant. His mother had shouted at her one day for breaking a dish and said that she would deduct the money from her salary until she had paid for it. David never treated her as a servant though, the two of them had a close relationship. She treated him like one of her own.

David bent down as she hugged him and stroked his face, looking up at him gently. 'What a big man you have become … my *Loku Baba*.'

'*Kohomada* Asilin, are you keeping well?' She was a young girl when his father brought her from a village in the south to look after him soon after he was born. Now a mother of her own children, she had become the family cook.

She looked at him with a worried expression. 'Yes, I am well. I am happy you came. I have something important to ask you.'

She spoke to David in Sinhalese. Asilin understood English and could even be persuaded to speak it occasionally but Sinhalese was the language of their earliest days together.

David placed his shoulder bag on the table next to the front door. 'Yes, *Loku Missi* told me you wanted to talk to me. What's the problem?'

She took him by his hand to the rear of the house. 'Come, come. Sit here with me.' The kitchen smelt of wood smoke and food. It had an open fireplace for cooking, its soot blackened chimney poking out through the tiled roof. Open cupboards lined the walls filled with bags of rice and different types of lentils. A four-legged wooden chest held an assortment of fresh vegetables.

David sat on a low stool next to the chest. Asilin walked over to the large refrigerator which sat proudly in the corner and poured him a glass of water. She knew his fondness for icy cold water.

She brought it over to him and squatted on the floor next to him, her lips twisted in anxiety. 'I am worried about Nalini. I have not heard from her. The last letter I got said that she was pregnant.'

Nalini was her daughter who lived far away in the north of the country. A pretty dark-skinned girl about David's age, she had fallen in love with a young man from the adjoining village and married against her mother's wishes.

'Do they still live in the Vanni?' David asked sipping the cold water. Before the war, the government encouraged young couples from the south to resettle in the north to farm the land and grow cash crops.

Asilin nodded her head. 'Yes, in Hunuwilagama.'

David knew the village. Not more than a collection of houses near the entrance to the Wilpattu Wildlife sanctuary, he remembered it had a small *kade* -store, selling supplies and an eating house.

'Is Thenu still working as a game warden?' Nalini's husband Thenu worked for the wildlife sanctuary as a game warden, but the sanctuary had been closed to visitors since the war began. David remembered the quiet young man who had helped him track down the terrorists who had kidnapped Priyani and Eileen.

'I don't know,' Asilin said looking at David sadly. 'It's been almost three months since I got a letter from her. I would like to go and visit her. *Loku Missi* will give me leave if I ask but I am getting too old to travel that far.'

Normally a very cheerful person, David could see that she was upset. He had grown up with Nalini and her brother Justin. They spent their school holidays with their mother in Colombo where they learnt to speak English. David benefited by becoming fluent in Sinhalese and learning about their culture.

Asilin stood up abruptly and walked to the open fireplace. She reached out with a tea towel for the blackened metal kettle which sat in the glowing embers, gentle wisps of steam floating out of its curved spout. 'Would you like a cup of tea?'

David liked the way Asilin made a cup of tea, thick and strong and sweetened with condensed milk. She consumed numerous cups of sweetened tea during the day and always had a kettle on the boil. Her sweet tooth was legendary in the household.

'Yes please, I miss your wonderful cups of tea,' David said, smiling at her.

Asilin smiled as she poured hot water from the kettle into a glass she had filled with a pinch of tea leaves. Leaving the mixture to brew for a few minutes she strained the tea through a small metal sieve and stirred in a heaped teaspoon of condensed milk, mixing it well until it frothed at the surface.

'Let me finish what I am doing, and I'll join you.' She bent down and picked up a broken half of coconut lying next to the wooden coconut scraper. Asilin had been scraping coconut when David rang the doorbell. The well-used kitchen implement was a low four-legged wooden stool with a sharp tooth-edged metal spur sticking out from one end.

David watched as Asilin sat sideways on the scraper and picked up half a coconut in her hand. The fresh coconut would have been plucked that morning from the back garden. 'Thenu is a good man but he has found it difficult to get any work,' Asilin said.

She leant forward cupping the half-broken shell in her hands, pressing it against the metal spur. Scrapings of tender white flesh fell in piles into the container as she rotated the nut, grating it against the tiny metal teeth. 'It's a hard life up there. I didn't want her to go but she is stubborn. If she is having a baby, she will find it very difficult. She should be with us when the baby is born.'

David had watched her scrape coconut a hundred times before. 'What do you want me to do?' he asked.

She looked at him pleadingly. 'Could you go and see how she is doing? I have saved a little money for her. I want you to give it to her.'

David considered her request. He was due back in Jaffna on the weekend. Perhaps he could drive past the village.

David nodded, 'Yes, I can do that. I have to be in Jaffna by Sunday and I will drive instead of taking the morning flight. I can give them the money then.'

Asilin digested what David had said. '*Bohoma isthuthi Mahathaya* -Thank you Sir, I knew you would be able to help,' she said, smiling at him gratefully.

David sipped on the cup of tea watching her soak the grated coconut flesh in warm water and squeeze out the thick creamy essence. She then poured the white mixture through a fine sieve producing a thick coconut milk she could use for cooking. A ritual she went through every evening, storing the fresh milk in a large glass container in the refrigerator to be used the next day.

Asilin washed her hands in the kitchen sink and dried them on her sarong. She went over to a narrow *almirah* –cupboard, in the corner where she kept her personal belongings.

She took out a crushed envelope folded in half and handed the few notes it contained to David. 'Can you give this to her?' She then walked over to the fireplace and poured herself a cup of tea before sitting cross legged on the floor next to him.

David looked at what she had given him. It wasn't a lot of money. David knew that she saved her monthly wage and sent it all to her family in the village. His mother provided everything she used in their home. Her food, clothes and any medicines she needed.

Asilin saw him looking into the money. 'It's not a lot of money but that's all I can afford to send them. I have to send money to *amma* –mother, as well.'

'It's good that you can send her something. I will make sure she gets it,' David said. 'Is there any message you want me to give her?'

Asilin looked at him gratefully. 'Yes, tell her that I cannot be with her during the birth of her baby. She should come back home to the village. My mother can look after her.'

David nodded his head. 'Yes, I will do that.'

David sat with Asilin in the kitchen until he heard a car reversing into the garage. His father always picked up his mother and they came home together.

David stood up when he heard his parents come into the house. 'I will let the *Missi* –Lady, know how they are doing. She will tell you.'

Asilin thanked him as he left the kitchen to greet his parents. He was hoping to take the two of them out for dinner.

℘

WILPATTU NATIONAL PARK

David drove down the dry, unpaved road that led to the game sanctuary. He'd left Colombo early to make the detour to the sanctuary. He wouldn't have another chance to deliver the money that Asilin had sent.

Sprawled across on both sides of the dusty road, huge coconut trees spread out like umbrellas, each one twisting and struggling to carry the large bunch of coconuts under its crown. Around a bend, paddy fields filled with young green paddy shoots, with water-filled canals snaking through the field.

David entered the small village outside the oldest and largest wildlife park in the country. There were no more than a cluster of thatched mud-wattle houses with *cadjan* –woven palm leaf, roofs. A couple of buildings in the middle were more substantial with brick walls and rusted corrugated roofs. Children came running out from their hiding places and followed the jeep when it stopped in front of a small *kade* –store- by the side of the road.

It sold basic supplies of rice, pulses, and vegetables and bottles of kerosene. Stands of green and yellow bananas hung from the ceiling and large jars full of colourful sweets stood on a small wooden counter. A short, fat man stood lounging in the shade of the structure, dressed in a stained white shirt his brown sarong tucked up and tied untidily below his bulging belly.

David leaned across the passenger seat and spoke to the man. 'I am looking for Thenu and Nalini's home. Do you know where they live?'

The man looked at David morosely and spat out a stream of red liquid in front of the jeep. David hated the uncouth habit some villagers had of chewing *bulath* –betel leaf. The blobs of red spittle they spat out left ugly marks on the ground.

'Why do you want to see them? They owe me money.' He stared insolently at David, his face shiny with sweat.

David came out of the vehicle in a fluid motion and walked quickly around the front of the jeep stopping a few feet away from the man. He wore army fatigues with the three crosses of his army Captain's rank on his epaulettes. He had his holstered pistol strapped to his waist and looked very intimidating.

'If you know where they live you'd better tell me,' he said threateningly.

The man's eyes opened wide in shock and beads of sweat appeared on his bald head.

'They live a few houses down this lane,' he said, pointing with his right hand at a side track that went past the *kade*. 'I'll get one of the children to take you there.' The man motioned to a young boy. 'Take this gentleman to Thenu's house,' he said sullenly.

David did not want to let his annoyance of the man's insolence to go unnoticed. He knew that shop owners like this man brought small goods and essentials to outlying areas and sold them to the villagers, who often had no money, while they waited for their crops to be harvested. The *Mudalalis* -businessmen, provided the villagers with easy credit and charged exorbitant interest rates or took their crops as payment, increasing the misery of these helpless people.

David stepped into the small structure. 'Have you got a permit to operate a *kade* here?' he said looking around.

David knew that the man would need a permit to sell goods on any government owned and operated road. The rough unpaved track at the entrance to the sanctuary may have not looked like a proper road but David knew that it had an official designation on the maps he had seen.

The man looked nervously at David. 'I don't need a permit.'

David nodded his head at the man. 'Yes, you do. This is a government road and you need a permit to sell goods here. I can have you arrested and your shop closed down.'

'Please don't do that Sir.' The man clasped his hands together and bowed his head to David. 'It's my only business and I have a wife and family to feed.'

David was pleased by his reaction. 'How much does Thenu owe you?' He asked.

The man looked scared. 'They owe me about 500 Rupees Sir,' he said uneasily. 'I have not refused to give them anything they wanted.'

David looked at him closely. 'What is the real amount?' He asked. 'Without the interest you have added?'

'It's about 350 Rupees sir.' The man nervously licked his lips and kept looking around.

The amount of money was very small. David had more than double this in his pocket. He pulled out his wallet and took out a few hundred Rupee notes holding them out to the man. 'Here is 400 Rupees. They now owe you nothing. You'll be sorry if I hear that you asked them for more.'

The man put his hand out and took the money. 'Yes Sir, thank you, Sir.'

David turned around and got into the jeep. The young boy who had been asked to guide him waved David forward and he turned the jeep down the narrow track which wound around trees and vanished into the surrounding scrub.

They soon came to the hut, a crude small structure a little more than a hovel. Its mud-wattle walls held up a thick mass of woven coconut leaves resting on a frame of rough timber. A faded blue plastic sheet held down by pieces of brushwood covered one side of the roof.

The hut sat in the middle of a neat sandy garden with blooming Bougainvillea plants growing in clay pots scattered around the structure. A small outhouse made of mud plastered on rough sticks stood in one corner of the compound. An *ekel* -coir broom, stood next to the door by a pile of dust and leaves.

Thenu and Nalini came outside when they heard the jeep approach with its noisy pack of children running behind the vehicle. A small child peeped from behind Nalini.

David got out and walked into the garden raising his hand in a greeting. '*Ayubowan* Nalini, Thenu. It's nice to see you. And is this your daughter?'

Both were emaciated, their clothes hanging on them. Thenu hung back as Nalini ran forward when she saw him. She knelt in front of David touching his feet in the traditional gesture of respect and greeting. David leant down and raised her to her feet. She did not weigh much at all. Concerned by her state he held her by the shoulders and looked at her carefully.

'David *Mahathaya*, it's good to see you. Is my mother okay?' she asked him with a look of concern on her face.

'Yes, she is fine. She sent me here to see how you are doing.' David could tell that she had been through much. She had been a pretty girl but had lost the spark of youth and looked much older.

'Please come in,' she gestured towards the hut. She gathered her daughter in her arms and waited for David to move.

David stepped around an untidy pile of firewood that had been collected from the jungle. It would be the only fuel they used to cook their food.

Surprisingly cool inside, the dark room smelt of wood smoke and food. Filtered streams of sunlight shone down from the makeshift roof allowing him to look around.

A crude, wide wooden bench on one side held a rolled-up reed mattress and personal belongs. The soot blackened fireplace which took up most of one wall held a few burnt clay pots turned over to drain on a reed mat. A shelf with a shiny brass vase containing flowers from the garden stood next to a small statue of the Buddha.

Nalini bent over and picked up a wooden pestle lying on a reed mat next to a *wangediya* –mortar, filled with small brown seeds. The tamped clay floor of the hut covered in a thin paste of mud and cow dung mixture, smoothed and dried to a dark brown finish had been freshly swept.

'I pound *kurakkan* seeds to make flour, she shrugged apologetically. 'It grows wild around here.' David knew that *kurakkan* was a finger millet that the poorer villagers ate to supplement their diet. Made into a flat bread or boiled into a paste, it could be eaten with a curry of some sort.

'Would you like some water to drink?'

Nalini poured water from an earthenware pot lying under the wooden bench into a glass. Wonderfully cool and refreshing from being in the pot David remembered visiting Asilin's home in the south and drinking from a similar container.

'Asilin is worried that she has not heard from you. She said that you are pregnant and hoped that you are well.'

Nalini nodded her head. 'Yes, I am well. The baby is okay. Thenu took me for a check-up last week.'

David glanced at Thenu who stood inside the doorway with a look of concern on his face. He owed the young game warden for helping track the Black Tiger team who had kidnapped Priyani and Eileen after their killing rampage at the Shri Maha Bodhi temple. Without his help it would have been extremely difficult to track them through the jungle.

'Do you have enough food? You will need extra nourishment during your pregnancy.'

Nalini glanced at Thenu who looked down with embarrassment.

'We have not had work for some time now. We are living on what the *kade Mudalali* is able to give us. We owe him a lot of money.'

'Your mother has sent you some money.' David handed the envelope Asilin gave him, to Nalini.

David looked at Thenu. 'I have spoken to my friend who has a farm near Nochiyagama. There is a driver's job available for you.' Thenu's head came up and he looked at David with a light dawning in his eyes. Nochiyagama was a major town on the Puttalam-Trincomalee road not far from where they lived. 'Go tomorrow to the farm behind the *vidyalaya* -school and ask for Fonseka. Say that I sent you. He will take care of everything. And Nalini, you go too. He needs someone to keep the bungalow clean.'

A bright smile lit up her face as she heard David. She rushed over to him and hugged him, her thin frame light against his strong body.

'Thank you so very much,' she whispered in English. She released him and stepped back, going down on her knees, before bowing her head and touching his feet with her forehead.

David bent down and raised her to her feet. 'There is no need to do that Nalini. If I knew things were so bad I would have helped sooner. My mother also sent you some money.' He gave her another, fatter envelope which his mother had given him.

Tears poured down her cheeks when she took the envelope from him. 'It's been very difficult, and we didn't have any money to even send a letter. You are like a gift from the Lord Buddha.'

David realised how difficult their life had been. A long time ago he had questioned his grandfather as to why Asilin's family did not have the same opportunities and benefits that they themselves enjoyed as a family. The old Scotsman explained to David that Asilin's family came from a very poor village and would have almost no chance of breaking away from the class that they belonged to. By working as servants for a European family they would be much better off as their status would be elevated in the village. According to his grandfather, this would lead to better jobs and would eventually improve their position since occupation governed the class they belonged to.

David realised that Nalini had married a man from a similar village she came from, whose circumstances were not much different to hers. He knew that Asilin had been against the marriage as she wanted her daughter to marry someone of a higher standing in the community.

Nalini had opened the two envelopes and showed Thenu the money they contained.

'Take this and pay off our debt to the *kade Mudalali*. He has been very patient with us.'

'You don't have to worry about him. I paid him on my way here. Keep that money for yourselves and make sure you eat well. You will need it.'

Nalini cried as she hugged Thenu. He looked at David over her shoulder nodding his thanks before burying his face in her hair.

David stepped outside the hut and took a few deep breaths. He felt emotional seeing the love the two of them had for each other. He suddenly missed Priyani and decided to call her when he got to Vavuniya.

Nalini and Thenu followed him outside. Nalini wiped the tears from her face and David could see the familiar sparkle back in her eyes.

'I have to leave now. I pass this way quite regularly and will come again to see you. If you need anything just ask Fonseka to send a message to me.'

Nalini nodded her head, holding tightly to Thenu's arm.

'Tell *amma* I will write to her today. Give her my love.'

He waved to them as he reversed the jeep and went back the way he came. He still had a long ride to Vavuniya ahead of him.

CHAPTER TEN

CENTRAL HIGHLANDS

Mukesh slept fitfully on the cool cement platform preferring to spend the night outside the stuffy room. He was eventually woken by the growling and whining of stray dogs that lived outside the lines. He rolled over, seeking a more comfortable position as he strained to hear what had disturbed the animals.

He raised himself on his elbows as the barking took on a more urgent quality. The animals often bickered and played, even in the early hours, but there was rarely such a note of nervousness in their barking. Mukesh remembered that today was the funeral of a worker who had died after being bitten by a King Cobra. The long, venomous snake usually avoided confrontation with humans, but the unfortunate worker had stepped on it while cleaning out the stone-lined drains which channelled rain water down the mountain slopes. Maybe the snake was still around.

Mukesh exhaled a sigh of relief when the commotion eventually died down, leaving him fully awake. Lying with his hands interlaced behind his head, Mukesh stared up at the stars partly obscured by fast moving clouds. His thoughts drifted wistfully to the time when he used to sleep with his father on the front veranda of their home in a neighbouring estate. He remembered his mother making *dhal puris* early in the morning, flinging them into the air, clapping them as they fell light as feathers like flakes of layered silk across her palms. The soft flattened dough smelled of warm ghee and aromatic spices and were so tender they'd melt in the mouth. So much had changed since then.

A gong from the metal tube hanging outside the tea factory above the lines signalled the time for the women to rise and prepare the day's meal. A watchman from the factory, holding a kerosene lantern to light his way, walked through the estate lines calling out the time. Lights began appearing inside the rooms as kerosene lanterns were lit. The sounds of wood being chopped, and pots being rinsed mingled with the occasional cry of children.

The pungent smell of spices permeated the air as women ground chillies and turmeric on granite stone mortars to prepare pastes for the day's curry. The food cooked fresh every day, was wrapped in sheets of old newspapers and carried to work.

A crowd began gathering outside one of the rooms. The dead worker had been washed and anointed with gingelly oil the previous evening in preparation for burial. His shrouded remains had been wrapped in a white cloth and were being carried on a plank to the *sudukadu* –the burning field, for cremation. The women let out a heartrending wail that pierced the air. This was their goodbye as they did not go to the pyre.

At the burial ground, the body was carried three times counter-clockwise around the funeral pyre before being placed on the structure. It was covered with wood, and long sticks of incense were burnt as an offering to the Gods. An oil lamp was passed in a counter-clockwise, circular motion over the remains – everything was symbolically reversed in death. The chief mourner of the deceased, his bare chest glistening in the morning sun, circled the pyre in the same direction carrying a clay pot on his left shoulder while holding a glowing firebrand behind his back.

At each turn around the pyre, a relative knocked a hole in the pot with a knife, letting water out, signifying life leaving its vessel. At the end of three turns, the chief mourner dropped the pot shattering it. Then without facing the body, he lit the pyre and walked away from the cremation grounds.

While some of the men stayed to tend the fire, the rest went back to their homes for the ritual cleansing of impurity. They exited into the misty morning, the sun trying to break through the low-lying clouds. Some of the men were barefoot, although if the hot earth scorched their feet, no one appeared to notice. The men bathed and cleansed the room. A lamp and a clay water pot were placed where the body had lain.

Mukesh sat on the stoop wondering what he should be doing with his life. He missed the danger and excitement of being an intelligence operative. Even though it had only been about three weeks since he left the north, he missed living on the edge. The tension, the adrenaline rush when he sensed danger, knowing that any false move would mean he would end up with his throat cut and lying on some stinking pile of garbage.

The workers lines were quiet that afternoon. The men and women were out working late, delayed by the funeral that morning. They still had to meet their quota for the day or money would be deducted from their wages. Apart from the dejected clucking of the chickens, he could hear children playing a game somewhere beyond the buildings.

It was almost dusk when small groups of men and women started trickling back from the estate offices. Cooking fires were lit and the smell of *dosa* frying on flat iron skillets permeated the air. The evening meal usually consisted of flat bread eaten with a mixed vegetable curry and a spicy coconut sambal.

A man riding a shiny new red bicycle, stopped at the entrance to the lines. He was wearing a clean white shirt and *dhoti*, a traditional cloth garment passed through the legs and tucked at the back, covering the legs loosely. A new bicycle was a rare sight and children came running out of the rooms excitedly to touch the shiny metal, their parents poking their heads out wondering what the commotion was about.

Mukesh knew right away by the man's bearing that he was the *Head Kangani* -Overseer. With the indentured system of labour on the estates, a *Kangani* was responsible for the livelihood of a gang of workers. All gangs on the estate reported to the *Head Kangani* who acted as an intermediary to the estate *Durai* -Superintendent. The *Head Kangani* managed the payment of wages for the *Durai* and wielded unlimited power over the entire estate labour force.

Mukesh studied the *Kangani* who was surrounded by children. He was a gaunt old man with a lined face. Above average height, he was still lean and fit, his body muscular. Mukesh wondered what type of man he was. While some *Kangani's* commanded respect from the estate communities displaying generosity and kindness, others were unscrupulous and corrupt.

'I wonder what he wants?' Rani said, coming out to the stoop.

Mukesh glanced over his shoulder at his sister Rani who was watching the man. 'He never comes here except to collect his portion of our salary on pay-day and that's on a Friday.'

Rani glanced at Mukesh sitting on the concrete stoop. 'The man's trouble', she warned him. 'He's probably heard you are living with us and wants us to pay him extra.'

Mukesh nodded his head in understanding. 'I will deal with him', he said quietly. 'Now go back inside.'

The *Kangani* had not even glanced at Mukesh sitting on the stoop but Mukesh's senses, fine-tuned by many hours of undercover work in the north, were tingling a warning. It sounded like the *Kangani* was one of those men who preyed on the helpless workers.

The *Kangani* eventually shooed away the children, enlisting an older boy to watch the bicycle, and walked in Mukesh's direction. Mukesh acknowledged the man as he drew closer, inclining his head in a respectful gesture. He didn't want to antagonise the man knowing his sister and her family would bear the repercussions.

The *Kangani* stopped opposite Mukesh, studying him for a moment.

'I heard that Rani's brother was visiting,' he said abruptly, almost rudely. 'Will you be staying long?'

Mukesh held his temper in check. *I am going to teach this overbearing pig a lesson,* he thought.

'And who are you to ask?' he asked guilelessly, knowing it would upset the man.

The *Kangani's* eyes met Mukesh's confidently. 'The *Durai* has appointed me to manage these dwellings,' the *Kangani* said arrogantly puffing out his chest. 'Anyone living here has to be a worker.' The man smiled, thinking he had the upper hand.

Mukesh knew that this was not true. Money was deducted as rent from the workers' pay and there was never any stipulation whether the people living in the dwelling needed to be an estate worker. Many of the workers had their brothers and sisters and their elderly parents living with them.

'Is that really true?' Mukesh asked, nodding to himself as if he had made up his mind. 'I think I will go to the *Durai* directly and ask for his permission to let a poor cripple stay with his sister.'

The *Kangani* looked at Mukesh in disbelief. He was not used to being questioned by the workers. 'You cannot do that,' the man snapped angrily. 'No one can address the *Durai* except through me.'

Mukesh knew that to be true. The workers only spoke Tamil and the estate *Kangani's* took advantage of the language barrier to control access to the men in charge.

'That is because they cannot speak his language,' Mukesh said, holding the man's gaze. 'I can speak it and I don't need you to translate.'

Mukesh decided he needed to get the upper hand. 'And I will remind the

Durai that we pay rent every month and that you also take my sisters money for her to live here.'

The *Kangani's* eyes narrowed dangerously. Mukesh knew exactly what was going through the man's mind. Someone speaking the estate manager's language would be a direct threat to his authority. He would not want Mukesh going anywhere near the *Durai*.

'I may have been a bit hasty,' he finally admitted shrewdly. 'You can stay with Rani and Kanan as long as you want. Will you be looking for a job around here?'

Mukesh waited a moment, deciding how to answer. He wanted to offer the man a way out, not wanting his sister to suffer any consequences. 'I don't think I want to stay too long.' He said truthfully. 'Maybe a month or two, maybe even less. As you can see I cannot do any physical work with my bad leg and will have to look for work elsewhere.'

The *Kangani* nodded his understanding of the compromise they had reached. 'You can tell your sister that I won't be charging her anything extra,' he said, watching Mukesh closely. 'I don't want you going anywhere near the estate office or the *Durai's* bungalow. If you happen to meet him on the road, you are to speak to him in Tamil and only if he addresses you.'

Mukesh nodded his agreement. It was a good arrangement. But he didn't trust the man and decided to keep a close eye on him.

CHAPTER ELEVEN

KALPITIYA REFUGEE CAMP

Sami thanked Priyani and went out of the room to the veranda. Sami had been impressed with Priyani from the very beginning. The first time he had seen her was when she and her friend crossed the rice paddy as a captive of Iyer and his bunch of thugs. There was no mistaking the inner strength she had displayed at the time, even after spending three days in the jungle. Sami knew instinctively that she would bring them trouble and he had been right.

He leant against the pillar thinking of the events over two years ago that had brought him and Suria to the refugee camp.

Rajan, Sami's second in command, had warned him that the Moors were going to be evicted from Jaffna and that the team he had put together would be disbanded. Hearing the news, Sami had decided to leave the Tigers and become his own man. But he had to warn his people first. After making sure his sister was safe with Priyani and the Captain, he had headed west, walking through the night. The area they had operated in varied enormously, from thick impenetrable jungle to wide, open, dry scrub to swampy, abandoned paddy fields.

Sami had only stopped once the next morning, at a mud brick shack with a woven *cadjan* leaf roof just outside a small farming hamlet at the edge of the jungle. To one side was an overgrown hedge, to the other a rusty barbed wire fence. In the small field next to the shack, a farmer worked calf deep in water, ploughing behind a mud-caked water buffalo who moved unhurriedly through the clinging mire.

A tattered piece of canvas, burnt white by the hot sun, kept the front of the shack shaded. In the dark interior, a middle-aged woman sat on a stool behind a small wooden counter, holding onto an infant. A young girl, not more than five or six years old, peeped shyly from behind her. The woman had fresh country rice and *dhal* -lentil, mixed with a leafy green vegetable that she sold on a banana leaf to Sami for a few Rupees. The meal had refreshed Sami and he left with an extra packet of food which he stored in his ammunition pouch.

He had approached the northern supply camp cautiously, suspecting that the group sent to replace him had already taken over. Sami climbed a tree in a dense thicket of jungle which allowed him to observe the camp without getting too close. He had used this tree once before to watch for army patrols from the north.

There was movement in and around the camp. He watched as people came and went, recognising Danika by the long plait of hair that hung down her back. Sami could not see any of the men who were under his command. He waited until it was dark, watching the activity in the camp until he could not see them any longer. He slid down the tree and moved silently in the undergrowth. He needed to get much closer and talk to one of his people. Sami remembered that Danika, unlike the others, always slept in the bushes away from the centre of the camp. She didn't see the need to huddle with the other women who slept close to the fire for safety and warmth.

Sami crept closer inch by inch. He found his way barred by a thorny thicket which resisted his attempts to push through. He backed away slowly and worked his way around the right side of the clump of bushes. Sami was so intent on the glow of the fire that he only heard the click of a safety being unlatched before he felt the barrel grind painfully against the side of his head.

'Don't even blink,' a voice breathed in his ear. 'It'll be the last thing you do.'

Sami felt his heart skip in his chest and a wave of adrenaline wash through his nervous system. He froze, cursing himself silently. He had come all this way and made the basic mistake of not spotting the sentry.

'Who are you?' the man whispered. 'Why are you sneaking up on the camp?'

The quiet voice triggered a reaction in Sami's brain. Something about the way he spoke reminded Sami of the young man who was part of his team. 'Ismail?' Sami gasped. 'Is that you?'

Sami felt the pressure of the pistol barrel ease back a fraction. '*Thalaivar*?' the voice breathed in surprise. 'We thought you were dead.'

'It's not that easy to kill me,' Sami said, slowly turning his head and looking over his shoulder. 'Where are the others?'

Sami felt the gun barrel being withdrawn. Dry leaves lightly rustled as a shape settled next to him. Ismail always had the ability to move in the jungle like a ghost. The last time Sami had seen him was when he had sent Ismail with Danika to collect ammunition and grenades from the dead soldiers.

'They are being held in the camp,' Ismail whispered into Sami's ear. 'The men from Jaffna said that they are no longer needed. There are only four left. And me. The rest are all dead.'

Sami felt a pang of regret shoot through his body. 'Who's left?' he asked. 'Where is Ratnam?'

'Ratnam is dead,' Ismail whispered. 'He was shot by Para when he refused to take orders from him. Kaleel is still alive but he is wounded. The others are Kabir, Haresh and Babu.'

'And the women? I saw a few of them when I scouted the camp.' Sami was thinking about Danika when he asked the question.

'They are okay,' Ismail said. 'I don't think they will be harmed. They are not like us.'

Sami nodded in the dark. Danika and the rest of the women cadres were all Tamils, not like Sami and his men who were Moors.

'What are you doing here,' Sami asked Ismail. 'You didn't get caught with the others?'

'No, I was with Danika when they came. She got me to hide in the jungle and not come out until she found out what the men wanted. She's smart, that one.'

Sami narrowed his eyes. 'Can we get our men out?' Sami asked Ismail. 'I don't want to leave them without at least trying.'

'It won't be easy,' Ismail said. 'They don't have any weapons and Kaleel is injured. I have been watching for two days now. Para's men are pretty good.'

'Will Danika and the women help?' Sami was hoping that Danika's loyalty lay with the men she'd fought with, rather than a group of men who came from Jaffna.

'I think she will,' Ismail said. 'She was very upset when she heard you were dead. We have to get close enough to talk to her, but I can do that. She knows I am watching and left some food for me once.'

Sami knew he had to do something to free his men. But he did not want to risk the lives of Ismail or anyone else. The only plan he could come up with which had the least risk to his people was to put himself in danger.

'Ok, this is what we will do.' Sami outlined his plan to Ismail who listened quietly. 'Can you do it?' He asked after going through what he wanted.

'Of course, I can,' Ismail said. 'My part is easy. You have taken the risky part for yourself and will have them all coming after you. Lead them into the southern part of the jungle, around the temple where we met Iyer and his men. There are many places to hide there.'

Sami nodded in the darkness and grasped Ismail's shoulder. 'Thank you, my young friend, I hope we both survive this,' he said, a catch in his voice. 'And tell Danika to look after herself.'

It had not been easy for him to leave his men to their fate. And he felt a sudden sadness that he would not see Danika again. He shook his head to clear it. He couldn't afford to get sentimental.

Sami moved back the way he came. He needed some space between himself and the camp. He would have to move quickly once they came after him and he went over in his mind exactly where he would lead them. He moved his hand over the breech of his rifle to make sure that the safety catch had been released. His eyes scanned the trees, looking through them to the bush beyond. His finger rested close to the trigger without actually touching it.

The gunshots, when they came, startled him. The plan was for Ismail to fire into the camp and double back around it and get behind where his men were being held. Para and his men would naturally head in the direction the shots came from. Sami would reinforce the subterfuge by shooting at the men and then drawing them away from the camp. He expected at least some of the men to follow him.

In the confusion, Ismail would free his men and with Danika and the women's help, take them to the coast where they could pay a fisherman to take them to safety.

Sami moved silently towards a patch of more denser cover next to a tree. The smell of wet, rotting leaves and earth was strong. He looked towards the south, covering the area he expected they would come from. He had struggled earlier with the thought of shooting at the men who'd come with Para but after he'd heard that they shot Ratnam, he had no doubts what he would do.

Time slowed to a crawl. Sweat poured off his forehead while he waited. He strained to watch and listen. He must not let them get past him.

Then he saw them, indistinct amongst the trees, moving cautiously in a half crouch. He raised himself, his eyes scanning the growth around him. There were at least three of them. Sami slid behind the tree and stood up, bending at the knees. He moved forward and sideways in a crouch, firing at where he had seen the first man.

A man screamed and crashed into the undergrowth. Bullets sliced all around Sami as he darted back into the dense undergrowth. He turned and fired again, holding down the trigger and aiming instinctively at a muzzle flash to the right of where he'd shot the first man. The gun stopped firing allowing Sami time to change the magazine on his rifle.

Suddenly there was no more gunfire. He heard the man he'd shot first, screaming for help and thrashing around somewhere to the left.

Sami knew it was time to move. If he stayed there he was dead. He slowly retreated backwards, his eyes scanning the forest around him. He moved like that for a number of minutes and then turned, moving at an angle towards the east. The men he was running from would take time to regroup. Maybe even wait until daybreak before following. He needed to put as much space between them as he could.

Sami hurried through the forest, not bothering to take any precautions. It didn't matter if he left a trail. He wanted them to follow him. After about an hour he crossed the main highway, just a dirt road now after years of neglect. He curved south in a wide arc, towards the temple where he had first seen Iyer coming across the rice paddies. It was just six days ago although it seemed much longer. So much had happened since then.

The moonlight that appeared from behind the clouds made it easier to move. Sami shivered in the cool night air. His clothes were soaked with sweat. He staggered towards the temple compound which couldn't be too far ahead. He would spend a few hours there resting and then keep moving south. He had more than ten days to get to the Giants Tank and meet the Captain. It was a long way away and he needed to preserve his strength.

It was still dark when he got to the temple compound and collapsed behind its moss-covered stone wall. He strove to listen for the slightest noise that was out of the ordinary but didn't hear any. He would rest here for a while and keep moving.

Sami's mind snapped back to the present as Suria came out to the veranda, closely followed by Priyani. For a moment he wondered where he was. The images in his mind were so real.

'Ah, there you are,' Priyani said. 'We were wondering where you'd gone. I've had a long chat with Suria and we've decided that she would be safer living in Colombo with me. At least for the moment. I'll also speak with Rohan and see whether we can have you moved back to your home. I think that after almost three years out here they shouldn't see you as a threat anymore.'

Sami nodded, a lump in his throat. He would miss Suria, but it was for the best. He couldn't do his job and keep an eye on her. He needed Priyani to convince her brother to talk to the President. It was his only hope.

CHAPTER TWELVE

JAFFNA PENINSULA

The rain came in a solid wall of sound that swept across the coconut plantation in Siruppiddy, crashing through their high crowns in great swollen drops. Lightning flickered in the darkness and thunder muttered incessantly, overshadowed by the steady roar of the rain.

David huddled under a rough shelter made up of four corner-posts with a roof of plaited coconut leaves, at the edge of the orderly rows of trees. Coconuts that were picked or had fallen from the trees were piled in the corner of the shelter. The roof dripped continuously, water running down the back of his neck making him fidget in discomfort.

The army had begun its offensive out of their enclave at Palali taking the Tigers by surprise. Most of their fixed defences were constructed to prevent a breakout from the Jaffna Fort and an advance up the Kandy Road from the main army camp at Elephant Pass. But the use of anti-personnel mines and roadside bombs had slowed the advance, and snipers were a constant menace. The Tigers had responded fiercely and halted the army's advance along the road to Achuveli across the lagoon.

It was the biggest military operation undertaken by the Sri Lankan armed forces, up to that time. The sheer logistics and planning that went into this operation were unprecedented. The air force had been using a couple of helicopters and fighter bombers for close-in-support of the ground troops but had quickly run out of air to ground missiles and bombs. They had resorted to using barrels filled with high-explosives, ball bearings and metal scraps to support the ground troops. These dangerous and inaccurate barrel bombs were pushed out of helicopters and slow-moving transport planes causing mayhem wherever they fell.

David was ordered to clear out a coconut plantation across an open rice paddy where snipers had killed three soldiers. His plan was to get across the fields to the tree line in the dark and wait for morning. The rain helped mask their approach as he waited with his men. He had sent Indika ahead, to scout around, knowing that he was the best man for the job.

The rain stopped towards morning as suddenly as it had begun. A monkey screamed in delight at the ending of the storm and the roar of the rain changed to the steady drip of rainwater falling from the trees. Frogs croaked hoarsely from within the rice paddy as the undergrowth stirred around them. It felt cooler after the rain and the smell of wood smoke hung in the air.

A grey blur materialised in front of him and it took all of David's will power not to shoot. The man moved like a ghost and took pleasure in startling members of the team.

'You're going to get shot one day,' David grumbled, as Indika crouched next to him with a wide grin on his face.

'There's a coconut-pickers hut up ahead,' he pointed. 'Someone's in there but I don't think it's one of them.'

They had been constantly hampered since the offensive began by the semi-rural nature of the country-side they were in. Filled with rice paddies and kitchen gardens tended by locals living in isolated mud huts, the use of mortar and artillery fire was prohibited to limit civilian casualties.

'Ok, let's move out.' David signalled the rest of the team by waving his hand and pointing in the direction Indika had indicated.

Indika followed an indistinct track which wound through the tall coconut trees. Steam rose from the wet ground forming a light mist about waist high, becoming visible by the growing morning light filtering through the tops of the trees.

'There', mouthed Indika, pointing ahead.

A ramshackle hut stood in a cleared area of the plantation, smoke wafting through the *cadjan* covered roof. The door of the hut was wide open.

David watched Indika as he scanned the clearing. Only the sound of frogs and cicadas disturbed the stillness.

The crack of a high-powered rifle and the stammering of a machine gun froze David where he stood. The sound came from deeper in the plantation, from the left of the hut.

The Tigers were using a tactic which was having a lot of success. They used the tops of trees as firing platforms to shoot at the soldiers. Under normal conditions the two major factors which helped detect where the shot came from were sound and dust that was kicked up by the weapon, or the muzzle flash at night. As these positions were carefully sited on treetops and well camouflaged, there was no trace of a flash or dust. But the sound of the gunshot gave away their position.

David circled his hand in the air to draw his team's attention and pointed in the direction of the gunfire. This was not the first time the team had done this, and his men knew what was expected of them. They would deal with the occupant of the hut later.

Indika, as always, led the way, moving soundlessly off in the direction the shot came from. David followed, the rest of the team moving into position behind him. His job, as second in the column, was to scan the trees while Indika guided them. It was possible that the Tigers had left someone on the ground to cover their backs, but they preferred not to as it would give away their position.

The loud crack of a shot echoed around them, followed quickly by another a bit further away. *They are close*, thought David, trying to pierce the gloom under the crowns of the coconut palms.

A loud thud to his right brought him to one knee, his rifle ready to fire. He scanned the area around the narrow tree trunks, his eyes searching for the source of the sound. He looked towards Sarath who pointed up and then indicated the ground.

A bloody coconut thought David. He instinctively glanced up at the tree he was under. A falling coconut would cause a pretty serious injury.

David focused back in the direction they were moving. Indika was standing next to a tree trunk looking intently ahead of him. By his posture David knew that he had spotted something. He signalled with his arm without looking back for David to move up next to him.

Taking his time, David sidled up to Indika. Pointing with his chin, the scout indicated an area of the plantation he was watching. For a few long seconds David could not see anything, but then a flicker of movement high up on a tree caught his eye. Straining to see through the drooping palms he could barely make out the outline of a figure sitting on a wooden platform. David started to move to his right to get a better look when Indika grabbed his arm, shaking his head as he did.

'Tripwire,' Indika mouthed, pointing to a spot a few feet away from where they stood. David could not see anything but trusted the scout's uncanny ability to spot anything out of the ordinary and if he said there was a tripwire, David would not dispute it. The thin nylon fishing line was just a foot off the ground and could only be seen by the glint of moisture dripping off it. David traced the line with his eyes and saw that it was anchored to the back of a tree trunk next to the track. David had seen this done before. The Tigers placed hand grenades, with their pins removed, in old tin cans to stop their levers springing open. Anyone following the track and walking into the wire would pull the grenade from its can, freeing the spring–loaded lever and setting it off.

David looked around and saw Sarath watching him. David drew his right hand, palm down across his neck signalling danger. Focused on what he was doing, the crack of the sniper's rifle made him almost jump out of his skin. Feeling stupid, David tapped Indika on the shoulder indicating that they should leave the track.

Indika nodded and moved to the left, away from the tree the sniper was using. The stammering beat of a machine gun and a rain of spent cartridges falling on the ground identified the tree the firing was coming from. Bullets fired from soldiers on the road snapped through the line of trees forcing David to duck for cover. Two high powered cracks coming almost simultaneously indicated a second sniper at work. The return fire grew intense as bullets shredded the branches and thudded into tree trunks around them.

The men hidden in the trees were well protected from return fire by the dense branches on the trees crown and its thick trunk. The sniper was sitting on a wooden chair tied to the tree. He had poked the long barrel of his sniper rifle through branches and flowers of the palm and was observing the road through its telescopic sight.

David quickly identified the three trees that were being used and positioned three of his men beneath each to take out the snipers. He and Indika kept watch to make sure no one would surprise them when they opened fire.

The three cracks of automatic rifle fire when David gave the signal were almost simultaneous, they sounded as one. Silence descended in the plantation as they watched and waited for any reaction. The soldiers on the road had stopped firing hoping that their wild volleys had taken out the snipers.

David walked beneath each tree and could see that each of the men had been hit. The one with the machine gun had collapsed off his platform and only a rope around his waist prevented him from falling to the ground.

'We better clear those trip wires before leaving,' he said to Sarath. 'And get Indika to scout the rest of the plantation. This won't be the last time we have to do this.'

CHAPTER THIRTEEN

VANNI JUNGLE

Danika absently rubbed her chin as she watched a flight of birds drifting over the open fields and settling into the darkening jungle. A peacock screamed in the distance as the sky quickly darkened into night. Her senses were on high alert as she knelt behind the sandbags her unit had stacked around the open window, clutching the brand-new T-56 Chinese made automatic rifle she had been issued recently. She was dressed in trousers and a shirt with dark socks and runners on her feet, an outfit that no civilian woman in these parts would wear.

Danika had watched earlier as a line of heavily armed men walked silently past the mud-brick house heading east. The men from the Vanni *Padaipirivu* Brigade, were part of an attack against an Indian army outpost less than a kilometre away. The stone-faced men, barely noticeable against the dark vegetation, wound along the edge of the jungle before disappearing into the tangled undergrowth. Danika and her unit were not part of the attack and were positioned at the edge of the village to cover the men when they retreated after the action.

Danika glanced across the room at the other occupant. She had met Parvathy during training and they had become friends. Parvathy had come from one of the islands off Jaffna after losing her home to the navy, who had turned the island into an armed camp. Danika was always envious of the way she looked. Her long brown hair, shining with oil was drawn back into a tightly knotted plait at the nape of her neck.

Parvathy's teeth gleamed when she felt Danika's gaze. 'I think we're better in here than out there in the stinking dirt and mud.'

Danika smiled. Parvathy always had a way of putting her at ease. But what she said was true. For the past few nights they had been scouting the Indian camp, sometimes right up to the surrounding barbed wire fence. The monsoon rains had turned the area into a quagmire and she had struggled that morning to get the foul-smelling earth out of her hair and clothes.

The small, two-room building they occupied reminded Danika of the home she lived in before the troubles began. Her home was small and crowded, especially after her sister was born, but she remembered it fondly. She still yearned and pined for the life she had lost, and every night she prayed for her parents and sister living in the refugee camp in India.

It was the nights when her dreams troubled her, with images of men brandishing flaming torches that seemed to come out of the dark. Danika hadn't forgotten the nightmare of that fateful day when men with swords and revolvers, carrying cans of petrol and kerosene, came charging down their lane looking for Tamil homes. Their home was burnt, and her father so badly beaten that he almost died. Only the intervention of the neighbours had saved their lives. Her sister had been so traumatised that she had cried herself to sleep for months. Danika had gone to India with her family in one of the refugee boats, parting with her family at the camp to come back and fight for her people. After undergoing basic training, she had joined a group of women who were being used to supply the men who fought on the frontlines.

Danika ran her fingers through her hair. Her parents would never have let her wear her hair this short. Some women fighters who were averse to cutting their hair, coiled the long plaits high on their heads. She did not have the patience. The short bob suited her, she decided. The prickly hair on her nape would unfailingly remind her that she was different from the other women, braver, with greater purpose.

Danika peered out of the open window as the moon disappeared behind high clouds cutting across the sky. Life in the north hadn't been easy. Landmines, bombs, gunfire, missile attacks and the almost constant shelling from army camps had toughened her up. She was not new to combat. She had been part of a team of women attached to a group of Tamil fighters near Mannar who were defending the western approaches to the north. The fighting had been intense, but they had held their ground against a superior military force and denied use of the Western Highway. Danika often thought about the man who led the group, Sami the *Marakkalaya* – the Muslim. He had treated her fairly, even though she had been extremely rude to him when they first met. She had been a single woman in a male dominated world and had built a series of walls to keep everyone out, but he had seen through her and had treated her with respect and kindness. A feeling of sadness enveloped her. She had lost friends in that battle and she wondered whether Sami was alive.

It had been only a few months earlier that a new women's military unit had been formed under an experienced and capable leader. The knowledge and proficiency she had gained fighting with the Tamil Muslim unit had made her an obvious choice. The unit she was attached to specialised in reconnaissance and the covert gathering of intelligence. Danika had also been trained in the use of a GPS unit and land navigation, but she had never used those skills.

Women had not been encouraged until then to take part in active operations although several of them had faced combat while working as communication specialists, support personnel or medical orderlies. Danika had undergone extensive combat training and had been integrated into a new women's military unit which had become a well organised, highly disciplined fighting force.

Danika had volunteered for special training as a combat scout. The shirt she wore was a man's shirt in shades of green with the tail out, belted at the waist with a sheathed fighting knife at her hip. An ammunition harness with two full pouches and a water bottle completed her attire.

A distant stutter of automatic weapons punctuated by explosions rolled across the neglected fields. Flashes of light silhouetted the trees and the firing got louder as the defenders responded. The attack was targeting a company of Indian soldiers who had taken over a school compound in a small town on the edge of the Vanni. Her unit had scouted the Indian army camp over the past week, taking notes and drawing a map of the Indian positions.

Waiting till darkness, they began their attack knowing that the Indians were hampered during operations at night. The use of their superior airpower to support the Indian *jawans* –soldiers, on the ground were intermittent, and attacks like this were happening across a wide area making it extremely difficult for the Indian air force to support them all. The sounds of fighting continued sporadically throughout the night as the Tigers probed the Indian defences, forcing the *jawans* to shoot flares into the sky illuminating large areas for several minutes.

There was nothing for Danika to do while the attack was in progress. The distant sounds of gunfire and explosions were a constant backdrop.

Just before midnight Danika heard the distinct sound of a helicopter as it arrived over the camp. The Russian-built helicopter gunship was a formidable weapon to which the attackers had no answer. The sounds of firing dropped off almost immediately after the aircraft appeared, until there was just an occasional round. After several minutes, the noise of combat died away as the gunship circled the camp.

The men trickled back in small groups, some of them assisting those wounded in the attack. As the pre-dawn light backlit the high clouds, slowly lifting the inky darkness at ground level, Danika and her team crept out through the rear of the building into the welcoming jungle.

CHAPTER FOURTEEN

KALPITIYA REFUGEE CAMP

The man barged into the room Sami used as an office in the Kandakuli Refugee Centre near Kalpitiya. 'I can't fucking believe that you reported me to the police.' Mahen's face was red, his veins stood out prominently on his neck. 'I pay those bastards to leave me alone, but you had to come along and rock the fucking boat.'

Sami had reported Mahen to the local police many times, but only after he'd threatened to take his complaint directly to Colombo through the relief agency did the Sub-Inspector in charge arrest the gang leader for suspected extortion.

Mahen was well used to using his anger as a weapon and intimidating bigger opponents by the sheer force of his personality. He walked up to Sami, thrusting his face forward until he was just centimetres from Sami's face. His breath stank making Sami grimace in disgust. He was at least ten centimetres shorter than Sami but appeared even shorter because of the way he pushed his head forward. But the lack of height made him no less intimidating. Sami could see flecks of spit on Mahen's moustache as the man glared up at him.

'Now how do you think I am going to explain to my fucking people that I allowed a *Mukaal* to have me arrested in my own village,' he yelled.

Mahen was capable of brutal violence, the results of which Sami had witnessed before. Stories circulated amongst the refugees that he had killed men from two families who had refused to pay what he demanded.

Sami moved his feet, waiting for any sign that Mahen was about to strike.

'My own fucking village,' he repeated unbelievingly. Mahen waved a fist under Sami's nose, and pushed him back with his other hand flat against Sami's chest. He pulled back his fist to strike but before he could land the punch, Sami drew his knee up sharply into Mahen's groin.

Mahen yelled in pain and bent in two, his hands instinctively grabbing between his legs. Sami used his elbow in a round arm action and hit Mahen on his temple, knocking him to the ground. Sami stepped forward and drove his foot hard between Mahen's legs hearing the man's fingers snap at the strike.

Sami stepped back and calmly observed the man on the ground. Adrenaline pumped through his body making it tingle, his senses heightened. He had not felt this way for a while and realised he missed living on the edge, the excitement, the rush. Combat was addictive and there was no feeling like it. Sami wondered whether he had gone too far and killed the man. He had attended close combat classes while in India and had been trained to take down an opponent with overwhelming force. *You must never give them the opportunity to stick a knife in your guts*, the voice of his turbaned instructor rang in his ears.

Mahen lay on his back semi-conscious, his hands between his legs moaning softly. Sami considered what he should do with him. Mahen would not let this matter slide. He had too much to lose and would come after Sami again, this time with some of his *goondas* - thugs. Going to the police was a waste of time. They would find a reason to release him again and the cycle would start all over.

He should kill the man and bury him where no one would ever find him, but Sami knew that he could never kill a man in cold blood.

Sami grinned as an idea popped into his head. The recent spate of attacks against the government by the hard-line communist *Janatha Vimukthi Peramuna* - People's Liberation Front party had created a state of panic amongst the ruling establishment. Politicians and party officials who had supported the peace accord with India were being killed or had just disappeared. Police stations had been attacked and there were rumours that elements of the military were involved in some of the killings.

The Special Task Force, an elite para-military unit of the Sri Lanka Police specializing in counter-terrorism and counter-insurgency operations, had been recalled from the eastern province to track down the insurgents and eradicate the problem, a job that they were doing with ruthless zeal. The latest was a succession of killings attributed to the STF when local men were found hanging from lamp-posts in the Kalpitiya town centre.

Sami dragged the unconscious Mahen into the parking lot outside the building. The night was dark and quiet, only the criminals and the so-called protectors of the peace busy with their nocturnal activities.

Sami tied Mahen's hands and bundled him into the car he had been given by the relief agency. The man was moaning loudly as he began to awaken. Sami went back into the office and scrawled a few lines on a sheet of paper which he took with him to the car.

The drive to the STF camp in the town took him just a few minutes. The roads were starting to empty of traffic. It had become too dangerous to be on the roads at night. Sami stopped the car in sight of the camp's front gate and pushed Mahen out onto the road, placing the piece of paper on his body before turning the car and driving away.

Stopping at the end of the street, Sami switched off his lights but kept the engine running. In the rear-view mirror, he could see activity at the entrance to the camp. The armed STF troopers were approaching the body on the road cautiously, fearing a trap. Once they realised the body was not booby trapped, they stood around examining the body. Sami knew that they would see the note he had left saying that the man was a JVP activist who had been involved in many attacks against the police in the area.

Sami had no doubt that Mahen, if he survived the beatings and the interrogation at the camp, would be incarcerated in the high security prison at Boossa in the south where all hardcore JVP prisoners were sent. Mahen's arrogance and over confidence had made it easy for Sami, but he'd better watch his back from now on.

CHAPTER FIFTEEN

JAFFNA PENINSULA

The sun hung directly overhead when they left the Palali airbase and headed south towards Jaffna. Fighting along the road to the east had died down after the Tigers blew up the bridge across the lagoon. The army had taken the opportunity to consolidate their hold on the western portion of the peninsula and began mopping up pockets of resistance in the villages around the town.

David's body still ached from the previous day's exertions. He looked up at the sound of a military aircraft overhead. The sky was such a tranquil blue, a sky that looked like it belonged to a happy country, not to one that was being torn apart by war.

Will the country ever know peace and tranquillity again?

They passed a couple of formidable looking armoured cars at the first road junction near the entrance to the heavily guarded base. Occasionally the flash of movement through the trees reminded David of the hundreds of soldiers patrolling the surrounding plantations, or lurking in ambushes, hoping to catch survivors from the fighting, trying to get back to their lines.

David could see a group of houses just ahead. Open fields of tobacco and corn hemmed in by coconut and Palmyra groves in small holdings, surrounded the agricultural village. The team was travelling in two new Isuzu long-base 4-wheel drives the army had acquired recently. The men fell silent as they approached the village, watching the thatched fences give way to run down houses and shops which lined both sides of the road.

The trees shading some of the houses drooped in the hot sunlight. A dog, listless in the heat, lay on the side of the road hardly looking up when the two vehicles passed. Nothing moved.

A sudden cold feeling crept up David's spine, like a precursor to something terrible. *Where is everyone?*

The Tigers had been trying to divert attention from the eastern district by stepping up their attacks in the areas controlled by the army, forcing them to deploy more troops into the area. Their hit and run tactics were working. David was ordered to take his team out to investigate a sighting made by a helicopter pilot that morning, of men hiding in a coconut plantation only a few kilometres from Jaffna.

This wasn't like other villages they had passed through. It was too empty. Where were the kids playing on the street, the ever-present cyclists, the women walking with bags of produce they had collected from their gardens, the old men crouching on steps, chewing betel and staring at nothing?

The windshield on the Isuzu spiderwebbed and suddenly exploded, splattering David's face with stinging fragments. Time slowed down, and everything felt surreally disconnected.

David's training took over the moment they came under fire. 'Get out!' He yelled, pushing the safety catch on his weapon to its firing position and flinging the door open. He tumbled out on the road, kneeling next to the vehicle, steam from its disabled radiator coiling noisily upwards. Noise, dust flying and muzzle flashes everywhere.

Nimal, who had been sitting behind David, crouched next to him on the road. 'Better call this in,' David said, glancing at him. Nimal had just come back from a radio technicians' course and oversaw all team communications.

'Base Alpha, this is Charlie-Niner. Contact at Urumpirai. Wait. Over.'

David scanned the area for movement. After the initial exchange of automatic fire, a dangerous, loaded silence descended on the area. Only the hissing and crackling of the cooling engine broke the stillness. The ambush had been well planned and executed. Almost daily there were reports of hit and run attacks by the Tigers against the army on the roads in the area. Usually the attacks lasted just a few minutes, the attackers disappearing into the surrounding coconut and vegetable plantations before reinforcements arrived.

The old dilapidated buildings of the village stared back at him, their low shop fronts tightly shuttered. He scrutinised the tops of the roofs, the trees, looking for shadows, movement, anything irregular. But there was nothing.

The burst of automatic fire stitched a line of geysers in the packed earth of the roads shoulder as the bullets marched across the open ground toward them. Rounds hit the vehicle like a handful of gravel being thrown against an aluminium sheet. The Isuzu tilted forward slowly, the front tires of the vehicle shredded by the incoming fire. David peeked around the open door. Up ahead, buried in a slit in the wall, the glint of a weapon.

'They're in that building with the cart,' he yelled, firing his weapon in controlled bursts, watching the bullets hit around the opening. The firing died down again, and David looked around. His men were only taking fire from the front. Something was not right. Either the Tigers had opened fire too early or they wanted them to stop exactly where they were.

David drew back into cover and ejected the ammunition clip, slamming another in its place in a practiced motion. He risked raising his head above the vehicle door for a moment.

'Watch both sides,' he yelled. 'I don't like this.' The words were hardly out of his mouth when he felt the vehicle shudder and the boom of an explosion blew out its doors and windows in an intense sheet of heat and fire. A super-human force lifted and threw David back several metres, his head and shoulder smashing into a concrete post by the side of the road.

David found himself lying on his side next to the post facing the road. The sound of small arms fire grew in intensity and the smell of scorched metal and cordite filled his nostrils. The Isuzu, its windows shattered and doors hanging open, was burning fiercely. Clouds of black smoke billowed into the clear blue sky. He tried to turn but any movement brought intense pain. He felt dizzy. He tried to focus on something to ignore the pain. The staccato bursts of a light machine gun firing close by made him wonder who it was. His mind was like treacle, he couldn't remember who in his team had one. Someone ran past him firing a weapon. David watched the boots as they disappeared down the road.

David's head throbbed, and his vision spun as a shape leaned over him. 'Shit, he's in a bad way.' David knew it was a familiar voice, but his mind was fuzzy, and he couldn't be sure who it was. 'We need an emergency evacuation. Call it in.' David wanted to say that he was okay but couldn't get the words out. He felt someone trying to turn him on his back and everything went black.

∾

COLOMBO

Priyani knew something was wrong when her brother Rohan called her at the office. He sounded different, almost scared. 'What's wrong, Rohan,' Priyani asked anxiously. 'Is anything wrong with *amma*?' Priyani's mother had been feeling unwell and had gone to the hospital that morning for a series of medical tests.

'No, no! It's David,' said Rohan. 'We just heard that he's been injured.'

The colour drained from Priyani's face and she clutched the edge of her desk. She closed her eyes and bowed her head. She always lived knowing that David had a dangerous job but refused to let herself think that she could lose him. Deep inside she had known that she may have to face the bad news one day.

Priyani opened her eyes and shrugged off her thoughts with an almost physical effort. Her chest felt tight and she struggled to take a deep breath. She latched onto the only piece of news which was good. 'Injured?' she asked forcing the words out fearfully. 'What do you mean injured? Is it bad?' Rohan worked for the President and was a close friend of David, so he would know.

'I am not sure Priyani,' Rohan said, the anxiety in his voice clearly noticeable. 'The report we got was that he was on a patrol that was ambushed. It happened this morning. That's all I know right now.'

'Is it something bad?' Priyani insisted. She realised that Rohan had ignored the question, but she needed to know.

'He's not in good shape according to the reports, but he's alive.' Rohan said reluctantly.

'When will he be arriving?' Priyani blew out a shaky breath as the appalling reality struck. She knew that Rohan wouldn't be able to tell her everything about David's condition, but she could tell that he was keeping something from her.

'The President authorised a special flight to bring him to Colombo. The plane is in Palali right now and will be leaving soon. It should land in Katunayake in about an hour.'

David had come to the attention of the President when he tracked and killed the Black Tigers who attacked the Shri Maha Bodhi temple, indiscriminately killing Buddhist monks, nuns and pilgrims worshipping at the holy shrine. David's actions at the time prevented a backlash against Tamils in the country. The President had taken a liking to the young Captain and had asked to be kept informed of all his assignments.

'I am going to the airport,' Priyani said, standing up at her desk. 'Can you arrange to get me into the military terminal?'

'Are you sure you want to do that?' Rohan asked uncertainly. 'It's better you go to the hospital and wait for him there.'

Priyani was determined that she wanted to be with David. She couldn't erase the memory of their last meeting together.

'I want to go,' Priyani insisted. 'I will go there with or without your permission. You'll have to deal with whatever happens when I get there.'

'Ok, ok! I'll send a car over to pick you up,' Rohan said. 'It's an official car and you won't be stopped.' Rohan knew how determined Priyani could be. Her work at the refugee agency had changed her and she wasn't the obedient little sister he once knew.

'Priyani,' he said, before hanging up, 'don't worry, we'll make sure he gets the very best care.'

∾

The doctor that Priyani sought oversaw the Military Hospital in the affluent suburb of Cinnamon Gardens in Colombo. She was determined to find out David's actual condition. She had been with him all morning and didn't like the way he looked. Something was not right.

The day David got injured was still fresh in her mind. She didn't remember the drive to the airport at all. She just knew that they were there. She had been allowed access to the air force terminal but was not allowed to go out onto the tarmac. She had to watch from the terminal building while David was lifted in a stretcher into a waiting ambulance.

The air force Medical Officer who had met her at the airport stood next to her. 'He'll be taken directly to Colombo for examination,' he said. 'It's the normal procedure we follow for medevac'd soldiers.'

'Do you know how badly hurt he is?' Priyani asked, without taking her eyes off the scene.

'The report we received said that he has suffered a severe trauma to his head.' The Medical Officer glanced at Priyani before continuing. 'Also, he has blast injuries to his upper body, but no loss of limbs.'

'What does severe trauma mean?' Priyani asked apprehensively, finally looking at the Medical Officer.

'I cannot answer that question without examining him,' the Medical Officer shrugged. 'It could mean a fractured skull, broken vertebra, broken facial bones. It could be a simple concussion or something more serious. He'll have to undergo a number of tests.'

David was surrounded by many men in uniform. 'Who are all those people with him?'

'We got orders to send a trauma team from the hospital to evacuate him. He's obviously someone important,' the Medical Officer said, raising his eyebrows at Priyani.

That was 48 hours ago. Today she needed answers. David was barely conscious, drifting in and out of a twilight zone that only he occupied. He lay drawn out and pallid against the starched sheets of the hospital bed with two sandbags on either side of his head. He wore a brace around his neck, his face badly swollen, his eyes small slits above an oxygen mask. An IV drip reached down into his arm. Priyani couldn't tell whether he knew she was there with him, holding his hand, talking to him. But what bothered Priyani most was the pallor of his skin which was clammy to the touch.

David's mother and father had spent the entire day in the hospital and had only gone home to get some rest after Priyani promised that she would remain with him through the night. David had been subjected to a series of tests during the day. A technician had wheeled in a portable x-ray machine which was used to take scans of his upper body and head.

Priyani marched up the stairs to the office of the Director of the Hospital on the 2nd floor. She left David with his parents who had arrived a short while ago. Priyani waited outside the Director's office for his secretary to tell her boss that Priyani wanted to see him. She had met the director when David was first admitted. She'd been impressed with his polished manner and the air of confidence he displayed.

The office door opened, and the Director stepped out. 'Please come in Miss Priyani. I was about to come down to see you.'

Priyani waited until the secretary came out and allowed herself to be ushered into the room. The director pulled out a chair for her before going around the desk.

'I presume you have come to talk to me about Captain Anderson,' he asked, glancing at Priyani over his glasses as he opened a file on his desk. 'I studied the latest reports on his condition and the news is not all that good'.

Priyani felt a stab in her heart as she held her breath. She knew just by looking at him that David was far worse than when he was first brought in.

'There's intracranial bleeding which is putting pressure on his brain,' the Director said. 'We will have to operate on him and reduce the pressure. But it's a very complicated procedure and we cannot guarantee that he will come out of his coma.'

Priyani's face fell as she stared at the head doctor. Even though she had steeled herself for bad news it came as a shock. 'But he's not in a coma,' Priyani said. 'I've been with him since he arrived, and he seems to be half asleep. He seems to drift in and out.'

The Director glanced at her sharply. 'If that's correct then it's good news,' he said, leaning back on his chair. 'This report does not say that. It's possible that he was in a comatose state when he was examined.'

'What do you mean good news?' Priyani asked, leaning forward in the chair. When David had first come in he had been drifting in and out of consciousness, but she had noticed that morning that he seemed to be more asleep than awake.

'What it means is that if we reduce pressure on the brain and stop the swelling, there is every likelihood that he will wake up,' the Director said.

'People with severe brain trauma take days, weeks and even years to recover. Sometimes never,' he added.

Priyani listened to the Director without saying anything. There was nothing she could do other than pray that David would be okay. It was left to the skill of the physician and whatever fate was written out for him.

'To complicate matters, he has two cracked vertebrae and a broken collar bone.' The Director stood up. 'I don't want to waste any time,' he said. 'We'll begin preparing to operate on him right away.'

Priyani left the room deep in thought. She needed to inform David's parents what was about to happen to their son and had to call Rohan. She would then go to the temple to make an offering and pray for David's recovery.

CHAPTER SIXTEEN

CENTRAL HIGHLANDS

The rain had caught Mukesh by surprise as he stood outside Cargills Food City in Nuwara Eliya collecting his thoughts. He shivered in the damp cold wishing he was back in Jaffna. He had taken the bus to Nuwara Eliya to withdraw some money from the bank account the Captain had set up for him. Mukesh had not realised that he was getting a wage from the government and was surprised at the amount of money that was in the account.

But the question that burned in his mind was why was Shankar here? Mukesh had seen him quite by chance when a car slowed down at the roundabout, almost opposite the supermarket. There was no mistaking him. The same dark round-face with a thin moustache.

Seeing the man brought a sense of unease to Mukesh. He suddenly remembered the conversation he had with Kanan the previous night and wondered whether there was a connection. They had been sitting on the cement platform outside their room drinking the cheap liquor that was sold in the estate store.

Kanan cleared his throat and spat out the betel leaves he was chewing. He had quarrelled with Rani about the quantity of food she had served him in his lunch packet that day. Rani had said that it was all they could afford given that the price of kerosene had gone up and that he was drinking every night.

Kanan glared at her angrily. 'We break our backs every day for this company and all we get is a pittance,' he complained bitterly, looking at Mukesh. 'I heard from the *Kangani* that they get over fifty thousand Rupees for each tree we cut. And they only pay us a few Rupees a day.'

Kanan worked for the estate Forestry Department which looked after forests of Teak and Eucalyptus grown on land that could not be used for the planting of tea. The government had recently lifted a ban on the harvesting of these forests for timber used in the construction industry or used to light the factory fires that dried the tea leaves.

'Haven't the tea pluckers got an increase recently?' Mukesh asked Rani who was sitting in the doorway rocking her daughter to sleep on her outstretched legs.

'Yes,' she nodded. 'They are giving us 285 Rupees a day now, but we have to pluck eighteen kilos a day. They want us to pluck two kilos extra for the water on the leaves.'

Mukesh knew that, though men carried out part-time odd jobs in the fields like fixing roads, cleaning and cutting of overgrown plants and fertilising, the heavy part of the work would rest on the women's shoulders. They worked longer hours and were paid less than their husbands.

Rani would go out onto the steep slopes, carrying a rattan basket on her back. She would carry a long slim bamboo pole which functioned as a sort of level. By placing the pole horizontally over an area of tea bushes, she would pick two leaves and a bud from the new growth on each plant that had grown over a certain height. It was hard, back breaking work, but she never complained. Like their mother, she had been on the estate and had plucked tea all her life. That was all she knew.

'But times are changing,' Kanan said ominously. 'When we take control of these hills we can all share in the money.'

Mukesh stared at Kanan in surprise. 'What do you mean take control?' he asked. 'We won't be allowed to own these estates. They won't even give us citizenship.'

'I know,' Kanan said, spitting into the garden. 'But when we become *Malai Nadu* –hill country- it will be a different story.'

'You are crazy,' said Rani, who had been listening to them talk. 'You really think the government will allow us our own country?'

'Why not?' asked Kanan aggressively. 'The Tamils in the north are fighting for one. We are organising ourselves and we will be getting help soon.' He tilted the liquor bottle he was drinking from, emptying it in one long gulp.

'Who are you getting help from?' Mukesh asked dismissively. 'The Workers Union? That'll never happen. The union is controlled by the government and it's the last thing they want.'

Kanan glared at Mukesh and Rani. 'We deserve better,' said Kanan, slurring his words. 'These tea companies make huge profits which all go to bosses in Colombo and London. They are living luxuriously from our blood and tears. That's all going to change when we take over. You wait and see.'

'*Aiyoo, Kaduvale,*' Rani muttered dismissively. 'That group of men he mixes around with will only bring us trouble,' she said glancing at her brother. 'And you,' she said addressing Kanan, 'you should stop drinking. They wouldn't want a drunkard in their ranks.'

Kanan glared murderously at Rani but did not say anything. Mukesh had thought at the time that Kanan was trying to impress him with his wild ideas. But after seeing Shankar that morning, he wondered whether the help Kanan was referring to was actually going to come from the militant groups in the north.

The more Mukesh thought about it the more sense it made. The Tigers would benefit greatly by causing problems in the hill country. The government would do everything possible to keep their lucrative plantations in operation. It would take their focus away from the north.

Mukesh needed to find out more. He would try and infiltrate the group that Kanan was talking about and would contact the Captain when he had more information.

CHAPTER SEVENTEEN

CINNAMON GARDENS

The cold, steady feed of oxygen through the mask was painful and soothing all at once. David opened his eyes slowly, and they adjusted to the dimly lit room. A strong chemical smell of disinfectant hung around him. He took in a couple of shallow breaths and blinked at the ache in his lungs. His chest felt as though it had been hollowed out and repacked with glass.

David lay unmoving trying to figure out where he was. His head was wrapped in something tight and it was night time, that much he could tell, but nothing else. He tried to look towards where the light was coming from but something hard and unyielding prevented him from turning his head.

As he lay there becoming aware of his surroundings, he could hear different noises; the sound of a wheezing air conditioner, the buzzing of an incorrectly screwed light bulb and a clicking noise from behind his head. *Where am I?*

David tried to think but his head was hurting badly. His mind felt fuzzy, like a badly focused camera. He strained to cling onto fleeting thoughts but could not grasp them before they vanished. He tried to talk but couldn't. Something was inserted down his throat. David wanted to remove it but couldn't move his arms. He was feeling helpless and beginning to get frustrated. Without any warning he felt the familiar fog drifting back in his mind.

∾

Priyani woke up with a start. There was someone in the room. But when she looked around in the semi-darkness it was empty. There was only the bed with its monitor showing David's vital signs pulsing across the green screen. Maybe it was the clicking noise from the ventilator sending oxygen deep into David's lungs that woke her.

Priyani walked over to the bed. David had not moved, his eyes still closed. There was no change in him since the operation two days ago. The Director had assured her that the procedure had gone extremely well. They had drilled into David's skull and drained the fluid that had collected there.

'The swelling will take some time to go down,' he said. 'Once it does, it will reduce pressure on his brain and there will be nothing to prevent him from awakening.'

Priyani was emotionally and physically drained. She had not been to work since David got injured, refusing even to go home in case he needed her. She spent most of her time on a chair in the hospital room, sleeping fitfully, often disturbed by nurses coming in to check on David's condition.

'How's he doing?' a voice asked from behind her. It was the night nurse who had been on duty every night since David was brought in. She walked past Priyani to the bed.

'There's no change,' Priyani said tiredly, looking at the nurse who was checking the saline bag hanging on a metal stand. 'I thought I heard something, but it wasn't him.'

The nurse glanced at Priyani and bent over David, observing him closely. 'I have dealt with these kinds of cases before,' she said. 'They awaken sometimes for a short time and go back to sleep.' She stepped away from David. 'He seems more relaxed today,' the nurse said. 'I might talk to the doctor about removing the ventilator.'

Priyani moved over to the bed and held David's hand. If he had woken even for a few minutes she wanted to be there for him, look into his eyes and tell him that she loved him. She felt like crying but she didn't want David to see her like that. Priyani fought the fierce stinging of her eyes, wiping the moisture that escaped with the back of her hand. She needed to get some fresh air. *But what if David wakes up?*

'Don't worry,' the nurse said, patting Priyani on her shoulder as though she was reading her mind. 'If he woke up it's a good sign and he'll wake up again. I'll get you a cup of tea.'

'I'll come with you,' said Priyani, making up her mind. 'I need to get some fresh air.'

The nurse nodded, and they left the room, walking side by side to the nurse's station.

Priyani stood next to the little kitchen as the night nurse made her a cup of tea. A large white board behind the counter had the nursing roster for the week and Priyani noticed that Chanika was on duty tonight. Priyani felt awkward as she had never asked the nurse what her name was.

'I am sorry, I never asked you your name,' Priyani said. 'Is it Chanika?' she asked.

'Yes,' the nurse nodded, glancing at Priyani. 'It's okay, you have other things to worry about.' Chanika poured the steaming brew into a mug, stirring in a heaped teaspoon of sweetened condensed milk vigorously. Chanika handed Priyani the mug. 'Here, drink this. It'll make you feel better.' Priyani nodded her thanks as she sipped the hot, syrupy tea. Chanika was busy behind the counter when Priyani finished so she decided to go outside for a little while.

The night was quiet, the traffic on the main road dying down to a dull murmur. A light wind rustled through the branches of the tree outside the hospital entrance, as Priyani stood next to a large Bougainvillea shrub looking up at the stars. Whatever was going to happen has happened, she realised, now they would have to live in its shadow. Priyani wrapped her arms around herself and squeezed tight, willing the strength she had found in the jungle to rise within her again.

The smell of cigarette smoke made her realise that someone else was in the garden with her. A woman dressed simply in loose blue blouse and white trousers stood framed under the entrance light, smoking a cigarette. She turned towards Priyani sensing her presence.

'Oh, I am sorry. I didn't know anyone was out here,' she said guiltily, waving her cigarette in the air. 'I won't be here for long.'

Priyani was used to cigarette smoke as her father was a two-packet a day smoker. 'It's okay,' she said. 'I am used to it. My father smokes a lot.'

'It's a horrible habit,' the woman said apologetically. 'And I am ashamed of myself when I give into it.' Priyani studied the woman who almost defiantly took a long puff, blowing the smoke out of her nostrils. She looked to be in her early thirties, with a long lean face and no makeup, her hair cut unfashionably short.

After a few moments of silence, the woman spoke, looking at Priyani from the corner of her eyes. 'What are you doing out here at this time of the night?' she asked. 'Are you a doctor, or a nurse?'

Priyani shook her head. 'No, I am here because my fiancé is in a coma and I want to be with him.'

'Oh,' the woman said, glancing sharply at Priyani. 'What happened to him?'

'He's in the army and the vehicle he was in got blown up in the north.' Priyani realised that she had been away from David for a while and began moving towards the hospital entrance. 'I came out to get some fresh air, but I better get back to him.'

The woman threw her cigarette on the ground and stubbed it out with her toe. 'Do you mind if I come with you,' she asked. 'I am a doctor. My name is Amanthi.'

Priyani nodded. 'Yes, of course. My name is Priyani and his name is David.'

CHAPTER EIGHTEEN

CINNAMON GARDENS

Amanthi did not know what prompted her to make the offer but the woman looked so sad and desolate standing by herself looking up at the stars, her heart went out to her. Amanthi often treated burn patients placed in an induced coma during the early stages of their treatment. She was familiar with blast injuries caused by severe trauma, and even if she could do nothing, she could keep Priyani company.

As a courtesy, she informed the Duty Medical Officer that she was accompanying Priyani to David's room.

'He's being treated as a special case,' the Duty Officer said glancing up at her. 'General Ratwatte has been involved and I've heard the President has made inquiries about him also.'

'What's his condition?' Amanthi asked raising her eyebrows.

'He had a cerebral-edema which has been drained,' the Medical Officer explained. 'He has two cracked vertebrae in his neck and a broken collar bone. His pupils respond well to stimulation and the prognosis is that he will come out of it. How long is hard to say.'

Amanthi nodded. Very often, burn victims had to be so deeply anesthetised that they were almost in a coma-like state. She had studied the effects of severe trauma to the brain.

'Ok, thanks. I won't interfere in his care. I just met his fiancé and she seems like a nice person. She's a bit upset, and I just want to reassure her that everything possible is being done.'

The Duty Officer shrugged. 'Go ahead,' he said. 'I have no objection. I'll place a note in his file. It won't hurt to have someone with your experience involved.'

Priyani was standing by the bed holding David's hand when Amanthi came into the room. She turned and looked at Amanthi hopefully. 'What did the Doctor say?' she asked.

'It's not completely bad news. He's stable and is responding to stimulation. These types of injuries take time to heal.'

Amanthi studied the readings on the monitor and picked up the clipboard at the foot of the bed, leafing through the various reports. She turned to the night nurse who had followed her into the room.

'Can you get me a torch please? I want to check his pupils.'

David's pupils dilated slightly when Amanthi shone a light into his eyes. It was a good sign, but she didn't want to raise Priyani's hopes too much.

'He could be much worse than what he is right now,' she said. 'He's being well looked after, and they are doing everything that needs to be done.'

Priyani nodded gratefully with tears in her eyes. Amanthi held her hand and patted it gently. 'Don't be upset. You have to be strong for him.' Amanthi could see Priyani's love for David shining through her eyes. She felt envious that she never had those kinds of feelings for anyone.

'You don't know what he has done for me.' Priyani said quietly, looking down at David. 'He has changed my whole life and saved me from being killed.'

Amanthi was intrigued by what Priyani said. 'What do you mean?' she asked. 'How did he save you?'

Amanthi couldn't believe the story that Priyani told her. How David followed the men who kidnapped her through the jungle and rescued her. It sounded like it was taken from an adventure novel. 'He did that for you?' she asked.

Amanthi looked down at the man lying on the bed. *He must be a very special person.* She wished for Priyani's sake that he would wake from his coma with all his physical and mental abilities intact. The chances were good if he recovered quickly but it would take time, and a lot of careful rehabilitation before he would be back to what was normal for him.

'I have to go now,' she said reluctantly. 'I've got an early start. I'll drop in again to see you tomorrow. You can contact me at the Burn Unit in the General Hospital if you need to talk to me.'

Priyani gave her a surprised nod of thanks and hugged Amanthi before she left.

Amanthi promised herself that she would keep in touch with Priyani after all this was over. She liked the young woman and wished she could do more for her.

❧

David wandered in the fog. It reminded him of a place he used to go to when he was a kid. It was his favourite place in the world. But it couldn't be. He had not been there for many years. Where was he? David heard voices muffled in the fog. They were getting closer. It sounded like someone he knew …

'David, David! Can you hear me …'

David struggled back to consciousness slowly. Little pieces of awareness ebbing and flowing, making him feel dizzy. *Why was everything so fuzzy?* He searched his recollection looking for specific memories. Someone leaned over him shining something bright into his eyes. David blinked in the harsh light wishing they would stop.

'He's awake …'

The bright light disappeared. David blinked a few times trying to remove the image it had left on his retina. He felt someone squeezing his hand.

'Oh, David. We were so worried about you …' A blurred face came into view. The woman's voice was familiar. David tried to say something, but it came out as a croak. His throat felt raw and it hurt to swallow.

'He's trying to say something …'

'Here, sip this …' Someone dressed in white leant over him and inserted a straw into the side of his mouth. He sucked, feeling the water trickle down his throat. The water felt cold and delicious. The best he had ever tasted.

David could not move his head, his neck seemed to be in some sort of a brace. The room seemed to be full of people. He saw someone in a white coat. Someone else stood next to him. They were all looking down at him.

Who are all these people? His head hurt so he closed his eyes and opened them again.

The people around him seemed clearer, less out of focus. He thought he recognised a couple of them, but he did not know their names. Someone squeezed his hand and leant over him, stroking the side of his face. The woman had a beautiful face. She smiled but her eyes were full of tears. *Why is she crying?*

For a long while, it was hard to do anything more than concentrate on breathing, but gradually he began to sort out his thoughts and get his head straight. David smelt her perfume … then suddenly, like a light switch had been turned on, it all came back to him. He remembered the ambush and the explosion but nothing after that.

He tried to speak again. 'Priyani …' It came out as a whisper.

'He said my name …' Priyani sobbed. 'He said my name!'

There was a commotion around the bed as people crowded around.

A man dressed in a white coat leaned over him. *It must be a doctor.*

'Do you know your name?' he asked.

David tried to nod but couldn't. 'Yes,' he croaked. 'It's David.'

The light was shone again in each of David's eyes and the doctor's face was replaced by Priyani's.

'Oh, David. We were so worried …'

David felt tired, his eyes started to close. He squeezed Priyani's hand. He wanted her to know he loved her and that she need not worry.

∾

Priyani was overjoyed. David was going to be okay, she knew that in her heart. He looked so helpless lying there, his head tightly wrapped in a bandage, electrical wires and tubes running everywhere.

Amanthi walked over to Priyani. 'I think you should go home and get some rest,' she said, holding Priyani's arm. 'You look pretty tired and you don't want to look like that when he wakes up again.'

Priyani nodded without saying anything. She suspected that David's recovery would be a long process and she needed to be at her best for him.

'Doctor Fernando believes that he will wake up gradually. He'll have longer moments of lucidity and will eventually fall into a regular wake, sleep cycle. This is all very normal in people with these types of injuries.'

'Will he be alright?' Priyani knew that accident victims with brain injuries ended up with severe disabilities.

'Well, he knew who he was, and he called you by your name,' Amanthi said smiling. 'That's really good news because it shows that the injury has not affected his memory. The rest we will only find out over time. The whole recovery process can take months, sometime many years depending on how badly affected he is. Head injuries are notoriously difficult to predict.'

Priyani ran her hand through her long dark hair and looked around the room. The nurse was standing next to David's bed replacing the bag of saline on the metal stand. The doctor stood next to the light, leafing through David's medical charts making notations as he did. David was in good hands. She would go home. But first she had to call David's parents.

CHAPTER NINETEEN

CENTRAL HIGHLANDS

The piercing wail of a *canku* -conch shell, at dawn signalled the *perattu* -the muster, was about to commence. Workers started lining up outside the factory waiting for the *Durai* to appear and give them their orders for the day. It was a familiar ritual repeated every morning on the estate lines.

Mukesh pulled Kanan aside before he left for work. 'I am very interested in what you said about us taking control of the estates,' he began. 'You know I was put in gaol for nothing and I have no love for the people in charge. Can you introduce me to the men you talk about?'

Kanan pulled Mukesh away from the lines, glancing around furtively as he did. 'Shhh, don't talk so loudly,' he hissed. 'I shouldn't have said what I did. They will kill me if they find out.'

'C'mon,' Mukesh said. 'The union has been talking for many years about trying to get more control. I remember hearing it when I was a kid. No one got killed then.'

'This time it's different,' Kanan said. 'The union does not know.'

Mukesh stared at Kanan, his mind racing. The union was like a father and mother to all the estate workers and if they were not involved it changed everything.

'So, who is in charge then?' Mukesh asked. 'If you don't tell me I can ask Rani.'

'No, no. Don't do that,' Kanan said looking scared. 'She doesn't know who it is and if she goes around asking questions they won't like it. It's not like before,' he pleaded. 'These men are different.'

'You're not explaining yourself,' Mukesh said. 'Why are they different?'

Kanan glanced around cautiously before answering. 'They were part of the *Great Uprooting* and have come back illegally.' Kanan leant in closer. 'Some of them have had military training,' he whispered.

Mukesh knew what Kanan was talking about. The period when families were forced to leave the homes they had lived in for generations was known as the *Great Uprooting*. It had torn families apart and those that found their way back illegally were prepared to do anything not to be sent back to India.

Mukesh nodded his understanding. 'Where are these people living?' Mukesh asked Kanan. 'Won't the *Periya Durai* –Head Superintendent, find out that they are not from this place?'

The rigid, hierarchical social structure of a tea estate required the *Kangani* to report all outsiders to estate management.

Kanan shrugged. 'I don't know where they're from,' he said. 'All I know is that each estate has someone who oversees recruitment. No one is spoken to unless they are verified by at least two people from the estate.'

'So, Rani and you can vouch for me,' Mukesh said.

Kanan shook his head. 'The women are not supposed to know' he said. 'But many of them do. They will be told what's going on closer to the time.'

Mukesh was surprised at what he had learnt. What Kanan said showed a level of organisation that had only existed with the estate workers union. If the estate Tamils were serious about breaking away from the rest of the country, they would not want to be under the Tamils in the north.

'There must be someone who's head of this movement,' Mukesh said. 'Who is it?'

'There is someone, but I don't know who it is,' said Kanan. 'I have heard that he is a *Durai* and is one of us. He will be the leader of *Malai Nadu.*'

'Is that what you're going to call it?' Mukesh asked. 'The Hill Country?'

Mukesh nodded excitedly. 'Yes,' he said. 'We will be a country of our own. We deserve better that this. We are human beings too and we have our rights.'

Mukesh could see that Kanan was nervous talking about it but at the same time determined. Mukesh sat and thought about what he had learnt from Kanan. It was obvious that the man believed that there was a movement being formed for the estate Tamils to break away and form their own government. If Shankar was involved, then they would have the support from the militant movements in the north who would supply arms and finance. Even men, thought Mukesh. He was not surprised that it had got this far. Many of the estate Tamils were stateless and had no rights. They were in effect indentured slaves working for private interests who made enormous profits on their labour.

It was time to get in touch with the Captain. He would be very interested in what was happening. He would go to Colombo and look for him there.

CHAPTER TWENTY

CINNAMON GARDENS

It had been six weeks since David's operation and he was recovering well. He still had problems with his balance and wore a brace around his neck and shoulders. His memory had come back, and he was not slurring when he spoke.

Priyani wheeled David out into the garden and sat next to him on the grass. It was a bright, sunny day and the garden was shaded by an enormous flame tree.

David had been getting one of the hospital orderlies to read the daily newspapers to him as he couldn't focus too long on the words. He wanted to talk about the Indian presence in the north. 'This is not going to be good for the country,' he said shaking his head. 'Has Rohan said anything to you about it?' Rohan had visited David in hospital a couple of times, but David had not seen him for over two weeks.

'No,' Priyani shook her head. 'He has not returned my calls either. Ever since the Indians came and the riots, he has been hard to catch.'

David nodded his head in understanding. 'From what I hear, the papers say that several Cabinet members are opposed to the Indians being allowed in, which doesn't surprise me. I don't think the Sinhalese people in the south will be too happy.'

The newspapers were reporting that there had been attacks on government buildings by groups of armed men claiming to represent the common people. He had noticed that morning that an armed soldier stood at the entrance to the Military Hospital. Not for the first time that day, he wished that he had access to top secret intelligence reports that he would normally be privy to. But according to the Medical Officer he still had a number of months of rehabilitation before he would be declared fit for any type of duty. David felt frustrated just sitting around when there was so much happening in the country, and deep inside was a growing concern that he would never be allowed to return to the work for which he had sacrificed so much.

David tried to be cheerful for Priyani's sake. She had remained with him all through the time he was in a coma and even now spent most of her free time with him.

'Where is Amanthi?' David asked Priyani. 'She's not been around for a few days.' David liked the doctor from the General Hospital who had befriended Priyani. She dropped in often after her evening shift when Priyani was with David. They ordered take away food from a local Chinese restaurant and sat talking in David's room until he got tired.

'She left a message that she's been very busy but will try to make it tonight,' Priyani said. 'She must be dealing with all this trouble that's going on.'

It was getting dark when Priyani wheeled David into the hospital. David had just settled in the bed when he saw Amanthi standing by the door. Priyani had gone to the restroom to wash her hands.

'Ah, Amanthi,' David said. 'It's good to see you.'

Amanthi walked into the room and David could tell right away that something was bothering her. 'What's wrong?' asked David. 'You don't look very happy.'

'How much have you heard about what's going on?' she asked, looking around the room. 'Where's Priyani?'

'She's in the washroom,' said David. 'She'll be back in a minute. What do you mean what's going on? I am locked in here and no one tells me anything.'

Amanthi nodded. 'Of course,' she said. 'I am sorry. How are you feeling?'

Priyani walked into the room at that time and the two of them hugged. David waited a moment. 'I am feeling fine,' he said. 'But they won't let me do anything until this damn neck brace comes off. I am getting quite frustrated.'

'You've had a very bad injury, David, and you were very lucky not to be paralysed or have permanent brain damage,' Amanthi said soothingly. 'It takes time to heal you know. You won't regret the time you spent getting better.'

David couldn't argue with Amanthi's logic. She was so practised in her bedside manner that he did not argue.

'Ok, ok,' David said with a lopsided smile. 'I knew you wouldn't be any help. So, what's going on?'

Amanthi pulled a chair forward, waiting until Priyani sat on the bed next to David. 'The JVP are active again and have started attacking government buildings,' she said. 'They are calling for a *hartal*, a strike action, and are threatening to kill anyone who goes to work.'

David leaned back on the bed thinking hard. The JVP was a Marxist-Leninist party which had led an armed uprising against the government in the early '70s. David was in Officer Training College at the time and had participated in military operations to put down the bloody uprising. Recently the group had re-emerged as a Sinhalese nationalist organisation opposing any compromise with the Tamil insurgency in the north.

'They must think that they have a lot of support after the peace accord was signed,' David said, thinking aloud. 'They will use the Indian presence against the government, I think. That's what I would do.'

'And that's why we miss you at the Joint Operations Command,' a voice said from the doorway, startling everyone in the room. 'It's good to see that knock on your head has not affected your thinking.' Colonel Ranasinghe walked into the room smiling broadly. 'Hello young lady,' he said, hugging Priyani who had got to her feet. 'You look as beautiful as ever. And who is this?' he asked, holding his hand out to Amanthi.

The Colonel was David's commanding officer and head of the Army Special Operations Group that David was attached to. He was a close friend of General Ratwatte, the Head of Joint Operations Command.

'It looks like I came at the wrong time,' he said to David after being introduced to Amanthi. 'Something has come up which I need to discuss with you. Perhaps I'll come back tomorrow.'

'No, no, Colonel,' said Priyani. 'We'll go for a walk outside while you talk to David.'

David smiled at Priyani, who ushered Amanthi out of the room. David looked up at the Colonel who came and stood next to his bed. The smile the Colonel had on his face when he came into the room was replaced by a grim expression.

'How far away are you from active duty?' he asked David brusquely. 'There are so many things going on right now that we need you back in some capacity.'

David looked up at the Colonel. 'I am afraid I am still weeks away from being released from the hospital,' he said. 'I still get dizzy spells and I can't move around until this bloody brace is removed. I have to get someone to read the newspapers to me, but I can still help.'

The Colonel grimaced. 'That's what I was hoping,' he said. 'I need someone like you to analyse the current situation and give us something we can work on. The President is under a lot of pressure and he needs our help.'

'I have been wanting to get my hands on all the intelligence reports since I got injured. Can you arrange to have them sent to me here?'

The Colonel nodded. 'Yes, I have taken care of that already. From tomorrow you will have all the files you want,' he said. 'I will also assign Sarath to stay here and read them to you. He's cleared to know their contents and he can keep an eye on them. They cannot get into the wrong hands.'

'What's the situation like up in the north,' David said. 'I can't help but think that it is the reason the JVP have decided to show their hand again.'

'We are restricted to the main bases in the north and east, but the bulk of our forces have moved south to confront the JVP. The Indians are sending in more and more troops, bloody shiploads of them mostly into Trincomalee to disarm the Tigers,' the Colonel said. 'And to make it even worse, they are such an arrogant lot.'

'Are there any local assets embedded in their forces?' David asked. 'We have been fighting the Tigers for a few years now and can teach them a thing or two.'

The Colonel shook his head in disgust. 'I was at a meeting with their commanders last week and it was a total waste of time. They think they know everything and won't take any advice from us.'

David looked at his Commanding Officer, surprised at the passion he was displaying. It was a part of him that David had never seen before.

'What gets me is that they accuse us of the persecution of the local civilian population, but they are acting like a bloody occupying force. We're hearing of rapes and atrocities, and what is especially frustrating is there are reports that their intelligence services are arming some of the smaller Tamil militant groups while the military are trying to disarm the Tigers.'

'What is Prabhakaran's thinking on all this?' David asked. 'He wouldn't be too pleased with what's happening.' David knew that the leader of the Tamil separatist movement would play a pivotal role in what was going on.

'We have been getting reports that Prabhakaran is refusing to play ball with them,' the Colonel nodded. 'We've heard that his idea of a *Tamil Eelam* does not include the Indians.'

'So, for once we have an alignment in thinking between the Sinhalese and the Tamils,' David smiled grimly. 'We both don't want the Indians here. I wonder whether that could be exploited?'

The Colonel looked at David thoughtfully. 'No one has come up with that kind of thinking,' he said. 'It's something worth pursuing.'

CHAPTER TWENTY-ONE

VANNI JUNGLE

Danika brushed aside a tear with the back of her hand and looked through the opening in the bunker. Smoke from the smouldering fire in the corner escaped through a vent built above the hearth, although small tendrils drifted across the enclosed space making her eyes water. The bunker had three levels: the dank ground floor, which was the safest but most suffocating section, an uneven mezzanine of rough logs for storing food and clothing, and a more open upper level covered with woven palm leaves for when immediate danger had passed. It also had a small alcove with a dry toilet. It had to be one of the more durable underground structures in the area.

It was not yet dawn, so the trees outside were visible only as a dark menacing mass. The familiar crackle of firewood and sizzling of flour paste turning into *rotis*, baking on a flat piece of metal, reminded her of her mother preparing their morning meal. All cooking was done during the dark to prevent the smoke being spotted by army patrols. By sunrise the cooking fires would be piles of cold ash but at times they had no choice but to light the fires during the day. To prevent being seen, they had engineered chimneys of bamboo which were thrust up into the low ceiling of vegetation. The top of each improvised flue fitted into a horizontal length of bamboo punctured with vent holes along its length. The smoke from the cooking fires would not rise in tell-tale columns but would exhaust into the forest canopy in thin trickles, dispersed efficiently amongst the dense foliage.

Indra squatted beside her making balls of the dough for Danika to flatten. Danika liked Indra. She was a soft-spoken, unassuming woman about Danika's age who did not say much. The Vanni's unrelenting sun had burnt her to a coffee brown, her hair cut short, almost like a man's. Indra had grown up nearby and knew these jungles intimately. She had survived the bombing raid on their village that had destroyed her family home and killed their parents. Forced to live with neighbours, her miserable existence had fuelled her hatred and fed a desire to exact revenge. Her history did not differ greatly from that of hundreds, even thousands of bitter young men and women trapped in the warzones of the north.

Indra stared at the flames confined between three stones laid on the bare earth supporting the cooking vessel. Danika noticed the tracks of tears on her shiny, rounded cheeks glistening in the firelight. It was probably because she missed her childhood lover. At the Tigers' inception, their leader, known to everyone as *Anna* –older brother, had banned marriage, relationships and sexual activity among the cadres. It was part of a rigid disciplinary code for combatants, which included bans on smoking, drinking and gambling. He enforced celibacy ruthlessly; carnal feelings were believed to distract combatants from the call of duty, and family life was considered corrupting, as it would make people selfish. Everyone knew that they would be defamed, excommunicated and even killed if they strayed from this rule.

They'd all heard of couples that had been shot dead. 'Both are not always killed,' Indra had once said to her tearfully. 'One is shot and the other is punished for life.'

Danika had not responded as she was grateful for the leaders' edict. A man who had arrived with a group of Tamil cadres to take over the western defence force she was with, was a heavy, thickset man from Jaffna by the name of Balan. He'd made it clear on more than one occasion that he wanted something from her. She was a woman. Putting two and two together wasn't difficult. He wanted her but had been cautious knowing what would happen to him if he was caught.

The Tiger cadre had treated the Tamil Muslim unit who had fought so bravely against the Sri Lankan military with contempt, even killing Ratnam for questioning his authority She had been very upset at the time after hearing that the man who led them, Sami, had been killed. Danika had helped the youngest member, Ismail, smuggling food to him after Balan and his men had taken over the defence of the area.

Danika had heard Balan boasting proudly that he'd killed the young *Marakkalaya* who had been trying to escape and she knew it must have been Ismail. Hatred burned in her heart for the man, but she had to be careful, not wanting anyone to know her feelings.

Danika shook her head in regret, her thoughts far away. She had never let her feelings control her life since she'd dedicated her life to the movement. But time had softened her, and she'd begun to regret the life she'd chosen for herself.

Danika sighed and slid a *roti* onto a cooked pile heaped on a cracked and chipped plate. There would soon be enough to feed them all.

Danika slipped into the class room and stood with her back against the wall. *Something big must be going on?* She had been in the village, talking to a woman who had returned from a trip to the north to see her parents and had just got the message.

The large class room was full. Sundara, the Sector Commander, turned in his chair and cast a dark look at her. Everyone turned to look as she stood frozen at the back of the room. She stared back defiantly. She had been here before. As one of the first women to experience combat, she was used to the smug arrogance that most of the men present wore like a badge of honour. But there was also respect on some of the faces that looked at her. After she'd slit the throat of the Indian soldier who tried to take her by force and stabbed another, she had been taken seriously by some.

As a member of the women's military wing, the job came with more than its share of narrow-minded issues. The Tigers had been a male domain since their inception and some of the men felt that women were being forced on them. Since her small team was the only operational female unit in the sector, she felt that they were sometimes seen as servants.

Danika scanned the room. All of those present were Team Leaders. None of the rank and file men were present. The only other woman in the room was Mala, her scout Team Leader. She was one of the first women to volunteer after her family had been killed when their home was destroyed by an artillery shells fired from within the Jaffna Fort. Women combatants like Mala and Danika had since functioned as an integral part of the Tiger's and had proven themselves time and again as an effective fighting force.

A large map, pasted on a blackboard the width of the class room, appeared to be the only item they were using. Danika thought she recognised the contours on the map which were on the edge of their operational area ... only one hill she knew of was shaped like that! Random words and phrases, she couldn't decipher from where she was standing, were written haphazardly on the blackboard on either side of the map.

The man briefing the team must have been someone important, at least a Senior Commander. Sundara deferred to him every time he addressed him. He was dressed neatly in a Tiger uniform and was by far the eldest in the room.

'The Indians have strongly established themselves at the Padaviya Junction and have fortified the camp. They forced the civilians out and have taken over their houses. We are planning an operation to take it back'. The Commander looked resolutely across the room. 'We want the Indian soldiers to go back with their tails between their legs like they did in Jaffna. We cannot let them establish a base so deep in the Vanni.'

The enormity of what he said filled the room. After failing to destroy the Tiger organisation during a major operation in the Jaffna Peninsula, the Indian army had turned its guns towards the militant bases in the Vanni jungles, transforming the entire area into a mammoth theatre of brutal and bloody warfare. Intensive search and destroy operations along the coastal areas took place on a large scale. Many civilians had been killed in these operations, but the Vanni militant forces had remained protected and active in the deep jungles. Until now they had avoided open confrontation with the Indian *jawans* to preserve their jungle sanctuaries. *Everything is going to change.*

The Commander pointed at a table covered in maps and photos. 'We have been gathering information about the camp and it's time to act. We are moving a brigade of experienced men and a complete mortar section to reinforce your sector. You will all be taking part in the upcoming battle, so you must prepare your men to sacrifice themselves for the struggle.'

Danika had heard about the locally made Baseelan mortars but had never seen them in operation. The warheads were locally made with pellets fashioned from the metal floorboards of buses.

Danika was breathing hard by the time she made it to the top of the steep hill. It was late evening and the sky was turning red behind her. The sound of the helicopter gunship that had been circling above faded into the distance.

Only the night before had the team been notified that the operation was going ahead, sending everyone into a flurry of action. All the planning and time spent masking their movements from the circling planes and helicopters had led to this moment.

She stopped a few metres short of the summit and adjusted her webbing. The wide straps from which the two ammunition pouches hung, were cutting into her shoulders. Sliding her hand into a side pocket of her cloth bag, she pulled a plastic bottle out and took a mouthful of warm water. Replacing the bottle, she tugged at the hessian sack she had tucked into her belt.

Danika looked behind her to ensure that she was not being watched. The large boulder where Parvathy had positioned herself was barely visible. She pulled the woven sack over her head, adjusting it so that the eyes holes were aligned on her face. The strong, light brown fabric covered the top of her body and was perfect camouflage against the greens and browns of the hilltop. Long slits on each side of the sack gave her complete freedom of movement, allowing her to crawl up to the summit.

The Indian army camp lay in the village more than half a kilometre away on the main road. The long range, military-grade binoculars she carried around her neck had been given to her only that morning. From the top of the hill, she could see through its wide-angle lens that the mud-bricked shops, homes and village school were clearly visible, but large neem and mango trees blocked her view in places. The junction the village straddled was blocked with 55-gallon barrels overflowing with earth. A few unarmed soldiers lazily kicked a ball around the schoolyard.

Next to the road, uncultivated paddy fields stretching into the distance were overgrown with weeds. In front of her, a pumpkin creeper with splashes of bright yellow flowers, spread across an untended vegetable plot next to some rotting plantain trees. Long spools of wicked looking barbed wire formed a protective ring around the entire village. Freshly dug trenches zigzagged through the reddish-brown earth behind the jagged barriers. Fortified machine gun bunkers, roofed with sandbags piled on freshly cut coconut trees, were located every 100 metres or so. Large areas bulldozed of all trees and ground vegetation right to the edge of the jungle made the camp look tough and menacing.

A small group of soldiers huddled around a pit in the school yard, the mortar's deadly black tube peeping above the sandbagged side of the mortar pit. She could see another sandbagged firing position through the trees but couldn't see the weapon clearly. There were supposed to be three 81-inch mortars located in the camp, but she couldn't see where the third one was located. It didn't worry her that much as she had been told that the weapon pits would be located close to each other.

The village had been cleared of all inhabitants when the Indians moved in. Three large army trucks were parked in the school compound next to a hibiscus in full bloom. A large pile of neatly stacked, wooden ammunition boxes, surrounded by a ring of sandbags, were next to the trucks.

Danika carried a walkie-talkie on her belt. When the shelling started, her job was to report where the shells were landing and make the necessary adjustments. The plan was to neutralise the mortar pits before the men could advance. The weapons were used by the Indians to shoot parachute flares which illuminated large areas for several minutes, taking away the cover of darkness.

The crump of a round leaving its tube behind her was the first indication that the attack was underway. She quickly pulled up the walkie-talkie, which was set to the operational channel, and readied to call out where the explosive projectile would land.

The whistle of the shell going over her head also alerted the soldiers in the village. The camp came to life like a disturbed ants' nest, men scurrying out of buildings and seeking shelter where ever they could. Through the binoculars she couldn't see exactly where the bomb landed, but the blast of high explosive which threw debris into the air, gave her a general idea. She estimated that it was about 50 metres away from the mortar pits.

'Down 50', she shouted into the walkie-talkie, while pressing the toggle switch. A squelch on the handset indicated that she'd been heard.

The next round was on its way before she looked through the binoculars, which had slipped down her face. This time she could see the bomb land about five metres away from the mortar pits.

'Up five, up five,' she yelled into the handset. Danika held her breath hoping that the next bomb would be on target as the Indian mortars were almost ready for firing. In the dugout, a soldier carrying a large mortar shell in his arms stood next to the mortar tube while another soldier adjusted a handwheel.

The geyser of black smoke and brown earth which erupted when the round hit the mortar pit was spectacular. The huge flash must have included the rounds that were stored in the pit and a split-second later the sound rolled up the hill until it reached Danika.

Danika shook her head trying to clear away the deafening sound of the explosion as she looked through her binoculars at the camp. There was nothing left of the mortar pit. A dull grey pall of smoke hung over a massive crater with the twisted remains of the mortar tube. A faint noise from the walkie-talkie made her realise that she had not reported the last round.

'On target, on target,' she shouted into the handset.

Explosion after explosion bracketed the area as dusk began to fall. She kept adjusting the fall of the rounds until she was certain the mortar pits had been destroyed and nothing could have survived in that area. As instructed, she switched targeting the rounds to the western perimeter of the camp where the attack would take place.

It was completely dark when the mortars finally stopped firing. Fires burned out of control in the centre of the village and the popping sounds of gunfire indicated that the ground attack was underway.

CHAPTER TWENTY-TWO

CINNAMON GARDENS

David's neck brace had been removed and he was finally allowed to go home more than three months after he was injured. His rehabilitation was progressing well. He could now walk without the aid of a walking stick and his dizzy spells had almost completely disappeared. He had strict orders from the Medical Officer to follow the rehabilitation program designed for him and had started jogging slowly to improve his aerobic fitness.

His physiotherapist at the Military Rehabilitation Hospital at Ragama always insisted that he stretch before doing any exercises and David took his advice seriously. He spent at least two hours in the gym every day building up his strength for when he would be able to go back to the field again.

The Medical Officer had cleared him for limited duty which meant that he could do a job that required no physical activity of any sort. David didn't mind.

His cognitive reading ability had returned and at least he could go to Joint Operations Command headquarters on Slave Island and keep on top of what was going on.

The latest intelligence reports he was reading were getting more detailed and it was a scary picture they were painting. The Tigers had been using the Indian state of Tamil Nadu as a logistical base for their operations against the Sri Lankan army since the beginning of their campaign. The long Tamil Nadu coast facing the Tamil-inhabited areas of Sri Lanka was the focus of attention for the militant organization. In the Indian hinterland there were twenty-six urban centres and over four hundred fishing villages, where the Tigers successfully co-opted or subverted the local administration, police, politicians, and more importantly, fisherfolk and farmers. The key area was in a two hundred and thirty-kilometre-long coastline covered in part with thick mangrove forests, innumerable creeks, and about one hundred fishing villages. This area had over the years been a haven for smugglers and drug peddlers as the Jaffna Peninsula was just twenty-eight kilometres away.

Fuel which was tightly controlled by the Sri Lankan government and critical to the ongoing Tiger operations, was often siphoned off the thousand-strong Indian fishing fleet made up of hundreds of small, mechanized fishing craft. The militant craft would merge, siphon off diesel at a hefty premium, and proceed to Jaffna. Diesel that cost a few Rupees per litre in India was reportedly being bought at exorbitant prices on the high seas, tempting more than a few to sell.

The Indians were training the militants in camps all over India, while in Tamil Nadu itself, mass training of cadre had begun. The reports indicated that up to five thousand persons were training in about fifteen well-run camps.

One report he read indicated that this increase in Indian involvement was because Indira Gandhi, the Indian Prime Minister, had begun to take an interest in the activities of the militants. Encouraged by highly placed militant supporters, a movement to detach north-eastern Sri Lanka into an independent state had begun to surface in New Delhi. She evidently saw in the conflict an opportunity to ensure that 'foreign western forces' were kept out of Sri Lanka and was not averse to extending India's influence in the region.

If this was true it was a game changer. David knew that the Indians had always been sympathetic to the Sri Lankan Tamil's plight and looked the other way, even supporting them to a degree, when it suited them. But what he was reading was quite startling. The Indians obviously felt that the current situation was favourable to create a friendly state to their south. This would give them access to the strategic deep-water port of Trincomalee which they had coveted ever since their independence from the British. It had to be the reason the Indian Peace Keeping Force had been deployed to the north. They were there to ensure Indian control!

David was reading a report that had come in one morning when he got a call from the guard post at the front gate. 'Sir, there is a man here asking for you,' said the Duty Sergeant. 'He wanted me to tell you that his name is Mukesh.'

David had completely forgotten about the man who had been his main operative in Jaffna. He felt guilty that he had made no attempt to contact him after being released from hospital.

'Yes, I know Mukesh,' David said. 'Bring him to the meeting room in the lobby. I'll meet him there.' David hoped that he had been contacted by someone from military intelligence.

David hurried down the stairs making sure to keep his hand on the side rail. He still had the occasional dizzy spell although he could barely remember the last time he had one.

Mukesh stared at David when he was brought into the room. David understood why. David had lost weight lying in bed for so long and was almost half his normal size. He was also completely bald, a legacy of his brain surgery. An angry pink scar ran from his temple to the crown of his head.

David smiled at Mukesh. 'I know, I know, I don't look the best,' he said. 'But I am getting better every day.'

'What happened to you?' Mukesh asked, his mouth still open in surprise.

'The vehicle I was in got hit by an RPG outside Jaffna and I was badly injured. I have just recently been released for some limited duties and I am trying to catch up. I am sorry, but I had completely forgotten about you.'

Mukesh waved David's apology away. 'Don't worry about it. I have been looking for you in the north and decided to try this place when I heard you had been transferred. I didn't know you had been injured.'

David waved Mukesh to a chair. 'Ok, you have found me,' he said. 'What's going on?'

Mukesh was a trained operative who knew how to give a concise intelligence briefing, but it seemed to David that he was getting something much more. Mukesh started at the very beginning, from the time he went back to the place of his birth after being evacuated from Jaffna.

David listened as Mukesh explained the conditions on the tea estate where his sister worked, the plight of the Indian Tamils who were stateless and the anger that many felt towards their masters. Mukesh talked about the workers organising themselves to demand better pay and conditions. He leant forward attentively when Mukesh said that some of the workers were talking about a separate state.

'A separate state,' David asked disbelievingly. 'You mean like *Tamil Eelam*?'

'No, like *Malai Nadu*,' Mukesh said. 'They already have a name for it. It means hill country.'

David was not convinced. 'There's no way it's going to happen,' he said, shaking his head. 'They don't have the leadership or the financing to do something that drastic. It's just the dreams of desperate men.'

'That's what I thought too,' said Mukesh. 'But then who do you think I see in Nuwara Eliya when I went there to the bank?' Mukesh regarded David smugly. 'Our old friend from Jaffna. Shankar!'

David leant back in his chair in surprise. He didn't doubt for one second that what Mukesh said was true. What was Shankar doing there?

David noticed that Mukesh was watching him expectantly as he processed the information. It did not make sense, but then again it did. If the government had to fight an uprising in the hill country and contend with a low-level insurgency in the south, they would have no resources to oppose the Tigers. David had seen reports of troops being withdrawn from bases in the north to cover trouble spots in the south.

'Hmmm, this is not good news,' he said to Mukesh. 'I will have to take this to my superiors. Where are you staying if I need to contact you in a hurry?'

David sat in his chair deep in thought after Mukesh left. He twirled the piece of paper with Mukesh's address absentmindedly. He needed to see the Colonel right away, but first he needed a plan. If he played this right it could provide him with an opportunity to get his hands dirty again.

∾

DIYATALAWA – CENTRAL HIGHLANDS

David breathed in the crisp air, enjoying the smell of tea and wood smoke. His comfortable room at the Officer's Quarters at the Diyatalawa Army Camp overlooked the well-groomed tea estates in the east. In the distance he could see the tea pluckers with wicker baskets hanging on their backs, plucking the tea leaves. The mist curled between trees of the deepest green imaginable. It was a sight that had always pleased him, and he was glad to be out of the heat and humidity of Colombo.

The Colonel had been sceptical about the estate Tamils' ability to form a separate state when David reported on his meeting with Mukesh.

'This has not come up at all before,' he said, leaning back in his chair. 'Are you sure that your man has not just made this all up?'

'No, I am not sure,' David concurred. 'But he has been pretty reliable before. And think about it. Just the thought of a million estate Tamils joining the Tigers scares the hell out of me. I don't know what that does to you, but don't you think that it makes sense for them to even try to get some sort of alignment.'

The Colonel steepled his hands deep in thought. 'Hmmm, yes, it's a worst-case scenario. With the Sinhalese Nationalists agitating against the peace accord in the south, the bloody Indians wanting us out of the north, and also out of the east mind you, it's a bad time for this to come up.' He shook his head. 'We cannot fight this war on all these fronts. Something will have to give. But if I am going to take this higher up I will need more than a brief sighting of a militant leader in Nuwara Eliya for it to be taken seriously.'

David nodded. 'I thought you would say that. How about if I spend some time in Diyatalawa and see what I can come up with? I'll be closer to Mukesh and can monitor what he's up to.'

The Colonel smiled at David. 'So, you figured a way to get involved did you?' He paused, looking thoughtfully at David. 'It's not a bad idea but you're not cleared for active duty yet. What will the Medical Officer have to say?'

'I have not spoken to him about it,' David shrugged. 'I don't see why he would have a problem with it. I can still do my rehab at the base hospital up there. I am sure he can get regular reports of how I am doing.'

'Ok,' the Colonel said. 'I'll get the ball rolling. But you have to convince him to sign off on it.'

Getting the Medical Officer to sign off on the transfer was not as difficult as David thought. But he got into trouble with Priyani when he told her of his plans.

'How did you talk the Medical Officer into letting you go?' she snapped at him. 'He was the one who put a six-month period on your recovery. It's been less than four months since your operation.'

'I can be more useful up there,' he said, taking Priyani's hands in his. 'You know I am bored just sitting around doing nothing. This will give me something important to do and put me right back in the middle of all the action.' David pulled Priyani into his arms and hugged her tightly. 'C'mon sweetheart, it's only until we find out what's going on.'

Priyani pushed him away, her eyes flashing. 'Don't try your little tricks on me,' she said. 'I know what you have been through and I don't want to see you in that state again. If you insist on going upcountry, then I am coming too to make sure you're not going to do something stupid.'

David agreed reluctantly. Having Priyani there would complicate things, but he liked the idea of having her around and they had not spent any time together at all. Priyani had applied for leave and would join him at the weekend. But before she arrived he had a few things to do.

CHAPTER TWENTY-THREE

CENTRAL HIGHLANDS

Mukesh wanted to join the meeting desperately. Kanan had too much to drink the previous night and let it slip that a meeting was being planned. But he had avoided Mukesh that morning, hurrying out of the room without even looking at him.

Mukesh brooded all day, wandering around the estate lines, cursing Kanan under his breath for being such a coward. He waited outside the estate office to accost Kanan when he returned from working in the eucalyptus forests above the tea fields, which were maintained mostly for a soil and water conservation.

'I have been thinking about your cause,' he said, grabbing Kanan by the arm. 'I want to be a part of it.'

Kanan looked around anxiously and pulled Mukesh aside. 'What are you doing?' he said angrily. 'Do you want to get me killed? I told you that these men will not stand for any disloyalty and by just telling you about it I have crossed that line.'

Mukesh could sense the fear in Kanan and realised he had been too anxious and needed to take a softer approach with him. 'Ok, ok,' he said quietly. 'I am sorry. But the more I think about it the more I like it and I am quite excited about what it all means. What's the best way for me to become a part of this venture?' Mukesh winked at Kanan.

Kanan looked around to make sure no one was listening. 'Wait here,' he said. 'I have to report to the *Kangani,* so I will get paid.' Mukesh watched as Kanan joined a line of workers who reported the number of hours they worked, to the estate office. The *Kangani,* dressed in a western-style jacket and sarong, would verify with the estate clerk that Kanan had actually been at the work site.

Kanan motioned Mukesh to join him and they walked down the rutted track to the estate lines where Rani would be preparing the evening meal. She would have gone through the same process earlier in the afternoon, having her basket of freshly plucked tea leaves weighed and recorded by the estate clerk.

'You cannot be a part of this,' Kanan emphasised strongly looking over his shoulder to ensure they were out of earshot. 'You are not registered as a worker on this estate or any other estate. You're not even a dependant. They are very careful to only recruit people whom they know and can be trusted.'

'You can tell them who I am,' Mukesh said. 'And that I served a term in Boossa for nothing. They cannot question my loyalties, can they?'

'I know, I know,' Kanan whined. 'But you don't know them. They are completely under the thumb of the *Durai* who is very ruthless, let me tell you. You are not only jeopardising my life, but your sister's life as well. I just won't do it.'

Mukesh realised that he was not getting anywhere with Kanan. 'Do you know who the *Durai* is?' he asked. 'Perhaps I can talk to him directly.'

Kanan shook his head miserably. 'No, no one knows who he is. He could be from any one of these estates or someone who lives in the city. I don't know who he is, and I don't want to know either.'

Mukesh watched Kanan as he hurried into the room which was his family home. He couldn't depend on Kanan as he seemed to be overcome by fear. He would have to rely on his own efforts.

∿

Mukesh approached the estate *kovil* -temple, from the rear, using terraced paths he knew from when he was a kid. A rocky outcrop of granite provided the perfect place to hide. Only a stream, gushing over a boulder-strewn bed lay between him and the building. The temple was very old, the intricately carved idols on the three-metre-tall *cobram* -tower, had weathered with time but lost none of its beauty.

As evening approached Mukesh could see small groups of two or three men walking across the estate towards the *kovil*. Mukesh pushed himself into a crevice between two rocks. *They won't see me here.*

The onset of darkness did not slow down the gathering as men carrying torches wound down the steep slopes, all converging at the *kovil*. There would have been over fifty men from different estates and divisions milling around its wide portico which extended out in front of the building. The space where devotees prayed was paved with dressed stone and painted in broad red and white stripes. From where he hid, Mukesh could see the winding, tarred estate road gleaming in the silver moonlight and the twin headlights of an approaching car.

The vehicle slowly turned into the *kovil* compound, the crowd of men parting before it until it stopped next to the elaborate structure, almost next to the portico. Three men got out from the car and entered the building. From the top of the rocky outcrop Mukesh could not make out who they were. The compound was slowly emptying as the workers entered the building.

Mukesh cursed to himself. He had confirmed that something was going on, had even witnessed a meeting but did not know what was said. He could try and sneak down next to the building to listen, but there were men with torches patrolling the area around the *kovil*. His eyes were drawn to the car that the men had come in. He had seen it before, but where?

CHAPTER TWENTY-FOUR

SLAVE ISLAND, COLOMBO

The meeting with the Colonel at Army Headquarters was not going the way David had expected. The Colonel had brushed aside David's attempt to report on the meeting at the tea estate and wanted to talk about something else.

'Your comment the other day about the government being in alignment with the Tigers was spot on,' the Colonel said, leaning back in his chair. 'This came up at the JOC meeting the other day and I have been asked to propose some ideas to exploit the situation.'

Open warfare had broken out between the Indian Peace Keeping Force and the Tamil Tigers who were resisting a major offensive by the Indians to capture Jaffna town. The Indians had been pouring troops into the peninsula and were expected to defeat the Tigers in the coming week.

David stared at the Colonel in surprise. 'What's brought that about?' he asked. 'It's been obvious that the Indians would eventually clash with the Tigers. The Tigers want a Tamil state without any outside control and it is never going to work. And to make it worse, the Indians sent in second rate troops from all over India. It only means that we were being replaced by a foreign military force that wants total control.'

The Indians had made a major blunder by sending troops from non-Tamil states. These troops did not speak the language and had no sympathy for the local population. There were many reports of rape and pillage.

The Colonel nodded. 'You saw that before anyone else,' he said. 'I have spoken with the General about what you said but he was reluctant to take it to the politicians as this is their mess. He wanted to wait until they figured it out.'

David didn't need the Colonel to tell him what was going on. 'So, the politicians have finally realised that the electorate won't stand for it,' he said. 'And if nothing is done they will lose control of the people.'

'Yes, you're right,' the Colonel sighed. 'Do you have any ideas?'

David sat for a while deep in thought. The Indians were playing a smart game. They had forced the Sri Lankan government into inviting them into the country and had quickly become a major player in a situation they had been manipulating for a while. The question that was foremost in his mind was what their ultimate motives were?

The Sri Lankan Tamils desire for a separate state seemed to be linked to the material support they got from India. It certainly did not include having the Indian Army patrolling the streets of Jaffna or forcing the mass displacement of civilians by shelling and bombing their neighbourhoods.

What concerned David was that even though the Colonel didn't seem to take the situation developing in the central highlands too seriously, to him it had the potential to disrupt the entire economic structure of the country in a way that the war in the north could not.

It was clear that the increased involvement from India was the far greater threat which had to be dealt with first. Building bridges with the Tamil separatist movement would require opening lines of communication which could eventually lead to cooperation and dialogue between the different parties. This would also stop the Sri Lankan Tamils from aligning themselves with the estate Tamils who all came from India.

'Yes,' David said finally. 'I think I know what needs to be done. The question is whether we will have the political will to do it.'

The Colonel listened intently, taking notes as David highlighted the current scenarios as he saw them, emphasising his concerns in each of the three areas he had identified.

'The question I don't have an answer for is whether the Sinhalese people will react favourably to a dialogue with the local Tamils if we support them against the Indians.'

The Colonel tapped the sheet of paper he had been scribbling on. 'It's a good start. We can get some good people on this right away. But how will we establish contact?'

∾

ROAD TO COLOMBO

Priyani's back and legs hurt. She had been travelling for days, the week full of visits to remote refugee camps, with dawn starts and nights spent alone in small nameless houses. She closed her eyes tiredly and rested her head against the car window trying to collect her thoughts.

The condition in the camps was growing intolerable. A modern tragedy in the making. All the camps now looked the same, a chaotic mishmash of tents and rough wooden structures that people now called home. The only irritation was the smell and sounds of people with not much clean water to drink and cook with, let alone bathe. But what concerned her the most as she travelled through villages in the Vanni, was finding an unreported humanitarian crisis in the making – people starving, no electricity, no telephone service, few medicines, no fuel for cars, water pumps or kerosene lamps.

Every time she thought about it her stomach knotted, so that her first instinct was to think of something else. But she couldn't do that. It was complicated, but she knew it was wrong to keep silent. The country had already been at war for seven years and now they waited to see what the Peacekeeping Force from India was up to. The clashes between the Sri Lankan army and the Tigers had petered out and it had become a war of rumours. The speculations and opinions changed in each refugee camp she visited, until she wasn't sure of what was happening. *It looks like the government has lost its way*, she thought gloomily.

The heavy rain which had lasted all evening, had lightened to a drizzle. Motorcycles and three-wheelers honking their horns incessantly, jostled for position as they took advantage of the break in the weather. She sighed as she watched the sodden street hawkers running alongside the vehicle, waving their wares with the hope of getting a sale.

Priyani felt her driver's concern when he turned his head to look at her. 'We should get to Colombo in an hour or so,' he said, his eyes back on the wet, slippery road.

That morning she had woken early and stepped out on the veranda. The pale dawn spread itself out over the sea, smooth as a fresh sheet. The last few stars shimmered on the horizon, and wind from the ocean set the coconut trees by the beach alight with the first of the sun's rays. She had stayed at the house the camp co-ordinator had been renting on the beach. It was a quiet, pleasant spot, away from the busy camps.

She thought about what she would have done if she hadn't met David. When she was younger, she thought that she would travel as soon as she could, exploring places she had read about. Places like France, Italy, Greece. She liked music and dancing and wanted to become a sparkling citizen of the world.

But the reality, as she grew older, was quite different. She had a traditional upbringing and had learnt to dread the endless afternoon visits to distant cousins and friends of friends, both of her parent's co-conspirators in their effort to ensure a suitable marriage for her. In the end she had given in to their wishes and agreed to marry an older second cousin, a man she had briefly met who was a lecturer in a university in England.

David had changed all that after she'd met him by chance at a dinner dance. He had made her come to her senses and realise that she was accepting her role in a traditional society, that alternately praised and condemned her, for the very same attributes. At first, she had been ashamed to go against her parents' wishes, so dependant had she become on them, but then she became defiant.

Everything had changed when she was kidnapped by a group of Black Tigers - special-operations commandos of the LTTE, who had attacked and massacred over a hundred devotees and priests at the Shri Maha Bodhi sanctuary, one of the holiest Buddhist temples on the island. Priyani and her Dutch supervisor had been ambushed on the road between Anuradhapura and Puttalam and taken forcibly into the jungle as hostages.

David and his team had followed them through the jungle for three days, finally rescuing them before they could be taken across the lagoon into the Jaffna Peninsula. Her parents had dropped their objections to her relationship with David and she had moved out of home with a new-found confidence.

Sami, who had played a major part in her rescue from the Black Tigers, was pardoned by the President and allowed to live in the refugee camp with his sister Suria.

Priyani thought about Suria. *I wonder how she is doing?* They had become closer since they started living together, as though Suria's own existence somehow held the key to her own continued sanity and survival. Suria missed her mother and Priyani had promised to do everything in her power to bring the old lady out of Jaffna.

But the arrival of the Indian Peacekeepers had upset the process which had been established to repatriate older residents of the embattled city. International aid agencies were banned from distributing food by the Indian Peacekeepers and the situation was dire.

Priyani gloomily looked out at the evening commuters huddling under bus stop shelters trying to keep dry. Others carrying umbrellas, stood back from the kerb to avoid being splashed by motor cyclists and three-wheelers being driven through large puddles of water.

She just couldn't believe the Indians who had almost invited themselves into the country, had the arrogance to pretend that they were not responsible for what was happening on the island. She had overheard snatches of conversations when she was held by the Black Tigers, about their recruitment and training in India. She didn't speak Tamil fluently but knew enough to understand what they were saying.

Priyani had met with an Indian Major responsible for administration in the north to discuss how the process could be restarted. Priyani's hands reflexively contracted into fists thinking about the meeting. She had come away frustrated at the man's conceit and superior attitude. *Who did he think he was? Wasn't this all their fault?*

The Indian Major dressed in olive grey battledress was a big, tough looking man. There was something heavy and menacing about him.

'We are now in charge and we'll do what's necessary to sort out this mess,' he said, studying a sheet of paper on his desk. 'We don't want any foreign agencies involved.'

'But it's a government sanctioned agency,' Priyani said sharply. 'We have been dealing with refugees since the war began. Money and relief supplies are collected overseas and distributed monthly.'

The Major looked up at her, his eyes cold and calculating. 'It's not sanctioned by us,' he said officiously. 'It'll have to be cleared in New Delhi.'

Priyani shook her head in disbelief. She knew how long it had taken for the agency to get the necessary government permits in Colombo and that was with the help of her brother. She couldn't imagine what it would be like dealing with a government body in a foreign country.

'That'll take too long,' she said doubtfully. 'How will these families survive in the meantime? Is there a way of getting approval here?'

The Major leaned back in his chair studying her closely. 'Perhaps you and I could come to an agreement,' he said. 'We can distribute the money and relief supplies for you in the camps.'

Rumours had been circulating among the relief workers that the Indians were confiscating relief supplies and shipping them to India to sell. Bribes were being demanded by some Indian *jawans* to allow the supply trucks through the Indian army checkpoints. It was one of the reasons she had travelled to the northern refugee camps, to see for herself whether these stories were true.

'But if we don't have the permits from New Delhi...'

The Major waved away her question. 'They don't need to know,' he said calmly. 'You will pay us to have the supplies delivered.'

'What do you mean pay you?' Priyani asked, trying to stay calm. She certainly had experienced her fair share of low-level officials asking for bribes to expedite paperwork down at the docks. But she had never met anyone at such a high-level so blatantly asking for a bribe.

'I want a percentage of everything that goes into the camps,' he said smugly, 'off the books of course.' The Major smiled, showing his teeth.

Priyani couldn't suppress an intake of breath. There it was. What she had feared. He had not even tried to sugar coat it in any way.

Priyani sat back in the chair. She needed to be careful. She thought for a moment before responding. 'I cannot agree to that without talking to my superiors,' she said frankly. 'They will have to decide how to handle such a request.'

The Major nodded understandingly. 'As far as I am concerned, this conversation did not take place.' He studied her through narrow, threatening eyes. 'However, you now know what is required for your agency to continue your work in these refugee camps.'

Priyani had summoned all her strength to control herself and uttered with as much composure as she could muster, that she would take the message back to her superiors in Colombo.

CHAPTER TWENTY-FIVE

KALPITIYA REFUGEE CAMP

It was getting dark when David walked up the path to a small house built on a block of land roughly thirty metres square. It sat amongst similar houses, all built by the government as refugee housing. He had been driven there in the Colonel's car.

David saw the curtain move in the window as he knocked on the front door. 'Who is it?' An unfamiliar voice called from inside.

'It's David,' he called out. 'I've come to talk to Sami.'

David heard the front door being unlatched but before the door opened, the porch light switched on brightly, blinding him for a moment. While his eyes adjusted to the light he heard a footstep to his right.

'So, it is you!' Sami stepped into the pool of light by the door hefting a rusted metal pipe about a metre long. 'I need to be careful these days.' David wondered for a moment why Sami had come around the house not trusting who was at the door. What was he worried about?

Sami was no more than medium height and did not look over-muscled, but his grip as he shook hands was like a steel band and there was something about his steady gaze that spoke of an inner strength and a will that would never give up. He had put on a bit of weight since David had seen him last and looked fit and strong.

David had got Sami's address from Priyani who kept in touch with Sami and his sister Suria. The relief agency that Priyani worked for provided them with food and medical supplies to supplement the allowance they were getting from the government.

Sami motioned to the front door which was partly open. 'Let's go in,' he said looking at the armed soldier standing by the car. 'Your man can keep an eye open for any trouble.'

'What kind of trouble?' David asked curiously, stepping into the front room that had a table and two chairs. A rolled-up mattress was propped up in a corner of the small room.

'Just some local thug trying to take advantage of these people,' said Sami, following David into the room. 'Nothing I cannot handle.'

Sami stood with his back to the wall, studying David warily. 'This is unexpected,' he said. 'What do you need from me?'

'Do you mind if I sit down?' David said, pointing at a chair. 'This is going to take some time.'

David sat down and studied Sami who stood leaning against the wall.

'Have you been following what's happening in Jaffna?' David asked. 'Have you had any contact with your mother?'

Sami shrugged. 'No, I haven't heard from her recently. Suria is worried because she reads what's happening in the papers.' Sami looked at David questioningly. 'Have you heard anything? Is that why you are here?'

'No, no. I haven't heard anything,' David said, shaking his head negatively.

'The latest is that the Indians have decided to take complete control in the peninsula and have attacked the militant positions. There are many civilians who have been displaced by the fighting and they are all being moved down to Trincomalee.

Sami nodded. 'Yes, I heard that from Priyani the other day. She said she'll check the lists, but I was wondering whether I should go and look for them in Trinco.'

David looked up at Sami curiously. 'I came here for a reason,' he said. 'But you knew that already. I want to talk about something that might interest you. Would you be willing to listen to what I've got to say?'

Sami studied David thoughtfully before nodding. 'I'll listen. But it doesn't mean I have to agree.'

'Yes, you don't have to,' David nodded. 'But I think you will be interested.' David hesitated before continuing. 'The government is under pressure from the electorate for allowing the Indians into the country, which has given the JVP a new lease of life. The government want to manage this and have decided to open a line of communication with the Tigers. The intention is to support them in some way against the Indians. We want to use you as the go-between.'

Sami looked at David in surprise. He started to say something, then paused for a moment, thinking. 'Why me?' he finally asked. 'I am not one of them. Remember that they tried to get rid of me once before. I would have thought you would want to use someone else.'

David shook his head. 'You are the best person to do this! Yes, you are not a Tamil but that works for us. You have many contacts in the militant groups. You know whom to talk to. We cannot think of anyone better.'

David could see that Sami was considering what he had said. 'You can look for your mother and grand-parents while you are there,' he continued. 'In fact, that would be a good cover story to get you into the militant controlled areas.'

Sami shook his head. 'There's still the problem with Suria. It's not safe for her here and I am not sure how long she can stay with Priyani.'

David pursed this mouth, thinking. 'She's very happy where she is,' he said to Sami. 'I know because I spoke to them yesterday. I am not sure how long the arrangement is supposed to last as I haven't spoken to Priyani about it specifically, but I am sure she wouldn't mind her staying longer. They get along very well together.'

Sami looked at David thoughtfully. David could see that he was going through everything in his mind. After a few minutes Sami nodded slowly. 'Yes, that'll work. But I need something from you before I agree.'

'Go ahead,' David said self-consciously. 'I shouldn't be saying this to you, but anything is possible. The government have got themselves backed into a corner.'

Sami nodded his agreement. 'I think so too,' he said, narrowing his eyes. 'I want to go back to Colombo. I am tired of this life and I want to make sure that my family doesn't have to live in these conditions again.' Sami took a deep breath. 'I understand that after having fought with the Tigers I should be grateful to be allowed to live here and not get a bullet in my head. It's time now to make a change. I cannot let my family suffer for the choices I made.'

David could see that Sami had made up his mind and was determined to make best use of the opportunity that had been presented to him. David had been there throughout the time Sami was debriefed by the military after walking away from the Tigers. Sami had commanded a special strike force composed of Moors who operated in the western areas of the Vanni with great success. Only the realisation that they were being used by the Tiger leadership as cannon fodder had made Sami decide to leave the militant ranks. He had provided vital information during the debrief which enabled the government to formulate their strategy for the peace talks in Bhutan. David doubted whether they had tapped all the information Sami had locked up inside him.

David nodded. 'It's a reasonable request and I will take it to the Colonel. I would be very surprised if he said no but he would have to clear it with his superiors and maybe even with the President. I can have an answer for you by tomorrow evening. In the meantime, you'd better get ready.'

CHAPTER TWENTY-SIX

CENTRAL HIGHLANDS

Mukesh crouched in the shadow of a large flowering bush at the edge of the stone and brick estate bungalow flanked by landscaped gardens. Built by the British as the Superintendent's home at the highest spot in the estate, its age-old opulence contrasted sharply with the grimy barrack-like estate lines that the workers lived in.

The long broad terracotta veranda extending right across the front of the house was empty. The only illumination came from green-shaded overhead lights hanging down from the ceiling. Two antique rattan recliners next to a gleaming ebony coffee table were the only pieces of furniture he could see. A few large earthenware pots held vibrant Anthuriums of different colours and hues.

Mukesh was here because he had realised that the car he saw at the *kovil* belonged to one of the *Durai's* living in the bungalow. The man was somehow connected to the movement.

Through the panelled glass windows, the long dining room with its French-polished ebony furniture and teak sideboard filled with flower encrusted porcelain tableware was a haven of luxury that he had never seen before. Only the very privileged workers could work in the house and tend the flower garden. Everyone else doing menial work in the kitchen or cleaning the toilets were expected to use the servant's entrance at the back of the bungalow.

Why would he do it? Mukesh, thought frowning in concentration. It didn't make sense that a person with all that power would risk everything for the *coolies* - workers.

A middle-aged man dressed in open necked shirt and long white trousers appeared on the veranda with a glass in his hand. Mukesh drew back into the shadow. He knew the man was the *Periya Durai* on the estate. They were granted the authority and power of a Police Captain and it wouldn't be a good thing to be seen by him.

The *Durai* stood leaning against the pillar looking over the garden into the distance while sipping from his glass which sparkled in the overhead light. Behind him, two servants bustled about the dining room, laying plates and bringing dishes of steaming food from a room at the back.

The peal of a gong echoed from within the bungalow, stirring the man on the veranda who turned and walked into the dining room. Two other men and a lady dressed in a lime green sari with a red border joined him, the four of them all sitting at the table while being fussed over by a white-coated servant.

Mukesh focused his attention on the three people who had joined the *Durai*. He had never seen them before. The woman was middle aged with silvery hair tied in a bun behind her head. One of the men was young, in his late twenties while the other was a bit older. They were all deep in discussion, drinking from glasses of sparkling crystal and eating with silver spoons and forks like the Europeans did.

Clouds scudded across the sky, plunging the garden into darkness one minute and then revealing it in silvery light the next. Mukesh waited for a moment of darkness and scurried across the lawn to the other side of the property, squatting in a drain behind a clump of Bougainvillea bushes with long thorny branches that swayed in the light breeze. Much closer to the veranda he strained to hear what was being said in the room.

Except for words or half completed sentences snatched away in the breeze, nothing could be heard through the half open window. Mukesh had seen enough. It had been a waste of time. The only bit of information he had learnt was that there were three others living in the bungalow with the *Durai*. One obviously was his wife, they looked about the same age. The two other men were either *Sinna Durai's* – Assistant Superintendents, or friends who had joined them for dinner.

A rustling sound to the right made him sink lower to the garden floor. The sound moved closer until Mukesh could make out the shape of a man through the bushes, his attention totally riveted to the scene inside the bungalow. Mukesh wormed closer to the base of the shrub he was under, ignoring the pain from the clinging Bougainvillea barbs that tore into his shoulder.

From where he lay, Mukesh could not see into the bungalow unless he raised his head. Time passed slowly. The man, not more than a few metres away, was completely still, forcing Mukesh to remain likewise.

The bright glow of light on the bushes alerted Mukesh that someone had come onto the veranda. Footsteps on the terracotta tiles stopped just a few metres away. The rasp of a match being struck was followed almost immediately by the unmistakeable odour of cigarette smoke.

'Are you there?' a voice asked in Tamil. Mukesh's heart pounded, not knowing what to do.

'Yes, *Durai*,' the man hidden in the bushes answered. 'I have come as you asked.'

'Good,' the *Durai* responded. 'Pass the word to everyone who attended the meeting that we have made good progress. Our friend from the north is leaving tomorrow and we will hear from him when the time is right.'

'Yes, *Durai*,' the man responded. 'I will do as you ask.'

Mukesh desperately wanted to see which of the three men in the bungalow was standing on the veranda but knew that if he moved the two men would hear him.

'I want leaders from all the estates to get their men ready as we planned,' he ordered. 'They'll be sent to the north soon for training. Go now, you have much work to do.'

The man turned and clambered down the slippery slope to the path beside the drain, turning away from Mukesh before disappearing from sight. The *Durai* stayed outside smoking until he flicked the glowing cigarette butt into the bushes, his footsteps receding into the bungalow. By the time Mukesh extracted himself from the clinging Bougainvillea bushes, the dining room was empty, only the servants clearing up the remains of the meal.

Mukesh was frustrated that he could not make out who the *Durai* was, but he had some valuable information that the Captain would be pleased to get.

CHAPTER TWENTY-SEVEN

KILINOCHCHI

Sami watched the dusty road from the window of the bus as they approached Kilinochchi. The Tamil town in the northern Vanni had become the centre of militant activities after Jaffna was overrun by the Indians. The intelligence that David had passed to him placed many of the militant leaders in the town and in outlying villages.

The last time he'd been anywhere near the town was when he helped Suria, Priyani and David escape from the Black Tigers. He had shot the Black Tiger leader who had threatened to harm his family. It had been the last straw which made him switch sides. He had left them with David and gone to warn his men that they had fallen out of favour with the Tiger leadership. Sami still couldn't understand why the Tiger leader had made such a foolish error. He was doing to the Muslims what the Sinhalese were doing to the Tamils. Expelling them from their traditional lands.

His thoughts turned back to the present as they reached the outskirts of Kilinochchi. The town, built by the British to ease the overcrowding and unemployment in Jaffna, was full of refugees from the north. Makeshift houses made of wood and plastic sheets concealed a school playground, covered in a smoky haze from open cooking fires.

The bus pulled up to an untarred, open area which served as the town's bus stop. Sami descended from the battered old vehicle, a cloth bag with a change of clothes and toiletries slung over his shoulder. He paused amongst the evening crowd, buffeted by the strong tide moving slowly into the main street. He sniffed the air, at once repelled and energized by the smell of burnt diesel, spices, sweaty bodies and food.

The street was full of small shops selling clothing, gold jewellery and food of various types. He looked for a veranda fronted wooden building with no signboard, next to a jewellery store. Sami walked to the left of the bus station as instructed, trying to hang onto his bag which was jostled continuously on his shoulder.

Sami stood on the opposite side of the busy road, looking up at the first-floor windows of the building crushed between the jeweller and a grocer, selling all types of dry goods and limp vegetables. Below the first floor, a narrow, grubby window displayed women's salwars and different rolls of coloured cloth, the colours brightened by a strong light focused from above.

Sami looked up and down the street, before thrusting forward into the stream of trucks, buses, bullock-carts and three-wheeler taxis on the main highway between Kandy and Jaffna. He bent to study the bright lengths of cloth in the shop window, trying to see into the store through the dusty glass. Establishing contact with the militant groups would be the most difficult part of his mission. He would first have to convince a few low-level functionaries before getting to meet the people who mattered.

The shopkeeper looked up when Sami pushed through the hanging strips of plastic used to keep out the flies which doubled as a doorway.

'*Vanakkam - Greetings,* what are you looking for?' The shopkeeper came around the counter. 'A nice cotton or nylex sari for your wife or girlfriend?' he said with a smirk. The shopkeeper was short and fat, with heavy jowls, making him look like a fierce and wrinkled watch dog.

Sami looked around the room before answering. 'I am here to arrange a meeting with Shankar,' he said. 'Tell him that the *Marakkalaya* is wanting to talk to him.'

When Sami had his briefing with David and the Colonel, they had decided that talking to Shankar would give Sami the best chance of success, but finding the elusive militant leader was not going to be easy. The shopkeeper narrowed his eyes, looking at Sami suspiciously. 'Who is this Shankar?' he asked aggressively, raising his voice. 'There's no one by that name here.'

The doorway behind him darkened as another man came into the room. He was tall and well built, his face pockmarked with scars. One eye socket was empty, the eyelid fused over the empty space making him look dangerous.

'I only want you to pass on a message to him,' said Sami aware of the doorway behind him and his exposed back. 'I will remain in Kilinochchi for the next few days. When you have heard from him, leave a red silk sari in the window where it can be seen. Remember to tell him that the *Marakkalaya* wants to talk.'

Sami backed out to the shop, turning and disappearing into the crowd. Sami had thought that he should first look for Rajan, who was his second in command when he lead the militant combat team in the western Vanni, but the others disagreed with him. Their argument was that they knew Shankar was alive and operating out of the area, while Rajan had dropped out of sight and may be dead for all they knew.

The sun was an orange-red ball behind the roofs of the bazaar where he went to get some food. Mounds of bright spices were spread out on gunny sacks next to bags of rice and lentils. Sami sat at a busy *kade* – tea shop, in the crowded bazaar with his back to a wall and ordered a *marsala dosa* and a glass of milk tea. He constantly watched the shifting crowd, looking for anything out of the ordinary. He felt invigorated by the need to be alert in an environment that could turn hostile at the blink of an eye.

With some food in his belly, Sami sipped the creamy tea, thinking back to the last time he was in the area.

The memories came flooding back. He had headed south after leaving the temple, walking through the night. He was bruised and chafed now, his clothes filthy with mud. It had taken him two days to get to the dirt road that cut across the jungle from Mankulam in the east to the main Jaffna-Kandy Road. The army was out in force after the massacre at the temple, their patrols criss-crossing the area looking for the men who had attacked the holy shrine. Helicopters thundered low overhead making it too dangerous to cross the open rice paddies.

Sami felt lonely and disconnected, almost a spectator, as he absentmindedly stroked his rifle, scanning the edge of the jungle across the road for any movement. He had finally made it to the road with great difficulty, hungry and tired, his clothes filthy and caked in mud. He was lying in a hole he had scraped out quickly behind a low bush which allowed him to see the road clearly. Fifty metres of open ground separated him from the dirt road and then another twenty metres to the opposite edge of the jungle. He had to get across the road, but something held him back. It was very quiet … almost too quiet. Even the normal sounds of the jungle were muted in the afternoon heat.

The quiet rolling sound of a vehicle broke into his thoughts. A light truck, it's open bed full of goods covered with a blue tarpaulin, jostled down the deeply rutted road. Long tails of dust rose from its back wheels. It was the first vehicle he had seen since he got here. He watched the truck disappear from sight. A jungle fowl scratching for insects wandered onto the road. Sami watched the fowl as it meandered down the road finally disappearing back into the thick grass.

Sami's nerves were still on edge. He did not want to cross the open area to the other side during daylight and decided to wait until it was dark. The swish of leaves to his right made him freeze. A shadow moved in his direction following the same route he had taken. Someone was following him.

The person stopped not more than ten metres from him, his attention focused on the road. From where Sami was hiding under the bush he could only make out the man's feet. They were covered in muddy, ankle high sneakers. Something about them reminded him of Ismail. Could it be him? What was he doing here? Sami needed to be careful. If he startled the boy, he could react by pulling the trigger. And what if it wasn't him?

Sami waited and watched as the man sank to one knee, observing the road intently. He wore a torn, dirty brown shirt, his trousers were tucked into his sneakers. A small pack was slung on his back. Sami was almost certain it was Ismail.

'*Allahu Akbar.*' Sami whispered in Arabic, a language Ismail was familiar with.

The figure stiffened as the man heard the words. 'Is it you, Ismail?' Sami needed to be certain.

'Yes, *Thalaivar* - Boss. It is me.' Ismail turned and looked around, not seeing Sami under the bush. 'Danika sent me with food and a warning. There's a man with Para who's very dangerous. You must be careful.'

Sami instinctively looked round. He had been right to be careful. 'Have you seen anyone trying to follow me?' Sami sensed Ismail shaking his head. 'No, I haven't but I came from the coast. I wanted to make sure our people got there safely. If anyone's following you it'll be from the north.'

Sami tried to think. Ismail was right. He was still a day away from where he needed to be. He would have to travel another forty kilometres before reaching the shores of the Giants Tank. It was an area full of arid, scrub jungle mixed with patches of dense vegetation the further south he went. Anyone wanting to stop him would try along this stretch of road. If he crossed to the other side of the road, he would be very difficult to find.

Ismail had located where Sami was hiding and crawled in next to him. 'This is where they'll try to stop me,' Sami whispered. 'We must be very careful.'

Sami felt a sense of relief now that Ismail was with him. He was thankful that Danika had the courage to send Ismail to him. Sami appreciated the loyalty she was demonstrating and hoped that she would come out of this ordeal alive.

'Let's wait until dark before crossing,' Sami said, glancing at Ismail. The boy looked tired, his eyes bloodshot. 'Why don't you get some sleep? I'll keep watch.'

Sami snapped back into reality. The bazaar was almost empty, and the proprietor was standing in front of him with his hand out. Sami dropped a ten rupee note and some coins into his hand before leaving the *kade* which clanged shut behind him. He needed to find a place to sleep. It would take at least a day to get a message to Shankar and another day to get his reply. He'd have to hang around for a couple of days, maybe more.

CHAPTER TWENTY-EIGHT

DIYATALAWA

David was sweating despite the chill in the air. He had woken up before daybreak and jogged along the main road which climbed up into the misty hills around the town. The hillside became increasingly covered in closely packed tea bushes sprinkled with shade trees. Terraced paths and gravelled roads wound through the steep slopes punctuated by large outcroppings of rock.

Turning into a narrow side road which twisted its way up the contours of the mountain, David could see the tea factory in the distance, clad in silver-painted corrugated-iron, shining like a beacon in the mist. The dim grey of dawn was developing into pale colours in the strengthening light, revealing wisps of wood smoke rising gently from the estate lines. A hooter from the factory echoed across the hills and lines of tea pluckers in bright saris beneath their dark head cloths, headed from their homes towards the muster yard in front of the estate office.

Hearing a motorcycle coming up behind him, David moved aside as the estate Superintendent riding a vintage Triumph rattled past him on his way to the morning muster. He waved as he accelerated over the crest of a small hill. Seeing the Superintendent, David was reminded of the reason he was in the hill country. Mukesh had come to see him at the base camp the previous day and briefed him on what he had learnt. It was clear that something big was being planned. Even though Mukesh had not been able to find out who the leader was, David was confident that it would only be a matter of time before they did. Out of the hundreds of Superintendents, visiting agents and estate owners working in the hill country, Mukesh had done well to pinpoint the estate where the leader lived.

David turned off the estate road onto a terraced path that led up the tea covered slopes. He pushed himself relentlessly the last hundred metres, arriving at the top out of breath and puffing hard. Bent in two with hands on knees and sweat pouring off him in steaming streams, he surveyed the vista around him while recovering his breath.

To his left, the estate factory where the tea pluckers and labourers had gathered for the allocation of the day's work was a hive of activity. The men were being methodically assigned tasks like replanting, pruning, fertilising, road and drain maintenance or weeding. Others would be sent to the Eucalyptus forests above the estate to cut firewood for the insatiable furnaces used to dry the fermenting tea leaves.

David couldn't imagine these people capable of revolting against their masters, but then again, how could anyone have predicted the revolt in the north. A seemingly well-educated and favoured ethnic group under the British had chosen to fight because they felt that they were losing their rights and were being disenfranchised in their own country. These estate workers were treated as serfs, traded along with the estates like chattel, and exploited like no other. They were stateless and were paid less than any worker in the country. They had nothing to lose. The same could happen in these hills.

Small estate lorries filled with tea pluckers and pruners, carried them to the far slopes of the estate to begin their work. Their special skills befitted their elevated status on the estate workers hierarchy.

The worker's union had become stronger since the country's independence from the British and had fought hard for better pay and living conditions for the labourers. David wondered whether the union knew about the involvement of the northern Tigers. *The union have to know what is going on*, he thought, although the key union leaders in Colombo may have been unaware of it. Maybe it was an avenue he could exploit. He resolved to talk to the Colonel about it.

To the right, the estate bungalow occupied by the Superintendent, sturdily built out of dressed granite blocks and brick, had large casement windows and a red-painted corrugated-iron roof over it. It was set in an attractive terraced garden with granite steps leading to a wide spacious veranda which ran down the front of the bungalow. The windows of the sitting room and dining room opened on to the veranda, with the front door leading to a passageway between them. The open veranda with colourful flower plants in pots and hanging baskets, looked out over a lawn bordered with flowerbeds and a stunning view over the lowlands to the south.

Between the two buildings, rolling hills of green tea bushes carpeted the hills and valleys of the estate, broken only by deep ravines of clear rushing mountain streams. It was a scene that David would never tire of. He loved the Central Highlands and promised himself that one day he would live in these mountains.

David recovered his breath much faster than he'd expected. He realised that he was ready to go for his final medical check up to regain the active status he had lost. He rarely had dizzy spells anymore, in fact he couldn't remember the last time he did.

He turned and started jogging down the terraced path, heading back the way he came. He would call the Medical Officer when he got back to his room and schedule the test. For the first time since he got hurt, he felt totally invigorated and alive.

CHAPTER TWENTY-NINE

KILINOCHCHI

The boarding house that Sami found for the night was cheap, but the lumpy mattress and the snoring and farting from others in the room had kept him up most of the night. Sami slipped out before daybreak, glad that he had only paid for one night.

The fresh air outside the cramped and squalid building revived him as he walked carefully down a narrow alleyway filled with refuse. A dog watched him warily as it lifted its thin leg against a wooden shack, urinated and moved away from him, almost in anticipation of being kicked.

Sami's nerves were twitching as he approached the main road. He had to find someplace to lay low for the next couple of days. But it wouldn't be easy. The town was filled with militant sympathisers and he would stand out if the men he was trying to contact came looking for him.

Then he remembered the refugee camp he saw from the bus. He was familiar with how they operated. He could lose himself in one until it was time. The school, where the camp was located, was just a short distance away so he decided to walk.

Dawn streaked across the sky with clouds tinged with orange and rose. Even that early in the morning, people walked purposefully to wherever they were going, ignoring the buses that passed them regularly. Cattle tethered with long ropes chewed cud on the grass verges, defecating complacently on the edge of the tarred road, creating lumps of grass filled cow patties which he had to step around.

The entrance to the camp was busy with people coming and going. The school playground was filled with faded army tents and wooden lean-to shelters, with bits of blue plastic draped over the top to prevent any rain from entering. Sami walked to the main school building which housed the class rooms. It was easy to find the Camp Coordinator's office, a short line of people standing outside a room giving it away. He poked his head through the unlatched door, but it was empty. Just a table and chair, and a locked filing cabinet making up the contents of the room.

'Hey, can you open the door for me,' a voice called out. Sami turned and saw a harassed looking European dressed in a white shirt and khaki pants walking quickly towards him. He carried a large cardboard box in both arms, his face red from the strain.

The man walked past Sami who held the door open for him, depositing the heavy box on the table with a loud sigh. He rubbed his arms and flexed them as he turned around. 'Thanks, I was wondering how I would get in.' The man looked Sami up and down. 'And who are you may I ask?'

Sami smiled and held out his hand. 'I am Sami,' he said. 'I am the Relief Coordinator at the Kalpitiya Refugee Camp. I work for the same agency you do. You can check with Priyani. I am looking for my mother and grand-parents who are from Jaffna. They are supposed to be in one of the camps here in

Kilinochchi. I was hoping that I could go through your lists to see whether they have been registered as refugees.'

'My name is John and I am the Coordinator here,' he said, shaking Sami's hand. 'See that box I just brought in. Those are all the government forms from refugees in Kilinochchi alone. And there are three more boxes like them. I bring that bloody thing in here every day to get them into some sort of order, but I have only made a dent. I am supposed to get help, but no one wants to come with all that's going on. Look at the line outside. It's like that every day.'

Sami nodded. It had been like that when the Tigers had asked the Moors to leave Mannar. This was the opportunity he was looking for. 'How about I go through the paperwork and sort them out for you,' he said. 'I did the very same thing when we got a flood of refugee families from Mannar. Just give me a place to work and I'll do all the boxes.'

John looked pleased at the prospect of handing the paperwork to someone else. 'You can use the room we store our supplies in,' he said. 'It's just next door. The forms are all there and it's even got a table and chair. Are you sure you want to do this?'

'Yes,' said Sami. 'I have to find out where my family are. That means going through all the forms. I might as well sort them out while I am about it.'

John nodded, lifting the box again. 'Get that door for me again will you. I'll show you the room where you can work.'

It was late in the second evening when Sami finally left the refugee camp. He had spent the last two days sorting out the government forms each refugee had to complete, grouping them into different categories to be entered into the relief agency's computer system. He had not left the room during this time, paying a young boy to bring him fresh food from the *kade* and sleeping on a thin foam rubber mattress John had tossed at him when he had said that he wouldn't leave until the job was completed.

Sami hadn't found his mother or his grand-parents' names on the lists. This concerned him, but he'd heard that the majority of refugees from Jaffna went to Trincomalee in the east where the large naval and air base would have given them a sense of security.

Walking on the opposite side of the street, Sami approached the clothing store cautiously. The shop window had been cleaned, the light from the display falling on the ground outside. A beautiful red silk sari draped prominently across the shelves obscured everything else from view. Looking around Sami quickly walked across the road, avoiding an onrushing three-wheeler, and paused at the entrance to the wooden building. Other than pedestrians moving about on the pavement there was no one showing any interest in him.

Taking a deep breath, he pushed aside the hanging strips of thick plastic and entered the cramped clothing store. There was very little light inside making it dark and gloomy and the smell of incense wafted in the air. He immediately sensed someone behind a stack of bales to his right but before he could move, he felt the impression of a gun barrel pressed against his neck.

Sami's heart started beating faster, adrenaline pumped through his body. He didn't hesitate the moment his body felt the gun. His hand pushed the gun up and away, the involuntary shot deafening him. His assailant hadn't turned his head away, his single brown eye blinking and unfocused. Sami head-butted the man, and he staggered back, leaving the gun in Sami's hand. As the man collapsed on the ground holding his broken nose, Sami turned the gun around feeling the heat from the barrel on his fingers. He spun in a half circle, the gun pointed menacingly in front of him, his eyes adjusting to the gloom.

The store owner behind the counter stared at Sami in shock. His eyes flickered between the man on the ground and Sami, as he stepped back fearfully holding up both his hands in submission.

'Don't shoot, don't shoot,' he said, with a tremor in his voice. 'We were told to check you for weapons before talking to you.'

Sami stepped aside, his back to a glass cabinet. From there he could keep his eyes on both men and the entrance to the shop.

'Ok, so you have a message for me,' Sami snapped at the store owner. 'What is it?'

The man on the ground raised himself on his elbow, his single eye glaring malevolently at Sami. He raised his hand to his nose and looked at the blood smeared on it. He made an attempt to raise himself but stopped when Sami waved the gun at him.

'Stay down,' Sami said menacingly. 'We have not finished our discussion yet.'

Sami scowled at the store owner, waiting for him to answer. The man's jowls trembled, the gleam of sweat on his face as he struggled to get the words out.

'Yes, yes,' he stuttered. 'I have a message for you. You are to be taken to Thamapuram where you will be met. That's all I have been told.'

'Where's that?' Sami asked. He had never heard of the place.

'It's not far,' the store keeper said, pointing to the east. 'Only about ten kilometres.'

Sami quickly made up his mind that he would go by himself. He didn't trust these men. But he would need very specific instructions on where to go. 'Where is the meeting going to be?'

'We are to take you to the main gate of the Maha Vidyalaya school on the Paranthan Mullaitivu Road,' the store keeper said. 'Someone you know will come and get you.'

'Someone I know?' Sami asked. 'Who's that?'

The store keeper was getting his composure back. 'I don't know,' he shrugged, looking irritably at Sami. 'That's all I know.'

Sami stared at the man until he lowered his eyes. He had got the information he wanted. 'I am going by myself,' he said. 'I don't want anyone following me. Do you understand?' Sami stared at both men. 'I am going to leave now,' he said. Sami waved the pistol at the two men. 'I am going to keep this.'

Both men watched as he clicked off the safety and pushed the pistol into his waistband under his shirt, moving towards the entrance as he did. Sami looked through the plastic strips to the street outside, then glancing at the two men in the store he stepped through the doorway and disappeared into the crowd.

CHAPTER THIRTY

SLAVE ISLAND

Colombo was grey and brooding. The monsoon had arrived early, and gusts of wind and rain battered the city streets from low hanging clouds. The rain was hissing down, washing the pavements and overflowing the drains. Traffic had come to an angry crawl, a dazzling confusion of lights and wet reflections in the premature darkness. Taxis vanished as the rain gained in momentum, forcing David to wave a three-wheeler over.

'Take me to Slave Island.' David dusted his trousers which were speckled with drops of water and settled in the back of the three-wheeler which wove in and out of the traffic. The suburb, bounded by the Beira Lake and canals built by the Dutch, was given its name during British colonisation. It referred to the period under Portuguese rule, when slaves were held on the man-made island, most of them black people from the Swahili coast and Portuguese East Africa.

David had an uneasy feeling about the meeting. The Colonel was in an ebullient mood when he walked into the office. 'You're looking fit and healthy,' he said, smiling up at David from behind his desk. 'How do you feel?'

'I am good,' David said. 'I am almost back to normal.' Other than a stiffness in his neck which he had to exercise every day, the effects of the wounds he had sustained in the ambush were not noticeable. He had been lucky to have come out with just a few injuries.

'Good, good,' the Colonel said, waving David over to the chair in front of the desk. 'We have a lot to talk about.' He waited until David sat down. 'Have you heard from that Mukesh fellow?' he asked. 'There has been some movement on that problem in the estates.'

David looked at the Colonel attentively. He had not been in touch with Mukesh for a few weeks. 'No, I have not heard from him. Why?'

'Your report caused a bit of a stir with the Plantation Minister and the Special Branch was ordered to independently verify what you had reported.' The Colonel leaned forward. 'The man they sent was found hanging from a tree with his throat cut.'

David sat back in his chair thinking hard. If the men who were behind the movement to declare a separate state in the hills had done this, they would know that they were being watched. It made Mukesh vulnerable.

'What does the union have to say about it?' David had read in the papers that the head of the Plantation Workers Union had been given a Cabinet post. It was the first time that an Indian Tamil had held such a high position in government.

'I have not spoken to the Minister myself, but I have heard that he is concerned,' the Colonel said. 'His people are not coming back with anything solid. He thinks it's just a small group of people who are being encouraged by the situation in the north. But he wants it nipped in the bud, so to speak.' The Colonel grinned at his attempt to inject some humour to the conversation.

'Do you want me to go upcountry and talk to Mukesh,' he asked, thoughtfully.

'No, no' the Colonel said. 'You've got too many things on your plate now. That's why I am pulling you out from the field back to Colombo. I want you to arrange for Sarath to head the team. He's due a promotion.'

David was disappointed, but this was what he had been hoping for. The army had withdrawn to their bases and left the Indians to control the militant groups led by the Tigers. But what David still couldn't understand was why the Indian Intelligence Services were still assisting an organisation that was fighting against their own troops. The insurrection in the south had reached its peak and the government was slowly regaining control, mainly by arresting or killing the JVP leaders and their hard-line sympathisers.

David nodded. 'It makes sense,' he said. 'But I'll need some help upcountry. If they are eliminating our agents, we'll need to be more careful.'

'Yes,' the Colonel agreed. 'It's really not a military matter. Maybe we can hand it off to the police. Let me talk to a few people and get back to you. I'll let you go back to Vavuniya and inform your team. But I want you back here by Monday.'

⌒

Priyani picked up the late edition of the Daily News on her way home from work. On the front page was a photograph of Rajiv Gandhi being attacked by a member of a ceremonial Guard of Honour. 'Only in Sri Lanka,' the headline screamed. 'Indian Prime Minister hit during Guard of Honour inspection.'

The Indian Prime Minister had come to Colombo for discussions with the Sri Lankan President on the presence of Indian troops on the island. When inspecting the ceremonial Guard of Honour at the airport, a naval rating reversed his rifle and used it as a club to hit the Prime Minister on his head. Only the Prime Ministers quick reflexes saved him from being badly injured.

The astonishing news had made the world headlines. Never in the twentieth century had this happened anywhere in the world, let alone to a head of state. She wondered when she'd heard the news whether it would have any effect on the funding they received from overseas and had quickly dismissed the thought. Most of the money that was received for the refugees came from aid agencies based in western countries and though the image of the Indian Prime Minister ducking while being hit by a rifle was not a good image for the country, she did not think they would hold back any funding.

Priyani had been on an overseas call that morning and had gone to work quite late. The meeting was about the bribes that were being demanded to take relief supplies into Indian controlled territory. They were very interested in hearing what Priyani had to say about the political implications of the Indian Prime Minister being assaulted by the military. After much discussion, the European Directors of the agency had decided to wait until the media frenzy died down before making any decisions.

Priyani was frustrated by the decision not to do anything. She understood firsthand the plight of the refugees and the implications of not receiving any aid. Her mind ached from concentrating on the telephone for so long and she had just got home. She was tiredly contemplating what she should have for dinner when the buzzer to her apartment went off.

'Yes, who is it?' Priyani used the recently installed intercom system in the block of flats she lived in. Previously she would just lean over the balcony and shout down at the person wanting to enter.

'It's me,' a familiar voice said. 'It's David.'

Priyani was surprised. She thought that David was up north. She walked down the stairs from her flat to the front entrance and unlocked the security gate to let him in. The renovations to the property had not come with a remote door opener.

'David,' she said, looking at the wet, bedraggled figure standing under the porch. 'You're soaking wet. Come in, come in.'

When they got to the apartment, Priyani handed David a towel and watched while David dried himself, combing his short hair with his fingers.

'I did not think you would be back for a while,' she said. 'What happened?'

'Something has come up,' he said. 'I am going to be transferred to Colombo for a while. And this time it may be permanent.'

Priyani was used to David not telling her everything. She understood that certain matters were classified, and he could not share them with her. But she was glad to hear that he would be based in Colombo.

'Really,' she said excitedly, grabbing hold of his arm. 'That's wonderful news David!'

'I have to go back to Vavuniya to hand over the Special Ops team. Sarath will be promoted to Lieutenant. So, he'll be in charge. I have to report for duty here in Colombo on Monday.'

Priyani could not help smiling. It was what she had wanted all along. She had grown up with her father in the army, a Lieutenant Colonel in the Engineering Regiment, and never got used to her father being away for long periods at a time.

'Why don't you stay here,' she asked impulsively. David normally stayed at the Bachelor Officers Quarters at the army cantonment when he was in Colombo.

David looked at her. 'I was hoping you would ask,' he said, a smile blossoming on his face. 'Are you sure? Will your parents mind?'

Priyani understood why he asked the question. It was not normal for unmarried couples to live together and her parents had been against their affair at the beginning.

'Yes, I am sure,' Priyani said, reaching out for his hand. 'I'll talk to my parents about it of course. I am sure they will have something to say but I don't care.' Priyani pulled David and hugged him. He smelt wet and musty, but she was happy. She had almost lost him and now she had a chance to spend more time with him. That couldn't be a bad thing could it?

CHAPTER THIRTY-ONE

KAMBAKKODDAI

Danika was seated outside the bunker listening to the sharp whine of military planes as they patrolled the grey skies above the army camps to the east. She felt safe sitting outside as the thick jungle canopy prevented her being seen. Sweat poured off her body, soaking her shirt in big wet splotches.

Mala walked purposefully back to their bunker. She'd been summoned that morning for a meeting with the leadership group. A rumour was circulating that an operation was being planned and their team would be involved. Danika watched her intently as she drew closer. Something in her manner spoke distinctly of bad news.

'We have been given an important mission,' Mala began, after gathering the team around her. 'We will be part of a group that will be sent to escort an Indian journalist to Trincomalee.' Mala studied them individually. 'The journalist has met with *Anna*. The interview will be published soon … but first we have to get her to Trinco.'

'A woman journalist?' Indra asked, fidgeting with her uniform. It was the first time they had been given such a mission. 'Where is she now?'

'Not too far,' Mala said. 'Near Mullaitivu.'

'That's four or five days march through the jungle,' Parvathy said, apprehensively. 'We'll have to go around the mined areas to get to them.'

They had all heard that the area around Mullaitivu was a no-go zone, tightly controlled by the Tigers. The small village of Puthukkudiyiruppu just west of the district town had become the commercial centre of the Vanni after the Tigers had been ousted from Jaffna. Over the past few months the Tigers had built a series of long earthworks as their main line of defence around the area, heavily mining a vast expanse around it. If the stories they had heard were true, a variety of anti-tank and anti-personnel mines had been planted in the fields and approaches to the east. Trip mines were used widely by the Tigers, many with locally made timing devices.

'They will be brought to Manal Aru.' Mala pulled out a map from her pouch, spreading it out on her lap. 'We take over from there,' she said tapping a spot on the map.

Danika and the others leaned over to look. The old settlement of Manal Aru she pointed to was on traditional Tamil land about twenty kilometres from the eastern coastline. It would cut the journey in half.

'You said we're part of a group,' Thangam said. 'Who else is going?'

Mala went over the plans she'd been given at the meeting. Their team would be divided into two sections. Mala, Parvathy and Thangam would go with the main group that would meet the journalist at Manal Aru and escort her south towards Trincomalee. Danika and Indra would go into Trincomalee to establish contact with the Tiger cell who would be responsible for the last leg of the journey.

'You'll have the more dangerous mission,' Mala said to Danika and Indra.

'Getting into Trinco will not be easy. There are both Indian and Sri Lankan checkpoints on the way, and we believe it'll be easier for a woman to make the crossing.'

Mala considered both Danika and Indra before continuing. 'It'll be far less dangerous for us. The army have stopped patrolling the area south of Mullaitivu when they started losing men regularly to the mines, and after the Indians came they have not tried. It's completely under our control.'

Danika and Indra exchanged glances. Crossing into Trinco without any support would not be easy. It could be done, but the chances of being caught and put in prison were very high.

'Explain why it has to be like this,' Danika asked Mala. 'I would have thought that we'd be better off together.'

'We want to make sure that the transfer goes smoothly,' Mala said. 'You'll be the only ones who know where it will take place.'

Sensing their hesitation Mala addressed both women. '*Anna's* interview must be published. The Indian *jawans* are no better than the Sinhalese soldiers. The world must know what they are doing to us. We are freedom fighters, we have chosen a path of danger, so it's normal for us to face such difficult situations.'

Danika's couldn't concentrate fully on what Mala was saying. Several thoughts flashed in and out of her mind. She was torn between loyalty to the cause, what she'd fought for so long and staying alive.

'We are prepared to take that risk, so long as we know it's not a suicide mission,' Danika spoke involuntarily. She was surprised how she felt. A month ago, she wouldn't have hesitated.

Indra nodded in agreement. 'Yes, I agree. We must make sure! If we get caught by either the *jawans* or the army, they will rape and kill us.'

'Maybe it's a mistake to send the two of you,' Mala said studying them thoughtfully. 'But I have no choice as I have been told to go north.' Mala paused thinking, then nodded, as if making up her mind. 'But then again,' she said deviously, 'you'll not take many risks with that attitude. Danika, you'll be in charge.'

∾

TRINCOMALEE

Danika adjusted the *dupatta* –shawl, hanging over her shoulders as the two of them walked arm in arm through the crowd. She felt almost naked wearing the thin cotton *salwar kameez,* missing the coarse rayon shirt and trousers she'd been wearing since she joined the militants. She knew Indra felt the same. They let themselves be enveloped by the city, drinking in the sights and sounds and smells. They were both nervous as they walked along the edge of the harbour but excited at the same time to once again be back in civilisation.

The colourful bazaars around the bus terminal were raucous with the cries of vendors, the fierce bargaining of women shopping, the barking of foraging dogs and the constant flutter of scavenging crows. The air was pungent with the odour of fruits, spices, dried fish, meat and the blood from butcher shops running into the open drains.

'There,' said Indra tilting her head subtly at a street running at right angles off the main road. Danika nodded, looking over her shoulder for a break in the oncoming traffic. They sidestepped the spluttering swarms of motorcycles, some carrying entire families. Children were perched precariously on the handlebars or mudguards of the overloaded motorbikes as they crossed the road. Lorries, vans and three-wheelers all jostling for space, struggled to get past men pushing or pulling carts piled high with goods and produce from the harbour.

It had taken most of the day to get to the eastern port-city. They had taken the bus from the village some miles away from their jungle hideout and disembarked at the central bus station in the city. The bus—which turned out to be just a van—was packed full of people and Danika was fortunate to get a seat.

Crossing the multiple checkpoints set up by the Indian *jawans* on the outskirts to the city, the Sri Lankan army and navy checking passers-by near the military-controlled dockyards, had been relatively straightforward. Everyone in the van was asked to disembark at each checkpoint, their ID cards inspected, some of the men even searched. When questioned, Danika and Indra said they were cousins going into Trincomalee for a family engagement ceremony that evening. The soldiers hardly paid them much attention, a couple of them even flirting openly with the two women.

The first thing they had done after arriving was to buy a bottle of water at one of the food stalls that lined the edge of the busy bus terminal. Danika took a mouthful, her body urging her to drink more, but she stopped after two mouthfuls and passed the bottle to Indra who took it with gratitude. The water was refreshing, without the sweetness of the water from the jungle stream they were used to drinking, but at least she was sure it was purified. Indra handed the half-empty bottle back and Danika screwed the lid back on, slipping it into the cloth bag over her shoulder.

They paused at the corner, looking up the street. It was no different to the others they passed. It rose in a gentle curve away from the port towards the wooded hills. In this part of town the streets were narrow, the buildings huddled together, the shops and domestic dwellings, many open to the streets, the activity of selling and living going on in the streets themselves. They had been given specific instructions on contacting the militant cell. Do not approach the area until after dark! Police and army patrols moved through the busy streets regularly during daylight, withdrawing to their camps only after the sun had set.

Danika nodded at a tea house at the corner which the two women entered, sitting towards the rear of the small noisy room which was open to the street.

Indra ordered a drink of 'cream soda' which appeared in a heavy glass bottle dripping with condensation along with two thin metal containers shaped like cups. Indra poured a portion of the drink into the container, offering it to Danika who shook her head. She had never loved the sweet drink.

'You don't know what you're missing,' said Indra, happily sipping the drink with a smile on her face. Danika grinned at her friend, her eyes focusing on a group of adolescent-looking soldiers dressed in khaki and carrying automatic rifles on their shoulders casually walking past the shop. She observed that the men were dressed in crisp, clean uniforms, their boots shiny with polish.

The soldiers paid them no attention, passing the shop in single file before moving out of sight. Danika waved her hand at the shop attendant, ordering four *paruppu vadai* and a strong glass of milk tea for herself. The deep-fried savoury fritters made from channa dal and spices was a simple, inexpensive street food found everywhere in the north. Danika savoured the warm, crispy delicacy with pleasure, sipping the steaming hot tea carefully.

'Eat your food slowly,' Danika whispered to Indra, their heads almost touching. 'We need to remain here until after dark.'

'Why do we have to wait?' Indra said grumpily. 'Let's go now.' Indra was always the impatient one and Danika dismissed the idea with a shake of her head, frowning at her as she did. 'We'll do what we were told to do,' she answered with an edge to her voice. 'We'll leave after it gets dark.' Indra nodded sullenly, not meeting Danika's eyes. They ordered more drinks, ignoring stares from the proprietor seated on his stool by the door.

Lights flickered on in the tea room as the late evening turned to night. The street was almost empty, and the pavements were empty too when Danika and Indra finally stepped out.

Beneath the dull yellow glow of the widely spaced overhead lights, the street looked threatening as they walked together up the gentle slope. Past the curve on the road the streetlights were spaced even wider apart, finally ending about halfway up the hill. Light filtered from a few of buildings as they walked into the pool of darkness beyond the last streetlight.

The night had become unusually quiet as the sound of traffic on the main road had died down to an occasional vehicle.

Danika tensed, straining to see what was ahead. The hum of voices from the dwellings around them and the sound of dogs barking somewhere close were the only indications they weren't somewhere in the jungle. They had taken about a dozen steps past the last streetlight when a familiar sensation ran through her body. *We are being watched.* Indra must have felt it too. She grasped Danika's arm tightly as they walked a few more paces.

'Stop there,' a gruff voice called out of the darkness. Danika's heart jumped at the sound of the voice, both her and Indra coming to an abrupt halt. Having experienced many night encounters in the jungle, they understood the importance of not making any sudden moves.

'What are you doing here at this time of the night?' the voice called out. 'Don't you know it's dangerous for anyone to be out after dark.?'

'We're looking for a man named Perumal,' Danika said cautiously. 'We have a message for him.' She could barely make out an outline of a man, deep in the shadow of an alley between two buildings. Indra grasped her arm so tightly that it was beginning to hurt.

'How do you know this Perumal?'

Danika had been instructed to meet a man named Perumal in a building at the edge of the wooded area. He would be easy to recognise as he had only one-ear. He would know they were coming.

'I was given his name and was told he has only one ear.' Danika said. 'We are to meet with him tonight.'

A man stepped out into the dim light of the street. He was of medium height and had a receding hairline. He wore street clothes and other than a peculiar twitching of his trimmed moustache, he had no distinguishing features of any kind. He studied them carefully through narrowed eyes.

'Who sent you?' the man uttered menacingly. 'Are you from Mutur?'

Danika shook her head. 'No, we're from Pankulam,' she said. 'Do you know Perumal?' Danika reached across her chest carefully, loosening Indra's grip on her shoulder. She had started to lose sensation in her fingers.

The man stared hard at the two women as if he was sizing them up. Danika held his gaze unflinchingly as Indra shifted her feet. Then suddenly as if making up his mind, his eyes flickered.

'Follow me,' he said, gesturing with his left hand. 'We'll take you to see him.'

A match flared in the alley, lighting up the face of a scar-faced man who had also been watching them. His cigarette glowed as he took a long drag.

'My name is Thiru,' the moustached man said. 'We've been expecting you.'

The two women followed uneasily, the scar-faced man falling in a few steps behind them.

'What are your names,' Thiru asked, turning his head to look at them.

'I am Danika, and this is Indra,' Danika responded. Indra did not say anything which was not unusual. Danika didn't want to say more until she was sure these were the men she was supposed to meet.

Thiru stopped abruptly and turned around. 'Are you the woman who cut the throat of that Indian *jawan*?' he asked, staring at her disbelievingly.

'Yes,' Danika said simply. 'I am the one.'

Thiru nodded after studying her for a moment. 'I have heard about you,' he said. The tone of his voice changed to one of respect. 'You also fought with the *Marakkalayas* near Mannar!' It was not a question, so Danika kept quiet. She was surprised that her exploits were so well known.

'Follow me,' he said, turning and walking up the street.

Danika's calves ached walking up the uneven dirt track from the city outskirts. The street had turned into a deeply rutted dirt road which climbed to the narrow path they were using. A sprawling run-down building huddling under enormous trees at the edge of the forest, loomed out of the inky darkness.

A candle flickered through the open doorway as Danika and Indra were ushered inside. The building had an overpowering smell of damp and decay. Danika's heart thumped against her chest and she heard Indra breathing heavily as her eyes adjusted to the dim light. Danika could sense the presence of others in the room.

'Are you sure these are the *pooralis* – troops, that were sent?' a voice queried out of the darkness. 'I was not told they would send women.'

'It's them alright, Muthu,' Thiru responded. 'This one I have heard about.' Danika tensed as a rough hand on her shoulder pushed her forward into the candle light.

A figure of a man stepped forward. He wore the distinctive camouflage uniform of the militant cadre. He held himself erect like a soldier. A scarf was wrapped high around his face, masking his mouth and nose.

'What's your name?' he asked authoritatively. His dark eyes flickered to Indra before switching back to Danika.

'I am Danika,' she replied, calmly. 'And this is Indra. We are part of the team assigned to ensure the journalist comes to no harm.'

Muthu's eyes widened at the mention of her name. 'Hmmm,' he muttered almost to himself. 'I too have heard of you.'

The man studied her curiously before stepping aside and gesturing with his right arm courteously. 'Come, he said, 'we'll get you some proper clothes for the jungle. We don't have much time.'

Danika was not used to be treated in this manner. The jungle cadre she interacted with daily were more arrogant and treated women like their servants. Thiru led them to a room running off a corridor at the rear of the building. Barely visible by the light of a sputtering candle were stacked piles of uniforms and assorted military gear, scattered around the room.

'Take what you want and come to the veranda when you're ready,' Thiru said, gesturing to the rear of the house. 'You'll get your weapons before we leave.'

The distinctive Tiger striped uniforms were not what they were accustomed to wearing. 'Just find something that fits you and wear it over your clothes,' Danika said when she saw Indra hesitating. 'We might need them later.'

Danika searched the pile and quickly found a set which fitted her loosely. Strapping a canvas belt with a green plastic canteen around her waist she selected a knife from a pile. Testing the blade for sharpness she slid it into its sheath and clipped it to her waist.

'You ready?' Danika asked Indra as she laced a pair of canvas topped trainers to her feet. Indra nodded at Danika's question. Indra had kept quiet the whole evening and Danika looked closely at her. She wondered whether Indra had ever experienced anything other than her normal scout duties and whether the mission they were given was a bit too much for her to take in. Danika smiled at Indra reassuringly before moving towards the door and stepping out into the dark corridor which opened out to a long veranda at the rear of the building.

Muthu, Thiru and the scar-faced man they saw in the city earlier were standing around a lamplit table. Two men dressed in tiger-striped fatigues and carrying automatic rifles, stood alertly at each end of the veranda.

As they came up to the table Danika noticed with a start that the scar-faced man they had met on the street had only one ear. He showed his teeth disconcertingly at her reaction.

'Come and show us where we make the pickup,' Thiru gestured impatiently at a map laid out on the table. Muthu stood back, his arms crossed in front of his chest watching.

Danika felt the men's eyes on her as she studied the map on the table. It covered the entire eastern district showing major and minor roads around the city of Trincomalee with its enormous natural harbour and densely packed streets. Outlying towns, villages, temples and important geographical features were also highlighted. She glanced across at Indra before placing her finger on a spot on the map.

'We're to meet them here,' she said, tapping the map with her finger. 'At the *kovil* at Kanniya tomorrow night.'

Muthu bent over, studying the map carefully. He straightened his back, nodding. 'It's a good place,' he said approvingly. 'We have a safe house close to the *kovil* but the journey there will not be easy. You must pass two camps – one is an Indian camp and the other is the army.' He hesitated before continuing. 'Perumal here will be your guide.'

CHAPTER THIRTY-TWO

KILINOCHCHI

There were not many people around. The *Maha Vidyalaya* – high school was closed, it's metal gate chained and tightly shut. The hamlet was just a collection of roughly constructed houses set back from the road, and a few *kades*. Only a board outside the Divisional Hospital indicated that a settlement was even there.

The sky was a shade of turquoise blue with fleecy white clouds low on the horizon. The morning bus to Mullaitivu had dropped Sami at the bus stop by the hospital, the driver looking at him strangely before accelerating away. Three Indian *jawans* stood warily by an open jeep at the junction, all holding their rifles alertly. Another was behind the wheel and had the engine running, fumes spilling out of the exhaust. Cyclists, men on motorcycles, women walking with children and carrying cans of water on their hips, drifted down the road. Sami coughed, as an overladen truck with a badly tuned engine belched a cloud of smoke as it rumbled past.

Sami felt the soldiers' eyes on him as he walked towards the *Maha Vidyalaya* on the further side of the hospital compound. He carried his cloth bag with the loaded gun and nothing else. Sami felt reassured by its weight but hoped desperately he was not going to be stopped by the soldiers. He moved to the side of the school gate and sat on a wooden bench under a large spreading mango tree, spotted with bird droppings. Sami could observe the main road on both sides of the school by just turning his head.

An hour passed, the road getting busier as the morning progressed. Sami watched as a convoy of Indian military vehicles passed the school. The heavily moustached, turbaned troops looked completely out of place as they peered from the back of the open trucks.

A young street urchin kicking a tattered round ball wandered down the road towards the school, a mangy dog with three legs limping along next to him. The two of them looked so odd together that Sami couldn't help but smile. The undersized boy kicked the ball towards Sami who trapped it with his leg. The boy stopped opposite Sami, his huge eyes full of cunning and street wisdom.

'Who are you waiting for?' he asked, in a nasally high-pitched voice. 'The school is closed.' His dog sat next to him and looked at Sami sadly, with his head tilted to one side.

'I am waiting for someone,' Sami said. 'It won't be long.'

The boy looked at Sami with a calculating look on his face. 'Do you have some change to spare,' he asked.

Sami felt compelled to put his hand into his pocket and pull out a few coins. He dropped them in the boy's outstretched hand and watched them magically disappear into his ragged clothing.

The boy winked at Sami, his teeth gleaming bright as his eyes. 'You are to go to the church at the next corner and wait inside,' he said, inclining his head to the east. 'Someone will come for you.' Without waiting for an answer, the boy turned and walked away, bouncing the ball in front of him, the dog limping closely behind.

Sami shook his head in admiration at how he had been played. The boy would have been given something to bring the message to him, and he had managed to extract more money from Sami by putting on his act with the dog. *Good for him!* Sami turned and looked towards the corner of the main road trying to see where the church was located. A number of trees obscured his view.

Sami's head and shoulders started burning as he left the shade of the mango tree. Getting closer to the corner, he could see a large red brick building with a cross above the front entrance. The sign outside read St Luke's Thamapuram.

Sami pushed the half-opened door and entered the building, glad to be out of the scorching sun. Light streamed in from tall narrow windows on either side of a simple wooden altar. Long wooden benches were untidily stacked one on top of the other in one corner, the rest of the church was empty.

A door creaked open near the altar and a figure stepped through. Sami immediately recognised the figure. 'Rajan,' he called out eagerly. 'I am glad that you are okay.'

Rajan walked over with a big grin on his face, clasping Sami by the arms. 'I told Shankar that only you'd have the balls to pull something like that off,' he said admiringly. 'Murugesu needed to be taught a lesson and I am glad it was you.'

Sami was delighted to see Rajan. His face had changed, his eyes older, wiser. A ragged scar ran across the left side of his face, from above his eyebrow to his cheek giving him a dashing look. Rajan had been at Sami's side ever since he joined the Tigers and became his second in command during the fighting to close the Western Highway. Sami owed Rajan for bringing Suria out of Jaffna.

Rajan put his arm around Sami's shoulder. 'So, tell me,' he began. 'How's Suria doing?'

Sami looked at Rajan sympathetically. 'Ah, I remember now. You had a soft spot for her. She is doing well but misses our mother.'

Rajan nodded in understanding. 'The first thing I did when I heard you were back was to try and find out what happened to your family,' he said. 'I sent a message to Jaffna, to your mother, and I should hear back in the next few days. The last time I spoke to her was before the army offensive. She was doing well and looking forward to leaving the city with her father and mother. But we had to get out of Jaffna quickly when the Indians attacked, so I didn't get a chance to see her before I left.'

Sami felt a twinge of disappointment that Rajan had no recent news about his mother and grandparents. But he could understand the pressure that Rajan would have been facing.

'I've been checking the refugee camps in Kilinochchi for them,' Sami said regretfully. 'But their names are not on the lists. I need to go to Trincomalee and do the same. Perhaps I'll find them there.'

Rajan nodded in agreement. 'Yes, that's the place to look. Many of the refugees from Jaffna ended up in Trinco.'

Rajan stepped back and studied Sami. 'But before we do anything I need to ask you what you have been up to since we last saw each other. Shankar thought you were dead and was very surprised when you showed up at the clothing store. What's the official story?'

Sami had prepared an elaborate cover story to account for the past two years. Rajan was the person to first warn him about the Moors being evicted from Jaffna, which was what made Sami leave the movement. Rajan had smuggled Suria out of Jaffna in a boat, handing her over to Sami before going back to work for Shankar during the government peace talks in Bhutan. The cover story needed to be airtight so that Shankar would not suspect what really happened.

'My cover is that I was captured after the fighting and held in a special camp with Moors who fought with the Tigers. I was released a few months ago under the peace accord agreement with India and now live in a refugee camp in Kalpitiya with my sister. I was approached only last week to take on this role and I wasn't given any choice. So here I am.'

Rajan looked thoughtful. 'That should hold up I think,' he said. 'They'll have no way of checking if you weren't in one of the main prisons down south.'

Sami nodded. 'That's what we thought. So, when do I get to see Shankar?' he asked. 'The government is running scared. The people want the Indians out and the JVP are using the situation to get stronger. They'll do anything within reason I think.'

'Soon,' Rajan said, nodding. 'He's on a special mission and should be back in the next few days. We are meeting him in Trinco, so it gives you time to look for your mother.'

Sami nodded gratefully.

'We will go with a couple of my men. We can't have you wandering around alone.' Rajan laughed as he said it.

Sami smiled at Rajan. He was lucky to have him as a friend. He wondered what Suria would think about Rajan now.

CHAPTER THIRTY-THREE

CENTRAL HIGHLANDS

The Ford pickup powered up the increasingly steep road, past a wheezing bus full of passengers who watched enviously out of open windows as the white vehicle drove by. Tilak sat with the window open, next to Chandra who was concentrating on the road. Two metal containers, one filled with half-a-dozen 9mm pistols, the other extra magazines, ammunition and a cleaning kit, sat hidden next to their personal kitbags under the retractable boot cover.

The air smelt healthy and clean after the pollution and humidity of the lowlands. The damp mist had settled in earlier than normal making the narrow road into the mountains more of an ethereal experience.

Earlier that day Tilak and Chandra were handed an assignment. A Special Branch informant had been found hanging from a tree in an estate near Haputale. According to the Special Branch Commander, the request to send someone to the estate sector had come from high up in the government. Tilak surmised that it would have been a request from a politician.

'We were asked to send an informer to find out what's going on with the Plantation Workers Union,' the Commander had said. 'There is some talk that the Tigers are trying to establish links with the Indian workers which is why we sent him. Military Intelligence already has someone in place, but we needed to verify the information as it's a civilian matter.'

They reached the top of the pass where the road crossed the saddle into the bowl of the hill country. To the south, sweeping views of the forested lowlands were punctuated by areas of glistening water and low rounded hills, set against the hazy backdrop of the distant ocean. As they crossed the saddle and started their descent into the central bowl of the highlands, soaring hills fell steeply into the carpeted green undulations of the tea estates with clouds of mist tumbling through the valleys.

Their destination that evening was the Officers Mess at the main army camp at Diyatalawa. Tilak knew it well. He had been the Senior Cadet in the Officer Training College when he was ordered into action during the first Marxist uprising in the early seventies. He was so proud when he was given command of a platoon of reserve soldiers and sent to the south to retake a town that had been overrun by the insurgents.

Their meeting the next day was with the local member of the Plantation Workers Union. He had arranged to meet with them in the hill town of Bandarawela. The large picturesque town set in the middle of a number of tea plantations had excellent road and railway facilities and could be reached from any part of the island in a few hours.

Chandra drove to Bandarawela in the morning, the road winding steeply up the hillside past flimsy wooden shacks with corrugated-iron roofs. Many of these small lodgings were surrounded by neatly planted vegetable plots which formed a patchwork of colour on the green hills. Men and women wrapped up in hats and scarves trudged up the road carrying sacks of vegetables and bundles of firewood on their backs to sell at the market. They passed a large, dusty bus station surrounded by market stalls selling all types of vegetables, bananas and fruits before turning into the Bandarawela Guest House opposite the colonial-looking Cargills building.

The guest house was a long colonnaded building from the colonial era. A spacious garden in front of the building afforded sweeping views of the surrounding tea covered hills dotted with white tea factories. The head waiter dressed in a white coat with a mandarin collar ushered them into the spacious lobby filled with wooden furniture from a previous era. Wide-bladed ceiling fans rotated slowly as they sat down on the comfortable, cushioned chairs.

'This is a strange place to meet anyone from the Plantation Union,' Chandra growled, looking around the room. Tilak stared at him in surprise. Chandra didn't say much and getting more than ten words out of him in one sentence was rare.

'Yes,' Tilak responded. 'I am a bit surprised as well.' They sat and sipped the freshly brewed tea the waiter brought for them. The area around the town was well known for high quality tea and the guest house always served the best.

Tilak was getting irritated as they waited for the union man to arrive. It was almost an hour past the appointed time when a car roared up the driveway and parked under the porch by the entrance to the building. A heavy man dressed in white shirt and slacks, wearing tan shoes, got out of the car and sauntered into the building. He was dark in complexion, clearly of Indian heritage. He was followed by a tall, thickset man dressed in a lightweight safari suit. He scanned the room alertly, pausing by the entrance watching Tilak and Chandra attentively.

The white-shirted man spotted the two of them sitting by the window and quickened his pace, coming forward with both his hands held high. 'I am sorry gentlemen,' he said, speaking English with a well-educated accent. 'I had to drive from Badulla and the road was blocked by a mudslide.'

The man, who was in his thirties, turned to the waiter who had followed him. 'Simon,' he said, speaking in Sinhalese. 'Could you bring me the usual?'

Tilak recognised the man. He was the son of the Plantation Minister who had recently been appointed as a sitting member of Cabinet. The Plantation Minister came from a well-respected family who had originally come from India to work on the tea estates. He now owned an estate of his own close to Badulla. The son exuded an air of authority and immediately took charge of the meeting. The man's bodyguard remained by the door watching the three of them.

'You know who I am,' The Minister's son said, looking at each of them in turn. Not seeing any dissent, he nodded and continued. 'My father is concerned about the possibility that a group of estate workers are fermenting trouble on some of the estates. He read a report from the military that talked about a few workers meeting with a militant group from the north and men being sent to the jungles for military style training.'

The Minister's son shook his head in disbelief. 'We cannot believe that this is actually happening, but we cannot afford to be complacent. We made a request to the Special Branch to find out who these men were. We have also asked our union reps to be more vigilant.' He considered Tilak and Chandra before continuing.

'But there is no word of any unusual activity,' he said, as he sipped from the steaming mug of coffee the waiter placed in front of him. 'That in itself is a worry because there's always something happening. There are close to a million estate workers and their families and not everyone is always happy,' he explained. 'Now we have heard that your man was found dead not far from here. For him to have been killed he must have discovered what was happening. We'll need to nip it in the bud, but first we have to know what it is,' he shrugged.

'I am sending a few of our men from Colombo into the estates. They are all from around here and will get to the bottom of it. I have moved up here from Colombo at my father's bidding and will meet each of the union reps.'

The Minister's son leaned back with his mug held in both hands, bringing it up to his face and sipping from it. 'I have been told that the two of you handle special assignments. That all I have to do is point you in the right direction and you will do the rest.' His cold, dark eyes studied them carefully from over the mug. 'Am I right in my understanding?'

Tilak had listened to the man speak with interest. This was bigger than he could imagine. If the Tigers got control of the Central Highlands it would be a disaster for the government both politically and militarily. Tilak remembered doing a training exercise in Officer Training College on this very same scenario. It was an easily defendable area as there were only five or six roads leading into the mountains. The government was right to be concerned.

'Yes,' Tilak nodded. 'Our instructions are to do whatever it takes to eliminate this threat. We obviously don't have any operatives in the area and have no access to any inside information. If you could provide us with anything relevant, we will do the rest.'

'Good,' the man said, preparing to stand up. 'Where will you be staying?'

'We're currently staying in Diyatalawa,' Tilak responded. 'In the Officer's Mess. But I was thinking that it's better for us to stay in a place like this. It's right in the town and an easier place to meet.'

'Yes, it will be,' The Minister's son said standing up. He held out his hand to Tilak and then Chandra, shaking each of their hands in turn. 'I apologise I have to rush,' he said. 'I am running late as you know. I have an office here, just around the corner in fact. You can reach me through them if you need to talk.' He paused smiling at each. 'Good bye gentlemen'

They both watched him as he walked away. Chandra sat back in his chair staring into the distance. 'He's a smooth operator … a politician,' he simplified his statement. 'No shit will stick on them.'

Tilak knew what Chandra meant. Playing with politicians was fraught with danger. But there was the bigger picture to worry about. He must try and get his hands on the report that the military had put together for the Minister. There may be something there they could use.

CHAPTER THIRTY-FOUR

NEAR PANKULAM

The village was dark as Danika, Indra and Perumal slipped through the shadows. There was plenty to be concerned about. One stretch, with an Indian army camp on one side and a Sri Lankan camp on the other, would be hard to negotiate without being seen.

It took almost three hours of stealthy and painstaking movement to edge around the camps. At times they knelt out of sight amongst the dried grass and deadfall for such long periods that their muscles burned and cramped. At other times they were forced to crawl on their bellies, dragging themselves quietly through the shadows thrown by the trees and folds in the earth.

The sentries, bored and restless, gave their locations away by their noise and movement allowing the two women and their guide to slip past undetected. Finally, as dawn approached, Perumal motioned them to stand up and the three of them walked quietly between the trees in a coconut plantation until they came in sight of an old abandoned *walauwe*, the rundown building a remnant from the colonial period.

'We'll spend the day here,' Perumal said gruffly. He hardly spoke during the night, only using hand signals to communicate. 'The army does not patrol this area after the Indians came. We'll be safe here.'

Danika nodded gratefully. Her mind still buzzed by the stress of crossing over from the military-controlled territory. They had not slept for over twenty-four hours and had not eaten anything since the previous evening.

The building echoed with emptiness when they walked through the rear door. But for the drone of insects and calls of birds in the trees around them, they were surrounded by silence. Danika wrinkled her nose at the sharp stink of bird droppings. Perumal gestured to the front of the house. 'Let's use that room,' he said. 'It overlooks the front gate.'

Soft morning light streamed through a large open window, the faded varnish peeling from the wooden shutters, one hanging from a single hinge and another fallen to the floor. The walls, cracked and crumbling, were dirty white with broken pieces of plaster littering the floor. A pile of broken glass lay heaped in a corner. The room overlooked an overgrown path leading to a rickety gate.

'One of us will have to stay awake and keep watch all the time,' Perumal said, his eyes scanning the area slowly. 'Sometimes villagers come into the plantation to pick coconuts,' he said, turning his head to look at them. 'They sell the coconuts at the *kovil*.'

Perumal pulled out two newspaper wrapped packages from the cloth bag he carried on his shoulder. 'Here's some food,' he said, scrutinising each of them. 'There's water in a small well at the back.'

Danika nodded, looking around the room for somewhere clean to sit. She felt drained and exhausted, her back and legs aching from the long crawl past the sentry posts. Danika looked at Indra, concerned that she hadn't spoken all night. Indra grimaced as she slipped the automatic rifle off her shoulder, leaning it against the window sill.

'What?' she asked, noticing Danika staring at her. Danika shook her head. 'Nothing,' she said. 'I was just wondering whether you were alright.'

'Why wouldn't I be,' Indra said grumpily handing a package to Danika. 'I am just very tired and hungry.' She pulled out her canteen and rinsed her fingers using water from the container. 'I'll take the first watch after eating,' she said, sitting cross-legged on the ground and opening the package.

Danika's mouth watered as the aroma of rice and curry filled the room. After rinsing her fingers, she opened the greasy parcel, devouring the tasty contents of red rice flavoured with a dry fish curry.

Wiping her fingers on the remnants of the parcel, Danika lay back on the dusty floor with a sigh. She felt energy slowly returning to her body as she listened to the sound of birds in the trees outside the window. She closed her eyes, sinking into a deep, exhausted slumber.

Danika woke to bright sunshine when she felt a hand on her shoulder. Indra crouched next to her. 'You take the watch,' she said, rubbing her face with the back of her hand. 'I can't keep my eyes open.' Indra lay down on the dusty floor with a sigh. 'Oh,' she said, sleepily. 'Perumal went to scout the temple.'

The heat had grown in intensity, radiating through the open window. Danika felt refreshed from her sleep as she walked to the rear of the building looking for the well Perumal had mentioned. By the position of the sun Danika calculated it would be sometime in the early afternoon.

The well was just an opening in the ground surrounded by heaps of scattered bricks. The cool water, only a few centimetres below the level of the garden, enabled Danika to drop down to her knee and scoop up cupped handfuls which she poured over her head. The water tasted sweet when she trickled a few drops down her throat. She filled her canteen with fresh water before taking a long drink. Topping up the canteen, she walked back feeling refreshed.

As she stepped on the veranda a movement at the corner of her eye made her start and reach for the rifle on her shoulder. She stepped sideways into the doorway, lifting the rifle to her shoulder, her eyes probing the edge of the plantation at the rear of the house. A figure barely visible through the trees, paused behind a Lantana bush at the edge of the garden. Danika flicked off the safety with her thumb as her finger took up the slack on the trigger.

'Don't shoot,' a voice called. 'It's me, Perumal.'

The sense of relief was overwhelming as Danika lowered her rifle, her finger releasing the trigger gently. It happened so quickly she had almost fired.

Perumal came across the garden, exhaustion slowing him as he climbed the steps onto the veranda. He swayed as he walked down the rear corridor, brushing past Danika who kept scanning the tree line. Finally satisfied he was alone, she followed Perumal into a room leading off the corridor.

Perumal sat on the ground with his back to the wall, his clothes filthy with mud. He stared up as her eyes held him, challenged him. He could have been shot if she had pulled the trigger. He nodded his understanding at her unspoken question and glanced at his watch.

'We'll be picked up after dark' he said. 'A team has been assigned to us.' She watched him give the slightest shrug and a small grimace. 'I need to sleep … wake me when the sun goes down.'

◦✖◦

The chorus of croaking frogs rose and fell with the wind as they walked in single file down the overgrown path through the abandoned rice paddy. The men escorting them in tiger-striped uniforms had suddenly appeared out of the darkness as they waited on the veranda overlooking the rear of the property. Perumal, who had been leaning against the back wall, had warned them, knowing somehow that the men were approaching.

Perumal conferred with one of the men before turning to the two women. 'They will be with us until the *kovil* and then escort the journalist to where Muthu is waiting,' he said. 'Your job is to establish contact with your team and make sure the handover goes smoothly. There's an army outpost on the main road junction at the entrance to the *kovil*, about a hundred metres away, so we'll have to do this without alerting them.'

Danika and Indra had been briefed on this part of the operation and knew what was required of them. Making contact in the dark was always dangerous.

The heavily armed men fell in around the small group as they left the old residence. After walking for what seemed like an hour or more, they halted, the men escorting them sinking to one knee. Danika followed, crouching on one knee, her gaze sweeping the surrounding area, faintly lit by a multitude of brilliant twinkling stars. A pale sliver of a moon glowed, distant and mysterious. All around her she could see the silhouettes of armed men.

Perumal was a dark blur just a few metres away. 'The *kovil* is just past those trees,' he hissed over his shoulder. 'We need to be very quiet from here.'

Danika nodded in the dark. Her mission would only be complete when the Indian journalist was safely handed over. Until then she would remain alert. She glanced at Indra before scanning the surrounding area. The silhouettes of trees and bushes less than fifty metres away were barely visible.

One of the men gestured with his arm, moving forward slowly towards the edge of the rice paddy. The rest of the team spread out around them.

The neglected fields were hard under their feet as they approached the tree line. Danika almost fell as she climbed up the side of the paddy field into the thick darkness beneath the spreading trees. Slipping through the underbrush overshadowed by gigantic trees, they reached a narrow track which they followed as it curved to the north. A faint glow silhouetted the trees, growing steadily brighter as they drew closer.

The path opened to a large sandy compound surrounding an ancient Hindu temple. The sound of chanting could be heard as they got closer. The area was lit by long fluorescent tubes fixed vertically on wooden poles connected by electrical wire hanging loosely between each post. Small groups of people, the men dressed in white and the women in bright colourful saris wandered into the temple. Two soldiers carrying automatic rifles on their shoulders leant casually against the wall, next to the front entrance of the temple.

Perumal hissed through his teeth in surprise. 'What are they doing here?' he whispered, almost to himself.

Danika realised that this was a complication they hadn't considered. The temple was usually closed after dark, opening at sunrise for the morning *puja* - offerings. If everything had gone as expected, Mala and the rest of the team would be with the journalist on the opposite side from where they were crouched. The original plan was to do the handover at the entrance to the temple.

'What shall we do?' he asked, glancing at Danika. 'It must be a festival!' Perumal muttered something angrily before resuming his scrutiny of the compound.

The groups of families and the familiar smell of incense wafting in the air reminded Danika of her childhood when she used to accompany her parents to the temple on holy days. She choked back a rise of emotion, *I cannot get sentimental*, she thought sternly to herself.

Danika turned her head and looked at Indra who was staring at her questioningly. 'We'll have to go around,' Indra said, shrugging her shoulders.

What Indra said made sense, Danika thought. They couldn't cross the open ground without being seen and they did not know how long the temple would remain open. Mala might consider it too dangerous, and retreat into the jungle to try again the next night. What would a delay of twenty-four hours mean to the news story that was supposed to be published right away? All these thoughts flashed through her mind.

A germ of an idea came to her mind. She paused for a moment thinking before turning to Indra. 'Remove your uniform,' she said abruptly. 'You're still wearing your salwar, yes?'

Indra's eyes widened at Danika's question. Then understanding dawned in her eyes. 'Yes, yes,' she said slipping the rifle from her shoulder. It took her just a few seconds to remove her uniform.

Perumal had a puzzled look on his face as he watched Indra smooth the creases on her green salwar. 'What's she doing?' he asked brusquely.

'She'll walk across to the other side and establish contact with Mala and the team,' Danika said simply. 'They may decide it's not going to work with those soldiers there and try again tomorrow. It's important that *Anna's* interview be published quickly so we must get the journalist tonight.'

Danika turned to Indra. 'Just walk across casually,' she said. 'Don't look at the soldiers. Just ignore them. Go into the temple if you have to.'

Indra nodded. 'What do I tell Mala?'

'That we're waiting here, and the transfer must happen tonight.' Danika looked across at Perumal. 'Do you have any ideas?'

'Maybe they can come back the same way,' a voice said out of the surrounding darkness. Danika turned her head to look behind her. It was the leader of the escort team. 'Why can't the women come back the same way?'

'Yes, that'll work,' Danika said. 'You can bring her across.'

Perumal bowed his head thinking before nodding his agreement.

Danika grasped Indra's arm. 'Don't take any risks,' she said quietly. 'If you don't think it'll work, bring her to the field where we entered the forest.'

Indra took a deep breath and stepped out into the open. The two soldiers were not paying much attention to what was going on in the compound as they were looking at the people going in and out of the temple. Danika watched as Indra joined a group of people and strolled casually past the soldiers. One of the soldiers turned his head to look at Indra before she disappeared into the temple.

'It's going to work,' Perumal said.

Danika sank to her haunches, anxiously watching the entrance to the temple for Indra to reappear. She would have to come out of the temple first before crossing the compound on the opposite side to make contact with Mala.

The compound was almost empty as the number of people entering the temple had dropped to nothing. Only the soldier standing by the door could be seen. The other wasn't in sight.

'Something's not right,' Perumal growled impatiently. 'She should be out by now. We must do something.'

The sound of people chanting, the wail of musical instruments and the rhythmic thump of beating drums rose to a crescendo before dying to silence.

'Wait,' Danika said getting back to her feet. 'The *puja* is coming to an end.'

People started streaming out of the temple at the end of the ceremony. The compound was awash with men, women and children some stopping in small groups to talk to friends and relatives.

A flash of green and Indra appeared out of the crowd heading in their direction. Beside her strode a tall woman dressed in shirt and slacks, carrying a bag on her shoulder.

'It's the journalist,' Perumal said glancing at Danika.

The two women had almost reached the edge of the compound when a voice called out loudly. Behind them a soldier appeared out of the crowd, his rifle held across his chest. 'Hey,' he shouted. 'Stop right there. I want to talk to you'

The Indian journalist looked over her shoulder at the sound of his voice, slowing down as she did. Indra grabbed the journalists arm and pulled her towards the edge of the compound, but the journalist shook off her grip.

The soldier reached them, manoeuvring his body to prevent them entering the edge of the forest. He stared hard at the two women, holding his rifle across his chest and almost pushing them back with the weapon.

'Where did you come from?' the soldier asked, addressing the journalist. He paid no attention to Indra, his attention fixed on the tall attractive journalist. 'I did not see you enter the temple.'

'What do you want?' the journalist snapped at him arrogantly. 'I don't have time to waste.' Some of the worshipers in the compound started edging away from the confrontation leaving an empty space all around them.

'Where are your ID's?' the soldier demanded, his eyes narrowing at the unfriendly tone in the woman's voice. 'I want to see them.'

Danika sized up the situation quickly. Perumal had started to bring up his rifle but Danika pushed it down. The last thing she wanted was to fire a weapon with innocent civilians all around and an army post just down the road.

Danika's nerve had never failed her yet. She stepped out of the undergrowth, coming from the edge of the soldier's vision. The soldier seemed unaware of her approach, fast, catlike in her canvas-topped trainers. Danika held her rifle firmly with both hands and brought the barrel down hard on the bridge of the man's nose. He squealed, almost an animal sound, dropping his rifle, his hands grabbing his face. Danika stepped between the soldier and the journalist, reached forward and pushed him hard, toppling him to the ground. He crumpled, then moaned, sprawling on the ground with his thighs apart. She kicked hard – and she did it again. Then she grabbed the journalist by her arm, dragging her aside.

'Run,' she commanded, gesturing with her rifle at Indra. 'Follow her!'

The three women ran together into the concealing jungle. Danika heard the escort team fall in around them as they hurried down the path, turning into the thick growth, heading towards the rice paddy.

They kept running, dodging through the undergrowth, Indra leading, the journalist and Danika following closely behind. There was no sign of Perumal.

'What happened in there?' Danika panted to Indra when they finally stopped at the edge of the rice paddy. 'We didn't see you leave the temple.'

'There was a door on the other side,' Indra said, gasping for breath. 'Mala thought it would be safer to bring her through the temple since there were so many people around. It would have worked if not for that soldier.'

The journalist was staring at Danika. 'That was a brave thing you did,' she said disbelievingly. 'I thought you were going to kill him.'

'I couldn't,' Danika said. 'Because to kill him I would have had to shoot him.' There was no emotion in her voice. 'There's no silencer on the gun. If I had killed him, the shots would have been heard.'

As the adrenaline-fuelled rush of flight began to fade, Danika realised that the journalist was safe and would be able to file her story.

CHAPTER THIRTY-FIVE

CENTRAL HIGHLANDS

The watchman walked along the terraced path shouting for the women to awaken after the factory *canku* -siren had sounded. The night had been cold, the monsoon winds blowing from the southwest making it feel colder than it was. Mukesh had lit a fire in an empty powdered milk can which he kept next to him to keep warm. The coals had burned down to grey ash when he poked it with a stick but the river stones at the bottom were still warm as he cradled the can against his stomach under the blanket.

The sound of tin buckets being washed, wood being chopped and the crowing of roosters, mingled with the sound of children crying and dogs barking. It was the time of day he hated the most.

Mukesh had not got any closer to finding who was the leader of the secret organisation being formed to wrest control of the hill country from the government. Mukesh was certain that the man discovered a few days ago with his throat cut, hanging from a tree near the factory, was meant as a warning.

Kanan was refusing to talk to him and his sister had asked him yesterday when he would be leaving. Mukesh wondered whether it was time for him to go. He knew that running away was not going to solve anything and knowing what was happening in Jaffna, he couldn't bear to think the same could happen in these hills. Did they know what it would mean, declaring a separate state in the hills? This place was not like Jaffna. They lived in a Sinhalese area, the heartland of the country. The area that had resisted the colonial powers for many centuries. The last bastion in the country to fall. The Sinhalese would never allow it to happen. It would be a bloodbath. He was certain of that.

Mukesh resolved to try to get more information one last time. In his mind he went over what he knew. He knew that men from many estates were involved. He knew that a *Durai* was involved. He knew which estate the man came from. Then it struck him. He knew his voice. He had heard the man speak that night when he hid in the bushes. Mukesh sat up excitedly on the stoop. He knew what he had to do. He would go to the estate pretending to look for a job. He would recognise the voice when the man spoke.

Mukesh limped up the driveway lined with flowering trees towards the low office building to the right of the estate bungalow. Built of the same material as the sprawling bungalow, the green roofed office lay nestled below a gigantic boulder that was almost twice as large as the building.

A man leaning against a carved veranda pillar in the bungalow watched Mukesh come up the driveway and turn into the pathway leading to the office. The man was in his mid-thirties, slightly overweight and wore a white shirt with button down pockets and a pair of blue jeans. Mukesh had never seen him before. He stepped off the veranda towards the office, flicking the cigarette he was smoking into the bushes. He reached the front door to the office the same time Mukesh got there.

The front of the office faced a small garden beyond which the tea covered hillside fell away down the slopes to the valley. A gravel path, bordered by flower beds, led from the office veranda to an inspection path which wound down through the tea towards the muster ground some distance below.

'What are you doing here?' he asked, looking at Mukesh suspiciously. He spoke rudely, almost aggressively, looking at Mukesh with a frown on his face.

'My name is Mukesh, *Durai*' he responded, bowing his head deferentially. 'My sister works here and lives in the lines as did my parents. I was working in the south and suffered a misfortune which has made it difficult to find work. I came back here hoping to find a job in the estate.'

'Your sister works here? What's her name?' the man questioned.

'Her name is Rani,' Mukesh said. 'She's a tea plucker and lives in the upper lines.'

'You said your parents worked here. Were you and your sister born here?'

'Yes sir, in those lines over there,' Mukesh said, pointing to the other side of the valley. 'My father was *karvalkaran* – a clerk, here on the estate.'

The *Durai* studied Mukesh thoughtfully before responding. 'So, what's wrong with your leg? What kind of work can you do?'

Mukesh had already discounted the man as the person he was looking for. It was not the same voice he had heard that night. He had to find something to do which would allow him to hang around the estate. Mukesh looked at his feet. 'I hurt it in a car accident,' he muttered. 'I was working in an all-night eatery serving people and they asked me to leave because I was too slow.' He looked up at the man. 'I couldn't find work, so I came back hoping to find work in one of the estates.'

Mukesh looked at the *Durai* pleadingly. 'I can read and write,' he said hopefully. 'I am used to working at night. I can be a *karvalkaran* if there is a need for one.'

The door to the office suddenly opened and someone stepped out into the veranda. It was an older, grey haired version of the man who was questioning Mukesh. He had an unlit cigarette in his hand. He stopped in surprise when he saw the two of them standing outside the office door.

His flinty eyes narrowed in irritation 'Sunil, what are you still doing here,' he barked angrily. 'You should have left for Kelburn. I told you it was an important meeting and I don't want you to be late.'

Mukesh recognised the voice instantly. It was the man who had spoken that night.

'I am going, I am going,' Sunil said nervously. 'I was just asking this man what he was doing here. He's looking for a job,' he explained.

The *Periya Durai* stared at Mukesh suspiciously. The man had a narrow, cruel face and his eyes glinted in the sunlight. 'Go away,' he said, dismissing him arrogantly with a wave of his hand. 'I don't want you coming here again.' Sunil shrugged his shoulders at Mukesh before turning and hurrying down the path to the estate bungalow.

The *Periya Durai* didn't even bother to look at Mukesh. He walked back into the office building, shutting the door firmly behind him. Mukesh didn't need to be told twice. He'd got what he came for. He limped back down the road trying to remember what time the next bus to Bandarawela would drive past the estate.

CHAPTER THIRTY-SIX

TRINCOMALEE

Sami sat with Rajan in the garden behind the church, out of sight from the road, catching up on what they had each been doing the past two years. Rajan, a university student who wanted a change for Tamils living in the country, had found himself in one of the more militant separatist groups. The students he had joined to protest by peaceful means were absorbed into their ranks. Not happy with where he found himself, he nevertheless threw himself wholeheartedly into the struggle against the government and became a trusted confidante of Shankar, one of the second-tier leaders of the now dominant militant group.

'It's not been easy,' Rajan said. 'The big army offensive forced us out of the peninsula into these northern jungles where our training camps were. We never expected to be forced out, but we had no choice. We lost a lot of people.'

'So, was the Indian involvement good for the movement?' asked Sami. 'I heard the Sri Lankan army had to go back to their bases.'

'Yes,' Rajan agreed. 'It was good at first but then *Anna* refused to join the peace talks with the Indians.' Rajan looked at the ground and shrugged. 'I was not sure it was the right thing to do at the time, but the Indians turned out to be worse that the army. They raped and looted, taking anything they wanted. The people were really getting very angry.'

Rajan stared into the distance, reminiscing. 'After the JVP uprising in the south, the army suddenly left Jaffna, so we just walked in and took over the city. It was a good time,' Rajan recollected. 'We could go anywhere, do anything we wanted, and no one would stop us. Then the Indians attacked us and here we are back in the Vanni. All we did is to exchange one army for another.'

Rajan looked at the watch on his wrist and rose to his feet. 'Come, it's time. We will be picked up soon.' Sami had been to Trincomalee when he was a child but didn't remember much about the place. His parents had brought him there when they visited his father's home in Batticaloa. He remembered being driven in a truck filled with coconut husks, which made for a comfortable ride, though the dry fibre dust made him sneeze continuously, much to the amusement of the others.

They were dropped off just before they reached the outskirts of the city, the lorry accelerating away in a cloud of noxious smoke. Sami followed Rajan who walked down a small narrow laneway between two houses. One of the men who accompanied them followed behind, the other remaining at the corner.

Cadjan fences lined the narrow dirt track which was overhung by branches from two huge jak fruit trees, round, green fruit like giant ticks clinging to the trunk. A property set well back from the laneway was their destination. The house, an old colonial-style villa with a dark red-tiled roof stood with its back to a thick growth of jungle. The city was full of such buildings, built during the four-hundred-and-fifty-year colonial era by European powers that viewed the deep-water port as strategic to their interests.

The building was yellow-grey with neglect, the paint peeling from wooden shutters hanging haphazardly from three sets of windows looking out into the yard. A large matching shed which was once the garage, stood on the left at right angles to the building. The yard in front of the house had two mango trees growing on either side which formed an area of filtered light.

The front door opened when they climbed onto the front veranda, littered with leaves and dirt. Rajan entered the house, beckoning Sami to follow. The house was dark, the only light filtering through the grimy windows. A loose shutter banged in the wind and the whole place smelt of mould and neglect.

In the gloom, Sami could make out the shapes of three men. Two were seated on the ground with their backs to the wall, their legs splayed out while the other stood by the door looking outside. They were all armed with modern AK-47 assault rifles, with a magazine loaded and another taped to it with dark green tape.

Sami followed Rajan to the back of the property, down a corridor to a large room lit by a spluttering lantern sitting on the floor. The mostly empty space smelt of kerosene and smoke. A stack of rolled up mats and a wooden box, overflowing with rifle magazines were piled in a corner.

'Ganesh, can you bring us some food,' Rajan addressed a young boy who stood in the doorway. Very young teenagers who joined the movement were often used in the militant cells to prepare food and carry messages.

'Is this where we are meeting Shankar?' Sami asked Rajan, looking around the room. Rajan tilted his head, studying Sami. 'It's better you not know,' said Rajan. 'He'll want us to come to him when he is ready. He has avoided being captured up to now by being extremely cautious.'

'Did you know there's a price on his head?' Rajan asked. 'He will be taking a big risk meeting with you. And by the way, I'll want the gun that you took from Murugesu. I can't let you go near him armed.'

Sami nodded and took out the handgun from the cloth bag on his shoulder, holding it by its barrel. Rajan took the gun from him and unchambered the round, putting the gun in his pocket. 'I'll make sure Murugesu gets this back,' he said. 'The man was very upset that he lost his weapon.'

Sami shrugged. 'He has to learn not to get too close,' he said. 'You would've done the same to him.'

Ganesh came into the room carrying a plate heaped with flat round *thosai* and a bowl with a thick lentil curry, placing them on the floor by the lantern. Rajan and Sami sat cross legged in front of the food and ate hungrily, twisting off pieces of *thosai* which they used to scoop up the fiery lentil curry.

Sami lay back on the floor contentedly after cleaning his oily fingers on square sheets of torn newspaper that were brought with the food. He crossed his arms behind his head, looking up at the shadows that danced on the ceiling.

'When can we go look for my mother,' asked Sami, burping gently. 'She could be anywhere in Trincomalee.'

Rajan looked at Sami thoughtfully. 'We still don't know whether they remained in Jaffna, but the chances are that they left during the fighting. There was a big battle near Kopay and the Indians shelled the area with mortars,' Rajan explained, shaking his head at the thought.

'I should hear back from Jaffna soon but let's assume that they are here. There are over a dozen refugee camps around Trinco,' he said. 'You find them in Pulmoddai, Kuchaveli, Thampalakamam, Kantale and in the city too. The army won't let any refugees come into the city unless they require medical attention. They are taken to the General Hospital under guard. It'll take time to visit each camp and we'll have to cross a number of Sri Lankan and Indian checkpoints.'

Sami sat up and looked at Rajan. 'We have to find a way,' he said. 'I am not going back until I know what's happened to them.'

Rajan nodded. 'I know, I know,' he said. 'It's been giving me a headache.' He paused for a moment, pursing his lips thoughtfully. 'I don't want to send any of my men into town. The Indians are picking up any young men they can find and are taking them in for questioning. It's not even safe to send our women out now. The *jawans* are molesting them and some have even been raped.'

Rajan shook his head in disgust. 'They came as peace keepers but all they want to do is rape our women.' Rajan glanced at Sami. 'Remember Danika, from the jungle camp?' he asked.

'Yes, of course I do.' Sami looked at Rajan questioningly. 'Is she alive?'

'She's become a bit of a legend.' Rajan grinned. 'After fighting with us on the Western Highway she became one of the first to join the new female brigade. She's now part of a scout unit.'

'What do you mean legend?' Sami questioned. He remembered her as a very capable leader of the group of militant women who supplied his team in the western jungles. Sami had never treated her any differently to the men under his command and had come, over time, to respect her intelligence and determination.

'Recently she was stopped by an Indian patrol not far from here and was forced into their jeep. They tried to molest her, but she fought back.' Rajan continued with a broad smile on his face. 'She stuck a knife into one of them and then slashed the driver's throat, making the jeep crash. She was able to get out and escape. People who saw what happened started throwing stones at the *jawans* and they had to send men from their base to put down the riot.'

Sami smiled, not surprised at what she had done to the *jawans*. They wouldn't have expected someone who looked like her to be so deadly.

'Where is she now?' Sami asked Rajan. He would like to talk to Danika about what happened to Ismail.

'She's is in a camp near Pankulam. The women's unit have been trained to fight and have proven themselves more than once against the Sri Lankan army.'

Ever since the mission began, Sami had been thinking more and more about those months he spent with his men in the western jungles surrounding the highway. The comradeship and the friendships they had made and how he felt when they had been betrayed by the Tigers. He began to recall events and conversations that had been repressed and long forgotten. It seemed that the more he replayed the memories the stronger they became.

Sami realised that Danika was one person who was always in the back of his mind. He remembered the fierce determination and the responsibility she had shown to the women under her command. There was no disguising her natural beauty and it had been almost a compulsion at times to crack that sullen exterior and expose the real woman beneath. He regretted not getting to know her better and felt a sense of relief that she was alive.

Sami shook away the unfamiliar feeling. 'So, what will we do then about finding my mother?' he asked. 'Is there any way we can find out?'

Rajan thought for a minute. 'I know what we'll do. I'll send Ganesh out to a few of the camps to look for your mother. He's too young to be picked up by the *jawans.*'

Sami nodded glumly. It was going to be more difficult to move around Trincomalee than he had thought. The government saw the city and its British-built military infrastructure as being important to their interests and had a strong army, navy and air force presence. The Special Task Force operated further to the south around Batticaloa trying to keep the Tigers from expanding too far in that direction. He'd have to be patient.

CHAPTER THIRTY-SEVEN

NEAR PANKULAM

The hand-tractor pulling a loaded trailer turned off the dirt road into an over-grown garden surrounding a burnt-out house set back from the road. Dusk had fallen quickly, and it was too dangerous to be on the road so close to the army camp. Only a few days back this area had been recaptured from the Indian army and the house had been partially destroyed by the fighting.

Danika's whole body ached. She had been jolted, bumped and shaken during the entire ride and her face and clothes were covered in dust. She was part of a detail transporting wooden planks to the men surrounding the army camp just a kilometre down the road. They would use the roughly hewn boards to construct dugouts and shelters from which to watch and attack the enemy.

The darkening sky was visible through the damaged roof, broken beams hanging dangerously twisted overhead. Some of the window frames were broken with glass strewn across the floor. The bullet riddled clay-brick walls which were still standing, were stained by the monsoon rains but it was the shelter it provided that attracted them.

She walked through what remained of the kitchen, it's roof still intact. Clay pots, charred and in pieces, lay scattered on the floor. A blue sari badly faded and in shreds, hanging from what must have been a washing line, spoke of the haste in which the owners had run away. She unslung her T-56 rifle, laying it down before sitting on the bare cement floor with her back to the wall. She adjusted the cloth bag she carried across her shoulder, letting it rest on the floor. It carried all her possessions.

Mala came into the room carrying her rifle and her bag. She was wearing running shoes with heavy socks, the cyanide capsule hanging by a black string around her neck was tucked neatly into her left breast pocket, with only the string showing. She cleared a space with her foot before sitting cross legged on the floor. Mala glanced sideways at Danika and smiled. Her demeanour was usually stern, sometimes far more serious and formidable than some of the men. But Danika knew that inside that tough shell was a good person, made hard by what she'd been through.

'I found some mangoes,' Mala said quietly, pulling out three half-ripe fruit from her bag. 'We can each have one.' Danika nodded her thanks when Mala handed a fruit to her. Danika remembered seeing a mango tree in the garden, charred on one side, with broken branches and leaves shredded by the heavy gunfire, laying scattered on the ground

The evening meal they normally ate would require a small fire but there was no way they could light one so close to the army camp. They would have to manage with the fruit and the *vadai* they each carried. She reached into her bag and pulled out a parcel wrapped in a greasy newspaper. Inside were half-a-dozen medium sized *vadai*. Made into balls from a paste of dhal and maldive fish chips and then fried in hot oil, they were easy to carry and did not spoil. The meal, though doing little to fill the emptiness in her stomach, was nutritious and would give her energy for the next day.

After eating two of the *vadai*, she unsheathed her knife and cut the fruit into slices, sucking out the yellow flesh, juice dribbling down the side of her chin. She'd not had any food since that morning when she had eaten a portion of boiled country rice and wild greens flavoured with a piece of lime pickle.

'Thangam will take first watch, I'll take the second'.

Danika nodded at Mala. Thangam was the third member of their team. Built like a fireplug, she was short but extremely strong, like a man. Her hair was plaited into two small braids which were pinned to her head making her look tough. The other two women who made up their small scout team, Indra and Parvathy had remained behind at the camp.

Danika snapped out of a deep sleep when a rough hand fell on her shoulder. Mala who had been on guard duty outside the building, muttered something incomprehensible and lay down tiredly across the room.

Danika rose to her feet clumsily, still groggy from sleep, almost knocking over her rifle before grabbing it by the barrel. Her lower back was so stiff she felt as if she would not be able to straighten it again. She slipped on her sandals and tumbled outside the building after taking a sip of water from the plastic bottle she carried. Her mouth felt dry even after swallowing the water, but she didn't drink anymore. The bottle in her bag was half empty and she was not sure when she'd be able to fill it again.

The position she selected was by the front entrance, next to the corner wall facing the direction of the army camp. If there was any chance of a patrol appearing it would be up the road from the direction of the camp. She knew that the camp was surrounded by militant positions and she would have ample warning of any attack.

Danika glumly contemplated her life. She had been forced to learn doggedness just to keep up with everyone else. She was a town girl and it had not been easy to keep up with the women born in the villages. Looking back, her past struggle seemed like such a little thing compared to where she was now, but back then when she had first decided to join the militants, she had to work twice as hard as everyone else and it had seemed so unfair.

She had found the selection process for the women's military wing quite easy to get through. The battle for the Western Highway had prepared her for the demanding training exercises. She soon found herself deployed, but it wasn't what she'd expected. The men who had been fighting on the frontlines for years first viewed the women cadre as a burden, which she hated. She'd been part of the newly trained group of women who confronted the army out on a search and destroy operation in the Adampan area of Mannar. The fighting was loud and savage and after several hours of fierce combat the Sri Lankan troops withdrew. In her new unit, you either carried your weight, or you were buried in some stinking mudhole, and it was too much for some of the women she'd graduated with. Danika had been under fire before and came alive in the fighting and everything changed for her. She, and the other women who had survived the battle, were no longer considered a burden. They were now an asset who had proven themselves under fire.

A feeling of uneasiness enveloped her as she watched the streaks of dawn light up the eastern sky. She eased herself onto her haunches, with her back to the wall, her rifle pointing to the ground, her finger beside the trigger. Her eyes searched the grey darkness wondering what was spooking her.

The trees in the garden began to take shape as a night bird flew overhead, screeching loudly as it headed for its nest.

A sudden burst of gunfire from the direction of the army camp broke the early morning stillness making her heart skip. It was quickly followed by a fusillade of automatic fire which grew in volume. Danika heard urgent movement behind her as Mala and Thangam gathered their belongings in preparation for evacuating the building. The three of them would abandon the tractor and disappear into the jungle if they had to, the cargo not worth the price of their lives.

'Can you see anything?' Mala was just a shadow inside the door frame.

Other than the lightening of the sky, which outlined the top of the trees, there was no movement she could detect. The volume of fire decreased, then abruptly increased in intensity after two loud explosions. It was much closer than she had expected.

'No, nothing, but the firing is getting close.'

Danika's chest tightened as she detected a flicker of movement at the edge of her vision. 'Something's out there,' she whispered, flicking off the safety catch on her weapon and putting it into burst mode. She felt movement as Mala took up position behind her. Thangam would be covering the back door.

The dawn light was getting brighter, and she could begin to see the outline of the two mango trees and the fence just beyond. A dog barked close by adding to the tension in the room.

'There ...' the sibilant whisper seemed loud in the small room.

For a moment Danika couldn't see what had provoked the warning but then dark shapes of sporadic movement caught her eye.

As the shapes drew closer she could make out individual turbaned soldiers leap frogging towards their position through the tattered Palmyra fence.

It was easy, much too easy. She aimed the automatic rifle sights at the enemy and gently squeezed the trigger. Two three-shot bursts tore out toward the Indian soldiers. She made a mistake with the first burst, and the jar of the recoil pulled the barrel upward, so the bullets sailed over their heads. Before they had a chance to react, she'd corrected, held the barrel tighter, and squeezed the trigger again. The second time, the burst slammed into one of the soldiers, and spun him to the ground. The other two men she could see stared in her direction in alarm, then dove for cover.

Mala had also fired although Danika did not hear the gunfire, being so focused on her own targets. The smell of cordite filled the room as Thangam continued to fire her weapon from the back room on full auto.

'Don't waste your ammunition,' Mala snapped over her shoulder. 'Shoot in burst mode.'

Bullets whizzed through the window and door, thumping into the clay brick walls, their energy absorbed by the thick walls.

'Keep firing ... they will rush us soon,' Danika yelled. 'They may use grenades if they get closer.'

Danika could see flashes as the soldiers fired, but she would have to raise herself above the level of the window to get a proper angle and to be able to hit them. She waited for them to make a move, but they stayed down. They needed to finish it soon, but it would be foolish to move just now.

Dawn had broken, and a soft light began to fill the room. 'We have to get out before it's too late,' Danika looked across the room at Mala who nodded her assent. 'Why don't the two of you make a break for the jungle through the back. Make as much noise as you can. I will cover you from here.'

Mala stared at her from across the room. 'Are you crazy?' she asked. 'You know what'll happen. You'll be killed or worse,' she grimaced.

Danika nodded furiously. They didn't have much time as the level of firing had begun to die down. 'I don't plan on being killed,' she said. 'Just go! I'll meet you at the *kalvettu* - culvert.'

Mala nodded before scrambling from the doorway and disappearing into the back room. After what seemed like an interminable period the sound of firing erupted from behind the building as the two girls broke cover and headed for the welcoming jungle.

Just as Danika thought, the Indian soldiers she'd been watching shouted in triumph, and leapt to their feet. Both men flung the butts of their rifles to their shoulders. She didn't wait any longer and squeezed the trigger. In the heat of the action, she'd nudged the selector forward to the full auto position, and a stream of bullets spat fury. The volley took one man in the chest. His body jerked and writhed as the lead tore into him. He was already dead when his body slumped to the ground. The remaining man had decided that he'd be next and turned on his heel and fled. He made fifty meters before she followed him with a further burst from the T-56. It clicked on empty. Every bullet had missed, and he dove for cover in a shallow depression, enough to shield him from her bullets.

Danika didn't even reload. She ducked through the doorway, feeling the familiar rush of adrenaline consume her as her body adjusted to the stress. She was keenly aware that she was exposing her back briefly to the threat behind her, but she had no choice. Mala and Thangam covered her all the way, shooting in short burst towards the Indian army positions. Only when she reached the edge of the jungle did Danika feel safe. They were in their element in the jungle and no soldier would follow them there.

CHAPTER THIRTY-EIGHT

NEAR TRINCOMALEE

Sami woke to a light being flashed in his eyes. He couldn't see anything past the blinding light. He had fallen asleep on a mat in the corner of the room. Rajan had gone out and the only other men in the house were the three guards.

'Get up,' a voice said. 'We're leaving now.' Sami's mind was still sluggish from being awakened so abruptly. He rose to his feet holding his hand against the wall to steady himself. The light left his face, but his eyes needed a few seconds to adjust to the darkness in the room.

Sami felt a hand grab his arm and pull him towards the rear of the house. It was pitch black, his eyes struggling to give him any vision at all. He felt someone run his hands over his body carefully, looking for weapons. The man grunted not finding anything.

Sami sensed they had left the house when he felt fresh air against his face.

His vision was coming back, and he could see the faint glow of the moon through the spreading branches. Leaves and small limbs brushed his face and body as they entered the undergrowth at the rear of the house. Sami could see the shape of a man in front of him. Another man behind him held onto his arm as they went deeper into the jungle.

They must have walked for at least thirty minutes, finally leaving the steamy jungle and stopping in an open area. Sami had lost all sense of direction, but his vision had cleared, and he could see that they were on a road of some kind. A dog barked in the distance as a cloud covered the moon for a few seconds.

'Come,' a voice said quietly. 'This way.' A hand pushed Sami to the right and they walked down the dirt road towards the sound of the barking dog. After a while the glow of a lamp shining through an open window became visible through the trees. The men quickened their steps as they approached the house. The dog barked excitedly, sensing them but quietened at a curt command from someone in the darkness.

Sami sensed they were being watched as they marched up to the house. He was searched once more before the door was opened by one of his guides who waved at him to enter. The room he entered was like a reception room with an open hallway leading towards the back of the house. The room also had closed doors on either side. The light from a kerosene lantern sitting on a table cast flickering shadows against the walls. Geckos moved randomly between the shadows. The table and three chairs were the only furniture in the room.

The door to his right opened and a man entered the room. Sami recognised him instantly even though he had not seen Shankar for a few years. He had lost weight, but his bearing was still the same. He clutched a steaming glass in his right hand. Rajan followed behind, smiling at Sami briefly before becoming serious again.

Shankar studied Sami carefully. 'You're truly a survivor,' he said, shaking his head in amazement. 'Saudi, Beirut, Jaffna, the jungles, a Sinhalese prison and now a messenger for the government. What will it be next?'

'It's nice to see you too Shankar,' Sami said respectfully.

Shankar nodded waving his arm at a chair. 'Sit, sit,' he said. 'What is it you bring from the government?'

Sami lowered himself onto a chair and waited for Shankar to do the same. Rajan stood behind Shankar watching Sami intently.

'I have come with a proposal from the government for which I will require an answer before I leave.'

Shankar glanced up at Rajan before responding. 'I cannot promise anything,' he said. 'Any proposal will have to be studied by *Anna* first. He will decide what happens next.'

'Yes, I am aware of that,' Sami nodded. 'I am prepared to stay for as long as it takes. It will give me time to look for my mother.'

'Rajan told me that you were worried about her,' Shankar said nodding. 'We will help you look for your family but tell me first what message you have brought.'

'The President believes, that for the first time, your goals and the governments goals are aligned,' Sami started. 'You want the Indians out and so does the government. They are looking for an unofficial agreement between the two parties.'

Shankar stared at Sami intently. 'Go on,' he said. 'What do they want us to do?' He blew gently into the hot brew he held.

'As you know the government is fighting Sinhalese extremists in the south. They cannot fight on two fronts. What they want from you is an assurance that there won't be any attacks against government forces in the north and east while the Indians are still here. The government will also agree not to attack any militant positions in the same areas. In other words, a mutual ceasefire.'

'So, they want us to fight the Indians while they sit back and watch,' Shankar said shrewdly. 'Sounds like something the President would have dreamt up. They don't call him the 'Old Fox' for nothing. He wants us to fight each other until one of us loses or is too weak to continue. Then the army march in and say, Thank you very much.' Shankar paused for a moment. 'Huh! I like the way he thinks.' Shankar shook his head in admiration. 'No, I don't think *Anna* will go for that.'

Sami shrugged. 'I am only the messenger here. I cannot negotiate for the government. If you have a counter proposal I will be happy to take it back with me.' Sami watched Shankar as he drank, draining the liquid in a gulp, pouring it into his mouth from above in the village fashion, without allowing the glass to touch his lips.

Shankar thought for a moment before nodding hesitantly. 'Yes, I will take the proposal to him and see what he says. In the meantime, you go look for your mother.'

∽

Rajan told him the next day that his mother and grand-parents had been found living in a refugee camp outside Batticaloa. The news came as a relief to Sami. They could after many years become a family again.

The taxi took Sami just a few kilometres out of town and stopped beside a small bridge. 'I cannot go further,' the driver said. 'It's not safe for me.'

Sami was surprised. He had chosen a Tamil driver so that he could be driven into the militant controlled areas. 'Why?' Sami asked. 'You're a Tamil. The boys will not hurt you.'

'It's not the boys I am worried about,' said the taxi driver. 'It's the STF. They have warned us not to cross into these areas and if they find out…' He drew an imaginary line across his throat.

Sami sighed. He would have to walk the remaining distance to the militant checkpoint. Sami had taken the taxi hoping that it would get him past the militant control point across the bay from Trincomalee.

The bridge had a checkpoint with armed soldiers. Several civilians, some on foot and others with bikes, were waiting to cross. The soldiers searched everyone's belongings and checked their identification. Sami showed them the card he carried from the relief agency.

'Where are you going,' one of the soldiers asked bad-temperedly. He was an older, heavy-set man wearing three stripes on his shoulders. The other soldiers seem to defer to him.

'I am trying to get to Batticaloa,' Sami responded. 'I am visiting a few of the refugee camps outside the town.'

The Sergeant scrutinised Sami's identification card carefully before handing it over. 'How are you going to get there?' he asked. 'It's over fifty kilometres from here.'

Sami shrugged. 'Maybe I can get a ride on the other side,' he said. 'I am not really sure how.'

'Hah, you should be able to find a push bike but not much more. All petrol and kerosene deliveries are prohibited. Maybe they can use their piss as fuel.' The Sergeant seemed to find that amusing. 'Let him through,' he said chuckling. The soldiers at the barrier, smiling at the Sergeant's humour, waved Sami through.

The road curved gently on a raised causeway, between a large paddy field on one side and a narrow lagoon on the other. Fishermen balancing on flat canoes flung round fishing nets into the water, drawing them in gently and picking the small fish caught in the nets which they tossed into a plastic bucket.

A small village at the end of the causeway gave Sami some hope that he would be able to find someone to take him the forty odd kilometres to the refugee camp.

Two women watched him as he got closer to the collection of huts and stores that made up the village. They were dressed in muted jungle green, their shirts hanging loosely over baggy trousers and belted at the waist. They were wearing rubber sandals. One woman had sharp, angular features, her older, more experienced eyes studying Sami suspiciously. The other's face was more open and friendly.

'Where you are going?' the younger one asked. Her hair was carelessly braided and tied up behind her head. A cyanide capsule hung on a black string around her neck tucked neatly into her breast pocket. She carried a fighting knife in a sheath on her hip.

'I am going to Batticaloa,' Sami responded. 'My mother and grand-parents are from Jaffna and are in a refugee camp in Vakarai.'

'From where in Jaffna,' the older woman asked distrustfully. Her attitude and demeanour reminded Sami of Danika when they had first met.

'From Kopay,' he said. 'I am from Colombo originally, but my mother is from there.'

The woman studied Sami thoughtfully. 'You're not a Tamil,' she said. 'What are you? A *Marakkalaya*?'

'Yes, I am,' Sami nodded. He was getting tired of answering questions. 'I am here with the permission of Shankar. I need to get to the refugee camp. Who do I have to speak to?'

The two women glanced at each other. 'Come,' the older woman said, motioning to Sami. 'I'll take you to see Sundara.'

CHAPTER THIRTY-NINE

CENTRAL HIGHLANDS

The only sound in the room was the hum of the fluorescent lights. Tilak leaned back on the bed with his hands behind his head. They had been at the Bandarawela Guest House for two days waiting. No one had come to see them and there was no message. He was getting frustrated. They were not going to find out who was heading this organisation by just sitting on their hands.

The Special Branch Commander had been insistent. 'You don't do anything without talking to me first,' he said, when Tilak had reported in that morning. 'There's something happening that you don't know. Just wait there until we tell you what to do.'

Tilak cursed all politicians and the games they played. He had no doubt that the Plantation Minister was putting pressure on the police not to act. What Tilak did not understand was why he was there at all. Tilak ran his fingers through the magazines on the table looking for something, anything, worth reading. He couldn't concentrate on the photographs of movie stars and television personalities and after a few minutes he threw the magazine on the table.

A quiet knock on his door awakened him from his stupor. He swung his feet off the bed and walked to the heavy wooden door. A houseboy dressed in a white jacket stood outside the door holding an embossed silver platter. On it was a folded sheet of paper.

'A message came for you sir,' the houseboy said, holding out the platter. Tilak had been amazed that even fifty years after the British had left, some colonial customs were still being practiced in places like this. Tilak took the message from the platter nodding his thanks. Closing the door on the expectant houseboy, he walked over to the window and read the message on the sheet of paper.

'Be ready at 8:00 this evening. You'll be picked up and driven to the appointment.'

Tilak stared at the cryptic message. Picked up by whom and to which appointment?

The Bakelite phone next to the bed thrilled loudly. Tilak crossed over to the bed and picked up the handset. 'Tilak here...'

'Are you alone?' Tilak recognised the Commanders voice.

'Yes Sir,' Tilak said. 'I am alone.'

'Ok, now listen carefully. Regarding the matter you are working on. It will be resolved today,' the Commander said bluntly. 'Your only involvement will be to verify what takes place. Do you understand?'

Tilak didn't understand what was going on but understood the order he'd been given. 'So, you want us to observe and take no action?' he questioned.

'That's right. Just observe and verify. I want you to report back to Colombo first thing tomorrow.' The Commander did not wait for an answer, hanging up abruptly.

Tilak looked at the handset in disgust. He'd rather mess with a bunch of Tigers than have to deal with politicians. He placed the handset back in its cradle and went looking for Chandra.

ॐ

Two white Toyota Pajero's with darkened glass roared up the driveway. The first vehicle braked to a stop under the front colonnaded porch. A man opened the passenger door and stepped out into the light. It was the bodyguard who had come with the Minister's son.

'My name is Alagar,' he said. 'You are to come with me.' The man looked at them distastefully, like he had found something nasty under his shoe.

Tilak instinctively didn't trust the man. He was glad he'd brought his personal weapon strapped to a quick release shoulder holster under his left armpit. He also had a fighting knife taped to his right calf.

'You sit with me. Your man can get into the other vehicle,' Alagar sneered, motioning to the vehicle under the porch. The way he said it made Tilak's blood boil.

Tilak shook his head, holding the man's gaze. 'We both go in the same vehicle or you can go fuck yourself,' he said in a flat hard voice.

Alagar looked shocked, then his eyes narrowed as he stared at Tilak angrily. Tilak figured that it had been a while since someone had stood up to him. He felt Chandra move to his left behind him forcing Alagar to shift his position to keep them both in front of him. It was clear to Tilak that the man had not expected him to react this way. He had made a mistake trying to intimidate the two of them without the backup of any of his men. They might as well have been on the moon for all the good they would now do.

Alagar shook his head angrily when he realised he had been given no choice. 'Ok, you both come with me.' He turned abruptly and walked to the open passenger door. 'Geethan, go get into the other vehicle,' he called out loudly. 'This old couple want to hold hands.'

Tilak let the insult pass without saying anything. He shook his head at Chandra who looked ready to tear the man apart. Chandra glared at the man as they both got into the back seat of the Pajero which took off before they could even close the doors.

The two vehicles circled the roundabout and turned on the road to Haputale. On one side of the two-lane highway was the rock face of the hillside, wet with water trickling down from the summit. On the other, a steep drop to the darkness of the valley below. Lights twinkled on the estate lines on the surrounding hills. The tea estate bungalows and factories were clearly visible in pools of bright light that could be seen for kilometres.

Other than a muttered command to the driver, Alagar had not said anything. His gaze fixed on the road ahead. But Tilak could see the tension in his thick neck and shoulders and sensed that the man would give them trouble.

They turned off the main highway onto a gravelled road leading to a tea factory across the valley. Almost at the summit of a nearby hill, a sprawling estate bungalow glowed brightly in the dark. Two sets of twinkling lights marked the estate lines a few hundred metres away. They approached a fork in the estate road where the *Karvalkaran* had his little hut. The watchman wrapped in a blanket and wearing a woollen hat, carried a long pole with a small axe head. He sleepily pushed open the white gate on the gravelled road leading to the estate bungalow.

The two vehicles slowly negotiated the narrow driveway. Flowering trees and bushes brushed the four-wheel drive vehicles as they drove into a large sandy yard big enough to turn a car in, a level below the brightly lit estate bungalow. The Pajero's headlights shone on a garage of roughly dressed granite with a green corrugated-iron roof, at the end of the yard. The three, dark green wooden doors were closed for the night. A terraced path lined with bushes led up to the bungalow on the left and down to the estate office, on another level, to the right.

'Stay here,' Alagar grunted before getting off the Pajero. He signalled to the second vehicle, watching as four men got out. They were all dressed like Alagar, in crumpled cotton safari suits which they adjusted as they walked up to him. The driver from their Pajero joined the group leaving the two of them alone.

'Keep your eyes open,' Tilak said, glancing at Chandra. 'I don't trust this lot.'

Tilak and Chandra got out of their vehicle while Alagar spoke to his men. Tilak could not hear what was being said. He signalled Chandra with his eyes to remain on the other side of the four–wheel drive. From where Tilak stood he could see someone on the bungalow veranda peering down at them.

Alagar finished giving his instructions turned to them. 'Stay here with Ravi,' he said. The man who had driven their Pajero detached himself from the group and walked up to the four-wheel drive and stood in front of it with his arms folded across his chest. Alagar signalled the rest of his men who followed him up the path to the bungalow.

The sound of voices speaking in Tamil drifted down from the bungalow, the deep questioning voice of an older man and the higher pitched voice of Alagar. The voices got louder as the older man raised his voice in anger. The sound of a fist striking flesh was followed by the thud of someone falling. An agonised cry from another man was suddenly cut off, the sound echoing in the night.

Tilak glanced at Chandra who had his eyes firmly fixed on the Pajero driver standing in front of the four-wheel drive. Tilak was uncomfortable with the situation he found himself in. Having the union take care of their own problems was a bit of subtlety that made sense to him but why he was asked to be here with Chandra didn't sit well with him.

A sudden movement at the top of the path made him look up. Silhouetted against the light of the bungalow, Alagar appeared, his thick set shape easily recognisable. He was followed by his four henchmen, each pair carrying a body between them.

'Ravi,' he called out. 'Go bring the *Durai's* car from the garage.'

Alagar reached the flat sandy area and watched while his men carried the bodies of the two men towards the garage. Tilak couldn't tell by looking at the men what condition they were in but by the limpness of their bodies and the way their heads flopped around they both looked dead. Alagar saw Tilak studying the bodies. 'They're both dead,' he said. 'We're going to make it look like an accident. The *Durai* had too much to drink tonight and it will look like he lost control of his car.' He watched as Ravi opened one of the garage doors and reversed the old Humber Hawk into the yard.

'You go with Ravi,' he said, waving at one of the men. 'Make sure it happens at that steep bend we passed on our way here. We'll pick you up on our way back.'

They watched as the two men loaded the bodies into the back seat of the Humber and drove it slowly back down the driveway.

'Go and bring the two houseboys down here,' Alagar called out to his men. 'And make sure that no one else is in the bungalow.'

Alagar dug out a pack of cigarettes from his pocket while he waited, lighting it and inhaling deeply. He looked up and blew a stream of smoke up into the night sky. He studiously ignored the two of them, studying the ember of his glowing cigarette.

Two of Alagar's men appeared at the top of the path, each clutching the arm of a houseboy. They were both men, one looked like he was in his late sixties while the other was half his age. They were wearing white jackets with buttoned down mandarin collars. Alagar's goons dragged the terrified houseboys in front of Alagar who studied them thoughtfully. The older houseboy stared back at Alagar bravely, but the younger man was visibly shaking.

'There's no need to be scared,' Alagar said, soothingly. 'You are not going to be hurt. All you have to say when questioned by the police is that the two *Durai's* went out tonight and they didn't say where they were going. The *Durai* had a lot to drink ... he was drinking all afternoon. That's all you need to say. Do you understand?'

Both men nodded nervously, looking down at their feet. 'We will know if there was anything else said to the police,' Alagar stressed. 'Now go and make sure any signs that they were drinking here this evening are cleared up.' The two houseboys bobbed their heads a number of times, relief evident on their faces. They scrambled up the path, both disappearing from sight.

Alagar looked around at his men. 'These two *Durai's* were going to bring untold damage to our people. Make us outcasts in our own country like the Tamils in the north. It will not be allowed. We will follow our own destiny. Make sure that this message is known by everyone.'

Tilak looked at Chandra who shrugged as if to say just leave it alone.

Alagar looked over his shoulder at Tilak and Chandra when they were all back in the car. 'You tell your people what you have seen,' he said. 'They must understand that this was just an isolated group being manipulated by one man for his own purposes. We will be more vigilant in future and not let it happen again.'

The watchman had disappeared, no doubt warned off by Alagar's men. Further down the road, the Humber was burning fiercely in a ravine. It looked like the driver had taken the hairpin bend too fast and gone over the edge. Alagar nodded at the two men who were standing by the side of the road, signalling the driver to continue. Tilak looked at his watch. He was surprised to see that it was not yet midnight. It seemed to him that they had left the hotel many hours ago.

CHAPTER FORTY

NEAR PANKULAM

Danika tried not to scratch the sutures sewn into the bottom of her arm. The neat row of blacklines reminded her repulsively of a hairless centipede crawling its way towards her elbow, but worse than that, it itched constantly. She had suffered the long, deep cut when she crawled through a roll of barbed wire to bury a landmine on a dirt track patrolled regularly by the army. The trail which started in the tree line opposite the camp, was an entry point the soldiers used at times and Danika's section was ordered to mine the track.

The track was deliberately dug up by the soldiers to create potholes. At some points they had placed old battered oil drums to block the track. A big water tank, turned upside down, sat on the ground in the camp. It was the tallest thing around. The soldiers had a sandbagged observation post on top of it which was always manned. It gave them good visibility all around the camp and all it took was one sighting for the soldiers to come boiling out of the camp like hunting dogs.

Being a scout had its advantages but being a woman in a male dominated culture was challenging. Danika had learnt the hard way that Tamil men in general had a huge problem taking orders from a woman. She found the attitude strange since they all followed a religion that worships both men and women as Gods. She knew it was a cultural anomaly and sometimes wondered whether it was the same in other countries.

Talking to the local women without a male being present, her team had soon developed a rapport with the women living in their sector. Before long they had a network set up that fed them information from the local villages. The wives and mothers who came in contact with the army would tell them anything they wanted to know.

Danika picked up her rifle and pulled the charging handle to the rear, even though she knew the weapon was not armed. It was a rule that had been drilled into her head ever since she was shown how to use one. She took a deep breath but couldn't shake the feeling that something was going to happen. Danika prayed that she was wrong but had learned long ago to trust her instincts. She had to be ready for the worst.

Danika walked back along the main road. She'd been on sentry duty at the entrance to the village since dawn. The houses built either with mud or brick were all damaged. One hut was totally burned down. Next to the hut a bigger house, its tiled roof completely shattered. Daylight shone through the large gaps making the inside look bright. A crown of a coconut tree next to the house had been partially lopped off and hung from its trunk. Various bits and pieces of debris lay scattered around the sandy yard.

Danika had seen similar scenes before; the devastation caused by barrel bombs dropped from a plane or a helicopter. She turned down a narrow track past the village that wound through a ruined cashew plantation before entering the jungle. The thick foliage overhead with its branches bent and interlaced with each other, turned the track into a green tunnel, making it totally invisible to any aircraft flying overhead.

The track led to the camp. It was had started to rain and no one was outside. Water dripped from the branches and leaves in a steady stream as Danika ducked into the roofed bunker, its entrance almost invisible in the concealing undergrowth. The underground room was dank and gloomy. There weren't any curtains or even a tablecloth to relieve the dreariness in the dimly lit space. Danika sat with the other women eating their first meal of the day. Indra had found some banana flowers in an abandoned field nearby which she had made into a *poriyal* with boiled *kadala paruppu* and rice.

'This is almost tasteless,' Thangam grumbled as she scooped up a portion in her fingers. 'It needs some chilli and coconut.'

Indra sniggered at her comment. 'I suppose we should go down to the army camp and ask the soldiers to give us what you want.'

Danika kept quiet, content to have some food in her belly. Supplies had to be brought from the coast, usually carried on the backs of new recruits or local villagers conscripted for the task.

By now the rain had become a dense noisy curtain around them. Danika huddled quietly in a corner where a thick plastic sheet directed the rain water away from the bunker keeping it relatively dry. It was hot and steamy, the spray from the deluge coating everything with a thin layer of water.

The rain began to ease and then finally stopped, though the sky remained grey. Danika felt her eyes closing and decided to remain where she was for the moment. She snapped awake when a man's voice called her name out loudly.

'She's in here,' Mala responded, looking at Danika questioningly. Danika shrugged not recognising the voice.

A slightly built, moustached man she had seen before dressed in shirt and trousers, poked his head into the bunker. He was a part of the sector leadership group, but she couldn't remember his name. The man grinned, recognising her. 'Ah, Danika! Sundara wants you to come immediately,' he said, glancing at

Mala apologetically. 'He has something to ask you.'

Mala nodded at Danika who pushed herself to her feet. Sundara was the Sector Commander and held complete command over all the units. Danika had no idea why she was being summoned. She hitched her rifle, settling it firmly on her shoulder before following the man who had started walking up the muddy track.

The heat was unrelenting at that time of the day. It seemed to beat upon them like a hammer, the humidity caused by the recent rains rising up like a steamy curtain. It radiated through even the thick shade of the forest canopy, pounding her mercilessly so that by the time they got to their destination she was slick with sweat and panting with thirst.

CHAPTER FORTY-ONE

PANKULAM, EASTERN PROVINCE

Sami followed the woman into the town. He couldn't believe that this was a contested area, the surroundings were too idyllic. But there were signs painted on the walls in Tamil declaring that he was now in *Tamil Eelam* and that it would be dangerous to cause any trouble. They walked up to a small veranda fronted house where three men sat watching them approach. The men were dressed in nondescript clothing and one carried an AK-47 rifle in the crook of his hand.

The woman militant ignored the men and motioned Sami to enter the front room of the house. An AK-47 rifle leant against the wall next to an ammunition harness with two full pouches. A man emerged from the rear wiping his mouth with the back of his hand. He was about fifty years of age, above average height and had the weather blown features of someone who worked outside. His dull grey eyes devoid of emotion studied the two of them.

'Sundara,' she began. 'This man claims to know Shankar and wants to visit the camp in Vakarai. What do you want me to do with him?'

Sundara regarded Sami impassively. 'How do you know Shankar?' he asked, watching Sami's face intently.

'He was my commander when we fought the army on the Western Highway,' Sami responded. 'Yesterday I met him after two years in Trincomalee. He has allowed me to travel to the refugee camp to find my mother, but I must be back in two days.'

'You are one of the *Marakkalayas* who fought the army,' he said, a ghost of a smile on his lips. 'I thought most of them were dead.'

'I was captured by the army and released only a month ago. I have brought a message to Shankar which requires an answer.'

Sundara stared at Sami thoughtfully. 'It's not that I don't trust you, but I want to make sure who you are. Wait here.' he said, leaving the room.

The room smelt of incense and was completely bare. The half-burnt stubs of incense sticks protruded from a small bowl filled with sand. No pictures or posters adorned the walls. Only a small table in the corner held a statue of Lord Ganesh.

Sundara came back into the room. 'I want you to wait here. If you are who you say you are then I will help you get to Vakarai. There's a tractor leaving at midday with some supplies for the camp. You can go with it and come back the same way tomorrow.'

Sami was pleased with the news. He was wondering how he could get to the camp and back in two days. Sami sat on the floor, his back against the wall. The woman who brought him to the house, leant against the door frame watching him. Sundara had disappeared into a room at the back taking his weapon and ammunition pouches with him. He sat staring at the wall, wondering how his mother was doing. Moving from Kopay with her two elderly parents would have been very difficult. They should have got out when they had the chance two years ago. Sami was happiest for Suria and could imagine her happiness when she was reunited with their mother.

Sami must have dozed as the sound of voices brought him out of his slumber. Sundara came back into the room carrying his rifle. He was followed closely behind by someone Sami could not see. Sundara stepped aside motioning the person forward. For a moment Sami didn't recognise her. Then he realised it was Danika. Her hair was cut short and she had matured into a beautiful young woman.

Danika recognised him instantly, her eyes opening wide in shock. She smiled broadly, her face lighting up in delight. Sami was captivated. He had never seen her look like this before. He had always known her to be angry, consumed by a fire that burned inside her. Their relationship had been antagonistic for a long while but had started softening over time.

'*Vanakkam* Danika,' Sami said with a grin, coming to his feet. 'Rajan told me that you were based around here, but I never expected to see you.'

The last time he had seen Danika was from afar, before he led Para's men away from the camp.

'*Thalaivar* ...' Danika took a step towards him and then stopped. She glanced at Sundara who was watching them closely.

'It is he,' she said, motioning to Sami. 'He led us in the fight for the highway.'

Sundara nodded, looking at Sami calculatingly. 'We have heard about the fight to close the highway,' he said. 'You and your men did well.'

'We couldn't have done it without the help of the women,' Sami responded, inclining his head to Danika. 'They did more than what was expected of them.'

There was a flicker of emotion on Danika's face which Sami almost missed. Without her help they would not have been able to accomplish what they did. He never had a chance to thank her before ... perhaps this was the chance.

Sundara shrugged and walked to the front entrance. 'Jega,' he called out. 'You'll be carrying someone to Vakarai when you leave. Make sure he comes back with you.'

Sami stepped out onto the veranda. The three men sitting outside looked at him with more interest, more respect. They would have heard what was discussed in the room.

'Have you eaten?' The woman militant who had brought him to the house asked him brusquely. She had been there the whole time.

Sami shook his head. 'No, nothing since last night.'

The woman looked at Danika. Something passed between them that Sami did not catch. 'Come with us,' she said, inclining her head to the right. 'Jega won't be leaving for another hour.'

Danika looked at him curiously. Her eyes, which were large and fringed with long lashes, sparkled with intelligence. 'Are you alright?' she asked softly. Sami nodded without speaking. He suddenly felt an enormous affection for this woman.

Sami followed the two women deeper into the village, which looked empty. Many of the houses were pockmarked with bullet holes, the tiles on their roofs shattered and broken. A mangy looking dog lay across the road in the hot sun, fast asleep.

The woman militant, whose name was Sita, led them down a side road hidden by trees, to a small house set in a yard. The ground was covered in smooth raked sand, a Margosa tree and other smaller trees shaded the whole yard. Within walking distance was a sizeable well next to a large vegetable garden. A woman in her forties dressed in a sari stood at the door.

'This is Santhosa,' Sita said. 'She will feed the two of you. Once you finish go back to where Jega was. He will pick you up from there.' Sita watched Sami to make sure he understood, then nodded. 'I have to go back to the guard post.'

The house had two small rooms with tiny windows and a small cooking area blackened with soot from the wood fires. The stove was just local clay moulded into pot supports. A photograph of a young boy hung on one of the walls. Sami wondered whether the young man had joined the Tigers. The Tigers demanded that each family give one child to the movement. But not every parent wanted their children to join the Tigers even if they supported the cause. The woman motioned Sami and Danika to sit on a reed mat on the floor and went to the rear of the house.

Danika had kept her head down the whole time, not looking around as they walked through the village. Sami had been struggling to keep his eyes off her. She was dressed like the other women he met that morning, although she wore a pair of dark socks and runners on her feet. Sami felt strange, as if an open wound had closed and another had opened.

'What happened to you that day after I left with Ismail?' he asked Danika. Sami felt a twinge of regret thinking of the young man. Ismail had saved his life in the jungle and Sami would never forget him.

Danika looked at him with clear penetrating eyes. 'We got away,' she said simply. 'One of your men was wounded and needed help. We stayed with them as far as the coast.'

Sami nodded. It was how they had planned it. But losing Ismail was not meant to happen.

'What happened to Ismail?' Danika asked. 'I heard later that they had killed a man and I thought it was you.'

'I know you sent him to help me and he was killed trying to keep me alive,' Sami said, his heart clenching in regret. 'He was killed by one of Para's men who followed me.' He shook his head regretfully. 'He was a brave young man.'

Danika turned and looked at him in the eye seeing love and warmth there. Her eyes filled with moisture. 'Until I saw you just now I thought you were dead.' Her voice choked. She lowered her head and looked at the ground. 'I have regretted all these years that I always pushed you away. I only realised what I had done after I thought I'd lost you.'

Sami stared at Danika in surprise. He had wanted the Tigers to think he had died in the western jungles so that they wouldn't extract revenge on his family. But he hadn't realised that Danika had taken it so badly.

Danika raised her head and looked into his eyes. 'You are going away again, and I don't want you to leave without letting you know how I feel.'

Before Sami could say anything, the woman brought in two chipped ceramic plates served with a fragrant pile of white rice and a mixed vegetable curry. She handed the plates over and brought a bowl of water which she placed on the floor between them.

Sami smiled gratefully at her and waited until Danika dipped her fingers in the bowl to clean them before doing so himself. Their fingers touched as she withdrew her hand sending a jolt of electricity through Sami's body. Danika must have felt it too as she glanced at him, blushing when she saw him watching her.

The woman stood and watched them eat. Sami wanted to say something to Danika and glanced at her surreptitiously only to see her doing the same. They both grinned at each other before concentrating on the food. They ate the rice and curried vegetables, mixing them with the tips of their finger and using their thumbs to scoop the mixture into their mouths.

Sami quickly finished eating, wishing to talk to Danika before he left. They washed their hands and thanked the woman before leaving the house.

'Danika,' Sami began as they walked back up the lane towards the main road. 'I have thought about you often and now that I've met you again, I have realised what you have meant to me.' He stopped and turned to Danika. 'I am going to Vakarai to look for my mother, but I have to be back in two days for a meeting with Shankar. I will have to take his answer back.' Sami reached for her hand and clasped it gently. 'But once I settle my family in Colombo I shall come back for you.' Sami looked deep into her eyes. 'Will you wait for me?'

Sami felt like pulling Danika to him and showing her how much he cared for her but resisted the temptation. He understood the strict code of conduct within the Tiger organisation and that public displays of affection were frowned upon. He didn't want Danika to get into any trouble.

Danika squeezed his hand in acceptance. 'There is nothing more I would want from this life,' she said, smiling through her tears. 'I am sorry for treating you so badly. You have always treated me with respect and kindness.'

Sami leaned forward and kissed her gently on her forehead before letting go of her hand and taking a step back. It wasn't a moment too soon as the rattle and roar of a tractor on the road signalled that Jega was on his way.

CHAPTER FORTY-TWO

NEAR PANKULAM

Danika tossed and turned, trying hard to fall asleep. The feeling that she'd worked hard all day to keep in check, had finally overwhelmed her and sat heavily across her chest. Turning onto her back, she looked up at the sky and the clusters of bright silver that filled it. She had never seen the stars so bright before. Thinking about the vastness of the sky made her head spin and she closed her eyes against its beauty for a moment.

She had felt her heart skip a beat when she recognised Sami. He looked different from when she last saw him but there was no denying it was the *Thalaivar*. His face had filled out and his calm, penetrating eyes looked at her in obvious delight. She had taken a step towards him instinctively, stopping when she realised there were others in the room watching. She had to take a deep breath and it had almost taken a physical effort not to reach out for him.

The time she'd spent with him had gone too quickly. She had gone over each moment in her mind and still felt the gentle kiss on her forehead. Thinking about Sami made her feel a delightful, warm sensation welling up in her. Her heart beat painfully, and tears clouded her eyes. It was a feeling she'd never experienced before. It had been years since she had allowed any of her emotions to surface. She couldn't believe that it had all happened so quickly.

Even now to remember the time when she'd heard that Sami was killed filled her with a choking, hopeless sensation. She remembered not sleeping a wink that night. The familiar sensation of anger almost overwhelmed her. Anger at what had happened. She had been told that the men she had shared food with, fought with, who saved her life, were dead. She had suppressed her feelings so much at the time, buried it so deep that it had taken the shock of seeing Sami for her to realise how she had felt.

On her way back, at the roadside shrine close to the camp, Danika knelt in supplication, her head bowed with arms raised above her head, her palms together in prayer. She ran her hands over the oil lamp flame, praying that she would survive the war and meet Sami again. She tried to focus on the future, a time when the war was over.

The entire team were lounging around the bunker when she finally got back that evening. Danika nodded her head in greeting, avoiding looking at the four women directly.

'What was that all about?' Mala asked Danika as she placed her rifle against the back wall. Mala was their leader and although she treated all the women with respect, she took her position seriously. Danika's heart beat hard against her ribs, and she tried to demonstrate control through her posture. She glanced at Mala and lowered her eyes when she saw the woman scrutinising her closely.

'You're acting strangely since you met that man,' Mala said with a half-smile. 'Is he the *Marakkalaya* you have talked about before? You said he was dead.'

Danika felt the intensity of their gaze and decided they deserved to know what was on her mind. They were like her family, women she'd fought with. As the emotion threatened to wash over her, she took a deep breath. 'Okay,' she said, returning with effort from her thoughts. 'His name is Sami and he was with us on the western front.' She paused, her eyes staring into the distance. 'I was told he had died.'

'He must be pretty special,' Thangam smiled, glancing at the others. 'What happened between the two of you?'

'It was about two years ago,' she began softly, looking down. 'We were together for months. They were all my friends and I was very sad when they died.'

'But what about the *Marakkalaya*', Indra asked impatiently, 'was there something between the two of you?'

'No', Danika shook head passionately. 'I was rude to him and actually treated him quite badly.' Her eyes filled with tears remembering. 'The truth was that my life was in chaos.' Danika took a deep breath. 'I had left my parents and sister in a refugee camp in India and I was all alone. He was the only one who showed me any kindness.'

The four women were looking at Danika intently. She had never opened up to anyone before, but she felt she needed to say what she'd been suppressing for so long.

'I was so tired and worn out. I couldn't think anymore and didn't want to.' Danika paused. 'The strength that was driving me all that time suddenly disappeared and I didn't know why.'

'It's because you love him,' Indra said, nodding knowingly. She was the only one in the team who had a secret lover.

Danika looked at Indra in disbelief. *In love...was that what she was feeling?* She'd never considered that she would have such feelings for Sami. But somewhere in all those jumbled thoughts and emotions, she sensed that Indra was right. She had found the root of her feelings.

CHAPTER FORTY-THREE

NEAR TRINCOMALEE

Sami sat waiting in the darkened room for Shankar to appear. The meeting had been arranged for that night and he was left with two armed men, one who watched him from across the room.

The trip down to the refugee camp in Vakarai hadn't been a total waste of time. Sami had learnt from the Camp Coordinator that his mother and his grand-mother had been in the camp and had moved to Batticaloa at their own request. He had missed them by just a few days. Sami was hoping that his mother had gone to his father's family home in Kathankudi, a Muslim town just south of Batticaloa. She would be safe there, but he had no way of checking. Sami wondered again what had happened to his grand-father. He was in his late seventies, perhaps even in his eighties. Sami couldn't remember when the old man had been born. It would have broken his grandfather's heart to leave Jaffna where he had lived all his life. He didn't want to think about the possibility that the old man hadn't made it.

Sami's thoughts invariably moved to Danika as they did hundreds of times every day. He had left her by the side of the road, watching him leave. His heart constantly ached for her and he couldn't stop trying to think of different ways to see her again. Sami tried to imagine how she must be thinking, the sudden joy that the impossible had happened, that Sami had returned from the dead. One thing was certain. He couldn't afford to lose her again. She filled an emptiness in his life and he knew that he would be devastated if he never saw her again.

A flash of light followed by the sound of muttered voices outside the room alerted Sami that it was time for the meeting. He sat on the ground waiting expectantly for Shankar to appear.

Footsteps receded, a door opened and closed. The man standing by the doorway was relaxed but alert. His eyes never left Sami. He would have heard the same sounds Sami was hearing but he was not distracted by them. It was very dark in the room. Only the diffused moonlight which filtered through the trees allowed some light through the small barred window.

Sami shifted his body, trying to get comfortable on the unyielding concrete floor. He was about to say something when he heard footsteps approaching. There was some movement by the door and someone entered the room.

'Come,' a familiar voice called out. It was Rajan.

Sami struggled from his sitting position, his right leg had gone to sleep. He flexed his leg and followed Rajan who had stepped out into the corridor. Rajan led Sami to an area which was lit by a kerosene lantern. The wick was turned down low, barely illuminating the whole space. The room was empty except for a table and two chairs. Rajan motioned for Sami to sit and pulled back the other chair, sitting opposite him.

Rajan leaned forward. 'Shankar cannot make it,' he said quietly. 'But he has given me a message for you.'

Sami looked at Rajan apprehensively. It didn't matter to him that Shankar was not there to deliver the answer. As long as there was something to take back to Colombo. Sami wanted to get out of the refugee camp he had been living in and bring his mother and grand-mother home. Only the success of his mission would determine whether he was going to get what he wanted or be discarded as he had been before.

'They have agreed to open talks with the government,' he said smiling. 'But, it must be without the knowledge of India.'

Sami grinned at Rajan. He knew that Rajan had never believed that a military solution would be reached, and the only way forward was through political and cultural reconciliation.

'Are they serious?' he asked Rajan. There had been the well-publicised peace talks in Bhutan which had failed dismally.

'Yes,' Rajan nodded. 'Having the Indians here does not give us a *Tamil Eelam*. We just become another bunch of people for the Indian central government to manage and New Delhi is thousands of kilometres away. I think *Anna* knows this and has always been opposed to them being invited here. But there are some in the movement who don't think it's a good idea,' he shrugged.

Sami considered what Rajan was saying. It was true that the Tiger leader had never given his support to the Indian peace accord and his men were now in open warfare, especially in the Jaffna Peninsula. If he was prepared to open discussions with the Sri Lankan government, it was a major concession and a big step forward. Something this momentous would have its detractors. Sami knew that it would be the same on the government side. But that was not his problem.

'Ok, I will take your message back.' Sami thought for a moment. 'We should also figure out a way we can communicate easily. We cannot have long delays for messages to get through and be answered when it's something important like this.'

Rajan nodded. 'We'll figure something out. When do you want to leave?'

'Tomorrow morning,' Sami said. 'On the first bus out of here.'

'Can't you send a message through the army camp in Trincomalee?' Rajan wanted to know.

'I can, I suppose but they don't know I am here and I am not sure how many people should know what's going on,' Sami said thoughtfully. 'And anyway, I want to get to Batticaloa which will be easier from Colombo.'

'I am glad to know that your mother is safe in Batticaloa,' Rajan said. 'She's truly a very wonderful person.'

Sami had not spoken to Rajan about what he had found out about his family, but he would have got the information from Jega or Sundara. For a moment Sami was tempted to tell Rajan that he had met Danika, but something held him back. It was not that he didn't trust Rajan, but he wanted to isolate Danika from everything that was going on. There would be time in the future to enlist Rajan's help with her.

∽

The bus station was crowded in the early morning. The bus stands were packed with people slumped on concrete benches staring vacantly at the buses pulling in and out of the busy yard. Stray dogs wandered between the bus stands looking for scraps of food. The overcrowded buses, their fuel tanks filled with cheap diesel, belched noxious fumes through which people rushed carrying all types of bags and packages.

Sami folded the ticket to Anuradhapura and placed it in his shirt pocket. The morning service to Colombo was already full of passengers who had prepaid for a seat on the bus. Sami was not too concerned; the Colombo bus went through the ancient capital and he didn't think he'd have a problem finding transport from the city whose central location allowed access to all parts of the island.

What occupied his thoughts was the short discussion he'd had with Rajan before he left the safe house that morning. Rajan had motioned him out into the predawn darkness of the garden. A rooster from a nearby house crowed loudly as it anticipated the beginning of another day.

'I want to tell you something important before you leave,' Rajan said seriously, looking around to make sure they were alone.

Sami, who had not slept much thinking about Danika, looked at Rajan who was just a dark shadow against the garden foliage.

'There's a Tiger cell operating in Colombo who are planning an attack,' said Rajan, leaning forward. 'I am telling you this at great personal risk.'

'Why would they do that?' Sami asked confused. 'This is not a good time to piss off the people in charge.'

'I know, I know.' Rajan responded fiercely. 'It's exactly the point I made. But there are some hot heads in the organisation who believe they can fight the Indians and the government at the same time.'

'Do you think Prabhakaran knows this?' Sami asked Rajan. 'I would think it will make it difficult to find any support for talks if bombs go off in Colombo.'

'I don't know if he knows. All I know is that it's going to happen in the next few weeks. You have to find them and stop them.'

Sami nodded in the dark. There was a lot to think about. 'I will pass on the news,' he said. 'But there is not much I can do. Can you give me any more information about the cell in Colombo?'

'All I know is that they are the same people responsible for the Central Bus Station bombing,' he said. 'So, they have done it before.' Rajan grasped Sami's arm. 'I know you met Danika. If you want to see her again there has to be a ceasefire between us. They must not take this threat lightly.'

Sami stiffened at Rajan's words. It sounded like a threat to him. Rajan reacted immediately to Sami's body language. 'No, no,' he said in a placatory tone. 'I didn't mean it to sound like that. What I am saying is that we cannot fight two forces. We're not strong enough to do that. Many of our people will die, so if you want to protect her, you have to make sure it doesn't happen.'

Although the darkness was receding, Sami could barely make out Rajan's features. Sami knew Rajan well. They had first met briefly in Lebanon and Rajan had been with him while he had trained and fought as a part of the

Tiger organisation. He had trusted Rajan in the past, but he knew that people changed.

'You must find out more about this cell,' Sami insisted. 'If you think it's that important, I will need more information. Names, location, target, how they plan to do it.' Sami ticked off each point on his finger.

'It will be a bomb for sure,' Rajan said nodding. 'The materials are already there, and the bomb maker is leaving soon. That's all I know.'

'Ok, I'll pass that information to my contact when I get to Colombo. If you have any more intelligence on the cell, you'll have to get it to me somehow. The police, the army … whoever you can use. Get them to send the message to Captain Anderson. He'll be the person I'll be talking to.'

Rajan nodded and then stared at Sami with a sheepish expression on his face. 'One more thing,' he said. 'Can you give this to Suria.' He handed Sami an envelope. Sami took the envelope from Rajan before folding it and sliding it into his trouser pocket. Rajan held Sami's gaze for a moment without saying anything before brushing past him and walking into the house. That was the last time Sami saw Rajan before he left.

CHAPTER FORTY-FOUR

COLOMBO

The news that a terrorist cell was operating in the city had pushed everything else to the background. The Colonel wanted to meet with Sami after his debriefing and David had raised it with Sami that morning.

Sami didn't understand why the officer in charge of military intelligence wanted to meet him, but David had insisted. 'I think it'll be good for you to meet the Colonel,' David said. 'We'll need his agreement to move your family to Colombo.'

The meeting was at the army headquarters building in Slave Island in the Colonel's office. The officer studied Sami from across the table. 'So, you're the one who was a thorn in our side for so long,' he said bluntly. 'Your small unit tactics have been studied and measures to counter them are being taught at the advanced infantry training course in Boossa.'

A slight smile was Sami's only reaction to what the Colonel said. David had heard that the army were studying all their clashes with the Tigers, trying to learn what went right or wrong. But he didn't know that the fight for the Western Highway was on the training school curriculum.

The Colonel waited a few seconds. 'I never got the opportunity to thank you for saving Priyani and this man here,' he added, waving his hand at David.

Sami nodded without saying anything. David could sense that he felt uncomfortable receiving praise.

'The reason I asked you here because I wanted to meet you face to face before I made up my mind.' The Colonel was observing Sami as he spoke.

David looked at the Colonel in surprise. *What was he up to?*

The Colonel glanced at David before continuing. 'I see that you have cut all your ties to the Tigers and become a good citizen. I have heard that you have been responsible for eliminating some of the criminal elements who were taking advantage of the refugees in your camp. You have anything to say about that?'

Sami shrugged. 'What is there to say? They were preying on the weak and took advantage of my sister. I did what anyone in my position would have done.'

'Hmm,' the Colonel muttered. 'I am not too sure about that. But the point is that you are no longer being manipulated by the Tigers. If your family is brought here, then you have nothing to worry about … is that right?'

Sami's eyes narrowed, and he glanced at David before replying. 'Yes, that's correct. You know I had to join the Tigers to protect my family. If they are out of harm, it won't happen again.'

The Colonel nodded, looking pleased. 'Then I have a proposal for you. I will have your family evacuated from Batticaloa immediately. In fact, it can happen tomorrow if we come to an agreement. In return I want you to join military intelligence.'

Both David and Sami stared at the Colonel in shock. Sami sat back in his chair, looking first at David and then back at the Colonel. He could see that

David was as surprised as he was.

The Colonel waited for the two of them to recover from their surprise. 'Think about it from my, well our point of view,' he said, including David with a wave of his hand. 'You're a well-trained soldier who's had military experience in more than one country. You have an intimate knowledge of the militant organisation and their tactics. You have fought with them and against them. You will be a great asset to us.'

David listened to what the Colonel was saying and could not find any fault with his logic. It was so obvious that David kicked himself mentally for not thinking about it himself.

Sami was clearly thinking about the Colonel's proposition. The Colonel watched him impatiently, waiting for him to respond.

Sami finally spoke; 'What do you mean by joining military intelligence?' he asked. 'I don't want to join the army.'

'You don't have to join the army,' the Colonel said smiling. 'We have operatives who are either ex-servicemen or people whom we have recruited off the street with some skill or experience to provide us with valuable information. You have both in abundance.' He laced his fingers and studied Sami for a moment. 'I am prepared to offer you a fixed-term contract. Like we do with the contractors we bring from overseas. You won't get the same benefits,' he shrugged, 'but you will become an official member of the armed forces. Your expertise will be recognised and rewarded.'

Sami's eyes flickered to David, trying to read his expression. David gazed frankly back at him. Sami would be an asset to military intelligence if he agreed to the Colonel's proposal. David did not have any problem with it.

'If you are looking for me to say anything,' David said, 'I am all for it. I can only see benefit for both sides.'

Sami nodded thoughtfully after studying David for a moment. 'Yes,' he said. 'I will do it. But I also want immunity for what happened before. I don't want someone deciding in the future that I am no longer of any use. Those are my terms.'

The Colonel sat forward enthusiastically. 'I wouldn't have expected anything less,' he said. 'General Ratwatte and I talked about what you would ask for in return and immunity from the terrorism act was the obvious one. He's taking it to the President and I expect an answer soon.'

David sat back in his chair thoughtfully. He had not seen this coming, but it opened many possibilities. He needed to sit with Sami and go over all the options open to them. However, before they did that, there was a terrorist cell to find.

CHAPTER FORTY-FIVE

CENTRAL COLOMBO

The phone rang jarringly, the sound intruding on his troubled dreams as he drifted towards consciousness. David groaned as he opened his eyes. It was dark, he felt as if he had just gone to sleep. Priyani shifted next to him, turning around and pulling the sheet over her head.

David reached for the phone on the bedside table. 'Yes,' he grunted. He cleared his throat swallowing a gob of phlegm.

'Captain Anderson?' the voice on the phone questioned. 'This is the operations room. We have a flash priority message for you.'

David struggled to clear his head of sleep. All matters relating to military intelligence came through the main JOC operations desk. There were specific procedures to be followed depending on the importance of the message. David struggled upright and sat on the side of the bed. The concrete floor felt cool beneath his bare feet.

'What time is it?' he groaned into the phone fumbling for his wristwatch in the dark. 'Shit,' he muttered, knocking it onto the floor.

An amused voice on the phone responded. 'It's a quarter past one, Sir.'

David gave up trying to feel for the wristwatch on the floor and bent his head, rubbing it sleepily with one hand.

'Ok, what is it?' he growled. It had been a while since he had been woken up at that time of the morning.

'Shall I read the message to you Sir?' the voice asked. 'It's from Bandarawela.'

David's mind cleared. It must be from Mukesh. With all the excitement of trying to sort out Sami and the valuable information he had brought, he had forgotten all about his operative.

David shook his head in annoyance. 'Yes, yes,' he responded. 'Go ahead.'

'The message reads ... Have identified head of the movement. My position is getting difficult. Need instructions on next step.' After a short pause the voice continued. 'It ends with the letter M.'

David thought hard for a moment. The bomb threat in Colombo was the immediate concern. But if Mukesh had identified the man who was heading the separatist movement in the estates, it was a big win.

'Do you want me to repeat the message?' the voice on the phone asked, not hearing a response from David.

'No, no, I got it,' David responded, thoughtfully.' Thanks.'

David quickly made up his mind. 'I want you to make sure the Colonel has a copy on his desk by morning. I'll be in early to brief him.'

❧

David woke up early. He had slept fitfully, images chasing themselves through his mind, one intruding on another until he woke up feeling irritated and tired. Priyani had woken up with him and watched him from the kitchen table as he filled the kettle and placed it on the stove.

'You were tossing and turning all night,' she grumbled, running her fingers through her luxuriant hair. 'What was the call about?'

David had moved out of the Officer's quarters and moved in with Priyani. They were still getting used to each other's habits and he was hoping that she would not object to him receiving phone calls at all hours of the day and night.

'It was a flash priority message from one of my operatives,' he said. 'I'll have to go in early to brief the Colonel.'

'Does this happen often?' She asked. 'The late-night phone calls I mean.'

'Only if it's a flash priority,' he explained. 'There are different types of messages and only the most important get that designation.'

David poured the boiling water from the kettle into two mugs, stirring in the instant coffee granules and handed one to Priyani.

'Urgh,' Priyani grunted taking a sip from the steam brew. 'There's no sugar.'

David grinned sheepishly while spooning in a heaped teaspoon of sugar. 'Is one enough?'

Priyani nodded, as she stirred the chocolaty brown mixture. She cradled the mug in her hands, inhaling its aroma and took a sip. 'Ah, that's better.'

They sat in silence, each lost in their own thoughts. David was mentally going over what needed to be done that day when Priyani spoke. 'Amanthi wants us to have dinner with her. She's seeing someone and wants us to meet him.'

'Ok,' David nodded. 'I can make dinner most days unless there is an emergency. This week won't be good but one day late next week should be fine.'

David finished his coffee and went into the room to have a shower and get changed. Priyani was still sitting at the table when he was ready to leave.

'You seem very preoccupied today,' she said, looking at him questioningly. 'Something's bothering you.'

'There's a lot going on,' he said, bending down and kissing her on the forehead. 'I'll try to come back for dinner, but I cannot promise. I'll call you if I am going to be late.'

David let himself out and walked to the main road, waving at a taxi which pulled up next to him. He was deep in thought as the vehicle negotiated the busy street. The Colonel was climbing the stairs to the second floor when David came up behind him.

'Good morning David,' said the Colonel. 'You're not usually in this early?'

'Morning Sir,' David responded. 'A flash priority message came in early this morning from up country,' he said. 'Mukesh has identified the man behind the movement.'

The Colonel raised his eyebrows and looked at David. 'That's good news,' he said. 'Do you know who it is?'

David shook his head. 'No Sir, the message did not say. He'll have to be debriefed.'

The Colonel opened his office door and snapped on the overhead light. He picked up the flash priority folder on his desk and studied its contents.

'Doesn't say much,' he agreed. The Colonel looked more carefully at the message. 'It's dated three days ago. It must have been held up by Special Branch.'

David couldn't understand why the message had been delayed. He had objected to getting Special Branch involved and they were already meddling in his case. Mukesh was his man and handing over an open case which had the potential to destroy the country did not sit well with him. But he had agreed it was not a military matter and was best handled by the civilian authorities.

'Ok,' David nodded. 'Shouldn't we be pulling Mukesh back to Diyatalawa for a debrief? We can do a proper handover to Special Branch.'

'Hold off on doing anything until I speak to my counterpart,' the Colonel said, shaking his head. 'I heard that they already have a team up there poking around. Mukesh would already have been interviewed by them.'

What the Colonel was saying made sense to David. The issue in the plantations had nothing to do with the military except for an unconfirmed connection to the Tigers.

'Ok,' he said. 'I'll back off completely and let you handle it.' David looked at the Colonel who had sat down and was leafing through a small pile of files on his desk. 'Have you heard back from General Ratwatte about the indemnity for Sami? I could use him right away.'

'I have a meeting with the General this morning,' the Colonel said, looking up from his papers. 'I'll make sure to ask him.'

David left the Colonel's office disappointed that bureaucracy and red tape was getting in the way. *Didn't they understand the importance of what was happening upcountry?* He would give it twenty-four hours and if he didn't hear back from the Colonel he would do whatever was necessary.

CHAPTER FORTY-SIX

NORTHERN SUBURBS, COLOMBO

The streets of the city were silent and dark. It was almost eleven thirty and the very large police and military presence in the city had driven many of its inhabitants indoors. Only the occasional person hurrying home from a late-night shift broke the stillness of the night. Young khaki-clad soldiers wearing green berets, their rifles strapped across their chests with the barrels hanging down, stood at every street corner watching.

Sami listened to the hum of the powerful Land Rover engine as David drove through an affluent area of large, white colonial mansions surrounded by walled tropical gardens. Large trees lined the wide streets, their branches touching overhead creating the impression of driving through a dark tunnel.

They were going to meet the person coordinating the search for the militant cell in the northern part of the city. Home to many small industries, warehouses and Colombo's biggest slums, most of the militant safe houses that were discovered in the city were from this area.

David stared alertly at the road ahead, wary of being flagged down by one of the many army patrols that roamed the city at night. The military vehicle they were in gave them some form of immunity against being stopped and questioned, but the threat of the militant cell in the city had everybody's nerves on edge.

The quiet drive gave Sami time to set things in perspective, to run through the events of the last few days in his mind. He had moved back into his family home at Wellawatte which had been empty since they left for Jaffna almost three years ago. Their neighbours, the LaBrooy's, had been looking after the house, using the money from the trust fund Sami had set up after his father's death, to hire a local woman to dust and clean the house.

'There's quite a bit of money in the account,' Michael said smiling. 'I was able to put pressure on your father's Middle East agent to pay up.'

Sami raised his eyebrows in surprise. The man had owed his father a lot of money for five or six shipments of fresh fruit and vegetables. Sami had given up any hope of repatriating the funds.

'I got him black listed from dealing with anyone else in the country,' Michael said proudly. 'He paid up what he owed, plus interest to get off the list. He'll be a good contact if you want to start up your father's business again. He's learnt his lesson.'

Michael was a chartered accountant working for a law firm in the Fort. Sami had left him to deal with his father's business after it had been burnt during the outbreak of violence that followed the killing of a patrol of Sinhalese soldiers in Jaffna. Sami had subsequently found out that his father and brother were killed by a gang of rivals who wanted to control the lucrative export of fresh food to the Middle East from the port of Colombo.

Sami had grown up with Michael at a time when race and creed were no barriers to friendships that lasted the test of time. Even though Michael came from a Burgher family of Dutch origin, the two families who lived next to each other were extremely close. Sami's Moorish and Michael's European heritages had no bearing on how the two families interacted, respecting each other's cultures and religions as if they were their own.

Michael's mother, Melanie had quickly taken command of the home, accompanying Suria to the local market and helping her buy provisions for the household.

It was clear to Sami that Suria was happier than she had been for a while. She had never wanted to leave Colombo and had missed her friends and the familiar, comfortable life that she was used to in the city. Jaffna had been an alien place, changing her into a sad, brooding young woman, which had broken Sami's heart.

Sami smiled knowing that the old Suria was returning. That morning, their cook, who they had known since they were children, had come back from the village to work in the household. Suria had danced around the room in joy, welcoming the old woman like she was a long-lost family member. She helped the servant put away her meagre belongings in the tiny room at the rear of the home built for that purpose.

'We'll have to show our passes here,' David said, glancing at Sami.

They were in the sprawling suburb of Grandpass, a collection of ramshackle shantytowns and commercial buildings covered with billboards of every size and description.

The two bridges which were the main gateway to the city from the north and central parts of the country were heavily guarded by both the police and the army. David drove up the old bridge, with its elevated causeway spanning a large area of slums. On either side of the road a jumble of corrugated-iron roofs fell towards the banks of the fast running Kelaniya River. Two checkpoints, one at each end of the bridge were covered by sandbagged, corrugated-iron sentry posts, out of which protruded the menacing barrels of heavy machine guns.

David lowered his headlights and flicked on the interior light of the Land

Rover as he slowly drove up to the barrier. The checkpoint was manned by members of the notorious Special Task Force. The troopers looked alert, studying the occupants of the vehicle warily as it cruised to a stop.

'Papers.' The trooper bent at the waist and looked into the Land Rover, scanning the interior of the vehicle before stepping back.

David glanced at Sami, who handed his new set of papers across to David.

'We're both from military intelligence,' David said, handing their papers to the trooper. The trooper scanned both sets of papers before handing them back, motioning for the barrier to be raised. The scene was repeated at the other end of the long bridge where army soldiers manned the checkpoint.

David took the Negombo Road and turned into the Wattala Police Station located near the bridge over the old Dutch Canal. The search was being coordinated by a Superintendent of Police who had control of a vast collection of police and military units. David, dressed in civilian clothes, acknowledged the senior officer by coming to attention.

'Captain Anderson and Sergeant Deen reporting as ordered.' They had decided to use a fictitious name to keep Sami's real identity a secret. His rank of Sergeant in military intelligence was assigned at David's request. It would make it easier to move around and avoid being questioned.

The Superintendent looked stressed as he frowned at the two men irritably. 'I've been wondering when you were going to show up,' he said. 'We have men moving into position right now and will kick off the operation at dawn.'

'What are we hoping to find?' David asked. He had not known that a specific operation had been planned. His orders were to report to the Superintendent at the Wattala Police Station by midnight.

'We have been investigating the recent bus bombing in Maradana,' the Superintendent said tiredly. 'A man and a woman were moving the bomb somewhere we think, and it went off prematurely. We traced the identity of the couple to a militant cell operating out of Batticaloa and raided the place. We found a stash of weapons and bomb making materials and captured a man who turned out to be the bomb maker.' He paused looking at David and Sami. 'It turns out he was the one who had built the central bus station and the Maradana bus bombs. And he was working on another.'

The Superintendent moved over to a large map pinned on the wall. He tapped on a location circled in red on the map. 'Under interrogation he revealed the location of the safe house here in Wattala.'

'Sounds promising.' David walked up to the map and looked at it. The address marked on the map was in a small narrow street leading off a junction on the old Negombo Road. The area was a rabbit's warren of low income housing built during the 1930's by private landowners for labourers who were engaged in the processing and shipment of tea and rubber from the thriving plantation industry.

'Hmm, have you sent anyone to take look at the place?' He asked. 'It's pretty congested and there may be other exits.'

'Yes,' the officer nodded. 'We have, but there's nothing much to see. We have cordoned off the area and will hold everyone within that circle for questioning.'

Sami looked around as David interacted with the Superintendent. It was the first time he had been in a military operations room. Men dressed in both khaki and camouflaged military fatigues huddled over radios and maps, while others hurried in and out of the room carrying messages and attending to other duties. It reminded him of a similar room in Beirut, from where Captain Shafiq had commanded the northern defence of the city.

David walked over to where Sami was standing. 'They seem to have it covered,' he said looking around. 'I think we'll stay here and wait for the operation to end. It doesn't make sense going over there. We'll see the big picture here.'

Sami and David walked over to the room that served as the kitchen. They prepared steaming hot glasses of tea for themselves and went outside the police station, sitting on a wooden bench in front of the building.

The sky was partially covered by dark clouds that loomed ominously in the west, though it had hardly rained that day. Sami wondered what Danika would be doing … whether she was also looking up at the sky like he was. She was never far from his thoughts. Getting her out of the clutches of the Tigers would be a major challenge and it kept eating away at him. There had to be a way. He felt David's eyes on him and turned his head.

'You were far away,' David said, looking at him sympathetically. 'Don't worry about your mother and grand-mother. All the arrangements have been made and they will be back in Colombo on Friday.'

Sami nodded thankfully. Now if he could only get Danika out. David was watching him enquiringly. It was like he was probing his deepest thoughts.

'Something has been bothering you since you came back,' he said. 'I thought you were worried about your mother but now I know it's not that. Do you want to talk about it?'

Sami shook his head to clear his mind. Getting Danika back would not be easy and Rajan might not be in a position to help. The Militant Commander outside Trincomalee, Sundara, had looked experienced and it would not be easy to fool him. Sami had helped David escape with Priyani when they were being hunted by the Tigers. Did it make sense to tell David about Danika and ask for his help? The more Sami thought about it the more sense it made.

Sami turned to David. 'Yes,' he said. 'Something has been worrying me and I need help.'

❧

David studied the sky above him with a certain sense of detachment. His face showed no emotion at what Sami had just told him. He remembered how he had felt when Priyani had been captured by the Tigers and completely understood Sami's feelings. He looked at Sami. 'I understand how you feel. It was the same with me and Priyani.'

David paused, trying to figure out how to answer. He would help Sami rescue Danika but first they had to find and stop the militant cell.

'I will help you,' he said finally. 'But we have to think this through carefully. And you will have to wait until we sort this mess out.'

Sami nodded. 'Thank you,' he said. 'I am a patient man and Danika has waited all this time. A few more days won't matter.'

David heard a sense of relief in Sami's voice. Sami had carried his love for this woman since he had escaped from his pursuers almost three years ago. David couldn't imagine how difficult that must be for him.

A light breeze rustled the leaves on the bushes separating the police station from the road, bringing with it the smell of rain. David looked down at his watch. It was after four in the morning. He hadn't realised they had been sitting outside for over two hours.

CHAPTER FORTY-SEVEN

NEAR TRINCOMALEE

For a while there was no sound but the chorus of birds and insects from the forest. Then, faintly at first, but growing steadily louder, they heard the noise of an aircraft engine. As it moved closer they could pick up the staccato beat of rotors. The attack helicopter passed within a kilometre of them, heading east as it made for the airfield at Trincomalee.

Mala, Danika and Thangam crouched under a giant Banyan tree, merging with the mesh of large roots which were characteristic of its species. Through the canopy of leathery, glossy leaves, the jungle camouflage paint of the aircraft made it stand out vividly against the grey sky. From a distance the attack pods on their stub wings, the bulbous shapes of the pilot's and gunner's cockpits, and the double air intakes, gave them the look of an ugly flying beetle.

The team had been given a mission to scout an area south of Pankulam known as the Naval Headworks Sanctuary. West of Trincomalee, the large forested area was regularly patrolled by the military to keep the Tigers from controlling the area. It was directly under the flight path for military aircraft landing at the China Bay Naval Station making it a hotly contested area.

The marks of war were everywhere: ruined buildings, burned crops and abandoned villages although a few orange and mango trees still grew, they were often surrounded by scorched marks where huts had been burned to the ground. The few people visible working the remaining rice fields all looked very old or very young.

In the distance Danika heard gunshots, the single rounds of a sniper. She looked across at Mala and forced a smile.

Moving with care, they paused often to listen, not wanting to get caught in the open if the helicopter came back. They were crossing an open muddy field when the mutter of a distant helicopter could be heard rising and falling with the wind.

Mala was the first to react. 'Get under cover', she shouted, turning and scurrying into the thin undergrowth at the edge of the field. The area, dotted with a few Palmyra palms, was not the ideal place to hide. The sound of the helicopter got louder. It would be over them in a few minutes, not enough time for them to get into the edge of the jungle and into proper cover.

Danika looked around, spotting a *cadjan* hut about fifty metres away. Made of thick wooden poles sunk into the grounds and mats woven from coconut palm leaves, the hut at the corner of the field would give them the cover they were looking for.

'We can be seen from the air if we stay here,' Danika called out urgently. 'Let's hide in that hut over there,' she said pointing.

They had just reached the hut when the helicopter came into view, flying very low over the trees. The three women crouched in the flimsy hut which was half-filled with torn and decaying jute bags. Only the woven mats used for the roofing and walls kept them from being spotted from the air.

'Did they see us?' Mala shouted.

The noise from the helicopter was deafening as it swung low, a wide, slow circle around the area.

Danika shook her head. From the angle the helicopter appeared she doubted they had been spotted. The helicopter drew closer, the hut shaking unnervingly from the tremendous downdraft. Thangam pointed to the jute bags, miming hiding under them before burrowing into a pile. Danika and Mala followed, barely getting under cover before part of the roof tore away.

The large assault helicopter hovered over the hut, the rotor wash beating down forcefully making the flimsy hut shake violently. Danika felt herself picked up and thrown brutally against the side of the hut, her head coming in contact with a wooden post. The hut filled with a swirling cloud of debris. Danika kept her eyes and mouth tightly shut as the tremendous downdraft from the helicopter blades just a few metres above the hut bounced her around violently.

Danika tried hard not to panic as she was convinced they would be spotted but after what seemed like an eternity the helicopter slowly moved away. The cloud of debris and their brown uniforms which merged with the jute bags had hidden them from sight.

Danika scanned her limp body for pain. Her shoulders ached, and her hips felt like they were run over, but it was her head where the pain was intense. Not daring to move too much, and enveloped in a fog of confusion, she sat up as the roar of the military helicopter receded. A groan sounded somewhere … somewhere close. She couldn't think straight!

The three of them lay dazed and stunned in the half-demolished hut. They waited for the roar of the military helicopter to subside then dug their way out from under the piles of scattered jute bags.

'Let's stay here until it gets dark,' Thangam stood up, flexing her shoulders while massaging her arm and shoulder. She searched through the messy pile of bags until she fished out her rifle. Mala coughed, spitting out a wad of phlegm.

'We should go into the jungle' she said, coughing again. 'If the men in the helicopter spotted something they may send a patrol to check.'

Danika closed her eyes and sighed. Every muscle in her body was aching from the pounding she'd received. She scrambled around for her rifle and forced herself to her feet, standing by the open door, her teary eyes sweeping the area.

'There's no one around but I don't want to get caught here,' she said, wiping her face with the back of her hand. 'Let's get moving.'

Dust and bits of jute fibre coated their uniforms turning the dark brown material a few shades lighter. Mala scooped up a fallen coconut as they staggered into the comforting gloom of the jungle.

They finally paused, deep in the jungle, under the comfort of a large Mara tree. Danika sat with her head between her knees, panting with exertion.

Mala used her long-bladed knife to lop off the top of the coconut, and they drank the sweet, fresh coconut water, cool as well water. Afterwards, she hacked the coconuts open and fashioned small spoons of husk so that they could scoop out the firm white inner flesh.

CHAPTER FORTY-EIGHT

KANTALE, EASTERN PROVINCE

The morning was warm, the sky heavy with clouds when Sami approached the structure cautiously, moving lightly on his feet. He didn't know whether it was occupied, although he doubted it.

Farmers built these wooden structures on trees, about ten metres above ground. They would sleep in the structure during the growing season to keep wild elephants and wild boar from entering and destroying their fields. The farmers would frighten the animals from the structure by blowing trumpets and beating drums.

It was a significant part in the cycle of life in remote areas of the country. A destroyed field would mean no harvest for the farmer and no money to be made at the market. They would have to live off the land and would have no money to spend on seeds, kerosene, sugar and other essentials for their family.

The empty lookout would make an ideal spot to rest during the night. This platform was constructed on the lower branches of a tall Mara tree in an open grassy area surrounded on three sides by dense jungle. It was built of dry wooden branches. Old pieces of canvas and cloth were draped over the top and sides to keep the rain from coming in.

Sami laid down on a piece of cloth left by the farmer. From there he could see all the way across open paddy fields to the north and the dusty dirt road that bisected it. The jungle, in a semi-circle around him, was noisy with the call of birds and the screeches of a family of monkeys as they hunted for food.

It had been a busy few days. The militant cell they were searching for had been located and neutralised. David kept his promise to help and the two previous days were filled with planning and preparation. David had dropped Sami off the previous day on the Kandy-Trincomalee Road just past the town of Kantale. He was dressed simply in a pair of faded blue jeans and a long-sleeved green shirt which blended into the jungle foliage. On his feet he had a pair of stout walking shoes.

David had offered him the choice of any weapon and Sami had chosen an AK-47 automatic rifle which was the weapon preferred by the Tigers. Sami had filled a kitbag with magazines and ammunition, a field medical kit, energy and chocolate bars and a set of clothing for Danika. A US Marine fighting knife, an automatic handgun for Danika, a waterproof ground liner and a water bottle completed what he thought was necessary.

Sami's plan was to hide the weapon and kitbag before crossing into militant territory. Carrying a weapon of any sort past the government and Indian Peace Keeping Force checkpoints would only land him in prison.

Sami felt that his life was changing again. His mother had arrived from Batticaloa with his grand-mother, much to the delight of Suria and the old servant woman. His grand-mother looked tired, the long, tortuous journey from Jaffna taking its toll on her frail body.

His mother was thinner than Sami remembered, but the familiar sparkle in her eyes was still there. She had smiled at him gently and cradled his face in her hands. 'You look so much like your father when I first met him,' she said, her eyes full of tears.

It was hard to leave his mother so quickly. When he told her why he had to go she took his hands in hers. 'Go with my blessing,' she said. 'May Allah protect you and guide you both to safety.'

Sami would cross into militant territory in the morning. He was going to be one man alone in hostile territory where no one was his friend. Above all, he must remain alert and be prepared to kill if necessary. He had cached the AK-47 and his kitbag, wrapped tightly in a ground liner, near some rocks along the escape route he planned to use. It had taken him more than a day to travel there and back but he felt comfortable knowing that he had access to food and ammunition if he was in trouble. He was not sure whether they would be able to get away without being noticed. Having access to a weapon and supplies would help if there was any pursuit.

∾

Sami joined the short queue waiting to cross into what the Tigers were claiming as their territory. The Sri Lankan soldiers were only interested in stopping any prohibited items like kerosene and weapons from being taken across. Once their search of his belongings revealed nothing they lost interest and waved him through.

The Indian *jawans* manning the check point across the invisible boundary were more alert. They insisted on searching Sami's belongings and asked him why he wanted to go to Trincomalee.

'I am looking for my sister,' Sami said. 'She's a refugee from Jaffna.'

The soldier said something in Hindi, turning and laughing at the other men. Sami shook his head, not understanding what the man was saying.

'He's asking you whether your sister is old enough to be married,' another soldier said in Tamil. 'He is getting tired of his wife and wants someone young and beautiful.'

The soldier stopped laughing when he saw the look on Sami's face. He came forward aggressively, glaring at Sami until a curt command stopped him in his tracks. An Indian soldier wearing the five-pointed, star insignia of an officer berated the soldier in Hindi, waving his arm in a gesture of dismissal.

The officer turned to Sami. 'You may go,' he said, in English. 'These men are second-rate troops and they have no discipline.'

Sami nodded his thanks and walked past the checkpoint. The dense jungle to the north of the road was in stark contrast to the fields of cultivated rice paddies in the south. Sami had studied the map that David had shown him. He remembered the area was a protected sanctuary with a set of low ridges running in a north-east direction towards Trincomalee.

David had pointed to an area on the map that didn't show any signs of civilisation. 'I've been in here,' he said. 'It's wild and it's desolate but it's a good place to hide. Everything north of this area is controlled by the Tigers. I am not allowed to go in there with my men, so you'll have to bring Danika out. We'll meet you to the west of this *wewa* – lake, by this rock formation.'

Sami looked down the road past the checkpoint. About a hundred metres away, a solitary three-wheeler was parked next to the road. It was what he was hoping for. The three-wheelers brought passengers to the crossing points and then waited for passengers who wanted a ride back into Trincomalee or to any of the smaller towns and villages in the area. The driver was asleep on the ground next to the machine when Sami got there.

He woke up when Sami nudged him with his foot. 'I need to get to Trinco,' Sami said. 'Are you waiting for someone or can you to take me?'

The man got off the ground and dusted himself. 'I will take you,' he said, grumpily. 'The man I brought wanted to cross early and we left before dawn.' The man stretched. 'Where do you want to go?'

Sami had to get to Pankulam, a little hamlet to the west of Trincomalee, but he was reluctant to divulge his destination to the man. 'I have to be in

Kanniya this afternoon. Can you take me there?' Kanniya was an outer suburb of Trincomalee on the old Anuradhapura Road. It was about seven kilometres from where he wanted to be.

The three-wheel driver nodded. 'That's about fifteen kilometres away,' he said. 'But I don't have enough gasoline to get there. These bastards restrict how much they give us. You'll have to give me some money.'

Sami nodded and handed a fifty Rupee note to the driver. 'I'll give you the rest when you drop me off.' The driver nodded and pulled out a glass bottle filled with a light amber coloured liquid from under the driver's seat. He poured the mixture into the small tank at the back of the three-wheeler. He started the two-stroke engine which sputtered into life in a cloud of acrid smoke.

The three-wheeler belched black smoke from its exhaust as it struggled all the way to the outskirts of Trincomalee. After stopping at the first petrol station to fill his tank and two empty glass bottles, he raced off happily on the road to Anuradhapura which passed through the small town of Kanniya. The three-wheeler was running much smoother which made Sami wonder what kind of gasoline mixture the driver had been using.

'Are you going to the hot springs?' The driver asked, breaking Sami's thoughts.

Sami had forgotten about the famous hot springs built by an ancient king who was said to have struck the earth several times releasing a fountain of water with each strike, each fountain with different water temperatures. Sami had visited the springs when he was young with his grand-father who had travelled to Trincomalee to attend a meeting of government agents.

'Yes, that's where I am going.' Sami could mingle with the crowds of people who usually visited the place to bathe in its healing waters and slip away unnoticed into the surrounding jungle.

After being stopped by an army checkpoint and then again by an Indian patrol, the three-wheeler turned into the road that led to the hot springs. The rundown stone-walled compound was crowded with people of all ages. The three-wheeler immediately picked up a fare and the smiling driver roared off with a family of five cramped into the back of the small vehicle.

Sami walked over to a food cart selling vegetarian snacks and bottles of colourful soft drinks. He bought half-a-dozen *vadai* and two cones of boiled *gram* wrapped in newspaper. He filled his water bottle from a tap next to the compound entrance and placed all the items in the cloth bag which he settled comfortably across his body.

Sami walked around the outside of the compound. Not seeing anyone, he stepped into the dense undergrowth surrounding the enclosure. From this point he would stay off the roads, moving to the northeast where Danika's camp was located

A young sapling from a Kumbuk tree gave Sami an idea. He bent the slender sapling and stamped on it near where it entered the ground, making a clean break in the hard wood. He stripped off a few of the lower branches and broke off the top. The walking stick of rough green wood he created would help him get across the mud flats of the streams and waterholes he would find on his way.

CHAPTER FORTY-NINE

PANKULAM

A few days after Danika's encounter with the helicopter, the entire scout team were ordered to the main camp to meet their Sector Commander.

The camp was a collection of thatched mud huts spread out under the forest canopy, clustered around a large open area. The men had already fallen out in two groups facing a small group of middle-aged men surrounding Sundara, the Sector Commander. They were all relatively young. A mixture of weary-eyed teenagers and young men not much older than university students. They wore tiger-striped camouflage fatigues and carried their weapons with practiced ease

Mala formed her small team of women next to the larger of the two groups, waiting for the Sector Commander to address them.

Danika had her first misgivings when she saw a thickset bald man with his back to her. He looked strangely familiar. He was wearing the uniform of a leader, a tiger-striped uniform with a holster attached to a crossed webbing.

Recognition came to Danika like a lightning bolt. *Is that Balan?* Danika stared at the man willing him to turn around, so she could see his face. She wished she was wrong, but she knew she wasn't.

Sundara stepped out from the cluster of men and advanced in front of the assembled company. He walked with a slight stoop, yet with that direct and purposeful gait of a senior officer. The men around the Sector Commander followed him a few steps behind. There was no doubt in her mind as Danika recognised the man who had killed her friend Ismail. It was a twist of fate that both Sami and Balan had come back into her life around the same time.

'*Vanakkam*,' Sundara greeted the cadre. 'I came here today to introduce you to your new Commander.' Sundar's eyes roved up and down the assembled cadre, stopping on the scout team for a moment before beckoning Balan forward.

'Balan is an experienced fighter who has fought in many battles,' he declared, studying the group. 'You have proven yourselves in many encounters and with the leadership of Balan, you will become the tip of the spear that will drive the invaders from our lands.' A murmur ran through the assembled cadre as they shifted restlessly.

Balan thanked Sundara before addressing them. 'I have been given the task of preparing all of you to fight the invaders,' he began. 'Not just to fight them, but to defeat them and send them back like dogs with their tails between their legs.' Balan began pacing. 'I have been told you are elite troops, ready for this, but I shall see for myself.'

His voice was harsh, peremptory, and commanding. To Danika's surprise, it seemed like the man was in charge, and the Sector Commander was an underling. Balan stopped when he came opposite the female scout troop, his eyes narrowing when seeing Danika in the front row.

'I know that many of you have seen action, some more than others,' he stood in front of Danika, his hands clasped behind his back. 'But once I have finished with you, you'll become the very best of the elite. Shock troops we will use to crush the enemy resistance.'

He studied the scout team before turning on his heel and walking away. 'You are just one company now,' he said confidently 'I have requested that we are reinforced by two more companies of experienced men … and women if necessary. *Anna* has chosen to grant me this request and our first task, starting from today, will be to construct more huts and shelters for the *pooralis* who will join us shortly.'

Danika felt her heart sink as she realized the implications of what he was saying. Hard physical labour before the monsoon period was tough and dangerous work. Heat stroke was common in the debilitating heat and humidity, and any physical work that was necessary was only done at night.

After being dismissed, Danika was walking away with the team, when she heard her name being called. She pretended she had not heard, but Indra grasped her by the arm. 'The new Commander is calling you,' she said, pulling Danika to a stop.

Mala stopped and looked back at the same time. Balan was gesturing for Danika to come over. Mala looked at Danika. 'Do you know him?' she asked, quietly.

Danika nodded. 'He fought with us on the Western Highway,' she said glumly. Mala looked at her sharply, hearing the unhappiness in his voice. 'Did you have a problem with him?' she asked tersely.

Danika shook her head. 'No, not really,' she said. 'It was nothing like that, although he tried. He killed someone who was close to me,' she paused trying to control her emotions. 'He's a very dangerous man.'

She glanced at Balan before addressing Mala. 'Can you wait for me?' Mala nodded curtly, her eyes never leaving Balan.

Danika walked slowly up to Balan who was staring at her closely. 'What do you want?' she asked him rudely. Danika had always treated Balan with disdain which clearly annoyed the man.

Balan glared at Danika, his face screwed up in a frown. 'Still the proud one I see.' Danika kept quiet, holding Balan's gaze, his eyes hard, unreadable. She didn't want to provoke the man into doing something stupid.

'Now that you're under my command you're going to do everything I ask you to do,' he said, with a leer. Danika bit her tongue. Her stomach churned, her cheeks flushed with anger. All those times he'd gazed at her, and she'd seen the longing in his eyes that repulsed her.

'Oh, we'll see about that,' Danika said, looking over Balan's shoulder at the Sector Commander Sundara standing just a few paces away.

'*Anna*,' she called out to him surprising Balan. 'Could I speak to you.'

Balan shot a hurried glance over his shoulder at Sundara who had turned and was looking at them strangely. It was not common for one of the *pooralis* to address a Senior Commander without first going through their Team Leader.

'Don't you dare address him directly,' Balan snarled at her. 'Any contact must be made through me.'

Danika shrugged. 'Let him tell me that,' she said, watching as Sundara walked to where they were standing. 'Yes, Danika' he said, looking at Balan curiously. 'What do you want?'

Balan's face changed when he realised Sundara knew Danika's name. 'Eh,' he stuttered. 'Umm…she wants to know whether there will be any more women assigned to the company.'

Sundara looked at Balan strangely before turning his head to address Danika. Danika could sense he felt the tension between the two of them.

'Yes,' he gestured at Mala to come over. 'We intend to expand your team with a few more women,' he said, addressing Danika. 'We're very happy with what your team has accomplished.'

Sundara turned and looked at Balan. 'Treat these women well. They have proven themselves on more than one occasion, especially this one,' he said, indicating Danika. Sundara held Balan's gaze for a moment before turning to talk to Mala.

Balan leaned forward as Sundara and Mala spoke to each other. 'It would have been better if you'd joined me two years ago. We could have made a good life together,' he whispered.

Danika looked at him in distaste. She had made an enemy of the man. Now she knew what he'd really wanted, standing in front of him, she felt both disgusted and appalled. Looking very satisfied, Balan smiled a creepy smile over his shoulder as he moved to join Sundara who had started to walk away.

CHAPTER FIFTY

PANKULAM

After struggling through the dense growth, Sami came in the failing light of the evening to the edge of the jungle. He looked over the flat, shining rice paddies towards the hamlet of Pankulam.

The small village was a random cluster of clay and cinder block houses gathered along a sluggish stream. A wide dirt track wandered to the north through flat open grasslands with a tinge of green after the recent rains. The only people visible were a group of children who were kicking a ball around a flat, dusty oval. Thin plumes of pale smoke rose up from many of the dwellings as the families prepared the evening meal.

Sami remembered Danika telling him that the militant camp was located inside the edge of the jungle, about a kilometre to the south of the village. He moved forward, keeping inside the edge of the jungle.

It was dark by the time Sami reached the camp hidden under the jungle canopy. The only way he spotted it was the flickering glow of a candle shining through an open window. It was pitch black under the jungle canopy, the moon completely covered by heavy dark clouds. Sami didn't want to go any closer in the dark, uncertain whether any traps had been set. He retreated to a small clearing he had just passed. He leant against a tree and took a sip from the bottle of water he carried.

Sami dozed fitfully listening to the sounds of the jungle around him. Cicadas and insects chirped in rising waves and the leaves rustled and shifted as night animals came out of their burrows. An owl hooted in the tree above him. Sami's senses were immediately heightened, his mind alert and focused. No light filtered through the dense canopy. He sat still as a stone statue. Only his eyes moved as he searched the darkness around him.

Faint voices carried by the wind drifted through the jungle. The sounds came from the direction of the camp. They were getting closer.

A patrol from the camp! Sami hoped that he was back far enough not to be discovered. His mind felt unusually calm, quiet and clear. The insects had stopped their incessant chattering and the voices seemed louder. Flashlights probed the deep shadows as the patrol moved along the undergrowth at the edge of the jungle.

From where he sat, Sami could see two flashlights. He tensed as one of them came into the jungle not far from where he was sitting. The person holding the flashlight headed towards the small clearing where he waited. Sami could clearly see the light from the torch bobbing around getting closer. Sami slowly got to his knees and crouched with one foot under him ready to move. He hoped his movement had not alerted the man.

'Get back here,' a man called out loudly in Tamil. 'You'll get lost in the jungle again. I am not going to spend the whole night looking for you.'

'Ok, ok. I am coming,' the man close to Sami grumbled, turning and walking back.

Sami began to relax as the patrol moved away from him working their way to the west. The night became quiet again, with only the natural sounds of the jungle to listen to. The leaves rustled softly as the breeze picked up.

The chirruping of insects started one by one, until it became a endless chorus once again. Sami could not sleep for a while, his eyes restlessly searching the inky darkness for any movement or light. He finally dozed as the outlines of the trees and bushes around him started to appear in the dawn light.

∿

Sami awoke with a start. It was morning and streams of sunlight filtered down through the branches of the trees around him. The jungle was alive with the call of birds. Sami reached into his bag and pulled out the bottle of water, swilling it around his mouth before swallowing it. He moved the muscles in his upper body feeling the tension loosen. He felt surprisingly good considering he'd only slept for a couple of hours at the most.

The smell of wood smoke drifted through the jungle, reminding him that he needed to find a place to observe the camp. Sami looked up at the tree he was under. It rose about ten metres in the air and was an aerial prop root of an enormous Banyan tree a little further back in the jungle. Climbing the tree would give him a good view of the camp.

Sami moved carefully to the main trunk, running his hands on its rough bark. The old tree was gnarled, its lowest branch only about three metres in the air. Wedging his booted foot into an angled protrusion, he hoisted himself up into the air and reached up for the branch, grasping it with both his hands. Pulling himself up was easier than he thought, and he balanced on the thick branch, holding onto another layer of branches above him. He clambered up slowly, taking care to always keep a foot wedged in a crevice or against a thick portion of the main trunk.

From the top of the tree he had an uninterrupted view of the surrounding area. The open flat area to the north-east was covered with muddy paddies. A man stood calf-deep in one of fields turning over clumps of mud with his hoe. To the south and west the unbroken jungle canopy stretched into the distance. Sami struggled to see the camp. Even though he knew where the camp was, there were no signs of any structures.

Sami slid down the tree. He would need to get much closer if he had any chance of seeing whether Danika was still in the camp. Placing his feet carefully so he would not step on a dry twig, he moved slowly towards the hut he had seen the previous evening. Sami finally squatted behind a dense bush, moving a small branch aside so only his eyes were visible.

The area where the huts were located had been cleared of all undergrowth except for a few large bushes around each of the huts. Tree branches, some pulled together to cover gaps in the foliage, provided a green canopy that made the camp invisible from the air. The thatched mud huts Sami could see were spread out haphazardly, each about thirty metres from its closest neighbour.

A troop of grey langurs were clustered around one of the huts. Females with their babies clinging to their backs chattered from the Palmyra leaf plaited roof, while the males, more vigilant and alert to danger, foraged on the ground for insects and roots.

The monkeys scattered when a woman almost ran into the yard from inside the hut. She waved her arms and shouted at the monkeys who climbed up into the canopy, hooting and calling out to one another. The woman was dressed in a brown shirt hanging over similarly coloured trousers. A wide brown belt encircled her slim waist. It was the same uniform that he'd seen the militant women wearing before.

Sami strained to see if the woman was Danika. He got a glimpse of her face when she turned and walked back into the hut and was disappointed when he realised it was not her. But he was reassured to see there were women in the camp.

The camp got quiet as the monkeys moved deeper into the jungle. A shouted command broke the stillness of the camp. Men and women poured out of the huts, jostling for position in an open space in front of the structures. They finally settled in some semblance of order, into two groups, one comprising only of men and the smaller one of women. The men were dressed in the striped camouflage uniform of the militant Tigers and were all carrying weapons. The women were not carrying anything although one woman, who was clearly the leader of the women's group, had a holstered gun on her hip.

Danika was standing in the front row of the smaller group. Sami's heart beat faster when he saw her, short hair framing a chiselled face with high cheekbones. It was exactly as he'd remembered her. Sami shook his head to clear his mind. He needed to think of how he was going to attract her attention. The enormity of the challenge he was facing almost overwhelmed him.

Sami studied the men. One group appeared to be two platoon-sized teams. There were at least twenty men in each. They were well armed with AK-47 assault rifles. A few carried Russian-made rocket launchers on their shoulders. The women were clearly in one group, about six of them. A small group of men were being addressed by a man who looked vaguely familiar to Sami. He was bald, of average height and thickset, his uniform straining across his wide shoulders. Sami could not hear what was being said but the men around him clearly deferred to him. *It must be a group of officers*, thought Sami.

The leader finished talking and dismissed the men around him with a wave of his hand. The officers broke apart and walked to the two squads. The leader turned to the women showing his profile for a moment. Sami recognised him immediately. He was the man who had followed Sami and Ismail into the jungle almost three years ago. It was the man who had shot Ismail as he lay wounded on the ground.

A jolt of adrenaline shot through Sami's body. It was like a switch had tripped in his mind. He had looked into the eyes of Ismail's killer and would never forget him. Only the empty pistol in his hand had prevented Sami from killing him. By the time Sami had reloaded his last magazine the man was gone. But here he was, standing not more than fifty metres away.

Sami took a deep breath. The fury that had almost overcome him still surged around his body. He couldn't jeopardise Danika's life for the sake of a personal vendetta. He needed to focus on what he'd come here to do. To take Danika away from these men and give her a chance of a real life, a chance to raise a family… maybe, if that's what she wanted.

The two squads broke into smaller teams of ten men, each commanded by an officer. The teams jogged off towards the other end of the camp, disappearing into the jungle. The women split up, some going into different huts while Danika and two others walked into an open structure, the thatched roof held up by wooden poles, and started to build a fire. A sheet of rusted corrugated-iron nailed to two posts served as wind and rain protection. Danika disappeared for a moment, then reappeared carrying chopped lengths of wood in her arms from a small pile behind the structure.

Sami saw an opportunity. If Danika went back for more wood, he might be able to attract her attention. He moved quickly to his left trying to get to the undergrowth behind the structure. He was sweating hard from exertion and anxiety when he finally crouched behind a thorny bush next to the woodpile.

The three women chatted to each other in the open hut. One of the women stirred two large round metal containers sitting on upright bricks, while the other scooped out dollops of buffalo curd from earthenware pots which the woman stirred into the mixture. Sami watched as Danika knotted the top of a half empty bag of rice and attended to the fire, poking it with a stick to make sure that the flame was even.

Sami retreated further into the jungle when one of the teams that had gone for their morning exercise returned, followed quickly by the other teams. The men stood in a row with tin mugs in their hands, talking and laughing with each other. The women ladled out portions of the curd and rice mixture into the mugs which the men took with them into their huts.

The three women were joined by the other women who ate their portions and helped wash and clean up the pots. Sami watched as Danika waved at the other women and after hefting an axe on her shoulder, walked into the jungle next to the woodpile. She didn't notice Sami who was waiting to see if anyone was following her. Not seeing anyone, he moved in the direction that Danika had gone.

Sami thought he had lost her after ten minutes of searching but the thud of the axe pinpointed her exact position. Danika was facing away from him, wielding her axe expertly at a half-grown tree about six metres tall. Stumps scattered around the area showed Sami that this was where she came to replenish the woodpile.

Danika must have sensed someone behind her, as she tensed and whirled suddenly, her axe lifted above her shoulders. Her eyes widened in disbelief when she saw Sami crouching a few metres away with his finger to his lips. Danika lowered the axe and Sami moved across to her and held her to him. She dropped the axe and clung to him fiercely, her head on his shoulder. She smelt of frangipani. Sami could feel her heart beating against his chest as they remained locked together for a moment.

Danika half pushed him away and looked into his face. 'I knew you would come for me one day,' she said, her eyes filling with tears. 'It is exactly how I thought it would be.'

Sami pulled her to him again, hugging her tenderly. 'Yes,' he said. 'I am here to take you away. But we must be careful.'

Danika nodded against his chest. 'Yes, Balan is here. He is a hard man and will not let me go easily. He thinks he can have his way with any of the women and I am afraid it won't be long before he will force one of us.'

Sami forced himself to remain calm. Balan! So that was his name. If only he could first kill the man. But that would be committing suicide.

'Is there a better time for you to leave or should we go now?' Sami asked. 'We'll have to travel about twenty kilometres through the jungle.'

'I am usually gone for about an hour, maybe longer gathering firewood,' Danika said. 'I will be missed if I stay out longer and they will come looking for me. I think it's better after dark. I can sneak out then and they won't know I am gone until morning.'

Sami nodded. 'That makes sense. I'll wait for you behind the woodpile. Try not to make them suspicious by acting differently.'

Danika nodded, as Sami caressed her face. A large teardrop fell down her perfectly chiselled face as she clasped his hand to her wet cheek. 'I will be there,' she said.

Sami gently removed his hand and stepped away from her, backing into the jungle until he couldn't see her anymore. After a few minutes he heard the thud of the axe striking the tree again and again and then the crash of the tree tearing through the canopy as it fell to the ground.

CHAPTER FIFTY-ONE

NAVAL HEADWORKS SANCTUARY

The jeep and truck turned onto a dirt track, leaving the main road behind. They passed by a small hamlet consisting of just a few mud huts and then it was open country. Grassland, patches of scrub jungle and rocky outcrops interspersed with bits of arable land and the occasional tree. Sweat dripped down David's face as the landscape began to shimmer in the morning sun. A few flies buzzed around, occasionally darting in through the open window to sit on their bare arms and legs.

The glare from the sun hurt David's eyes, even though he wore wraparound sun glasses. He seemed to be more sensitive to light since his injury.

The Colonel had shaken his head indifferently when David told him about Sami's plan to rescue Danika. 'I am totally against this, you know, but I have been overruled,' he muttered, almost in disgust. 'You have too many friends in high places.'

'However, what I do insist on is that you pass a fitness test before going out into the field. All this running around looking for the bomber is nothing compared to what you will be facing in the jungle.'

David had passed the fitness test and the Medical Officer reluctantly signed the form that permitted him back on field duty. 'I am doing this against my better judgement,' he said, handing the form to David. 'Usually these types of injuries take longer to heal, although in your case it seems to have happened much faster.'

The Medical Officer studied David thoughtfully. 'If there is a problem it will show itself in times of extreme stress or tiredness. That's when you will have to be careful. I've prescribed a tablet that you should keep with you at all times. Take one if you are feeling strange or disoriented. It will calm you down. If the symptoms persist, you should go to the nearest medical station.'

David nodded. 'Yes, doctor, I'll do that …' David grinned, pleased that he had passed the medical so easily. He felt good, the fitness and core body strength he had before the injury had all come back.

They left the vehicles at the end of the track, the team gathering under an enormous Banyan tree which shaded them from the hot sun. The vehicles would go back to base and wait for a radio message to pick them up.

David had brought the whole team along. All twelve of them. They had been used sporadically in small teams for reconnaissance missions while David was recovering. He sensed that their morale needed a lift. Going out into the jungle to hone their skills and bring back the feeling of excitement and danger was just what they needed.

The Headworks Sanctuary was east of the town of Kantale and well known for elephants and leopards. It provided a buffer between the militant areas to the north and government-controlled territory in the south. The Indians were focused on controlling the Jaffna Peninsula and areas around the major cities and towns. They hardly ventured into the jungles.

David divided his men into two teams. Sarath commanded one and David took the other. They would remain together for the moment but operate as two separate teams.

David was glad that they had been issued with new tactical radios with a longer range. He had made sure that Sami had been issued one of the new handheld models keyed into their frequency. It wouldn't have the range of the team radios, but they could communicate over a ten-kilometre range.

The vegetation in this part of the country was like the arid forests further to the north. The dry forests were a combination of a thick evergreen undergrowth with a taller, single layer, deciduous canopy. The two teams moved forward, slipping into the gloom of the forest through which light shone down in filtered streams.

As he walked silently down the trail following Indika, David thought about what he had been through the past few months. His close brush with death and enforced absence from the field had been very frustrating. Uncertainty whether his injuries would leave him handicapped had been his greatest worry.

David visited Priyani before he left. She was been taken by surprise when David arrived at her flat. Priyani wasn't working that day and she wasn't wearing any makeup. She looked so healthy and glowing. She wore a floor length, long sleeved cotton robe, open at her throat. David could see that she wore nothing under the robe.

Priyani had insisted on cooking for him. Each time she bent, the cotton robe parted from her body and David could see her lovely breasts and nipples. They ate and talked and then sat on the floor and listened to records and talked some more. Gradually they moved closer and closer until they touched and kissed. She led him to her bedroom. They kissed and hugged until she removed his shirt and helped him remove his pants. She let the robe fall from her shoulders and they came together, not breaking apart until the morning light streamed through the bedroom window.

It made David's head whirl just thinking about it. He felt thankful that he had been able to make love to Priyani. It was the first time since the ambush in Jaffna.

David jerked his mind back to the present when Indika froze, squatting on the leaf covered floor. Palm fronds crossed the path at shoulder and waist height and branches draped with vines crisscrossed overhead. David felt a momentary twinge of embarrassment that he had not been alert, he had been wool gathering as his US Special Forces Trainer Mike would have pointed out caustically.

David became focused. He didn't need to turn and look at his team. He just knew the men would have ceased moving as he did, checking the jungle brush on either side of the trail for any movement.

Time passed slowly. Nothing seemed out of the ordinary. Just the normal sounds of a jungle going about its business. But the men did not move an inch. They trusted Indika's instincts. They had saved them before.

The sky greyed as dark clouds approached from the west. Indika remained still. Only his eyes moved slowly as he checked the trail and brush ahead of him. David was sweating, the humidity rising as the afternoon sun turned the air around them into a furnace. An explosive rumble of thunder sounded in the distance, a gust of wind rustling the branches and palm fronds in waves of sound.

Indika looked over his shoulder at David, signalling that he was ready to move. Whatever had spooked him seemed to have disappeared. David signalled to the man behind him, his message repeated by each until the last man in the team had seen the signal. Indika nodded at David's readiness and slowly, very slowly, moved forward, studying each step before he made it. One pace every five or six seconds, ten paces a minute, less than 300 metres in an hour. He was moving like he knew something was out there.

Leeches hanging from leaves and stems twisted towards them as they sensed the heat of their bodies. A water-snake traced the sinuous course across the surface of the water course in front of them and clouds of mosquitoes hovered everywhere.

Indika moved off the trail, heading in the same direction along a path of least resistance through the jungle. David was glad they were off the trail. It was an obvious place for an ambush or a booby trap. His sense of hearing and smell was heightened. His eyes probed the greenery, his mind cleared of everything but the jungle around him.

∾

It had been a very long night and they were moving again. The light rain that had fallen during the night had made it uncomfortable. David had slept less than four hours. Soon after he'd fallen asleep, the night was split by an agonised shriek, the hideous tortured cry of someone being sadistically disembowelled with a blunt knife. The scream broke and cracked, diminishing into a burbling sob and for a moment there was silence. Then the night sounds of buzzing flies and vague shufflings from amongst the trees and bushes resumed.

The first time David had heard the *Maha Bakamuna* –large horned owl, he was a child staying the night in a rest house with his father. He had been petrified by the blood-curding sound and had jumped into his father's bed in fright. He hadn't slept a wink that night despite his father's reassurances that it was only a bird. David sighed knowing there was nothing he could do. The 'Devil Bird' as it was known by the locals, would complete its hunting and eventually leave the area. The silent predator let out its night-shattering cry three more times before finally subsiding sometime towards dawn.

They had fallen behind schedule after their slow movement the previous day. Indika had not given any specific reason when asked by David what he had seen, other than saying that it had not felt right. David hadn't questioned him further. He trusted Indika's instincts and didn't want the scout second guessing anything.

David wondered whether Indika sensed that he had been struggling a little. He wasn't a hundred percent since he'd been injured but he thought he'd done a decent job of hiding it. The encouraging thing was that he felt better than he had been for a while. He had regained the rhythm of life in the field, clearing everything but the mission from his mind. The lack of adequate food or water, or the threat of going against a dangerous enemy didn't bother him. He looked forward to it. He thrived on it. He had prepared himself for it. He was a good soldier. He loved tactics and loved playing the game.

As they silently followed Indika deeper into the National Park, the radio crackled quietly. David could barely hear it. He hissed at Indika who paused and looked back at him. David signalled a stop and watched as Indika slowly sank to his haunches.

The sun was directly overhead when they approached the rocky outcrop adjacent to where they had planned to meet with Sami. They were walking along a dried watercourse that meandered to the west, then swept in a gentle arc half a kilometre below the outcrop. It was about twenty metres wide with a flat bottom that was smooth and sandy from whatever seasonal rains had swept through it during the year. Its edges were steep and craggy in places, with plenty of rocks, clumps of Acacia thorn, Lantana grass and trees scattered along both sides of the depression.

Indika came to a sudden halt. From his posture David knew he had seen something. David's eyes scanned the lip of the watercourse for movement. *Not a good place to get caught in an ambush.*

The leopard lay about twenty metres away, on the top of the depression amongst the thorny bushes. Only his head and upper body were visible. He was resting in the heat, his eyes half closed. He yawned but must have sensed something as his eyes snapped opened, and he glared down at them with sudden interest. The leopard was a tawny yellow, every black rosette on his body clear as ink. Under that exquisite skin, rippled muscles of unimaginable strength.

After studying them for a while, the leopard relaxed, still watching them warily. A moment later the animal got up, stretched, and in a single bound disappeared into the clumps of Lantana grass lining the watercourse.

David had seen leopard before but never that close. And never without the protection of a vehicle. He looked down and clicked back the safety on his weapon. He couldn't remember having pushed it forward. David looked around the watercourse. It was not a good place to get trapped but it would also hide their presence from anyone looking from the forest. He signalled for his men to spread out.

David crawled to the top of the watercourse, near where the leopard had been sleeping. He raised his head slowly from under the Acacia thornbush looking in the direction the men had travelled. A field of Lantana grass spread out ahead of him ending at the edge of a thick growth. Termite mounds, coloured red by the rich soil, peeped above the clumps of tall grass.

David studied the impenetrable jungle beyond the grassland. He knew it was extremely difficult to know if there was someone watching. David remembered the Special Forces training he had completed a couple of years prior. The instructor was a grizzled Sergeant who'd fought the Viet Cong in the jungles of Vietnam and Cambodia. *'There's a knack to seeing beyond the surface of the foliage. The trick is to focus on the nearest leaves and then re-focus the eye to look through them. It takes time to learn it but keep practicing and it'll suddenly click.'*

David had practised the technique of looking through the foliage that the instructor had described to him and to his surprise, he had found that it was relatively easy to master. It enabled him to see through what had seemed impenetrable jungle, glimpsing any suspicious shapes that might be lurking in cover.

The outcrop rising about a hundred metres out of the jungle was scattered with rocks of different sizes, but bare of vegetation. It wouldn't conceal an approach from that direction. David looked up at the blazing orb of the sun which had started to dip towards the west. They would remain where they were until they heard from Sami.

CHAPTER FIFTY-TWO

PANKULAM

The day seemed to drag on forever as Sami waited for night to fall, controlling his excitement and his fear. He climbed the same Banyan tree and wedged himself high up in the canopy knowing he couldn't be seen from the ground. He tried to rest but the thought of Balan being so close kept his mind active and chased away any hope of sleep.

His mind went back to when he had last seen the man, almost two years ago. Sami had gone back to help his men after the firefight at the old fort in Pooneryn. He had been right not to cross the road that day. He had waited until dark with Ismail and they were just about to move out from under the bush when Ismail grabbed his arm, pointing. A shadowy figure crossed the road less than a hundred metres from where they were hiding. The moon suddenly appeared from behind a cloud catching the man out in the open. Sami had only seen him for a split second before he disappeared into the grass verge, but it was all he needed.

'He cannot track us in the dark,' Sami whispered to Ismail. 'He'll be watching the road to see whether we cross.'

Sami considered the situation in his mind. The man would be hiding close to where he crossed the road. It was obvious that his plan was to catch Sami out in the open when he crossed. But he did not know about Ismail.

'One of us should get across the road further down and try to flank him,' Ismail said. 'Once we pinpoint him we can take him out. He doesn't know there are two of us.'

Sami thought about what Ismail had proposed. What the boy said was correct. He didn't know there were two of them. But it was a risky move to get the man to reveal himself without putting themselves in danger. They had to find a place to ambush him. Get him to play by their rules.

'Looking for him in the dark will be too risky,' Sami said. 'I don't care how good you are. Let's both cross about a kilometre to the east and let him come to us.'

They crossed without incident where the road dipped into a small gully, moving south. They took separate paths in the dark, Ismail moving a hundred metres to the west keeping parallel with Sami. Their hope was that once the man found Sami's trail, he would follow it, not looking for Ismail's trail further away.

Sami remembered looking over his shoulder nervously. He could feel the uncomfortable threat of someone on his trail, although he knew he was just imagining it. The man would not realise they had crossed till morning and it would take him time to find any signs they had passed.

The land sloped downwards, and Sami felt his boots sinking into thick mud. *Must be a tank*, he thought to himself. The area was full of ancient irrigation works which had been neglected and unused for hundreds of years, but still provided wild animals with an ample supply of water in the dry months.

The vegetation stopped abruptly by a large open area. Light from the moon reflecting off high clouds shone brightly on the shape of toppled trees and broken branches, making him pause in surprise.

A loud trumpeted warning had made Sami jump in surprise. A dark rounded shape moved forward aggressively, the sound of flapping ears loud in the stillness of the night. He had stumbled onto a family of elephants resting for the night. The elephant trumpeted again making him retreat in fear. He would have to go around the tank, away from the elephant herd.

Thick clusters of reeds and mangroves sprouted from the edge of the water, the ground wet and marshy underfoot. The air was thick with insects. Sami knew he was leaving a trail a blind man could follow but he had no choice. He was dripping with sweat when he finally stumbled onto dry land, feeling weak and drained. He had not eaten for a while, the packet of food in his pouch only half eaten. The leaves rustled around him and the shower of rain caught him by surprise. He opened his mouth and looked up at the dark sky, letting the moisture trickle down his throat.

Sami stood for a while, the rain water tasting fresh and cool. He felt revived. He reached into his pouch and pulled out the half-eaten packet of food. He hunched his head to keep the rainwater from the packet, hungrily scooping up the remaining rice and pieces of vegetables.

Feeling slightly better, he continued heading south hoping that Ismail was close. Their plan depended on each supporting the other until they could set up the ambush.

Dawn came, as it did in the jungle, quickly, with just a hint of light. The usual chorus of insects and birds had gone quiet. It was strangely silent. Sami knelt on one knee by a thick bush, unslinging the rifle from his back. He had learnt to listen to the sounds of the jungle. He sensed rather than saw the movement when it came. A bush moved to his right and a dark face peered out. The man was completely bald, his head glistening with beads of sweat. They both saw each other at the same time, before disappearing.

Sami scurried around the bush, falling onto the mat of rotting leaves and debris. He flicked off the safety switch, his eyes searching the jungle. How had he followed him so quickly? Sami needed to warn Ismail but how could he do it without exposing himself? He looked around. A narrow trunk of a Palu tree a few steps away gave him an idea.

Sami aimed his rifle and pulled the trigger, sending a stream of bullets into the jungle where the man had disappeared. He immediately rolled three times to his left almost crashing into the Palu tree. Bullets thudded into the spot from where he had just moved, the winking muzzle flash of a rifle showing him where the gunman was hiding. Sami fired again, aiming to the left and right of where the flashes came from. Sami scrambled behind the tree trunk just in time as a burst of return fire hit the trunk above his head, bits of bark and torn leaves falling in a cloud around him. The man knew what he was doing. He wouldn't be easy to kill. Keeping the tree between him and where the firing had come from, Sami slithered backwards, trying to put some space between him and the gunman. He tried to listen to any unusual sounds but all he could hear was the creaks and groans of the forest as the heat from the sun warmed the air around him.

Where was Ismail? This was their chance to catch the man in a crossfire and kill him. The silence stretched as Sami nervously looked around, turning his head a centimetre at a time. A burst of fire to the right made him duck but no bullets came his way. A thrashing in the bushes ahead of him made him almost pull the trigger but something made him pause. The gunman had proven to be quite resourceful. He could be trying to lure him out into the open.

Through the trees to his right he saw Ismail step into view, his eyes fixed on a spot ahead of him. 'No...,' Sami's involuntary cry was drowned by the clatter of a weapon firing on full automatic.

Ismail was lifted like a puppet and thrown back into the undergrowth. Sami couldn't believe what had happened. He stared at the spot hoping to see any movement and lowered his head onto the ground when he realised the boy had to be dead.

A rustle in the undergrowth made him look up. The bald gunman stepped out from behind a tree and walked towards where Ismail had fallen. He paused, looking down at the body. The man was broad and thick, but not with fat. Yet he moved smoothly, like an athlete. Sami had known such men before, but not often. What they had was power. Sami moved his rifle around slowly, centering it on the man before pulling the trigger. The gun didn't fire. In his haste to get away, he had not checked his weapon and had run out of bullets. Sami tore at the pouch on his chest, attempting to get at a loaded magazine while trying to eject the empty one at the same time.

The shot was loud, making Sami look up at the gunman who was lowering his smoking barrel. He had fired a shot at Ismail as he lay helpless on the ground. The man looked down and then glanced around, giving Sami a good look at his face. Then without a sound, he slung his AK-47 over his shoulder and disappeared into the jungle away from where Sami was hiding.

Sami finally got a fresh magazine into his rifle, his nerves screaming with fear. *Where did he go?* His eyes nervously scanned the undergrowth but there was no sign of movement. After a while the birds were back, calling to each other as they perched on the branches above him. The man must have left thinking that Ismail was the person he had followed. It was the only explanation that made sense.

A couple of hours passed before Sami had felt confident enough to move. He felt a wreck. His face was itchy with a three-day growth. The clothes he was wearing were matted with wet leaves, his trousers and boots caked in mud. Sami buried Ismail in the soft earth where he'd died, his tears falling on the boy's muddy face. Sami muttered a few words from the Koran and swore that if he ever saw the bald man again he would kill him.

Sami's thoughts returned to his present situation. He knew what Balan was capable of. The man was experienced in the jungle. It was a big risk they were taking. The two of them would have maybe five or six hours head start but they would be travelling by night and wouldn't get very far. Sami tried to put himself in Balan's shoes. He tried to imagine the area they would be travelling in. The road to Anuradhapura curved in a semi-circle to the north around a sparsely inhabited area. It would be filled with arid jungle interspersed with rocky outcrops, *vilu's* -waterholes, and wild animals.

If Sami was organising the search, he would divide his forces into two. He would send the smaller group consisting of his best trackers to follow the trail through the jungle. The larger group would travel in vehicles to a point on the main Anuradhapura Road and enter the jungle, moving directly south, hoping to catch them in a trap.

Balan was intelligent, dangerous and unpredictable ... that's probably what he would do. Sami smiled coldly. He hoped that Balan would be one of those pursuing him. The hunter could very quickly become the hunted.

The sound of insects was deafening, the air plaintive with the sound of birds when Sami climbed down the Banyan tree to the ground. The sun disappeared in a red glow to the west, silhouetting the trees as it slid out of sight. Away in the still depths of the jungle, monkeys chattered and shrieked as they retreated high up into the canopy, away from the predators that came out at night.

Sami stood at the base of the tree listening for any unusual sounds. His eyes moved constantly, his nerves on edge. Every bush seemed to move in the velvety darkness. He moved forward in the direction of the camp. Several times he paused to listen but heard nothing but a slight breeze, rustled he leaves around him. It helped mask his movement. The glowing light of a candle visible in the uncovered window of the hut gave him his bearings.

The woodpile had grown, it's bulk a dark shape in the blackness of the night. Sami crouched behind it not quite sure when Danika would be able to get away. The jungle settled for the night and eventually he dozed.

CHAPTER FIFTY-THREE

PANKULAM

Sami woke with a start. The low, throaty roar of a leopard hunting reverberated through the stillness, then silence, and again a little closer. Sami's mind screamed at him to run. He could imagine it walking through the darkness scenting the air as it searched for its prey. Sami backed up against the woodpile and held out the long pole he carried, jamming one end into the earth. It was the only thing he had to keep the predator away. The leopard called again. It seemed very close. The plaintive cry of a frightened deer away to the right made Sami take a deep breath. He had forgotten to breath, so absorbed was he listening to the leopard on its stalk. The roar of the leopard and the call of the deer moved around intermittently, away from the camp. Then came a long silence.

It must have been around midnight when Sami sensed movement in the camp. A dark shape detached itself from one of the huts and moved towards the woodpile. Sami got the faint scent of frangipani and knew it was Danika. He rose up from behind the woodpile. She did not see him for a moment and then came to him in a rush.

'We all heard the leopard,' she whispered, grabbing one of his arms. 'Everyone was awake. I was scared for you.'

'He was close, but he's gone now,' Sami replied, looking around.

Fire-flies flitted round the tree tops, appearing and reappearing like dancing stars. A light breeze rustled the topmost branches of the trees. 'Are you ready to leave?' Sami sensed her nodding. It was too dark to even see her face.

'Follow me.' Sami turned and moved into the jungle, pushing aside branches and hanging creepers that brushed against him. Danika hardly made any sound at all. Sami remembered that she always moved like a forest wraith, instinctively knowing where to place her feet and angle her body so that she could slip through the jungle without being observed.

They moved slowly through the deep shadows, avoiding the bright silvery patches where moonlight shone through the openings in the jungle canopy. Sami felt a tug on his shirt and stopped, crouching as he did. Danika moved up next to him, her mouth close to his ear.

'We need to move much faster,' she said. 'Balan won't hesitate to send his men after us. I know of a better way to the south.'

Sami looked at Danika who stared back at him. He knew that they were taking too long. He wanted to get to the banks of the Naval Headworks reservoir which was about eight kilometres directly south. From there they would move in a south-westerly direction to where he had his kitbag and weapons cached.

'Ok, you lead the way,' Sami said, realising that Danika had been living and moving around the area for some time and would know the area much better than him.

Danika turned at a right angle, towards the east. It was not where Sami wanted to go but he trusted Danika and followed her. The ground began to rise, the jungle thinning out making it much easier to move. The sky became visible as the jungle canopy disappeared. On the eastern side of the small hill Danika turned to the right, following a dry watercourse that meandered to the south. Sami was glad that he had let Danika take the lead. They had made more progress in the past hour than they had the previous three.

The watercourse was dry, the mud caked and cracked. In the rainy season it would be difficult to negotiate but it kept them out of the jungle and provided the perfect path forward. The land on either side of the watercourse was sandy and dry, covered with scrub jungle. They stopped on the banks of the reservoir to eat *kadala* and drink water. Huge Kumbuk trees lined the banks, their drooping branches providing a sheltered place to watch the sunrise.

'We can't stop here for long,' Sami said. 'We made better progress than I thought, but we have to keep moving.'

Danika sat very still and straight, lost in her thoughts. There was an air of calmness about her. Sami had always noticed that she had that quality in her during times of stress. She saw him looking at her and smiled.

'What's your plan?' she asked, her eyes studying him steadily. 'They would have realised by now that I am gone.'

'We have to head towards Kantale,' he said, pointing to the south-west. 'Into government territory. It's about twenty kilometres away. We should go as far as we can during the day and find a place to rest tonight.'

'I am ready,' Danika said, standing up and dusting her hands by slapping them together. She was dressed in the same brown uniform she had worn the previous day. A knife in a leather sheath hung from her belt.

They walked along the banks of the reservoir until they came to an indistinct track leading in the direction they wanted to travel. They followed the tortuous path into the jungle, winding around trees, roots and rocks. The jungle was getting thicker the further south they went. Sami led the way, keeping the sun behind his left shoulder. They walked without speaking, their attention totally focused on getting through the jungle.

The sun was directly above when Sami saw a flat rock right next to the path.

He pushed at the foliage around its base in case there were any snakes and sank down on it thankfully. His feet were aching, and the lack of sleep was making his mind woozy. Danika climbed onto the rock and lay flat on her back, staring at the foliage above them.

'We must eat something,' Sami said rummaging in his cloth bag. He pulled out the paper wrapped *vadai* he bought from the food cart at the Kanniya hot springs, holding out the package to Danika. They were quiet while they ate, the lentil snack tasting delicious even though it was a bit hard.

'Let's go on until late afternoon and then find a place for the night.' Despite all his training and fitness Sami felt exhausted. Danika nodded without saying anything, her face taut with strain. Sami had set a fierce pace and she had kept up. He estimated that they would reach his hidden cache sometime the next morning. They still had the night to get through.

It was very hot, the heavy undergrowth preventing any breeze from reaching the ground. The sweat poured from his face and it ran down his cheeks and his nose, dripping off his three-day growth. Danika unbuttoned the top of her shirt, fanning herself in the oppressive heat. The top of her shirt slipped free and Sami found himself looking at her small, round breasts. For a moment he stared at the dark studs of her nipples, then turned away abruptly.

When he looked back, Danika had buttoned up her shirt. A hint of a smile played across her lips. 'It's time to go,' she said, standing up on the rock.

The sun beat down relentlessly as it moved towards the west. The path had petered out some time ago and they had to push their way through thorn bushes and brambles, skirting those that looked too big. Areas of open grass would look easy to move through, but the tall grass was slippery, and they stumbled through, careful not to put a foot wrong and twist an ankle.

'What about our tracks,' Danika asked, moving through a damp patch of underground seepage under a large Kumbuk tree. Sami had been thinking the same thought as he turned and looked at the marks they had left on the leaf strewn earth. It pointed like an arrow in the direction they were travelling.

'Let's move to the south-east and then turn west again,' Sami said. 'But let's make sure that we don't leave any sign that we have turned away from the direction we were going.'

A small Banyan tree just a hundred metres away gave them the perfect opportunity. Its roots had spread out in a circle around the tree giving them a place to change direction without it being obvious. Sami removed his boots and, in his socks, stepped on the above ground roots in a right angle to the direction they were moving. Danika did the same, removing her sandals and stepping on the roots barefooted. They walked like that for a hundred metres or more before putting their footwear back on again.

Sami motioned Danika to go ahead of him and followed, making sure that any sign of their passing was obscured. It was slow going. Trying to slip through the jungle without leaving any signs needed concentration. The light was beginning to fade when they finally turned back in the direction they were heading earlier.

'Let's look for a place to spend the night,' Sami said. 'The safest will be on a tall tree, but a cave or an overhang will do as well.'

A stream running to the east gave them another chance to hide their passing. They climbed down carefully using an overhanging branch to let themselves down into the water. The eroded banks were steep in places indicating the level of the water during the rainy season, but now in the dry season the water was sluggish and low. The wet sand was soft but firm, the marks they left in the sand quickly washed away by the flowing water.

The exposed roots of a tree leaning over the water gave Sami an idea. He tapped Danika on the shoulder and pointed. The sandy area under the roots provided a natural cave which would be ideal for them to spend the night.

Sami looked back upstream, at the way they had come. It had been a very long day and they must have covered at least half the distance to where David would be waiting. They could try and make the rendezvous by late the next day if they pushed. Sami also knew that the chances of running into anyone pursuing them would increase dramatically. They both needed to get a good sleep and get to his cache in the morning.

Danika crept into the small hollow, half concealed by an overhanging branch. She manoeuvred her body into the space allowing room for Sami, who crawled in after her. He turned his body, smoothing out any marks they had made before leaning against the back wall of the sandy cave. From his position he could see upstream as the bank curved towards where they were hiding.

'We should be safe here until morning,' he whispered, pulling out two hi-energy bars from a cargo pocket and offering one to Danika. Danika nodded her thanks, tearing open the long bar and taking a small bite.

Sami patted the ground beside him as he leant back wearily, taking a sip of water before biting into the energy bar. 'Come, sit next to me,' he said. Days of constant moving with too little food and little rest had drugged him with weariness. Slowly his muscles relaxed, and he rested easier as the sugar in the energy bar started to work.

The wind was rising, rustling the leaves of the tree they sheltered under. Somewhere out in the growing darkness, something moved, something other than the wind, something big and ominous. Sami leant forward alertly, tilting his head to listen.

Danika shook her head at Sami, smiling as she did. 'It's an elephant,' she said quietly. 'It will warn us if someone is too close.'

Sami raised his arm pulling Danika closer. She came willingly, laying her head on his chest, snuggling under his shoulder. Sami felt his heart beginning to pound as an unfamiliar feeling swept over him. It had been years since he had let anyone get this close to him. His arm tightened around Danika.

'I want to know everything that happened to you after I left,' he said, burying his face into her hair.

CHAPTER FIFTY-FOUR

NAVAL HEADWORKS SANCTUARY

The sound of Danika moving woke Sami from an exhausted sleep. The smell of rotting wood and earth hung heavy under the tree. There was just enough light to see her adjust her clothing and slip out of the cave. Sami lay there on the warm sand thinking about the previous night. They had spent what seemed like many hours whispering their stories to one another, wrapped in each other's arms, until they had both fallen into an exhausted sleep. Sami could not help but admire the courage and fortitude of the young woman. Their two stories were so similar that he felt he had known her all his life.

His thoughts quickly turned to the day ahead. It would be hard, more challenging than the day before. They would have to be very careful from here. His priority was to get to his cache. He needed his weapons and the radio to contact David. Once he had them he would feel much better.

Danika was taking a long time to come back. Sami got to his knees and peered out from behind a root that curved into the earth in front of him. He frowned when there was no sign of Danika. He gathered up his bag, stuffing the left-over food into it before slinging it over his shoulder.

Movement on the bank above him made him tense. He gasped in surprise when a pair of feet dangled right in front of him, the person dropping lightly to the stream bed. Danika's face was calm as she put her fingers to her lips, then waved him urgently forward into the stream. Sami didn't ask any questions but followed her into the placid water. She moved fast, downstream, away from where they had slept. Sami followed, trying not to splash. They moved quickly, following the stream bed, trying not to step on the exposed sand banks.

Danika pointed to a mass of granite extending out into the stream. They climbed onto it carefully, trying not to leave any scuff marks on its mossy sides. Sami followed Danika into the jungle, almost bumping into her when she stopped abruptly.

'What did you see?' Sami asked, breathing heavily.

'I went back towards the place we turned east. To the Banyan tree ...' she explained. 'I saw a group of men passing the tree. They didn't notice we had turned off.'

'Ok, so they have followed us this far. How many were there?'

'I saw about six men,' she said. 'There may have been more, but they were moving fast.'

Sami nodded. It was exactly what he'd thought would happen. When the militants discovered they'd lost the trail they would backtrack and look for signs where they had changed direction. The two of them needed to move quickly to keep the advantage they had.

'Good work,' Sami said. 'I've got a cache hidden about three kilometres away. I was expecting this to happen the way it did. We need what's in there to get away.'

Danika nodded. 'Ok,' she said. 'You know where to go so lead the way.'

They moved off again, this time not bothering to conceal their tracks. They were fresh after a good night's sleep and the thought of the Tiger scouts coming up behind them spurred them on. Sami tried to take some basic precautions to delay the trackers, but he knew that it would not take them long to pick up the trail.

The rounded rock formation that Sami had hidden his cache behind, appeared suddenly out of the surrounding jungle. He had chosen it so that he would not miss its distinctive shape. The cache was undisturbed, and Sami felt a sense of relief when he slapped a magazine into the AK-47 rifle and chambered a round.

Sami handed the automatic pistol in its shoulder holster with two magazines to Danika. She strapped the holster to her body and slid its magazine into her palm to make sure it was loaded correctly, before chambering a round. Sami pulled the tactical harness around his shoulder and fixed the Velcro straps firmly in place. The pouches held his spare magazines, the cleaning and medical kits and four grenades, with their pins taped down. Sami strapped the knife over his trouser leg and hooked the handheld radio to his belt. Hoisting the kitbag on his shoulder, he buckled the strap around his waist and shrugged it into position.

They didn't wait a minute longer than they had to, moving away down the slight slope back into the jungle. He paused about twenty metres in the jungle letting Danika get ahead of him. He reached into a side pouch of his combat harness and pulled out a reel of fish wire. Cutting off a length using the inbuilt cutter on the reel, Sami tied one end firmly to a tree across the trail they had moved down. He carefully tied the other end around a grenade he pulled out of his pouch. Sami then removed the pin and the tape that held it down, careful not to release the spring-loaded lever that armed it. He pushed the grenade into a clump of saplings about half a metre off the ground making sure that the lever remained closed.

Sami backed off from the trap he'd set and looked at his handiwork. Anyone coming down the trail from the bright open area into the darkness under the canopy would walk into the fish wire without noticing it and pull the grenade off its perch. Hopefully it would wound one of the trackers, maybe more than one. It would slow them down as they would have to be more careful following the trail.

Sami signalled to Danika, who was keeping watch while he worked. She smiled at him knowing what he had done. She remembered the fight in the western jungles when they used similar tactics against the army who was trying to open the highway.

Changing direction, Sami headed due west. With the compass on his wrist he could change direction often and keep his pursuers guessing. About an hour later he stopped in a small clearing. The canopy overhead was thick but the ground fairly clear. The smaller trees around them were covered in large palm leaves. Sami unclipped the hand-held radio from his belt and turned it on. He was glad to see the tiny green light next to the short antenna flicker to life.

'Calling Home Base, come in. Over' Sami waited for a response.

Not hearing one he tried again. This time the crackle of an answer came through the speaker.

'Home Base-Actual receiving loud and clear. State situation. Over.'

'Err! Pursued by a small group. Larger group heading to intercept from north. Over.'

'Understood. Will move into blocking position. Inform ETA. Over'

'Sometime early morning. Will check in later. Over.'

'Understood. Home Base-Actual. Over'

Sami handed a couple of energy bars to Danika who nodded gratefully. They moved further into the jungle and came across a faint trail which headed in the general direction they were moving. The crump of an exploding grenade made them pause. They both glanced at each other and set off again, moving a bit faster. They moved in an arc, keeping under cover but moving steadily to the south-west. They came to an area of scattered scrub and Sami signalled for

Danika to stop before stepping out into the open area.

A flight of birds burst into the sky about hundred metres away. Sami grabbed Danika and pulled her behind a thick clump of bushes. He pushed her to the ground and crouched low behind her looking towards where the birds had taken flight. A camouflaged Tiger appeared from behind a tree, followed by another and another. The man in front scanned the ground ahead of them for any signs that they had passed. Sami didn't know how they had got there so quickly and wondered whether they were from another group.

Sami's muscles were screaming in protest at his unnatural position, the weight of the AK-47 heavy across his bent knee. Danika looked anxious, only her eyes moving as she watched the camouflaged men move slowly away from them. Sami realised that they were in trouble. They had Tigers ahead of them and behind them. David and his team were still a couple of hours away. He needed to think of something, and quickly.

CHAPTER FIFTY-FIVE

NAVAL HEADWORKS SANCTUARY

David held the handset out to Nimal who clipped it to his harness. Sami's information meant that he would have to change things quite a bit. The Tigers coming from the north were a threat that needed to be addressed. David couldn't have them join up with the group that was following Sami. The question on his mind was whether he should keep the team together or send one squad to meet Sami and the woman.

He looked around and saw Sarath watching him. David motioned to Sarath who joined him at the bottom of the watercourse. 'We've established contact with Sami,' David said. 'He's got the girl out and is being followed by a small group which is what we had expected. But he says that a larger group is moving in this direction from the north.'

David should have expected it to happen that way. He would have done the same if he was in the same position. A slight ache behind his eyes made him shake his head in annoyance.

'I don't want to break up the team,' he said. 'We don't know how large the northern group is. I want to hit them hard … make them think twice about moving south. Once we stop them I will take Indika, Nimal and Jayasuriya with me to meet Sami. You remain and keep hitting them. Call in a helicopter strike if you have to, but don't do it unless you have no choice. I don't want to raise red flags all the way to Colombo.'

David signalled to Indika who duck walked over. David explained the situation to him. Indika nodded his understanding. 'I want to find a place like this across their path we can hit them from,' David said. 'I want you to locate them first so that we know their line of march.'

Indika had been born in the south and knew how to move in the forest without being seen. He waited for further instructions and not hearing any, moved to the top of the watercourse and looked around. Then crawling over its crest disappeared into the field of Lantana grass.

∽

Indika slid back into the watercourse more than an hour later. He was panting and sweat poured off his forehead. 'They're about a kilometre back and moving fast in this direction,' he said. 'We'll need to move further to the east, to the other side of these rocks if we are going to stop them.'

David didn't need to be told twice. He signalled the team to gather around and explained what they planned to do. Even though he had been in action before, the anticipation of combat always made him nervous. One wrong move and they'd all be dead. David looked at each man carefully, searching for signs of strain or weakness. From the expressions on their faces David could see they were ready.

One thought worried him constantly. What if Sami could not get away from the militants who were after them? David knew from experience what the young man was capable of, but it would only take a single mistake.

They moved quickly up the gully and around the rock formation. David positioned two of his men about halfway down the slope. A smaller, steeper gully to what they had been in earlier curved away to the south, giving them a good defensible position. David watched as Sarath positioned the men, placing the squad machine gun in the middle.

The ache in his head grew stronger and David remembered the doctor's words about putting himself under extreme stress. He promised himself to take one of the capsules the doctor had given him.

The sun had passed its zenith when a group of armed men dressed in striped green uniforms hurried out of the jungle. There was no semblance of order to their movement. Some of the men were intent on crossing the open area with their heads down while others looked around at the large rocky outcrop they were passing. Frankly David was surprised at the behaviour of the Tigers. He had heard so much about their discipline that he wondered who commanded them.

David and his men were spread out across the lip of the gully about ten metres apart. He had positioned Indika on the flank to prevent anyone surprising them from that direction.

David felt a flutter of panic as he counted the Tigers. There were over twenty of them in the open, with more emerging from the jungle. They were all carrying the AK-47 automatic rifle, easily recognisable by its curved magazine. A few also carried rocket propelled grenade launchers on their backs. David had expected a dozen, maybe a few more but this looked like there were double that number. David took a deep breath to stifle his panic. The militant soldiers were walking into an ambush and the advantage was with him and his men. But with only twelve soldiers there was a limit to what they could do.

David felt the thrill of anticipation course through his body as the Tigers passed the termite mound he had designated in the middle of the killing zone. David thumbed off the safety, consciously relaxing his muscles and steadying his breathing. He lined up the sights on the militant who was leading the group, waited until he had drawn a full breath and closed his finger around the trigger in a gentle squeeze.

The surprise was total. The squad light machine gun mowed down a number of the Tigers before they even realised they were under fire. Others were hit by individual bursts fired by the rest of the team. The Tigers had all gone to ground at the sound of the firing. Some of the men who had been shot were out in the open, but the others were hiding behind tall clumps of Lantana grass and the large termite mound.

A few of the Tigers fired blindly towards them but none of the bullets came close. David was impressed by his team's fire discipline, the experienced soldiers only firing when they spotted a target. From the sound of the return fire David realised that the Tigers were retreating under cover of the Lantana grass back from where they came from.

'Cease fire,' he shouted, waving his hand in the air. It was exactly the direction he wanted them to go.

After the cacophony of the firefight the silence was deafening. Birds that had taken flight as the firing began, settled back on their perches, noisily complaining to their neighbours. An anguished cry from one of the wounded gradually lowered to a low moan and then silence.

'Anyone hit?' David didn't think so, but procedure demanded he ask the question. Not hearing a response, David moved over to where Indika was. He nodded at the soldier who turned and slithered down the watercourse before disappearing. Indika would follow the men and make sure that they were not regrouping.

David would wait for Indika to come back. If the militants had enough sense they would just keep running.

CHAPTER FIFTY-SIX

PANKULAM

Sami tapped Danika on the shoulder and pointed to the jungle behind them. Danika nodded and crawled into the thick undergrowth waiting for Sami to join her.

Sami crouched next to her with his mouth close to her ear. 'We'll head south,' he whispered squeezing her arm reassuringly. 'There may be others around.' They would abandon their attempt to link up with David and head south, towards the Trincomalee-Kandy Road. He'd get David to come to him.

They crept into the dense undergrowth of bushes that stretched away on either side of them under the canopy. They wormed their way on their stomachs and got to their feet careful not to make any sudden movements. A family of grey langurs in the canopy above them made them pause. If the monkeys spotted any movement on the ground, they would raise the alarm thinking it were a predator.

While they waited for the primates to move Sami thought about the position they were in. The abrupt change in direction would confuse the militants and give them a chance to get away. He needed to let David know the change in plans but right now they had to get away from the immediate area.

The monkeys, intent on feeding on insects and fruits, did not notice them on the ground and moved to another tree further away. Sami and Danika pushed their way through the thorny branches that grabbed at their clothing and any exposed skin. They did not take any of the faint animal trails which seemed to be heading more towards the west but kept moving diagonally south. The ground started to slope up gently as they climbed a low ridge that ran at an angle from the north-east. They traversed its summit and dropped into a shallow valley. Sami pushed through the bushes and almost fell into a hidden gully. The rains had carved out a narrow channel through the hard soil that was about a metre and a half deep. The channel was lined on either side with a dense screen of bushes making it extremely difficult to see.

'Let's stop here,' Sami said, looking around. 'I'll try to contact David and let him know we are moving south.' They jumped into the channel, crouching below its lip.

Sami tried to contact David on the radio but got no response. 'The valley we're in must be blocking the signal,' he said, glancing at Danika. 'We'll need to get higher up.'

Danika nodded. Beads of sweat dripped down her face which was scratched and bleeding from the thorny bushes they had crawled through, but her eyes were alert and confident. The sun was close to its zenith and the heat and humidity sapped the energy from their bodies.

A series of sharp sounds like firecrackers echoed from the north. *Gunfire!* The firing intensified until it finally died out. *David must have run into them,* thought Sami. It sounded some way off, but Sami didn't want to hang around. He motioned with his head and they scrambled out of the channel and back into the undergrowth. The dense growth by the edge of the gully gave way to more open country and they were able to make good progress.

Sami was starting to think that they were going to make it. Another couple of hours and they would be in Kantale. But they would have to walk around the ancient reservoir used for the irrigation of crops in the region. He was getting tired and could see that Danika was struggling as well. They had been on the move since daybreak and carrying a pack on his back did not make it any easier. He spotted a large clump of rocks on a small rise in the ground and moved towards it. The boulders would conceal them and give them a chance to rest. They would move once it got cooler.

A smooth, sandy depression behind a flat boulder was exactly what Sami was hoping to find. It could only be approached from one direction. The rocks above them would create a slight overhang which protected them from above. Pug marks on the sand showed that leopards used the space. To the south, light glinted on the reservoir a few kilometres away. On the other side of the water, the main road to Kandy ran through the small town of Kantale.

Sami placed the rifle next to him and removed his backpack, leaning it against the rock before sinking down next to it. 'We'd better keep a lookout,' he said. 'You keep watch while I get some supplies out of the bag.'

Danika nodded and moved to the opening, settling herself comfortably, keeping a lookout to the south. Sami rummaged in his pack and pulled out the chocolate and energy bars which he piled on the ground next to him. He tossed one over to Danika who nodded gratefully.

Sami pulled out the radio and turned it on. 'Home Base come in. Over.'

The answer came back almost immediately. 'Home Base-Actual receiving loud and clear. Report situation. Over.'

'Was forced south. Cannot make home base. Heading alternate. Over.'

'Understood. Home Base-Actual. Over.'

Sami allowed himself to relax for the first time since that morning. The change of direction to the south seemed to have worked, but he didn't want to get complacent. He remembered the time three years ago, when he had thought that he'd got away only to run into Balan. There was a remote possibility that Balan would think that Kantale was their main destination and send a team to intercept them. They needed to be careful. They were not completely out of danger.

Sami crawled next to Danika and looked out over her shoulder. The ground fell away in front of them to the edge of the jungle which gave them a good defensive position. But it was very hot, the sun reflecting off the rocks made it feel even hotter than the air that flowed around it. He was beginning to think that maybe they needed to get out of the sun when something moved at the edge of his vision. A man dressed in camouflage pushed a branch aside and stepped into view. He paused at the edge of the jungle and looked up at the rock formation. Sami's heart sank, and he crouched lower, pushing Danika below the crest of the rock.

'Wh..?' she grunted in surprise. Sami looked back at her with his finger to his lips. The sound of voices would be amplified by the rocks that surrounded them.

Sami raised his head carefully. The man had been joined by three others and Sami thought he could see an outline of another man in the undergrowth. They were all wearing the striped camouflaged uniform of the Tigers.

Sami motioned Danika forward. She took in a sharp breath when she saw the men. One of them lifted his face and looked directly at the pile of rocks. Danika clutched at Sami's shirt. 'It's Balan.'

There was no doubt it was Balan. Sami felt like the man was looking directly at him. He watched as Balan waved his arm, signalling one of his men to check the rock formation. The man walked forward looking around at the ground. He was tall with a mop of unruly hair. He carried an AK-47 slung over his shoulder, its barrel pointing at the ground. He walked directly towards where they were hiding.

Sami ducked his head pulling Danika back. 'Give me your pistol,' he asked Danika.

Sami checked the weapon and slowly chambered a round making sure that the slide closed back slowly. He flicked off the safety and looked down the slope. The man was almost half way up. He looked around at the surrounding jungle and was not paying any attention to anything ahead of him.

What Sami planned was simple. He would wait until the man was within pistol range and shoot him. It would be an easy shot, but he had to remember to compensate for shooting downhill. By using the pistol, he hoped to not give away that they carried an AK-47 assault rifle with them. It could change the odds in their favour later.

Sami knew that the militants didn't wear body armour, so he aimed at the center mass of the man climbing the hill. He was not more than ten paces away when Sami got to his knees, arms outstretched holding the pistol with both hands, aimed at the man's body. The militant saw Sami, his eyes widening in surprise. Sami pulled the trigger twice, the two shots sounding almost like one. The man was thrown back violently, collapsing in a heap next to tuft of grass.

The militants standing at the bottom of the hill scattered, a couple of them scampering back into the dense undergrowth. Sami watched Balan as he crouched on one knee, his eyes sweeping the rock formation. Sami's tactic had worked. The militants did not know exactly where the shots came from.

Sami handed the pistol back to Danika 'Make sure no one creeps up behind us,' Sami whispered out of the side of his mouth to Danika. He heard her shifting around so that her back was against the rock he was leaning on. Sami was confident that Danika would cover his back in case anyone climbed up the slope behind them.

Sami reached into the pouch on his combat harness and took out two magazines placing them next to him. He took two of the three remaining grenades from his side pouch and placed them next to the magazines. Sami glanced at Danika sitting next to him. She looked back at him calmly.

The militants were getting ready to come up the hill. Sami could see Balan talking to the men around him. He picked up the AK-47 and checked that the safety was off. He settled the butt against his shoulder. He was ready.

Balan and one of the militants opened fire with their rifles, spraying the rocks around them. Three others moved up the hill. Sami didn't want the men too close and he wanted to take out as many of them as he could. Either injure them or kill them, he didn't care.

Sami centered the rifle on one of the militants and let off a short burst. He could see dust flying off the man's body where the bullets hit. He switched his aim and targeted another militant. In his hurry he pulled the trigger too quickly, the stream of bullets hitting the ground in front of the man. A bullet must have ricocheted off the ground and hit him as his leg gave way under him. He crawled behind a rock just as Sami pulled the trigger again.

When he looked back down the slope the other men had all disappeared. He cursed under his breath. He had been too sloppy. He had killed one and injured another. He could have got all three of them if he hadn't hurried.

'What happened,' Danika looked at him questioningly. 'Did you get any?'

'Two are down. But I should have got another,' he said, still angry at himself for missing. 'I hurried too much.'

'It's alright,' she said, positively. 'They may leave us alone.'

Sami shook his head. Balan wouldn't give up. He had thought the same thing three years ago and had got Ismail killed. He wouldn't make the same mistake again. The wounded man moaned from behind the rock, calling out to the others to come and get him.

Bursts of gunfire probed the rocks around them. Either the militants knew where they were hiding, or they were trying to provoke a response. Sami held his fire. He couldn't see anyone and the occasional bursts of fire from inside the jungle made it difficult to pinpoint where the shooter was.

Sami keyed the transmit button on the radio. 'We're taking fire. Trapped on rock outcrop north of Kantale in sight of tank. Need help. Over.'

The response was immediate. 'We're on our way. Sit tight. Over.'

The volume of fire increased, the bullets ricocheting around them. Sami risked a peek over the rock. The wounded militant was being dragged down the hill by another man. Sami let them go. Maybe they would take the wounded militant with them back to the camp.

CHAPTER FIFTY-SEVEN

KANTALE TANK

David could hear gunfire coming from the other side of the rocky outcrop. From the sound of the rifle fire he estimated not more than two or three men firing. He signalled Sergeant Jayasuriya to take Nimal and circle to the right while he went left with Indika.

The ache behind David's eyes became a blinding headache. He shook out a tablet from a small plastic bottle in his pocket and swallowed it, throwing his head back to get the tablet down his dry throat. Indika watched him take a quick sip from his water bottle. David stared back at him, but the soldier did not say anything.

'I want you to make sure there are no more coming from that direction,' David said. 'Cover the area to the east where they came from.' Indika nodded his understanding and slipped into the undergrowth like a ghost.

The firing had died down to the occasional burst when David spotted movement amongst the trees. He watched as a man came into view, moving quickly in his direction. The man's attention was focused totally on the hill where Sami and the girl were hiding. He carried an AK-47 rifle ready to fire and did not see David until he was almost on top of him.

The man grunted in surprise when David's arm wrapped around his neck, almost lifting him off the ground. The knife entered the man's body exactly where David wanted it to go. Between the ribs and straight into his heart. A twist of his wrist and he felt the man go limp. David lowered the man to the ground slowly.

The militant was young, not older than in his early twenties. Some were forced to fight because they wanted to, to avenge atrocities committed against their families or because they wanted a land of their own. David hated killing someone like that. But it was the way he'd been trained as a professional soldier. To weigh up the opportunities that presented themselves and be ruthless in its execution.

David loosened his neck muscles. He began a careful, clockwise movement to his left, staying inside the thick vegetation, always keeping the rocky hill in front of him. He studied the slope ahead of him. The sun was setting in the west and it would be dark soon. He'd covered a third of the distance to where the firing came from. Sami and the woman would be hidden somewhere in that pile of rocks. As long as they remained hidden they would be safe. He shifted his attention down the slope to the thickening undergrowth. The forest normally alive with the sound of birds had fallen silent. The firing had scared them all away.

If there was anyone hiding there, they were being pretty quiet, or they had left. David doubted the latter. He couldn't take any chances. David swatted an insect that had landed on his face. He'd have to wait until the militants showed their hand. He trusted Indika to keep away any reinforcements from the east, or at least to warn him if there were too many for him to handle. But the longer they waited, the worse their chances were of running into another group.

Twilight was followed quickly by darkness, the shape of the rock formation only visible against the twinkling stars. David waited with grim anticipation. His head still throbbed but the pain had not got any worse. The ache behind his eyes had not gone away but it did not bother him as much as before. He had no illusions about what was going to happen. The militants, if they were daring enough would try and sneak up the slope in the dark and try to catch Sami unawares. Not for the first time David wished he knew how many of them there were.

Sergeant Jayasuriya and Nimal were across on the other side of the hill but David didn't think the militants would make an approach from the west. They'd try from the east, from the side he was facing. The sun would be behind their backs when they attacked. But that was only if they waited that long.

The night was well advanced when David heard the first sign of movement. It came from where he was expecting. He lay perfectly still in the dark. The sound came closer, then stopped. David could hear someone breathing deeply. Then the sound started again, moving away up the slope. David turned his head but in the pitch dark he could see nothing. He could hear his heart beating like a drum.

David had to act before the man got too far ahead, otherwise he would lose him in the dark. David had memorised every rock and every clump of grass the man could hide behind when he went up the slope. There was one flat rock jutting out of the ground slightly that he would have to pass. David got to his feet and threw two bullets he had ejected from one of the magazines he carried in his pouch, as far up the slope he could. He snapped the safety off and waited for the bullets to land. The bullets hit the rock as he had intended and rattled to a stop. For a moment he thought the trick hadn't worked. Then the long muzzle flash of a rifle firing on automatic broke the stillness of the night.

David only had to move his rifle a few inches to the right and pull the trigger. The sound of bullets hitting a body was unmistakeable. David didn't wait to see whether the militant was dead or wounded. He immediately scampered away from his position deeper into the forest, crashing into a bush and dropping to the ground before rolling away to rest against the side of a tree. The silence was deafening. Every sensory organ in his body was strained to the limit of alertness.

A crashing in the undergrowth to his left almost made him pull the trigger. The sound receded, getting fainter until finally he could hear it no more. David didn't know whether it was a man or an animal. The headache had come back but he would stay where he was until the dawn. His only safety was in silence.

CHAPTER FIFTY-EIGHT

NAVAL HEADWORKS SANCTUARY

Sami was losing his battle with fatigue, just able to keep his eyes open when the gunfire erupted, the flashes lighting up the rocks for a moment. He couldn't look in the direction it came from without exposing himself.

He'd taken the first watch while Danika dozed next to him. The men they faced were hardened fighters. They could be waiting for him to fall asleep before they moved in. But nervous energy and the sapping heat had taken its toll and he was almost certain he had dozed off a couple of times.

Danika looked up at him, the whites of her eyes gleaming in the dark. He patted her arm reassuringly. The firing had not been directed at them. Something else was happening out there. But what could it be? Was it a ploy to draw him out?

There was something about the sound of gunfire that nagged at him.

Something he couldn't put his finger on. Danika struggled to her knees and knelt beside him.

'Were they shooting at us again?' The bursts of gunfire aimed at their position all evening had been sporadic, coming without any warning, although there had been no firing for a few hours.

'No,' he whispered. 'The firing was from the left.' Sami heard two bursts. Then it struck him. One was an AK-47 assault rifle. The clatter it made was distinctive. But the second burst sounded different. Sudden tension gripped him. Who else was out there? Had David made it with his team. Sami was wide awake now. But he needed to be wary. He would not leave this position until he was sure.

Sami bent down and put his lips close to Danika's ear. The smell of frangipani still lingered in her hair. 'The Captain could be out there with his men. I cannot be certain but that's the only thing that makes sense. We have to remain here quietly until morning and then use the radio.'

Sami felt Danika's head nod against his lips in agreement. She turned her face to him. 'I'll keep watch,' she said. 'You must be tired.'

Sami didn't argue. He felt the exhaustion creeping over him again. He sat down on the warm sand behind the rock and leant back. He remembered looking up at the stars …

ॐ

Sami woke up feeling groggy and disoriented. It was still dark, but the sky had lightened, and he could make out the shape of the rocks around them. The call of a night owl hunting its prey echoed through the rocks.

Danika shifted her position next to him. She had let him sleep longer than he had expected. She felt him move and glanced down at him before looking up again. Sami levered himself up and knelt next to her.

'You let me sleep for long.' His mouth was dry, and his throat felt raspy and hoarse.

'There was no reason to wake you up,' she said smiling at him affectionately. 'It's been quiet, and the birds have come back.'

The forest around them was alive with the sound of birds awakening to the dawn. The cat-like call of a pea hen some distance away mingled with the softer tones of songbirds roosting in the trees below.

They knelt shoulder to shoulder and watched the rays of the sun light up the tops of the trees below them. The land covered in dense jungle, undulated in rolling waves towards the enormous body of water to the south. Large flocks of birds lifted off the trees in waves, moving towards the sparkling water of the tank.

'It's beautiful,' Danika said watching the scene unfold before her.

'We have to get to the other side of the tank,' Sami said. 'But we can't risk it until we know what happened last night.'

The bodies of the two men he had shot the previous afternoon were clearly visible on the slope leading down to the tree line. The man he had wounded was nowhere to be seen. Sami worried about Balan. He had proven once before to be a dogged and dangerous adversary.

The only warning was a scratching on the rock above them. Something slammed into the two of them from above. Danika was thrown aside, crashing face first into the rock, her body going limp. Sami was driven forward, his body almost catapulting over the flat rock they were kneeling behind. His shoulder smashed into the rock, numbing his arm, his rifle slipping out of his grasp and clattered down the rocky slope.

Sami collected his feet under him and swivelled on his haunches. A figure dressed in Tiger camouflage loomed above him. It was Balan, there was no mistaking his dark bald head. He must have climbed up behind them in the night when they were distracted by the firing. A dangerous looking hunting knife glinted in his left hand.

'Ah, the *mukaal*,' he growled, recognising Sami. 'I thought you were dead.' His eyes glinted with madness as he looked at Sami.

Sami was consumed with a mixture of rage and helplessness. Balan was doing it again, taking away someone he cared about, someone he loved. This had become a personal war between the two of them. Sami forced himself to control his emotions. Balan was a cold-blooded killer. Sami had killed men like him in the past. He could do it again. Sami couldn't help glance at Danika hoping that she was alright. She had not moved after hitting her head on the rock.

Balan's eyes shifted to Danika when he saw Sami glance in that direction. Sami saw his chance and launched himself at the man. They went down in a tangle of arms and legs, Sami landing heavily on his right side grazing his arm and elbow under the long-sleeved shirt. He curled into a ball and rolled into the sandy depression, barely avoiding the full force of a kick thrown by Balan which glanced off his left shoulder and hit him on the side of his head. The next blow was better aimed, landing just below his rib cage. The breath shot out from his lungs with a painful burst as he rolled to his right-side gasping for breath.

The big man jumped to his feet, his eyes never leaving Sami. 'You're going to die *Mukaal*,' he snarled. 'And then I am going to fuck your woman.'

Sami had a split second as Balan stepped forward confidently, his knife held in front of him. Sami grasped the haft of the fighting knife strapped to his calf with his right hand and jumped to his feet, rushing the man and hitting him on his chest with his shoulder. Balan flailed with his knife but he didn't have time to move his arm high enough to swing it down with any force. A sharp pain shot down Sami's left shoulder blade as the edged weapon penetrated his clothing, slicing open his skin. Sami struck upwards feeling the blade go deep into the man's body.

Balan grunted and fell back clutching the left side of his stomach. A dark stain appeared on his shirt as he looked down at himself in disbelief. Sami stepped forward and swung his foot hard into Balan's solar plexus. The man's breath shot from his lungs as he doubled over, dropping to his knees, his head bowed in agony. Balan still clutched his knife and Sami jumped back to avoid being within easy reach of the man. He used the space to deliver a brutal kick up into Balan's jaw, snapping his head back and knocking the Tiger leader to the ground.

All the anger and hate Sami had stored for Balan burst out in a frenzied cry as he stepped up to the man, kicking him solidly in the head, again and again. His bald head gashed, and bleeding flopped lifelessly when Sami finally ran out of energy. Sami leant over totally drained, his hands on his knees, taking in quick gulps of air through his open mouth.

'Remind me never to let you get mad at me,' a voice said from behind.

Sami spun around at the sound, his knife held out in front of him. David stood beside the flat rock, a grim expression on his face. He was scratched and dirty, a rifle hung across his chest ready to fire.

Sami blinked. The rage he had felt a moment ago drained away, leaving him shivering and weak. Thinking of Danika, he crossed the depression in two steps falling to his knees by her side. She lay face down in the sand and had not moved.

Sami turned Danika on her back, cradling her in his arms. Her face was pale, blood flowing from a deep gash on her head. Sami stared at her, anguish written all over his face. Had Balan taken her away from him? He couldn't prevent the grief-stricken cry that tore from his throat as he hugged Danika to his chest. He felt David's hand on his shoulder in sympathy but could not accept that he had lost her.

A faint flutter against his chest made him lay Danika gently back on the sand. He bent over her holding her face between his hands, willing her to live, to show him some sign that she was alive.

Danika moaned as colour came back to her face. Sami's eyes filled with tears when she opened her unfocused eyes.

'It's okay,' he whispered. 'You're safe. It's all over now.' Danika tried to smile, and Sami bent down and kissed her, not wanting to let her go.

'You're hurt,' David said from behind him. Sami felt his shirt pasted against the back of his body from the knife wound on his shoulder blade. He felt blood running down his back.

'It's nothing,' Sami said. He turned and looked over his shoulder at David. 'Danika has a bad head wound and looks concussed. We have to get her to the base hospital at Kantale right away.'

Sami fumbled in the side pocket on his vest and pulled out the medical kit. It contained everything he needed to stop the bleeding on Danika's forehead until she received proper medical attention. He tried to open the zipper that held the medical kit closed and dropped it clumsily on the ground.

He leaned down to pick it up and felt himself topple over.

∾

TWENTY-FOUR HOURS LATER ...

The helicopter flared for a landing in the garden beside the base hospital. David stood waiting outside staring out across the main road towards the ancient reservoir built in the seventh century. Flocks of birds lifted gracefully into the sky framing a lonely fisherman tending to his nets. It looked so peaceful and serene from where he stood.

The Colonel wanted them back in Colombo immediately. David's team had gone back to Vavuniya and he had thanked them individually before they left, knowing in his heart that it was probably the last time they would be together in the field.

The hospital door behind him opened. Danika stepped out supported by a nurse. She looked small and vulnerable, her head wrapped in a thick white bandage. Sami followed the two women protectively, favouring his bandaged left arm which was in a sling. A dark bruise covered the left side of his face.

'You'll be admitted to the Military Hospital in Cinnamon Gardens for a full check-up,' David said, looking at them. 'Danika will be interviewed by military intelligence before she is released into my custody. I am afraid there's no getting around it. She'll have a lot of valuable information we can use.'

Sami nodded. David knew that Sami had been through a similar process when he left the Tigers.

David sighed. The events of the last week had been draining and though the ache behind David's eyes had disappeared, he knew he needed a good long break. David was looking forward to seeing Priyani. Maybe he could persuade her to take a holiday and they could go to the Maldives.

CHAPTER FIFTY-NINE

CENTRAL HIGHLANDS

The old man watched carefully from behind the squat tea bushes. He had selected the scrubs closest to the lines in which to hide. His instructions had been very clear. Rani's brother was becoming a problem. They couldn't let him leave with news of what was happening.

At least the man wasn't a policeman, he thought and grinned evilly to himself. He had enjoyed killing the bumbling Sinhalese they had sent from Colombo. Who did the man think they were? Village idiots! He didn't want to hang the man up near the factory but the *Durai* had insisted.

'We must show these people that we cannot be pushed around,' the *Durai* said angrily. 'I want to make an example of him not just to Colombo but also to our people. There cannot be loose talk, and sacrifices will have to be made in the future. They have to be prepared for it.'

The old man continued to watch carefully but could not see the man he was looking for. The one thing he did regret was that he had to kill one of his own kind. He could even remember Mukesh as a young boy playing outside the lines with his sister.

He steeled himself. He was fighting for a cause. The old man despised the men in their far away offices who had exploited his people for so many years. He thought about the damage done by the foreign thieves over the centuries, their arrogance and their conceit. *It's time we took control of our own destiny.*

At last the man he was looking for stepped onto the yard outside the lines. The old man noticed that Mukesh had a limp which would make it easier when the time came. He watched Mukesh, following his progress to the shared toilet. The old man reached into a pouch he had created by folding a section of his sarong over. He pulled out a *beedi* – cigarette, which he lit with a butane lighter. He sucked in the aromatic smoke deep into his lungs. It would be dark in a few more hours.

The old man had been told that Mukesh slept in a hut on a small-holding next to the bus station. He was glad Mukesh was not living with his sister. He didn't want to hurt her and her family. Although the old man knew that Kanan was a hot head, the man wanted the same thing as he did.

The old man had honed his *kavvattu katti* – pruning knife, to a fine edge. The knife was his friend and his enemy. The short-handled blade was straight for about twelve centimetres, then curving sharply, almost into a semi-circle with a very sharp point. He couldn't remember the number of times he had cut himself with it. But it was what he was. A master pruner. It required skills and dexterity to be one. He would wait until Mukesh fell asleep. All it would take was one skilled swipe.

∾

Near the estate, next to the bus stop, Mukesh had found a local small-holder who lived in a brick house surrounded by his vegetable gardens. Mukesh negotiated with Abbas, the small-holder, to rent a *cadjan* hut at the back of the house for a minimum sum.

Staying in the overcrowded lines on the estate had become more and more difficult. The tiny rooms that Rani and her family used were too small to accommodate more than a small family. Mukesh could see that Rani was getting agitated by the constant whining of Kanan who kept asking when Mukesh would be leaving. Kanan had been doing more complaining than usual recently and Mukesh would often hear them arguing in the room while he slept outside on the stoop.

Rani didn't complain when Mukesh told her he was moving. She was hunched over the fire cooking the evening meal. 'You can always have your meals here,' she said, wiping her sweaty forehead with her forearm. She paused what she was doing and looked over at Mukesh. 'It's not that you are not welcome here,' she said, quietly. 'Actually, the money you give us has made life a bit easier. But Kanan does not want you here and he is my husband.'

Mukesh nodded. 'I know,' he said. 'I think it'll be better for you if I leave.'

Mukesh found the arrangement to work quite well. He would spend most evenings with Rani and Savitri while Kanan was out drinking. At other times the two of them would bring cooked food for him and they would eat together. He made sure Kanan was never around when he gave Rani money for food and other living essentials.

The hut he now occupied was set away from the lines and he could slip in an out of the place without anyone noticing. There was nothing much in the hut except for mat and a cardboard box in which Mukesh kept his meagre belongings.

Mukesh struck a match and lit the lamp which he placed next to him on the ground. The dim warmish glow gave just enough light in the small room. Mukesh was feeling a sense of accomplishment as he stretched out on his mat. He'd briefed the Inspector on what he had discovered, and the man had thanked him for what he had done and asked him to return to the estate and wait for further instructions.

Talking to the Inspector from Colombo was not what he'd expected, thinking he'd be debriefed by the Captain. Evidently, he was on some important mission and could not be contacted.

The Inspector was young and inexperienced. Not like the Captain. Mukesh wondered whether Colombo was taking the threat seriously. But it wasn't his concern. He had completed another mission and he'd look forward to his next one. The time he'd spent with his sister had really opened his eyes to the poverty and exploitation that the estate workers were facing. It was not for him. It was too cold, and his foot ached almost every day. He would go back to the warmer climate of the lowlands and find a wife. Yes, that is what he should be doing.

The weather was unusually warm. Mukesh pushed away the blanket after turning down the wick in the lamp. The stars were out as he fell asleep, lying on his back, looking out through the open door. A sound from the doorway woke him from a deep, dreamless sleep. He raised his head to see who it was. Mukesh spotted the dull glint of a knife blade and felt a sharp pain under his ribs. His eyes lost focus and a mist descended over his vision. Mukesh felt himself void his bowels as he lost control, not understanding what was happening to him. He felt himself falling …

ABOUT THE AUTHOR

Roderic Grigson was born in Colombo, Sri Lanka where he was educated and lived till he was twenty-one. Rod's family were Burghers, descendants of the Portuguese, Dutch and British colonials who ruled the island nation for 450 years. With no prospects in the former British colony of Ceylon that had become a socialist state run by Sinhalese nationals, he left the country of his birth with a few dollars in his pocket and entered the United States on a tourist visa. He found work at the United Nations Headquarters in New York where he worked for the next twelve years.

After studying information technology at New York University, he volunteered and joined the United Nations Peacekeeping Forces in Egypt and Lebanon, serving on the Suez Canal during the signing of the Israel Egypt Peace Accord and in South Lebanon and Beirut during the Lebanese Civil War. After spending two years in the field, Rod came back to New York in 1980 and joined the UN Technological Innovations team. He spent the next six years helping develop and implementing office information systems in six languages in UN regional offices around the world.

Rod migrated with his wife to Australia in 1986 where he became a senior executive for a global IT company with responsibilities across the Asia Pacific region. In 2012, after choosing to retire early from corporate life, Rod completed a 6-month Creative Writing course and began writing his first novel.

This book, *'The Sullen Hills'*, is Rod's third book. His first book *'Sacred Tears'* was released in 2014 and his second, *'After the Flames'*, in 2017.

All of his books are available for purchase on Amazon.

To keep up to date with Rod and his writing, please visit:

rodericgrigson.com

36888341R00216

Printed in Poland
by Amazon Fulfillment
Poland Sp. z o.o., Wrocław